THE
COUNTING
GAME

THE COUNTING GAME

INTO THE WOODS.

COUNT TO TEN.

ONLY ONE OF US
COMES HOME AGAIN.

SINÉAD NOLAN

Harper
North

HarperNorth
Windmill Green
24 Mount Street
Manchester M2 3NX

A division of
HarperCollins*Publishers*
1 London Bridge Street
London SE1 9GF

www.harpercollins.co.uk

HarperCollins*Publishers*
Macken House, 39/40 Mayor Street Upper
Dublin 1, D01 C9W8, Ireland

First published by HarperCollins*Publishers* Ltd 2025

1

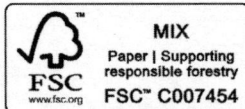

MIX
Paper | Supporting
responsible forestry
FSC
www.fsc.org FSC™ C007454

This book contains FSC™ certified paper and other controlled
sources to ensure responsible forest management.

For more information visit: www.harpercollins.co.uk/green

To my Mum and Dad, who always
believed in me

Drumsuin, Ireland
1995

The Rules

1. Count slowly to ten with your eyes closed. One player hides.
2. The seeker or seekers call out: 'Creature of the forest, will you play the Counting Game?'
3. Try to find the hidden player while seeker(s) counts out loud. Walking only. No running.
4. Once you find the hider, they must tell a scary story about what the Creature was going to do before they were found (e.g. steal their voice box, bury them alive).
5. The game is a test. To figure out if the players have been good to the forest. If they haven't, the hidden player won't be found.

Prologue

Branches rustle in the wind. They speak to Jack. They say something, but he cannot understand what. At times, he does not understand the forest; other days he understands it perfectly, like when it sends him messages about himself, telling him he has been wrong or bad.

Jack's fingers cover his eyes. It is dark underneath. Muggy breath fills the cavern of his palms. The seconds pass as he counts. *Two potato, three potato, four …*

The blanched October light streams through a gap in the trees and when he opens his eyelids from behind his hands, he can see the flesh of his fingers lighting up. In the afternoon air, he can taste the pine musk on the tip of his tongue. Drizzle floats through the forest and finds its way to the back of his neck, where he feels it crawl. A trail of ants on his spine, gooses on his arms. He hears a screech close by and he starts – drops his hands on *nine-almost-ten*. He opens both his eyes fully and looks up. It is an owl or a mourning dove. He calls out into the cold, still air. His voice shakes.

'Creature of the forest, will you play the Counting Game?'

Jack turns and looks around at the landscape.

'One!' he calls out as he begins to walk up the mountain. 'Two!' he shouts even louder. Birds flap away, startled. 'Three!'

He scrambles uphill, breathless. He is near the tractor now, far from the treehouse. 'Four!'

He can hear the sound of the river from here. The wind howls and booms like smoke up a chimney. He stops, turns around and looks down the hill through the myriad of trunks.

Jack lowers his voice. 'Five …'

He can see a shadow to his right, hiding behind branches. He can hear voices now. Then, as suddenly as they had started, the voices stop.

'Six,' he whispers.

Jack is dizzy. He is now looking down on himself from above. A little boy, all alone and lost between hundreds of pines. Then his stomach drops. In the distance, there is another scream – this one is prolonged and howling. Livid as the goat Jack had seen dragged into Fergal Duffy Junior's barn for slaughter, one day when he was not meant to be watching. The kind of scream which his mother would have said had a weight to it; a cry made from fear and agony. This scream sounded like it belonged to a person. The sound would stay in Jack's nightmares for weeks.

Perhaps Saoirse heard it too. They'll stop the game and together they'll find the scream. After all, it was too far off to be Saoirse – a field's length away, or more. She can't have got that far in so short a time. But Jack knows that the scarlet scream, between the waves of sound, the tidal, earthly graveness of it – he knows in his bones that it *is* Saoirse.

Jack feels a hollowness inside himself. She isn't nearby any more – he can feel it. They are always connected, like people talking on the phone. Now it's like she has put down the receiver. Disappeared. The very same way he felt when his mother died. Jack needs to search now but the trees feel closer, more crowded than before.

Thunder rumbles. Left and right there are only the brown bark teeth of giant monsters, the dark gaps between them full of eyes. The Creature is watching him. Jack can feel it. What comes next is a far worse feeling. Like he is under threat. Like whatever had caught his sister is about to catch him too. He turns and looks up. There it is all at once. The shrouded figure. It hovers above. Black, human-shaped, but much larger than anything human. Terrifying.

He can feel warm water trickle down his inside leg. So scared, he has wet himself. He pinches his own hand to check if he's having a nightmare, but it stings. He is not asleep and he cannot stay here; he must run away – but where to? As he sprints down-hill, he gasps for air. He is surrounded by firs now. The air is hazy, and filled with a ghostly hunger. *Samhain.* One week now until the souls will return to roam the earth.

Jack races through the forest away from the Creature, trying to find Saoirse. He runs for what feels like hours. He stops from time to time, hunting for signs of her in the gloom. His back is sticky with sweat. He calls her again and again. Big sister Saoirse. *Sir-shaaa.* Roaring and desperate, then fitful and quiet. Whispering, shouting, howling, sobbing. Yelling her name. She can't be gone, he won't believe it.

Jack finally reaches a gap in the trees and stumbles out onto the winding country lane. He waits there until nightfall and listens carefully for a sound of someone, anyone, but all he can hear are the birds. Eventually, as light turns to dusk, a car comes with a person inside. All the person sees is a little boy, standing in the middle of the road.

PART ONE

PART ONE

1

Day One

Jack

Things start and things end. When things start they are usually happy, and when they end they are usually sad. One is for start, ten is for end. When you reach ten, the game is over.

Jack's hands are bright from the orange poster paint. He's in the kitchen painting a picture. Footsteps make him jump. Older sister Kate appears in the doorway, her face pink, her eyes swollen shut from crying. Her blonde hair has been chopped short like a boy, uneven at the ends. She is wearing the same green jumper she had on yesterday evening when he saw her passed out asleep. When he had crept back in without Saoirse.

Jack can tell by her expression they are no longer alone in the house. They must have a visitor.

The Garda bends as he comes through the doorway even though he doesn't need to, holding his hat in front of him with flat palms. He nods a hello to Jack and sits next to Pearl's empty bed which is rumpled, covered in flecks of white fur. The chair makes a loud creak like it is complaining about the weight.

'My name is Garda Morris. Mind if I smoke?'

Kate shakes her head. She starts to tidy the kitchen table, shuffles the old newspapers into a pile, and throws a piece of turf onto the dying fire. The Garda lights a cigarette as the kettle shrieks. Jack watches as the bags float to the surface of the cups like little bodies in the sea. Tea sloshes over the cup's rim as Kate passes it to the Garda, who takes it from her, places it down, and begins to root in his briefcase. After putting his painting in the corner, Jack washes and dries his hands at the sink. Jack picks up his stuffed toy and takes the seat furthest away at the table. He can see now that one of the Garda's eyes is missing. A sunken bed of skin. Jack has lots of questions about how it happened, but he also feels worried that this is the person who has been sent to help. How could anyone be useful in searching for a missing girl with a missing eye? The Garda gives Jack a blank stare with his remaining eye and nods to Jack's lap.

'Who's this little fella then?'

Jack tightens his fingers around the sloth's woollen fur.

'Wilberry.'

'And does he go on adventures?'

'Ye.'

'Not ye, yes,' Kate corrects.

'Yes,' repeats Jack.

The Garda looks between Kate and Jack over his glasses.

Jack turns Wilberry around, to check he is not upset, and arranges his blue floppy feet next to one another. His mouth is a sewn-on, straight line with a little twist upwards on one side. He has a steepled nose and red tartan dungarees – a glassy button eye and an X where the other one fell off in the forest yesterday.

Jack says nothing. He draws an invisible S for Saoirse on Wilberry's front with his finger. Picks at the quick of his fingernails. There is still bright orange paint in the crease.

'And how old are you?' the Garda asks.

'Nine and three quarters.'

'A big lad altogether. And your sister Saoirse, who is missing?'

'Thirteen.'

'Bigger than you – is she the boss of you both?'

Jack nods.

The Garda laughs a little.

'Aye, I've a big sister too and she's the very same. And how did you get separated from Saoirse yesterday?'

'I lost her in the forest.'

The Garda writes something on his notepad, then takes another drag of his cigarette.

'Kate tells me you were playing hide-and-seek, and your sister was hiding at the time?'

Jack nods.

The Garda pauses.

'Why didn't you tell anyone last night that she was missing?'

There is a long silence.

Kate leans in and whispers to the Garda. Jack can't hear what exactly, but the Garda nods. He makes his voice softer.

'Could she still be hiding?'

Jack does not respond.

Garda Morris sighs.

'Could someone have taken her? Did you see anyone nearby at the time?'

Jack tries to recall what he had seen but it quickly disappears, like a ghost. Something is stopping him remembering. He had been so upset yesterday – it is like he can't see it now, as hard as he tries.

'The forest was the last place you saw your sister, was it?'

Jack thinks back to yesterday before they had started playing the game, standing near the clearing in the strong breeze. Wisps of hair dancing, feet planted solid like trees. He had covered his eyes then and counted. The Garda repeats the same questions Kate asked him this morning, though the Garda doesn't shake him by the shoulders like she did.

'Where could she be?' *I don't know.*

'Could she have run away?' *I don't know.*

'Did anyone take her?'

Jack wants to go back to the closet and sit among his mother's dresses. To hide away until it's all over.

'Do you know any other details, anything at all?'

Jack lowers his chin. Peers out from under his eyelashes.

'What was Saoirse wearing when she went missing?'

'Blue jeans, a red jumper, a navy coat,' Kate replies. 'Isn't that right, Jack?'

Jack nods. Kate bites her lip, traces a finger over the back of one hand. She still has blackberry juice under her fingernails from the jam they made two days ago. Jack had the same reddening purple colour around his mouth earlier in the week, as though he had been eating tar.

'She has snakes for hair,' Jack says. 'Like Medusa.'

'I'm sorry, Garda Morris, he has a wild imagination.'

Kate gives Jack a stern look, her mouth in a firm line.

'Have you got a photograph of her?' Garda Morris asks her. 'Just so I can confirm her hair is not *really* made of snakes,' he says, giving Jack a small smile.

'Of course,' replies Kate. She goes into the other room. Jack looks out of the misted window and down at the logs near the fence at the back of the house where the chicken coop used to be. Now it is just grass.

'Here,' Kate says, coming back into the room.

Jack looks at the photo Kate has chosen – it is one of Saoirse. In it, her smile looks frozen on, lips parted in an unsure way, like she does not trust the person behind the camera. Her red wavy hair is loose about her shoulders, rather than in her usual plait. Her shirt collar is two bright white triangles, in contrast to the blue of her jumper and the brown paper backdrop.

'Blue eyes, red hair, freckles …' Garda Morris mutters, looking at the picture and writing on his notepad. 'You say she was wearing a navy coat – how did it look?'

Kate's eyes dart to one side.

'It is tweed, with wooden buttons and … a hood.'

Jack thinks of the coat. He remembers seeing it when he and Saoirse went to play on Fergal Duffy Junior's land. They were not supposed to be there, annoying the cows. Fergal stood at the edge of his barn, in the mud, hand-bellows for smoking bees in one hand, mesh hat in the other.

'The shoes she went out in yesterday were her only pair, apart from her wellies,' Kate says. 'They are canvas, not great for the rain.'

'Any health conditions?' Garda Morris asks.

'Asthma.'

Fergal had been watching them from the barn. Jack had given him a wave, but he had not waved back. He had just glowered, face ruddy, like an angry bee himself who had been disturbed from his hive. Was that the same day as yesterday, or not?

Garda Morris is still asking questions. 'Would she have had an inhaler with her?'

'Yes, a blue one, I think – Jack, do you remember?'

Jack tries to think about yesterday, as they sprinted towards the forest in the drizzle. Saoirse had sprayed the inhaler into her mouth. He could hear the wheeze of her breath. They had climbed over the metal fence of Fergal's field and then ducked under the boundary of gorse, scraping their hands.

Jack nods.

'Does Saoirse have any favourite hiding places in the forest? Any kind of shelter, like a treehouse?'

This is a new question. The Garda puts down his pen and watches. The seconds pass slowly and the air is thick with a feeling Jack has never felt before. It stretches on.

Jack is careful to keep his eyes focused away from Kate.

'They do have a treehouse,' Kate says, 'not far from here. I can tell you exactly where it is.'

Garda Morris turns a new page and scribbles something in the corner. He reaches into his pocket and takes out a packet of Black Jack sweets.

'Do you like these?'

Jack nods. 'But I'm not allowed.'

Older sister Kate glances at him sideways. 'Don't worry, the Garda is safe.'

Jack takes one slowly. He unwraps a Black Jack, and puts it into his mouth. Jack likes Black Jacks, especially because they share his name. He strokes Pearl's coarse fur under the table with his bare foot, examining the strands of fibres in the wooden table, how the pattern curves and spirals into knots like the number eight.

There is silence. Jack rewinds like a cassette tape in his mind. They had been playing their usual game. He draws a selection of invisible numbers on the table. Then he draws a big circle around them. Kate places the cup down near the number three. She sits between Garda Morris and Jack on another chair. Jack's fingers crawl over his arm and hand, and he remembers the feeling of pine needles against his skin.

'It sounds like, you were playing hide-and-seek, and you never found her?' the Garda says, gently.

Jack doesn't nod or shake his head. Instead, he spins around in his seat and kneels up, teetering on the edge. He grips the chair, looks out of the window into the garden. Fear rises in him again, a suffocating feeling – so much, he can barely breathe. From here he can see a line of trees in the distance. Kate touches his shoulder.

'Come down now, the Garda needs your attention.'

Jack keeps looking towards the trees, waiting for a sign. Eventually, he sees it. Black pieces of something soar and dive. Into the wind, flapping their wings, swooping and scattering wide across the sky until they move closer to Jack and he cannot watch them any more – they are warning him not to speak. He turns away quickly and sinks low down in his seat so they cannot see him. He presses his chin on his chest, breathing fast. When he turns his head to look back, they have gone.

Visitors come and go, and Kate paces up and down. Everyone is worried and upset. They keep asking Jack why he never told anyone until this morning. Jack doesn't know why, only that he hadn't wanted to worry Kate, what with her sleeping at strange times, and he hadn't wanted to get Saoirse in trouble. Jack himself hadn't slept well at all. He kept waking and thinking he heard her coming home. Her key in the door, her soft steps creeping up the stairwell. Her whispering in his ear that it was okay, she was home now – but it never happened.

A few hours pass in the stuffy kitchen with Garda Morris, and outside the wind is picking up. Jack rubs his bare feet together, hides a black toenail like he is burying a clue, wraps his arms around Wilberry and squeezes. They are still asking him questions. She has been gone for twenty-four hours now – 'a long time', said Garda Morris. On the radio, beside where Kate's music cassettes are kept, a melody plays. It is interrupted with headlines of a missing girl. The world had got wind of his sister's disappearance. The news had spread around Drumsuin and the whole south-west of Ireland like flames in a tinder fire.

Kate had been asleep yesterday evening when Jack got home. Snoring on the sofa after a long day at work. The man who had found him on the road had dropped him off outside the house and Jack had pleaded with him not to come to the door and not to speak to Kate.

Jack had run inside, waving to the man, before he watched out the window to make sure he had driven off and his car lights had disappeared down the lane.

This morning, Kate was so angry with him. Angry for not telling her Saoirse was missing when they could have still found her easily last night. *How could you do that to her? To Saoirse?* she had exclaimed. Jack could tell that he was not just bad, he was very bad indeed. So bad, Gardaí are here now and might arrest him.

Jack closes his eyes and tries harder to erase any memory of yesterday. He feels the wool of Wilberry's dungarees running along the inside of his arms. When he opens his eyes again, he sees Garda Morris lean back on the chair. Garda Morris pushes his half-moon glasses up on his nose, takes a gulp of tea, puts the mug down and reaches for a new packet of sweets. The packet rustles. It has been there a while, a promise or a bargain. He chews with a slack mouth, extends the packet of red, yellow, and violet worms and offers them to Jack. They look like a mass of squirming fish, all wrapped around each other's bodies, their tails long, spineless and small with telescoping eyes. *Whipsnout sorcerers. Muddy arrowtooths. Pelican eels. Barreleye fish.* The Garda is a barreleye because he looks like he has one eye closed. Like the men in Western films, staring down the barrel of a gun, and the barreleye fish is camouflaged, like Jack.

Jack does not move for a minute. Eventually, he stretches one hand out across the table to the gaping bag and picks out a few squirming worms. They cling to his fingers. He holds them in his hands until they turn sticky. When Garda Morris is not looking, he lifts one to his mouth and swallows it whole. Garda Morris jots some words in his notepad. Jack cannot read what they say.

'As we know, your mother, Lucy Kellough, has passed,' he says to Kate, who nods. 'So that'd make you the most senior member of the household at the moment?'

She nods again.

'And Saoirse and Jack are minded full-time by you …' he says, as though he hasn't realised this until now.

She nods a third time.

'Right so,' Garda Morris says, rubbing the bridge of his nose. 'Any history of self-harm from Saoirse?'

'Not that I know of.'

Garda Morris looks up at other photographs hung on the wall. He rolls his shoulders back.

'We've already been in touch with your father, Cahill, in Dublin. Your Aunt Bronagh has told us she is on her way back from London, she is trying to get a flight as we speak. Anyone else she could be with – any other friends or family?'

Kate looks up to the ceiling.

'No. Most of our extended family are in Seancarrig. They're largely disinterested in us.'

Staring into the distance, Kate fiddles with her heart-shaped locket.

'You sure there's nothing you're not saying?' Garda Morris asks.

Kate suddenly looks more frightened and sadder than before.

'I think, somehow, I knew this would happen. I mean, I'm not surprised, with everything that's been leading up to today ...'

'What do you mean?'

'It's a long story.'

'I have time.'

He gestures around the still room, to the fire crackling away.

Kate clears her throat.

'Since our mother died, things have felt really ... out of control. This feeling of doom, the feeling of being watched by something in the forest – I can't shake it. I've tried everything. We even had the local priest, Father Maguire, around to the house to cleanse the place. This game our Mam taught them ...' Kate looks at the wall, as if looking into the past. 'It hasn't helped. Jack has been counting ever since our mother died, hoping if he does, she will come back.' She seems far away for a moment. 'The priest said it's us, not the house.' She takes a deep breath. '*We* are haunted. I'm unsurprised she is missing because it feels like it would always happen this way, you know?' She closes her eyes. 'The missing women in there ... all of the ones in the past few years. I feel like it's connected somehow. That forest wanted one of us, and now it's got what it wanted.'

Kate gives him a searching look, her eyes full of tears.

Garda Morris looks back at her with a worried expression. 'It's been twenty-four hours. Although it's very concerning, she may just be hiding – the way children do. Let's hope so, eh?'

Kate puts her face in her hands. Jack hears a high-pitched sound like a sob escaping.

Next to the table, Jack watches the fish tank in the corner of the kitchen. The fish swims around, turquoise flecks on his paint-spatter scales. Into his cave and then out again, hiding under a log, changing to blue, then green, then gold. Jack remembers the day his mam bought him, what the woman in the aquarium said as she scooped him into a clear plastic bag full of water. *It is recommended the Jack Dempsey fish is provided with plenty of places to hide.* Jack Dempsey had spun around in his clear plastic bag, searching for a way out.

Jack feels the sadness of Kate, deep in his gut. Wrenching around like his feelings are attached to something. Like a ghost has gone inside his stomach and is moving things about. It gets hot in his throat and behind his eyes, but he does not want to cry, not in front of Garda Morris. Someone is calling him now, as though in a dream.

'Jack,' calls Kate softly.

'Can I assume you won't tell me any more at this time?' asks Garda Morris. Jack's eyes feel wet now, but he does not say anything, he just nods Wilberry's head with his fingers and slides down off the chair. He puts him on the chair instead, Wilberry's face still smiling dimly, and walks over to the fish tank. He puts his hand to the glass. His reflection reaches out, from a backwards world. Plenty of places to hide, that was true. Jack can see Garda Morris watching him in the glass. Behind it, the fish looks out from under the log. It watches Jack for a few seconds until it turns and swims away.

2

Day Two

Jack

Garda Walter Morris has a red car. It is called a Beetle although it does not have crawling legs. It has a front that bulges out like a nose and wide eyes as though it is searching for someone who hurt it. Jack sits on the front doorstep with Wilberry and watches the glimmering Beetle crawl in and out of view through the trees, which separate their garden from the country road to Drumsuin. The trees are protectors, his sister Kate says. They shield you, so people won't tell on you for things they consider a sin. Jack knows the oldest and wisest of his two sisters is right; trees are good protectors – but they can trap you too.

The air smells clear this morning. The fog has lifted overnight and the forest is visible again. The pointed pines wave in the breeze. Morning rain blisters on the tips of the ivy leaves which climb up the side of the house. A spider scuttles across the stoop and sits on the cold step to wait with Jack. Garda Morris does a sharp turn towards the house and drives down the rocky turf. Jack feels a creeping fear on his skin about what he has come to say. Saoirse has been missing for two whole nights now. Last night, after Jack came home from searching through the forest with the villagers, the Gardaí stayed out with their torches and helicopters. Now Garda Morris is back. Will he arrest Jack this time?

'No need to be scared,' Jack says aloud to the spider. 'The Garda is safe.'

Garda Morris turns off his headlights, then begins to attend to some papers on the passenger seat. Jack squints. The number plate starts with nine and zero, which means his car was made in nineteen ninety, and that means it is five years old. The Garda opens his door. He pulls himself out like a seal out of the water and slams the door shut again, locks it, puts the jangling bunch of keys deep into his pocket and squares his shoulders. He slides a pen into his front pocket and gives Jack a look with his one eye, then fixes his Garda hat, moving it from side to side a little over his brow.

'You'll catch whooping cough sitting on that step,' he says, tapping Jack on the shoulder.

The Garda wipes his feet on the welcome mat and steps into the musty hallway, looking around at the yellow wallpaper and old radiators. Jack follows him into the house and points to a faded photo on the side cabinet.

'Your mother, Lucy.' Garda Morris states.

Jack casts a glance up at the Garda. In the photo, his mother is holding a chubby toddler on her hip, while an older child stands beside her, gripping her floral skirt. The Garda bends to examine it more closely, picking up the frame. When Jack looks at pictures of his mother for too long, he wants to cry, so he swallows a stone in his throat and looks away.

That's when he notices a ring on the Garda's hand. It's a bit like his mam's ring, the one she used to wear before their dad left. Just then, there are footsteps on the stairs. Garda Morris straightens up and turns to face Kate, who has stopped on the third to last step.

'Journalists have been calling all morning,' she says. She tucks a piece of hair behind her ear and glances at Jack.

'Don't feel obliged to help them,' says Garda Morris in a deep voice.

'Is there any news?' Kate asks.

Garda Morris shakes his head.

'The Gardaí and our volunteers searched all night, but there's absolutely no trace of her.'

Kate slumps and then tries to pull herself together.

'We'd … like to go out and look today. We both want to get out. To help.'

Kate's voice sounds panicky and fearful. Jack has noticed she keeps bursting into tears since last night. Pacing back and forth and speaking to herself about Saoirse as though Jack is not there.

Garda Morris shifts from foot to foot.

'I'd prefer from now on that you stay here. We're getting extremely concerned – two nights is a long time for a child her age to be unaccounted for. I need to see if I can get any more information from you – does that make sense?' Kate's eyes glisten. She nods. 'We have notified the sergeant in charge of Drumsuin Station of all relevant details in respect to your missing sister, and now the nearby detective branch is involved. The district superintendent, Superintendent Ridgeway, has been briefed both orally and in writing and she will now oversee the investigation. The Garda sub-aqua unit have been called in too.'

Kate's brows rise, her eyes terrified now. 'Sub-aqua? You mean water?'

'That's right.'

Kate's voice turns more high-pitched. 'You don't think she's drowned?'

'We hope not,' replies Garda Morris, in a reassuring tone.

Kate pulls at her dressing gown, tying it in the centre. She rubs both her hands over her face. Jack peers down at Wilberry. When he looks up, Garda Morris and Kate are heading for the kitchen. Jack follows them and watches as the Garda sits in the same seat as yesterday, petting Pearl's head. He takes out a metal case from his pocket and picks out a long white and yellow cigarette, then lights it up. Jack watches as a plume escapes from the Garda's lips.

15

Jack sits at the table while Kate runs the tap into the kettle. Pearl ambles over to the Garda and sniffs his boots.

'My head didn't touch the pillow,' says Kate, taking an apple from the basket on the side and tossing it onto the table for Jack to catch. Jack watches it roll towards him like a hand grenade, and reaches out and snatches it before it can explode. He sinks his teeth through the skin to defuse it, and tastes its bitter tang.

'The Dog Unit are on their way,' Garda Morris says. 'Can we take Pearl, too? He'll know her scent well, so he might lead us to her.'

'Yes, of course,' Kate says.

Garda Morris lowers his hand to scratch Pearl under the chin. 'As we already have some of Saoirse's clothing to familiarise the other dogs with her scent, and the *dee-en-ay* from her hairbrush, we don't need much more from you for now.'

Kate nods. A tear hovers in the corner of her eye and then falls. She quickly wipes it away.

Jack takes another bite of the apple, trying to rid the image of a pack of angry dogs from his mind. He hopes the other dogs will be nice to Pearl. Jack places one of Wilberry's paws over his button eye as though he is searching for something.

Pearl bounds over and puts his head on Jack's lap. The whites of his eyes are showing, and his ears are down. Jack strokes the soft part of his head, counting under his breath.

'Would Jack be willing to talk to me again today?' asks the Garda.

'You can try, but he's never been a great talker. It's been worse ever since our Mam died.'

The Garda's tapping foot suddenly goes still. He clutches at his notebook and shifts in his seat.

Jack draws on the table now with his finger. He writes some invisible numbers then the letter M. Then he draws a large X over it. Garda Morris looks from Jack to Kate, who takes a pained breath and averts her gaze downwards.

'Perhaps we will have to get a professional in to talk to him. Someone adept at dealing with children who struggle with talking. Would that be all right?'

Kate turns her gaze to the counter. There's a half-completed jigsaw puzzle on it, made up of butterflies, dotted with dramatic blues and pinks. On one side, three butterflies congregate on a tulip. Saoirse had been working on the jigsaw for the past few weeks.

'Of course,' she says, 'whatever it takes.'

Garda Morris tilts his head. 'It's been … so much responsibility for you to take on since your mother died, looking after the children,' he says. 'What age is on you?'

'Twenty. Handing them to social services wasn't an option. I wanted to keep our family together.'

Kate picks up a tea towel from the side next to the jigsaw and folds it – once, then a second time – and places it back on the counter.

Garda Morris looks worried. 'It was so sad when Lucy passed,' he says. 'It was such a … tragedy in the community. I was glad when I heard the young ones didn't end up in care. Still, I had assumed you were older.'

Kate goes to get a pair of cups from the press, turning her back again. 'Well, life doesn't always give us the luxury of choice, does it? I am doing the best I can. Working at Hope's Café in the village, trying to mind the children. It's not been easy.' Kate opens the fridge to grab the milk.

'Ah yes. I know I've already asked this, but I wanted to check this detail again. What time did you say you got home from work on the day Saoirse went missing?' asks Garda Morris.

'Around six. Usually, I'd make dinner. We'd all watch TV or read and they'd be in bed by ten. That day, though, they weren't home so I went and waited for them on the sofa. That was how I fell asleep – I was exhausted.'

'It sounds like a lot of work for you. Were you finding either of the children a struggle to deal with lately?'

She flinches. 'Not Saoirse,' she says.

She closes her eyes for a moment, opens them again, then sags back in the chair. Jack feels the ringing in his ears again.

'But Jack … well, he has changed since our mam died. First, he began this obsession with counting under his breath. Then the dreams started.'

'Dreams?'

'Nightmares. He wakes up and screams the house down. He sleepwalks, sometimes even leaving the garden and disappearing out to the forest. And in the daytime, he paints frightening pictures.'

'Did you ever get him any help?'

'What sort?'

There is a long pause. Jack can feel his breathing grow shallow, like a tiny animal hiding in a corner. He imagines the knot in his belly as a real thing that he could unravel like string, though he does not know where to start. Maybe he *should* run. Maybe he *should* scream.

'I never thought to,' she says.

Garda Morris writes something on his notepad. 'Any reason for that?'

Kate glances around uneasily. 'We're not the type of family to speak about our problems.'

She smooths her hands over her jeans.

'Did you try to speak to him about it yourself?'

She picks at her nails and shakes her head.

'Any reason for that?'

She examines her cuticles closer. 'I'm afraid of what I'd find if I tried to understand him. I threw away a few of his paintings, burned some. I let him keep the others in the attic. You're right though, he should speak to someone objective,' Kate adds, looking at Garda Morris at last. 'Someone outside the family. I don't have the same close bond with him that our mother had.'

Garda Morris is quiet a moment.

'Is there anything you're not saying,' he asks, gently. 'Anything you might have left out?'

'No. I've told you, the reason she is missing is because of that forest. There's nothing more I can tell you.'

The Garda scribbles something on his notepad, then looks at Jack who is sitting very still.

'All the same, Kate, I can't tell that to the superintendent – "it's just the forest". She's a human girl, there has to be an explanation. This is a human crime – we need human evidence and witnesses.'

Kate freezes a moment. 'But I've told you everything I know.'

'Right,' says Garda Morris.

Jack feels his ears start to ring. The worry for Saoirse was back. Last night he had another nightmare about her being gone. He had woken up only to realise it was true. He feels the sadness welling up in his chest again.

'I think it might be a good idea if we get a professional here to speak to Jack, and yourself. I'll see if we can sort someone here as soon as possible – a counsellor or a therapist. In the meantime, how about you, do you have support?'

Kate points out of the window.

'Just Aunt Bronagh. She helps out here a lot. When she's back from the UK she'll be around.'

The Garda shifts his attention away from Kate now.

'You're a strong big lad, aren't you?' he says to Jack. But he seems distracted, looking around the kitchen.

Jack swings his legs, trying not to feel scared, and looks at Kate, who has caught sight of a piece of paper on the sideboard. She goes over and takes it away, pushes it into her pocket and looks back at Jack over her shoulder. Garda Morris doesn't seem to notice.

3

Day Three

Freya

A flat-topped garage appears around the corner and I hit the brakes. Indicating, I glance in my mirrors, trying to ignore the debate on RTÉ radio.

'... *The Taoiseach John Bruton has been quoted as saying another "No" vote for legalising divorce would damage Ireland's image as a tolerant, progressive country.* A second voice crackles over the airwaves. *I believe it would increase tensions in Northern Ireland linked to the Catholic Church's sway on the country ... It would be very wrong not to allow our law to express forgiveness to those whose consciences permit them to remarry.*'

I turn off the ignition. The radio silences with the engine. I grab my keys and walk around to examine the tyres and hubcaps one by one. The potholes have been destructive over the last two hundred miles or so from Dublin. As I straighten up, I wince. Sitting in the same position for hours has not been kind on my back. It has been a while since I've driven long-distance.

This type of case, the Gardaí had said, would be familiar to me – the younger brother of a missing girl, who perhaps won't talk, but more likely *can't* talk due to the fact he is traumatised.

It sounded similar to an investigation I had worked on last year – the infamous Boland case, which had turned into a media circus and a public murder trial. A young girl had witnessed her father brutally stabbing her mother to death, and burying her body in the back garden. The child couldn't talk about it for months. Finally, I managed to get out of her what she had seen, and her father was convicted and sent away for a long time.

Taking the nozzle from the pump, I click open the petrol tank lid, and watch as the numbers dance like pictures in a flip book. Tiredly, I turn my head away for a moment, and the hinterland comes into focus – miles of fields, rocks, and gorse. I inhale my first lungful of Atlantic Ocean air. This might be the last garage for a while. In the distance, the mountain road undulates before zig-zagging towards the sea. I must be only twenty or thirty minutes away from Drumsuin now.

Inside the garage shop, I wander over to the fridge section and pull out a packaged sandwich. I grab some nuts, an apple, and then a KitKat from the confectionary stand too, and walk to the till. The man behind the counter has a rounded stomach which strains against his off-white shirt, and a badge that reads *Dave*.

'That everything?' Dave says.

'Pump two as well.'

Below the counter, Saoirse Kellough's face stares at me from the front cover of the *Drumsuin Examiner*, her gaze intense. I pick up the newspaper and stare back at her freckled face and red hair. My heart speeds up.

'And this, please,' I say, adding it to the pile of packaged food.

'Twenty-three fifty.'

I scrabble in my purse for some notes and hand the cash over. Dave slings me the change from the till and I thank him, and head towards the door.

'Wait,' Dave calls. I turn. 'You dropped something.'

He is pointing to the floor behind me. There is a child's toy on the scuffed lino. Tiredly, I shake my head to show it isn't mine.

'Oh. Must belong to the family who was here before you. Dublin number plate.'

I pick it up, inspecting it more closely. It is a plastic penguin. I turn it over and look at the trademark logo.

'It's just a McDonald's toy,' I say, walking towards the till with it.

'I'll throw it away, so,' he says, extending his hand. But when I look into the penguin's shining plastic eyes, for some reason, it catches at me.

'No, I'll keep it if you're throwing it away.'

'Fair enough,' he says, shrugging.

I can feel his eyes follow me as I return to my car. There are no other cars here. Exhausted, I slump into the front seat and open the sandwich. Part of me wonders what I am doing here, so far from Dublin, from my comfortable flat. It wasn't like I had planned to end up working on these types of cases in the long term. I had fallen accidentally into this line of work because of one criminal investigation years ago. One twist, another turn and here I am: the Gardaí's first port of call for some of the strangest and toughest of cases that involved traumatised children.

I stuff the sandwich into my mouth, hungrily. I start the car again and pull away from the pump.

'*... And that's right, at least 80,000 people are affected by marital breakdown – the divorce referendum does not reflect the reality of what our people are experiencing. I've spoken to a lot of married people who say this is wrong – that they couldn't vote in favour of divorce while honouring their own vows to their husband or wife.*'

I switch the radio off. The silence is easier to listen to.

4

Day Three

Freya

I get out of the car and cast my gaze around the village. The village of Drumsuin has one narrow main street, which slopes to the rocky coast. It is lined by two- and three-storey terraced shops, pubs, and houses, all in different colours. Lemon yellow, sky blue, emerald green, and blush pink. I get a haunting feeling as I park my car on the kerb, and suddenly it sinks in that Saoirse is really missing, not just from her family, but from her whole community.

This place feels familiar, but curiously alien all at once. Have I been here before? Perhaps years ago, on holiday? Then the memory comes as I begin to walk down the street and peer in the shop windows – a family day out. Me, Violet, Melody, and my ex-husband, Daniel. We were in Bray, Co. Wicklow, on the seafront. I was holding Melody's hand – she was only five at the time – and Violet was just a toddler sitting on Daniel's shoulders. All of us had '99' ice-cream cones. I remember us stopping at the seafront and looking out towards Bray Head, the wind whipping at my hair. That was the moment Daniel had chosen to tell me that he wanted a separation. It was one year before the holiday where the unthinkable had happened. I often think about how, if Daniel hadn't left, fate would have taken a completely different turn. I wouldn't have been in that villa on that day in Spain, alone with two young children.

In the distance, the otherworldly bell of the church chimes. I look at my watch. Four o'clock. The light is already beginning its glib descent into dusk. I breathe in the salty scent of fresh fish from the harbour. Seagulls dive and squall around the buckets of catch, and I notice a yellow boat near me, water lapping at its sides. I read the name on the side. *Saoirse*. A strange coincidence. Or perhaps not, considering that the name Saoirse means *freedom*, and how much freer could you get than sailing on the open sea?

I check the time again, and guilt trickles into the pit of my stomach like sand in an egg timer. I have permitted myself too long of a wander – it is time to go and speak to them now. It is time to find the Garda station.

Inside the station, it smells like pencils and erasers mixed with the lemon scent of floor cleaner. There is a clear, plexiglass cover on the hatch in reception. On the other side are two Gardaí in stiff navy-blue uniforms, deep in conversation: one rotund officer whose uniform strains around his stomach as he leans back in his chair, and a slight woman with a serious expression. Their eyes do not shift to look at me. Nervously, I knock on the plexiglass and the freckled woman with ringed, tired eyes seems to rouse. She stands and walks to the hatch, observing me with an uncomfortable gaze.

'Yes?'

'I'm here to see Detective Inspector Walter Morris.'

She stares at me, eyes flat. 'And you are?'

'Freya Hemmings,' I say, attempting a smile.

She nods and turns, looking irritated. She leaves the room, assumedly to get the detective. My smile fades. The other Garda watches me. I stand, unsure how to hold myself, and read the posters on the wall about drug use and how to report crimes. With a feeling of being observed, I look up instinctively at the security camera. After a while, I hear a door bang shut from the corridor behind and then the double doors swing open into the reception area.

'Dr Hemmings?' the detective says, and introduces himself. I try not to stare at the wrinkled, burned skin of his missing eye as I extend my hand. His grip is tight, almost knuckle-breaking. Garda Morris is tall, and about my age, with salt-and-pepper hair. I imagine meeting him could induce relief or intimidation depending on what mood you found him in. He seems to me like a stately old tom cat, who has seen a few scraps in his time.

'Thank you for coming,' he says in a thick accent. I try to place it. More northern than these parts. Donegal, perhaps? 'You're very cheerful, aren't you,' he says, 'for someone coming into a cop shop?'

'I'm just glad to be here at last,' I reply.

I follow him through the double doors. I catch a faint whiff of cigarette smoke as I follow him. He holds the door for me and leads me down a dim corridor to a quiet meeting room, full of chairs around an oblong table.

'This is our incident room,' he explains. 'Most stations don't have one – we only have four in the southern region. We had a conference in here this morning.'

He gestures to the seats, and we sit opposite each other. An awkward silence fills the room. He breaks it first.

'Would you like some water?'

'No thanks,' I reply.

'Was your journey down all right?'

'Yes, but they need to build better roads!'

He laughs. 'The back roads of villages can be a winding way to come, but we're very glad you did. We need someone like you. You sound like you're from England?'

'Nottingham.' I nod. 'Moved to Dublin to be with my husband a long time ago and stayed. Despite the fact that the relationship didn't last, I liked Dublin …' I trail off, unsure why I am divulging this to him.

'Well, you'll draw some attention around here with an accent like that. Some people don't like the English over here, you know.'

'Yes. I am aware.'

He pauses a moment, then his demeanour turns solemn. 'How much do you know about what has happened?'

'Not much.' I instantly feel silly, as though I should know more. I try to appear composed as Garda Morris explains a few details about the case and about Saoirse.

'The search was upscaled when she didn't show up after twenty-four hours, though unfortunately we didn't know about her disappearance until she'd been missing a whole night. We've got the civil defence, mountain rescue team, and the dog and sub-aqua unit on the case and have appointed a Garda officer to instruct the tens of local volunteers who've been scouring the area. There are various methods used on these cases and we are throwing the book at it – sweep searches, grid searches, the lot. Superintendent Ridgeway is leading the case, and she has drawn up a plan. This also includes a media appeal and a door-to-door questionnaire while we look for her, boots on the ground, inside the forest.'

'Do you have any suspects in relation to her disappearance?'

'We are interviewing a few persons of interest. We haven't involved the National Bureau of Investigation, not yet, anyway, as there is no evidence of foul play. The strategy we use is TIE – Trace, Interview, Eliminate – but that takes time. I am reporting to Superintendent Ridgeway; you will report to me. All make sense?'

'Yes,' I say, but my head spins as I try to absorb all of these details.

'Are you able to confirm an initial contract of seven days, and we will evaluate this on a weekly basis? Of course, we hope that we'll find Saoirse before then.'

I nod.

'Good' he replies, his expression tired. 'Just an hour ago, I had a phone call from a witness who claims to have rescued Jack on the day Saoirse went missing. A salesman who was travelling from Ballybunion to Cahersiveen. He found Jack in the middle of the road a few miles from the house – the boy was quite disorientated and upset, apparently. The man said Jack didn't mention a girl being with him. Just that he was lost and wanted to find his way home. The salesman dropped Jack back at his property around 7 p.m. Apparently, Jack pleaded with him not to speak to his sister about it in case he got in trouble, and the witness agreed, leaving him at the front door. He feels awful now, obviously, knowing he could have done more.'

'Could he have anything to do with it?'

'We did wonder. But no, he's not a suspect any more. He has alibis for where he was before and after he picked up Jack. Everything he told us adds up.'

Walter holds up a book. 'This is the Jobs Book. It's the bible of our case – everything we do is in here. You have allocated jobs in here, too – mainly around speaking to Jack and getting information from him, but also giving us tapes of your recordings of the sessions at the end of each day. Understand?'

I nod again.

'We want to pull together a picture of Saoirse – what makes her tick, who she is friends with, who could have taken her, why she ran away if she did run, that kind of a thing. Try talking to Jack one-to-one. When his sister Kate's around, he can be closed off. I am wondering if he might say more if he's alone.'

'Okay,' I reply.

'Do you usually work cases like this?' he asks. 'You came highly recommended by a colleague in Dublin.'

'I've plenty of experience on these kinds of cases, getting children to open up about difficult things.'

'That will be helpful. Back when I worked in Dublin, I did lots of missing person cases but this isn't our usual type of case for around here, as you can imagine … Just last week we were investigating a cattle theft, but of course, every once in a while, something big happens. You got family yourself, any children?'

I feel my palms begin to sweat, and I shift uncomfortably in my seat.

'Divorced, two kids. They – well, one of them, Melody – is grown up and gone to university, studying nursing. The other, Violet … died when she was small.'

I wait for his reaction, a part of me expecting him to recoil in judgement, but his face stays concerned, empathic.

'God, sorry.'

I look down at my hands, relieved at his reaction, and that he didn't ask me how. I'm not ready to explain that yet, not today.

'It's okay. Talking about it doesn't make it any more difficult. In fact, if anything, it makes it easier.'

'All the same,' he sighs, seeming lost for words. He leans back, folding his arms.

We sit in silence. I take a deep breath: *In and out.*

'I saw the photograph of Saoirse – she looks young for her age. I felt awful imagining her not coming home … imagining her out there somewhere, alone.'

'I know, it's very sad,' Walter replies, his face tightening. He looks at me intently. I feel uncomfortable all of a sudden. He looks away, as if sensing the discomfort too and not liking the intimacy of the moment. 'Until now, the case has been mainly depending on myself, and a few other detectives who have been brought in from Dublin. I've not slept much the past few days.'

'How about their parents?' I ask. 'How are they managing?'

'Unfortunately, the children's father left and their mother passed. It was ruled a suicide. We found her at the bottom of a cliff six months ago, near the forest. I covered the case myself – had to guard her body for several hours while the scene was investigated.'

My stomach churns. 'Do you think Saoirse could be acting out due to her mother's death?' I ask. 'Maybe she's run away?'

Walter rubs his good eye with his knuckles and lets out a sigh. 'That's what I've been thinking, but we've spoken to all of her school friends. She didn't mention planning anything of the sort to anyone.'

'So it could likely be someone local who has done this?'

'Yes, we need to consider that. It's not the first missing person case we've had in the area, as I'm sure you're aware?'

'No,' I reply. I'm not up to speed on the history of this area. I watch his Adam's apple bob as he swallows. He loosens his collar with one finger. I notice a scar around his neck.

'There have been three in the past twenty years. Two of the more recent ones I worked on myself. Maeve Murphy was the most prominent story in the national press, back in 1988. She was a seventeen-year-old girl who had an argument with her family and walked to the forest to cool off, and was never seen again.'

'The name rings a bell,' I mutter.

'Well, we never found her, nor her body. Though in her case, we really believed it was a one-off, as she had a strange boyfriend at the time. No evidence ever convicted him, but lots of people think it was him. He was very controlling.'

I shiver.

'Then there was one in 1981, a very sad case altogether. Ashling McGill, keen local camogie player, beloved by all her friends and family – with a lively, sunny personality – no strange boyfriend, no enemies, no reason to run away. She was only fifteen. She had been hiking with a group of Girl Guides when she went off on her own to relieve herself and disappeared. Volunteers and Gardaí searched for weeks. She never showed up. Not a hair or even a piece of her clothing. But the first case is perhaps the saddest of the lot, because of how young she was – in 1975 a child aged nine, Ellie O'Connor, went missing while playing in the forest. Her parents were on holiday and had been picnicking nearby. She just disappeared into thin air.'

I calculate quickly. 'You're averaging a missing girl every six or seven years around here, then?'

'I suppose you could say we are.' He looks at me as though hiding something. An invisible veil seems to drop over his face.

'Anything else?' I ask.

'Sort of. Years back, there was the Magdalene Laundry nearby, on some of the land that is now forest. Women who were pregnant out of wedlock in the forties, fifties, and sixties – they were taken away and hidden from society there. Some perished. Their bodies were buried in a mass grave nearby. Some fell off the cliffs, drowned in the sea or are lost throughout the forest, their bones and ashes scattered. There was a baby graveyard discovered in the eighties there too, with the bones of babies who had been buried illegally. Rumour has it, a woman ran away from the place in the forties. Her name was Mary Brady. It was said her baby was sick and she'd had enough of the poor treatment she'd had at the place. She tried to escape, carrying her newborn, but was chased and found by the nuns while hiding in the forest. After they found her, they burned Mary and her baby alive at the stake at the Hollowing Place, a clearing of trees near the old graveyard. At least that's what people call it now: the Hollowing Place – nothing will grow there now, not even grass. There's a local whose aunt survived the laundry and she witnessed the whole thing. The smoke rising, the screams of agony, saw her tied to the stake … the baby swaddled next to her.'

'Burned alive?' I repeat dumbly.

'It's just a story. A myth. Though I suppose it might be true.' He shuffles his papers together.

'And because of that, people say it's haunted?' I ask.

'Yes. They say the missing girls are not a coincidence. That the place is inhabited by the ghosts of Mary Brady, her baby, the other tortured souls from the laundry, and the evil nuns who did such cruel things. The 'creature' the local people believe in is supposed to be the embodiment of all those restless spirits – something terrifying that can make people disappear. As a result, most locals don't go in there, but our main source of income is tourism. That's where the problem lies – the locals don't want tourists here. They litter … they ignore the signs outside the forest and go on hikes. The signs clearly say *Keep Out*, but the catch-22 is, we need the tourists – they bring cash to the area.'

Walter sighs again. He looks exhausted.

'Do you believe in ghost stories?' he asks.

I pause, wondering whether I do. It's hard to say you believe in spirits or an afterlife if you don't believe in ghosts, and I want to believe in my daughter Violet having a spirit.

'I don't know,' I reply honestly.

'Well, I don't,' he says with emphasis. 'I believe there is always an explanation for things …' He trails off. 'But the people of Drumsuin, they don't think like me.'

I watch him. The veil had risen for a moment but now it drops back over his face, and he is gone again. He scrapes back his chair, slaps his thighs, and rises from the seat.

'I'd better get back. The media are going mad, and I've a good many tasks still to complete today. The villagers are putting intense pressure on too – after all, she is one of our own.'

I leave the room and walk back to reception. He follows and watches as I push open the glass front door. Before I leave, he speaks again, just loud enough for me to hear.

'Drumsuin is a strange place. Will you be able to cope?'

I give him a light-hearted smile, but I do not feel like smiling. In fact, as I walk away from the station, the feeling I had this morning only becomes stronger. The sense I should turn back and go home, that I should not get involved with Drumsuin or anyone in it. That something awful has happened to Saoirse, and it is going to break all of our hearts in the end.

5

Day Three

Freya

I park near the end of the driveway and look up. The bones of the house are beautiful. From here it seems to have many bedrooms, with a vast garden. An enviable property, at least to someone who's limited to a small apartment in the city.

My eyes scan over the nearby swing set and the disused barn which lines the perimeter of the garden, its metal panelling half-collapsed and bent. A yellow tractor sits not far from the front door, part-sunken into the mud, covered in rust. A fine mist of rain begins to fall again, as it has on and off all the way here.

I fumble for my belongings. As I get out of the car, I glance sidelong towards the line of dark pines with pointed helms. The forest seems to go on forever. It stretches tight across the mountains, like a woven blanket. A bird takes off from the trees and flaps into the distance.

Clutching my portable sand tray and briefcase, I stride to the front door and knock. I hear footsteps approach on the other side. The young woman who appears does not look much older than a child herself. A bleached-blonde bob sticks out in odd directions from her head, as though she has hacked at it herself with scissors. She is wearing her dressing gown, which is tatty at the edges. Her eyes are a startling blue, heavy-lidded. She looks fixedly at me, dipping her chin, then retracts her hands into her sleeves, pulling the material taut around her fists. This must be the older sister they had mentioned – Kate.

'Who are you?' she asks, in a frightened whisper.

'I'm Freya, a psychotherapist – I've been sent here by Garda Morris,' I say gently, and I give her a tentative smile. 'You must be Kate?'

She nods slightly and looks at me, as if sizing me up, then she steps back. I shuffle my feet on the mat and shiver a little. The air in the hallway is bitter, almost colder than outside.

'Chilly out there,' I comment.

She nods. 'Can I get you a cup of tea?'

'No, I'm okay, thanks,' I reply, looking around. 'If you could just show me to Jack, that would be great.'

The hallway smells like burning turf and bonfires, together with the mulch of old trees. On the wall next to the door there are photographs, and my eye is drawn to one of a knock-kneed, white-haired boy next to a spindly girl with a shock of red hair. The girl stands in the mud in wellington boots. Kate follows my gaze.

'God knows where she's gone.' Her eyes brim with tears.

I cast my eyes over a mahogany chest of drawers with brass handles. On top is a figurine, moulded with clay, painted green, brown, and black. It looks to have been created by a child, and to be part-tree, part-human. I reach out and pick it up.

'You couldn't have known this would happen,' I say, gently.

She shakes her head. 'I should have watched closer. Shouldn't have let them play in that forest.'

'This isn't your fault,' I reply. 'I'm sure of it.' I hold her gaze a moment, then look back at the figurine. 'Is this one of Jack's creations?'

I examine it, running my thumb over the rough, unfinished edges.

She nods. 'He's always making things.'

'Jack was with your sister Saoirse when she went missing?'

She nods.

'But he won't say what he knows?'

Her face crumples. 'I don't know what I'll do … if she never comes home,' she whispers.

'Now, now,' I soothe. I can feel my motherly instinct kicking in as I lean forwards and pull her into a hug. 'It won't come to that. Everything will be okay.' She sniffles on my shoulder, as I look towards the warm glow of the kitchen at the end of the hallway. 'It won't come to that …' I repeat, as if singing to a child.

Even as I say it, I realise I might be wrong. Happy endings don't always happen. Children don't always come home alive. And I know better than most that these losses can change a person forever.

6

Day Three

Jack

Ghosts live in the hallway, inside the statue of Mary that watches the door and everyone who comes and goes. The statue has no tongue, but can speak. It has a shawl and flat, open palms. Its head is tilted to one side. It has eyes without dots and little naked feet. It is carved from white stone, never painted, so it looks like a ghost itself. Saoirse says that at night, the lost souls inside the statue shake and tremble. Jack sometimes hears it rattle on the side table when he is trying to sleep. Saoirse says Mam bought it from a sale in the churchyard, that the woman who sold it got rid of it because it was haunting her house too. Jack turns the statue to face the wall. A moth flutters from it up towards the light. As he stands there, another knock happens at the door. Who could it be now? Jack runs into the sitting room and waits for Kate to answer it. He can hear Kate talking to the person for a while, out in the hallway, and then the door opens.

Jack thinks the woman doesn't look like the people from Drumsuin at all. She has pale olive skin and wavy hair that brushes her shoulders. Her face is heart-shaped and fragile-looking, as if carved from marble, and she has a long, proud neck. She's carrying a leather bag in one hand and a tray of sand in the other. Her brown eyes seem to see him fully, unlike most people.

35

But still, he keeps his hands on his ears and does not stop counting. He sees her lips move.

'Jack? I am Freya. Can you stop?'

Jack shakes his head and continues counting quietly.

She gives him a closed-lip smile, lifts one finger, then she turns her head.

'It might be easier if you leave,' she says to Kate, who's standing behind her, her face blotchy from crying.

'How long do you need?'

'An hour should suffice,' Freya replies.

'Grand – after that Jack and I will have our tea.'

Kate leaves the room. Jack scans his eyes over her peacock-blue jumper and pink scarf. A calf-length purple skirt and purple shoes. He notices that her fingers are delicate and bony with short nails, clipped and clean. Freya pulls up a chair, puts a worn cushion on it and sits down, placing her coat and briefcase on the nearest couch. Now she is a few feet away from Jack, not too close but not too far away. She takes out a tape recorder and presses the red button, leaving it on the side table next to her, then she leans back, rests one hand on each armrest. Eventually, Jack takes his hands down from his ears. He pulls Wilberry onto his lap.

'Hello, Jack,' Freya says again, in a softer voice this time. 'How are you feeling today?'

Jack feels empty now. Closed and shut, like a shop. He does not want to speak to this strange woman, he wishes she would leave. He counts on his fingertips. He looks up at the grandfather clock which is on the opposite side to the fireplace, between him and Freya. The long hand is pointing down at the six and the shorter hand is in between the three and the four. He looks at the box on the mantelpiece where the little keys to the cellar door are. He remembers the time when a little robin fell down the chimney, into the fireplace. It flapped about the room until Kate got it out the window. He remembers the robin flying into the glass, again and again, the light thud of its body a desperate drumbeat to escape. He feels sad thinking about the robin.

'After everything that has happened these past few days, I imagine you feel a little overwhelmed,' says Freya.

Jack listens to the hum of the heater. The tap-tap of the rain on the windowpane behind him. He looks at the cut on his wrist from where he'd scraped it in the gorse hedge.

'I heard your sister is missing.'

Jack stretches out his fingers in the number three, for three days.

There is silence. She uncrosses her legs and crosses them the other way around.

'I am a *sigh-co-terapinst*,' she says. 'Do you know what that is?'

Jack shakes his head.

'I listen to people as a job.'

Jack slides off the chair. He walks to the sand tray Freya brought with her. The sand in it is soft, unlike the sand on Drumsuin strand. There are also little figurines inside. A tiny plastic house with four windows and a door. A car. A man with a shovel, who looks like Fergal Duffy Junior, the farmer. A woman in a dress. A baby with a dummy in its mouth. Different townspeople with all sorts of trades.

'Would you like to play with it?' she offers, extending her arm.

Jack nods, his bottom lip still sticking out.

'Go ahead,' she says.

Jack lowers himself onto the carpet. Carefully, he picks up a figurine of a little girl and studies it. She is dressed like Little Red Riding Hood. Saoirse was not wearing a red coat, but it looks a bit like her.

'My mam listens,' he says quietly.

'She does?'

Jack puts his fingertips to both his earlobes and squeezes them.

'Where is your mam?'

'Gone.'

Jack begins to move the figurines around. He picks up the sheep and puts it next to the butcher. Then he moves the fireman next to the house.

'What do you tell her?'

He places the little girl next to the house and puts the farmer next to the tree. He places the woman in the bathtub.

'My fears.'

Jack rubs the scab on his wrist very gently, running his fingertip over the ridge of it. Jack thinks he might like Freya. She reminds him a little of his Aunt Bronagh, who is his favourite adult. Bronagh is safe.

'What are your fears, Jack?'

'Lots of things. Do you listen to fears?' Jack asks.

'That's exactly what I do. You could say I'm a professional listener, and anything you tell me stays right here. Unless I'm worried for your safety, or that of your two sisters.'

Jack looks at Wilberry for a while, taking in his dim smile. Then he looks back up at Freya, who is watching him carefully.

'Do you listen to Garda fears?'

Jack looks down and moves the doctor next to the woman. He puts the boy next to the tree, by the farmer.

'I do … and teachers and nurses and firemen.' She lists them off on her fingers, then fixes her eyes back on his.

'Do you listen to priests?' asks Jack.

'Hmm, not so far,' she says. 'What makes you ask that?'

Jack lowers his voice. 'Priests listen too, in confession. They listen to everyone in the village who has things they've done wrong. They give you prayers to say to make it go away.'

'Do you tell things to a priest?'

Jack thinks. 'Sometimes,' he says, moving the girl from beside the house to where the tree is on the other side, next to the boy and the farmer.

'But I don't really like Father Maguire.'

'Why not?'

'Saoirse went to his house one day with a load of other kids. For lunch.'

'Oh yeah?'

'Ye. She said he was weird. She said she didn't want to go back there again.'

Freya frowned. 'Did Saoirse say anything else about Father Maguire?'

Jack shakes his head. He pulls Wilberry from the chair and places him onto his lap. Freya writes something in her notebook.

'That's a nice toy. Does it have a name?'

'Wilberry.'

'Great name. Where did you get him?'

Jack frowns. 'I found him in the forest.' He pauses. 'Wilberry has fears too.'

'What fears has Wilberry got?'

'All sorts. Same as me. He is scared Saoirse will never be found.' He does a big sigh, then turns Wilberry to face Freya. 'Wilberry lost his eye,' he says, pointing. 'See? Now he only has one. Like Garda Morris.'

'Where did he lose it?'

Jack looks into the sandpit. 'Inside the forest,' he says.

Freya is quiet for a moment. 'Was your sister Saoirse there when he lost his eye?'

Jack shakes his head. He cannot open that box. The lid is locked. He cannot remember everything that happened after he heard the scream that day, but he does know it is the day Wilberry came home without an eye. He moves his gaze to Freya, and gives her a blank look.

'Do you know why I'm here?' she asks.

'No,' replies Jack, looking at her shoes, which look like they belong to a doll. He remembers Saoirse's shoes then, trampling through the mud.

'I'm here because of your sister Saoirse being missing. All of the people want me to find out where she is. I guess it's a bit like I have a mission to complete, and you can help me. But I'm guessing you can't tell me where Saoirse is right now.'

Jack holds his breath, then he lowers his voice to a whisper. 'I don't know where she is.'

'But you were there when she went missing. Can you tell me about that?'

'I don't remember.'

'That's understandable. Sometimes when things are really frightening, we block them out. Why don't you tell me about the forest instead, and that day – anything you *can* remember?'

'It's not that I don't *want* to tell you about the forest and things, it's that I *can't*.'

'Could you say a bit more?'

His heart begins to thud a little faster. He puts his hand up to his mouth in a C-shape and whispers again. 'It's a game. I can't really tell.'

Freya picks up a ballpoint pen and some paper and scribbles something on it, passing it over to Jack. It reads: *Tell me how the game works.*

Hesitantly, he takes the pen and paper. His handwriting is not good and he holds the pen wrong. His mam spent hours trying to teach him how to hold it properly, but he still can't. It comes out like a spider with ink on its feet, crawling across the page.

OK, he writes.

Ready when you are, she writes back.

Jack takes the pen and scrawls, then tucks the page between his fingers and passes it back to her. She scans it, reading it aloud.

'The Counting Game,' she says softly. 'Sounds interesting.'

Jack takes another piece of paper and writes on it. He leans over and hands it back, shaking his head.

No. Scary.

He points to the sandpit. 'Start,' he says quietly, pointing to the house. He writes some more. 'End.' He points to the tree figurine.

Freya cups her elbow with one hand and taps her lips with the other. 'Can you tell me any more?' she asks, then she writes something else.

Why can't you tell?

Jack feels the fear rise in his stomach. He turns to the window and points out towards the trees.

'It's the forest,' he whispers. 'It knows.'

7

Day Three

Freya

The hotel overlooks the ocean. *Cois Fharraige*, it reads on the front, which I know in Irish means *seaside*. In the lobby, a hunched, narrow-shouldered woman in her seventies looks up at me from the desk. She has sparkling eyes with a hint of curiosity in them, and her hair looks as though it has been coloured crudely with a chestnut home dye, her roots showing an inch of grey. Several necklaces adorn her neck, layered over one another above a faded floral top. Clutched between fingers which are slightly swollen is a novel with a painting of a man embracing a woman on the front. She puts the book down. 'Hello there! How can I help?'

'I'm looking for a room.'

I observe the array of staplers and office equipment stacked behind the reception desk and a printer in the corner.

'Of course,' she says, pulling up a ledger. 'You're looking to stay in the busiest village in the country at the moment, do you realise that?'

I frown, feigning ignorance. I don't need her to know I am working on the case.

'It's all anyone is talking about here at the moment. The villagers are devastated. A young girl went missing a few days ago, only thirteen she was. 'Tis awful. She was out playing and just disappeared into thin air.'

I nod and pretend to remember. 'I think I saw it in the papers.'

'Sure, you'd have to be living under a rock not to know,' she adds.

I glance around the timeworn lobby – a couch with a wicker coffee table on which lies a pile of women's magazines. My legs ache to sit. As if sensing this, the woman flicks through the ledger quickly and picks up a pen.

'I'll get you checked in as quick as we can so you can go and rest in your room. Mary's my name, by the way. Have you travelled far today? England, I assume?' she says.

'Actually, I live in Dublin.'

'Ah,' Mary says, pushing up her glasses. She raises her eyebrows and consults her book again. She traces her finger along the line.

'A holiday on your own ...' she says, in a tone as though she were narrating the beginning of a story. 'The world, or Drumsuin, is your oyster.'

I smile in agreement, but my stomach churns with anxiety.

'Room twenty-three is free. Is the ground floor okay?'

'That's fine.'

I clear my throat, which suddenly feels tight. 'Is it okay to leave my car outside?'

She takes out a book of tickets.

'If you give me your registration number it will be fine. I can give you a ticket to put in your window.'

She begins to write in her book.

'Registration?'

'89-D-3478X.'

'Name?'

'Freya Hemmings.'

Mary stands up and takes a key from a hook next to the desk. 'Follow me,' she says.

She sways down the corridor ahead of me, arrives at the room and puts the key in, turning it. It sticks and she curses, jiggling it several times. 'Fecking thing, excuse my French,' she says.

Finally, she gets it open and moves into the room, flicking on the light. She gestures to the double bed, and ensuite bathroom. The room is similar to the lobby – old-fashioned in its decor. The room feels cosy, nonetheless, and the bedspread and carpet look worn but clean.

'Here you are. Before I leave you to it, will you be wanting breakfast in the morning?'

'Yes, please.' I nod quickly. 'I'll want to eat before I spend the day hiking. That forest looks like it takes some energy to get around!' I think this might be what she wants to hear, a plan a tourist might make, but instead Mary's face darkens. Her mouth twitches a little.

'Right so,' she says flatly. 'One full Irish in the morning. Enjoy your night.'

With that, she closes the door behind her firmly with a click, the pleasantries over. I remember what Walter had said at the station: *The place is inhabited by the ghosts of Mary Brady, her baby, the other tortured souls from the laundry …* Could it be true?

Outside the window, I catch sight of the agitated sea and the seafront, white waves dotting the surface of the Atlantic. The curtain blows a little and I close and lock the window. I sing a little to myself as I begin to unpack my suitcase. A song I'd heard on the way here on the radio. Carefully, I lift out the framed photograph of me and Violet that I always carry with me and prop it on the bedside table next to the bed, then unpack everything else.

It had been difficult to leave my apartment in Dublin and come here this time. Home has become something of a safe haven in recent years. The anxiety of being in an unfamiliar place rises in my chest, and instinctively I look around for the mini bar. I am relieved to see there isn't one. Before, I would have raided the mini bar for alcohol and woken up the next day surrounded by bottles. I glance at the clock and realise it is almost time for my weekly AA meeting. I'll miss this week's, but that can't be helped.

I switch on the light in the gleaming white bathroom. The toilet roll end is folded into a neat V, and there are some wrapped soaps on the shelf beneath the mirror, along with some cotton earbuds and a shower cap. I wash my hands and splash water on my face.

Finally, I change into comfortable clothes then relax onto the soft mattress. I decide to call my daughter, Melody, under the guise of letting her know I arrived safe but mainly because I want to check she is okay. Somehow this case had gotten under my skin and made me feel a little less secure of my daughter's safety. I pick up the phone and dial reception.

'Can I call England from here?'

'We charge for any calls on check out. Just press 1 first to dial out.'

'Great, thanks.'

Melody doesn't answer my call. I imagine the phone ringing out on the other end into an empty hallway, and wonder what she might be doing. Perhaps she's on shift at her placement, or late home from classes; in a pub with her friends, knocking back pints and giggling over private jokes. All while I worry that she'll be the next girl or young woman to end up missing. Like Saoirse. I replace the receiver with a click, feeling for a moment like I could cry.

The clock reads 17.56. The sky is gloomy and dark. I think back to my conversation with Walter. The last thing he said has stuck – *Drumsuin is a strange place. Will you be able to cope?* I wonder if I will.

Then there was the session with Jack earlier. The icy, empty feeling in the house. The frustrating feeling of secrets being held just below the surface. I have worked with children who found social interactions difficult before, but Jack's quiet way didn't seem to be part of his condition – there appeared to be another reason he was holding back. The older sister, Kate, in the brief meeting we had, seemed on edge – fragile, like she might shatter at any moment. She had broken down into tears as soon as I had arrived.

I open up my notebook and scribble down some notes from the session today. *The Counting Game*, I scrawl, then underline it. *What is it?* When Jack was speaking about the game, he said he thought the forest knew something. *What does the forest 'know'?* I add. Is it about what had happened to his sister, or something else? It is odd how the adults here are frightened of this forest too. Strange that everyone in Drumsuin believes in this 'creature', and in the game Jack and Saoirse were playing that day. *'Curse', or just a myth?* I write below the other questions. I think about Father Maguire, as he is the only person Jack has mentioned so far who I've felt is a suspect.

I consider writing down my thoughts on him too, but then decide against it. I don't have any real evidence against him, and the Gardaí are looking into his involvement. I snap shut the notebook and my stomach rumbles. It is probably time to find somewhere to eat nearby. These cases always sound glamorous. Hotels, travel, restaurants, exploring new places, but they rarely are. I try to sit up but a wave of tiredness hits me, stronger than the hunger.

I lie back down and rifle in the drawer but there are no leaflets for takeaways, just a leather-bound Bible. Rooting out the nuts I bought earlier from my handbag, I lie back on the bed, snacking on a few. I take a drink from a bottle of mineral water next to the bed, and close my eyes. The pull of rest is too strong. I let the bed hold me in its palm, and feel myself drift off into an uneasy slumber.

8

Day Four

Jack

The next morning, Jack presses his ear to the sitting room door, clutching Wilberry in his hands. He can see Saoirse's pink roller skates on the floor near the coat rack. She had not worn them since two summers ago. He remembers her journey down the pier, limbs flailing, as she tried to keep from rolling into the sea. That's right – it was the same day they had seen Father Maguire on the pier. Father Maguire had spoken to Jack and he had felt scared. Jack doesn't like Father Maguire. People in the village say he is odd. He tries not to think about that, pushing down the fearful feelings again. Instead, he listens.

'… the search party has been out for another night … nothing found just yet … it's extremely worrying … we need to ask a bit more …'

It sounds like Garda Morris's voice.

Then the sound of sniffling, a muffled voice that starts quiet and soon turns angry.

Garda Morris speaks again as if trying to calm the frustrated voice.

'We know that, we are trying our best.'

Jack squints one eye and peers through the keyhole. He can see the painting of geese hanging above the mantlepiece. Below, Kate is sitting in the armchair, her eyes cast down, her cheeks flushed.

She is talking but her voice is not as loud as Garda Morris's. Jack tries not to breathe too heavily. He can feel his heart, fluttering like a hummingbird in his chest. What if they caught him listening in? Would Garda Morris take him to prison?

'And men who live locally, men who visit the house?' Garda Morris asks.

Kate counts on her fingers. 'More than five, I think.'

'And their names?'

Jack can see Garda Morris leaning his elbow onto his knee. He scribbles something in his notebook.

Kate says something in a low voice.

'Mr Fitzgerald?' Garda Morris echoes.

He sees Kate nod.

'Father Maguire?'

Kate nods again.

Jack feels some dust blow out from the keyhole. His nose tingles and before he can stop himself, he sneezes.

Garda Morris turns his head to face the door. Jack feels a zip of energy run through him. He sprints back down the hall, and sits on the scratched wood stairs. There are voices, then Garda Morris emerges. Hollow footsteps approach. Jack watches the stained-glass halo over the door and counts on his fingertips. The pictures are like sea monsters or a storm, or a stag on fire, though Saoirse says it is no picture at all. Garda Morris stands over Jack, his hands behind his back.

'You'd make a terrible spy,' the Garda says. 'Kate says you have an attic room you might like to show me, with paintings in?'

Jack breathes out, relieved he isn't in *big* trouble, and leads the way up the gloomy stairwell. Garda Morris holds the handrail as he follows. Jack's painting room is just off the half-landing, through a crawl space in the wall.

Garda Morris takes off his hat and dabs at his forehead with a tissue. He puts the hat on the step, then he stoops and peers into the attic, through the little hatch doors.

'Is there room to stand up in there?'

Jack nods. 'You need to bend to get in though.'

'No kidding.'

Garda Morris crawls through first. Jack follows with Wilberry sandwiched under his arm. Garda Morris stands up with a grunt and turns around on the spot, with his head back, looking at Jack's pictures. Every part of the wall and ceiling, apart from the skylight, is covered in them. Jack shows Wilberry the paintings too. He spins around so he can see it all. Some of them he remembers painting, and some he does not.

'These are excellent. *An-mhaith* indeed,' Garda Morris comments. 'You should show these to Freya – the psychotherapist – later, when she arrives. Do you think you could do that?' he asks.

Jack nods.

He smiles at Jack, who crosses his fingers on both his hands, because Kate says crossing fingers can ward off bad or evil things.

'Can you explain about this one?' Garda Morris says, pointing to one of a little boy standing next to a pile of luminous stones, boulders next to a tangle of branches.

Jack shrugs. He sits on a little wooden chair in the middle of the small room. Garda Morris sits down on the matching chair opposite. It is so tiny he looks funny on it, like a polar bear on a bike. Jack thinks he might like to talk to Garda Morris, but then he thinks he might not at all. He can't remember the day Saoirse went missing at all now. It has been erased. Garda Morris fixes him with his one-eyed gaze. Jack shifts a little, getting comfortable on his seat, staring at the gleaming gold buttons on the Garda's shirt, and the way his socks poke out from his shoes.

'Are you okay? Things with Kate, everything at home here?'

Jack looks away and takes out something from the pocket on the front of his jumper. It's a figurine he made of the Creature. He holds it up very carefully. It is brown and green, with long arms and a tongue. Feet with roots on them like a tree. He knows he should not show the Creature to Garda Morris, but he cannot help himself.

'What is that?' Garda Morris asks.

Jack is quiet.

'Can I see it?' he says, reaching out his hand.

Jack snatches it back and hides it in the front of his jumper again.

'Looks like a monster of some sort, is it from a cartoon?'

Jack shakes his head.

'Odd,' says Garda Morris. 'Jack, now we are alone, I'd like to have a serious conversation if we can. Does that make sense?'

Jack nods. He knows about serious conversations – he's already had a few in his life, and they are never fun. A conversation with his mam about his dad leaving, with Kate about his mother's funeral, and with the headmistress about his bad behaviour at school.

'Your sister mentioned there were some men coming to the house before your mam passed away?'

Jack nods.

'I don't suppose any of these men were … you know?'

Jack doesn't reply.

'*Interfering* with Saoirse?'

Jack does not understand the question. He gives Garda Morris a blank stare. The Garda sighs. 'I need to know if any of these men had an eye on her?'

'Were there any men you didn't like?' he tries again.

Jack wants to say Mr Fitzgerald, but it's difficult to speak. Mr Fitzgerald never did anything bad, but Jack didn't like him around – he doesn't know why. Some strange feeling that he cannot explain to a Garda.

'I have a sister,' Garda Morris continues. 'I mentioned that earlier, didn't I?'

Jack nods.

'Well, we used to be quite close, me and her. We used to play around near the beach – all sorts of games we used to make up.'

Garda Morris smiles a little as if remembering something happy. But then he frowns.

'One day, my sister was down on the beach and a man attacked her. I saw it all, but when we got home, she told me not to tell anyone it had happened. I never did. You know why?'

Jack shakes his head.

'I think you do. I think you know that siblings have unspoken loyalty.'

'What's *loy-al-tee*?'

'It means I won't tell on you, and you don't tell on me.'

Jack racks his brains. He had seen Saoirse at the gate to their house, waving to someone outside. He had seen the boy walking off. She had sworn him to secrecy.

'Well, she does have a boyfriend …' Jack whispers with a smile, covering his mouth. He feels excited now, and puts his hands in the air like a creature. 'He's this big!' Jack jumps up on his chair and stands on his tiptoes. He pulls a horrible face. 'And he's ugly with big spots and his name is Paddy LIONS, like a big cat with a *rooooarr*!'

Garda Morris smiles now. 'A boyfriend?'

Jack nods. 'Their faces were stuck together one time behind the shed in school!' He sticks his fingers in his mouth like he's getting sick.

'Paddy Lyons, you say … and where does he live?'

'Down by Slieve Doon, the state.'

'The estate?'

Jack nods. He jumps back down off the chair and sits down, swinging his legs.

'Is he in her class at school?'

Jack nods again.

'She writed *I love Paddy* on one of her copies. And they used to play a dare game together – to see who could climb the highest tree. One time, Saoirse climbed a tree a hundred feet high, though Paddy said she couldn't do it.'

'Is that right, now?'

'Ye.'

'And might she be with her boyfriend?'

Jack shook his head. 'They don't see one another *too* much.'

'Thank you for sharing that, Jack. I'll go and have a word with the lad and ask him if he knows anything.'

Jack looks at the paintings. He focuses on one of him and Saoirse rowing in a sapphire lake, the oars slicing through a constellation of numbers.

Garda Morris looks around himself, then stands up from the little chair. Jack watches as he takes a few paces to the other side of the room.

'Do you have any paintings here from the past few days?'

Jack points to the small table in the corner. It's his drying table, where he leaves his pictures until they are ready to be pinned up.

'This one here?'

Jack has a look. Next to his painting of a starfish Jack had found on the beach, there is one of Saoirse with her red hair standing near a river. Beside her stands a little girl in a yellow dress under a bleak grey moon.

'Ye.'

'Who is this girl in the dress – a friend of yours?'

Jack shakes his head.

'A friend of Saoirse's?'

'No. She lives in the forest.'

'Might she know where Saoirse has gone?'

Jack thinks for a moment, then shakes his head. 'She can't really talk ...'

'No?'

'No.'

'Is she imaginary?'

'I can't tell.'

Garda Morris moves his finger to point at another painting. A little boy in the torchlight, magical footprints trailing behind him.

'And this picture?'

Jack remembers that night. There was a swirling blackness behind them. He and Saoirse were running, carried by the momentum of the wind, their feet almost lifted off the ground in the swollen storm.

'Do Gardaí keep secrets?' Jack asks suddenly.

Garda Morris hesitates, and glances at the hatch. He seems to think for a moment. 'They do,' he replies eventually.

'Do you ever get tired of it?' Jack asks.

Garda Morris hesitates. 'Of keeping secrets? Oh, all the time. But those secrets are to keep people safe, so it's the best way.' He squats down, ready to crawl back out. 'Secrets that hurt people are different. You do know that, don't you Jack?'

Jack remembers what his mother had told him, that secrets were like elephants. Each time you told something, the elephant shrank. Pretty soon it went from a humungous beast to something you could carry around in your pocket with you, like a figurine. Secrets don't feel like elephants to Jack, more like tigers that would eat you alive. He does not want to be eaten alive.

Garda Morris looks up from the entryway, and his gaze settles on the painting of Jack and Saoirse in the forest, with the Creature looming behind them. Then he turns and disappears. Jack takes the clay model out of his pocket and inspects it again, running his fingertips over its roots. He closes his eyes.

Erase.

9

Day Four

Jack

Jack's house feels like a heart. Full of throb and thrum, of blood which runs through the arteries of staircases and hiding places. A loud house, if you listen to it closely enough from the inside. Worries and fears rush around and back, never escaping.

As Jack sits on the couch in the sitting room, hands over his ears, he notices little lines like veins in the floorboards – they carry his fear down so it drips into the cellar. Jack counts. *One, two, three, four … seven, eight, nine, ten …*

There is a loud knock. *Ra-tat-tat.* Jack places his figurine of the Creature on the chest of drawers, licks sherbet off his lollipop and opens the door to see a woman standing in front of him. Behind her, a group of people from the village stand holding casserole dishes covered in tin foil. The red and brown trees wave from the garden, and the sour-lemon sun tries to poke its head out from behind the clouds.

'Any news?' an older woman calls out from the group of villagers. 'We thought we'd come by with some food for you all. Send our love to your big sister, Kate.'

'I will, Mrs McCarthy,' Jack replies, watching as she draws nearer and leaves a dish on the step. The other villagers follow her and leave a dish each next to hers.

'We won't bother ye all, but we want you to know we are praying for Saoirse, and lighting candles – lots of them. Breda over here nearly burned down the church with the amount she lit.'

Jack glances at Breda who is hunched over, her old face worried. Jack knows her from Mass. He nods again, unsure what to say.

In front of him at the door is the woman he doesn't recognise. She has high cheeks and a bright stare. She is thin, like the wind could blow her away, but her welly boots seem heavy, as though she is rooted to the spot. Jack feels curious. Is she looking for Saoirse, too?

'I think they could probably benefit from some space now,' the woman says to the small group, who nod and walk away back down the driveway.

The woman seems to know Jack already. She calls him by name, says her name is Alice and she is a *vol-in-tear*, helping to look for Saoirse. She bends slightly and presses something into his free hand. It is a pebble from the beach. A little gift, she says. A touchstone. 'Hold on to it tight, now,' she says, patting his knuckles. Jack nods and looks down at her hands, which are a bit wrinkled, like his mother's used to be.

She takes her eyes off Jack and he studies the pebble. It is a rare-looking one, with reds and oranges like the planet Jupiter, with calcified threads of white running through it. Sand pushed together for thousands of years, smoothed off by the sea. Jack closes his fingers around it, feeling its cool weight. Her feet shuffle mud onto the mat. Jack stands back and she passes him. He closes the door and digs his lolly back into the sherbet as she disappears into the sitting room.

Now Kate, Alice and Garda Morris sit around on the couches and chairs. Alice sits opposite Jack. Jack is sitting on the floor, drawing with his pencils. He could go to the kitchen but he does not want to be alone.

'This is my girlfriend, Alice,' Garda Morris explains. 'She's been a great help. I thought she could join us here today as you could use another pair of hands? The past few days have been very overwhelming for you all.'

Alice nods. 'Can I make you all some tea or maybe I can sit with Jack and help entertain him for a bit?'

'That would be great,' Kate says, her face suddenly relieved. 'It has been a lot, and I am worried about Jack,' she adds.

Alice sits down on the floor in front of Jack. 'What are you drawing?' she asks, pointing to the monster on the page.

Jack notices the heater has been brought in. When Jack stares at it, the glow of the filaments burns into his eyes so when he closes them bright lines are all he can see. There is some *báirín breac* on a plate in the centre of the coffee table, sliced and buttered for the guests. They only ever ate it around October time. Every year, Jack would bite in and hope for the metal ring, hidden among the raisins. Last year, Saoirse got it. If you got the ring in your slice, it meant you would be married soon. Jack didn't want to be married soon, but it was exciting to bite into the cake, not knowing if suddenly your teeth would hit metal. Tonight, he didn't want any at all, though. Not without Saoirse.

'Can you draw me something?' Alice asks.

Jack nods. 'What will I draw?'

'How about ... a funfair?'

Jack tries to think about what a funfair looks like, with a circus tent and rides. It is hard to focus on drawing when everyone is discussing Saoirse's whereabouts in hushed tones. Garda Morris sits on the old green sofa, his legs spread wide with his navy socks in full view. He leans on his knees with his elbows, adjusting his glasses every so often and peering closer at some of Jack's paintings which are laid out on the floor, as though they are clues. The ones the grown-ups had selected are a strange bunch and Jack cannot understand why they picked them.

'Kate,' Garda Morris says. 'I haven't talked to you much about your mother's ...' – he glances at Jack hesitantly – 'death ... and how it might link to all of this? Alice, actually, can you take Jack outside a minute please?'

'He's fine,' says Kate. 'He's heard it all before.'

Garda Morris frowns. Jack remembers the day their mother had died. It was the thing they most avoided talking about, though every second without their mother was a reminder that she was gone forever. Kate looks upset. Alice is ready to stand up, but Jack keeps drawing.

'She didn't kill herself. It was that forest, that bloody game. They were playing it that day ...' She sounds angry now.

'What are you saying?' asks Garda Morris.

'I am saying she didn't jump off that cliff ... Something must have happened to make her fall!'

Garda Morris looks at Jack for a moment. 'I'd really prefer he didn't hear all of this.'

'He's already completely traumatised. What's one more conversation going to do to him?' she says dryly. Then she goes quiet for a long moment. 'You think our mother's death might have something to do with this?'

'Perhaps. Did Saoirse recently find out something about your mother's death, that she didn't know before? Or did your mother's death lead to Saoirse becoming overwhelmed and running away? I mean ... You say you don't know anyone who could have taken Saoirse, or enabled her to leave the village?'

'The only person I can think of who might have reason to do that would be our father, as I've said.'

'Yes. Officers have already visited his residence in Dublin – he claims he knows nothing about her disappearance and there was no sign of her having been there at all.' Garda Morris pauses. 'Jack mentioned Saoirse has a boyfriend?'

Kate raises her head slowly. 'A boyfriend?' She looks at Jack. 'I didn't know that. Who is he?'

'Paddy Lyons?' Garda Morris says.

'That's someone in her class at school,' Kate says.

'Well, I'll be getting over to his house to ask the lad questions. Do you know where he lives?'

'The school will know.'

Garda Morris stands up, and nods to Alice to do the same.

'Thanks for your help today, Jack. Don't be giving your big sister Kate any hassle, now. You hear?'

But he smiles as he says it, so Jack knows he is joking. He turns to Kate.

'That *sigh-co-terapinst* will be arriving shortly. Can you make sure to let her in? I think it's a good idea that she talks to Jack as soon as possible, rather than leaving it another day.'

'Of course.'

Jack closes his eyes and feels the din rising inside.

Erase.

10

Day Four

Jack

They are upstairs in Kate's bedroom now. Garda Morris has gone away to find more clues. Kate presses her fingertips to the side of Jack's head, so he'll look straight ahead. The fog has arrived outside again, and the sun is about to fall for another night. All Jack can see out of the window is the broken-down tractor in the front garden, with rust on the wing mirrors and moss on the wheels. Usually, from here, the treetops of the firs are visible but today they are not. Maybe the forest is scared of being found out, too.

Beside the window is a mirror. In it, he can see the pink and white lines on the inside of Kate's wrists. When people are around, she hides them with a jumper, but now they are alone she's letting them show. Jack remembers the time he found her, before – in the bathroom, covered in blood.

As if she senses Jack is looking, her hands drop for a moment and she begins to fiddle with her locket again. Jack's shoulders tense up. He looks away and after a while he feels the comb grazing his head, hears the cold scrape of the scissors.

'You know, Jack … keeping things hidden that stop Saoirse from being found is not okay.' She told him this last night, too, adding that it was especially not okay when there are *Gardaí up here, judging us and the state of everything.* 'Garda Morris said you knew she had a boyfriend,' she says. 'Why didn't she tell *me* that?'

'I dunno.'

'How do you know she has one?'

'I saw them kissing.'

'Is he a nice boy?'

Jack shrugs. 'Saoirse says he's nice, but he always wants to win.'

'In what way?'

'In their games.'

'Christ …' Kate mutters. 'Is there anything else you know? Any other strange men you've seen hanging around lately?'

'Just Fergal.'

'As in, Fergal Duffy Junior, our neighbour, the farmer?'

'Ye … he was out with his bees. Last week. He always looks angry when he sees us.'

Jack doesn't mention the other thing he knows about Fergal, the thing they had found in his barn a few months ago. He doesn't want to scare Kate too much.

Kate suddenly seems energised. 'When the Gardaí searched Saoirse's room, they wanted to know if she kept a diary. She always told me she didn't … but if she has a secret one, I'll bet you're clever enough to know where she might have hidden it?'

Jack thinks hard. He had seen her writing in one, but it was meant to be a secret. Where did she hide it? He remembers her closing it once, as he walked into the room. Sliding it behind the painting of Drumsuin in the hallway, where their dad used to hide cash notes in the wall.

'In the cubby,' he says.

Kate clamps her hands on Jack's shoulders and begins to cry again. 'Christ, the Gardaí were looking everywhere, I can't believe it!' This time it sounds like she's relieved. She puts down the scissors with a clatter on the tray, and runs from the room. Jack hears her go down the stairs to the cubby to fetch the diary. He watches Wilberry, who sits on the windowsill with his back to Jack. He is on the watch for visitors.

'Can you see anything, Wilberry?' Jack whispers. There is no reply, and Jack feels the fear again, the kind he feels during the game. Kate has played the Counting Game sometimes too, in the past – their mother taught it to all of them – but now she hates it. She hasn't joined in since their mam's death. And Saoirse always said, how could she and Jack end the game if they didn't play?

Finally, he sees Kate in the mirror behind him again, and he feels her cool hands tucking the rough edges of a towel inside his T-shirt. She puts the diary on the bed. Jack wonders if she read the whole thing in the time she was downstairs, but Kate's face doesn't give anything away. Her lips are pursed like she is trying not to say something. She then sprays some water from a bottle over his head. The droplets land on his ears and the tip of his nose. Jack scrunches his face and rubs his eyes then looks at the bed and a dress of Kate's which hangs on the edge of the wardrobe. It is navy with light blue doves across it. Jack remembers her wearing it the last time they went to Mass in Drumsuin. He remembers her taking his hand, gripping his fingers too tight. She had nodded to Father Maguire, pushed Jack into a pew and slid in next to him. Jack had spoken in a hushed voice to Kate, so no one else could hear.

'Why do I have to come to Mass?'

She had opened her mouth to reply but just then, Father Maguire had come over to say hello.

'The young one not here today?'

His hands were tucked one over the other. Jack looked down at the priest's shiny shoes, which poked out from under his cream-coloured robe. The robe had gold embroidery on it of a chalice.

'Not today. Studying for her tests.'

'Ah right. She'll do well, please God,' he said.

He continued walking towards the altar, where he bent his knee and bowed. Kate had muttered under her breath some rude words, and before Jack had a chance to ask questions about the words and what they meant, everyone had stood up.

Jack is brought back to himself as Kate turns his head to face forwards again. He tries not to think about how much he is missing Saoirse. The emptiness in his chest where the feeling of Saoirse being nearby should be. She would know what to do, and what to say to people about what had happened.

Kate snips some more, and Jack looks at his pale blonde hair on the floor. Kate had said they may as well trim their hair as long as they were stuck here, waiting for Saoirse and going mad. With all these people around, they need to look presentable. The hair flutters down and settles on the floorboards, like dried-out pine needles. It reminds Jack of something that happened a few weeks ago.

He crouched under the tree. Saoirse had her hand on his arm, and they watched the shadow move towards them.

After a minute Kate stops and snatches the diary back up. She tells Jack she will finish cutting his hair later, then she sits on the bed and begins to read it, like it's the most interesting book she's ever picked up. Jack's hair is half cut now – in the mirror, he sees that one side is long, one side short. He can feel the hot din rising in his chest again, and the images from the forest starting to come back, so he closes his eyes. *Erase.*

COUNTDOWN

Ten ...

Nine Months Ago

Saoirse

Saoirse's thoughts feel like freshwater here, immersed and complete. Her heart is brackish and meandering. Her mouth is a cave, lips pressed shut in an oxbow shape. Her fingertips coil and press around the cold boulder. Saoirse keeps her body on the muddy bank, grips tight and plunges her whole head backwards, submerging it in the river. She hears Jack's voice quaver as she drops back.

Down here it is silent. Too silent, except for the glug of the water in her ears. The cold tightens around her skull. She begins to count. The last time she reached forty before resurfacing, so today she would like to reach forty-five. Something tickles her face, a plant of some kind, soft like a finger. It forces her to open her eyes, her mouth. The taste of river pours in before she can close it again. Fresh, earthy, metallic. Bubbles escape from her lips and rise, a shimmering collective. She keeps her eyes open, not wishing to give up yet. Her hair hovers about her – orange dancing strands, amniotic and close. Forty-five is not too far away. There is something strange about looking at things underwater, something peaceful. The light fractures on the surface and enters with an amber hue. The water moves in distinct layers. It is not all that it seems on the surface, the river. Her gaze flicks around: the wizened stem of a cattail, a spatterdock, a sprout. Greens, whites, golds. *Twenty-five.* Her chest throbs, just a little at first. A slight discomfort. Like needing the toilet. She lists things to pass the time. *Bilgewater, blackwater, firewater, greywater.* Ten seconds left now. She can manage it if she counts down. Her lungs cry out. Then she sees the girl. She thinks she might be imagining it at first. Her mind playing tricks. But no, the girl seems real, moving towards her. Dark hair, wavy and long. Skin translucent in this light. She wears a cardigan and a yellow dress, and she swims breaststroke underwater, her face desperate and angry, or perhaps sad. The girl's mouth opens and closes.

Saoirse thrashes the riverbank with both hands, and her brother drags her up to sitting position again. She gasps as her head emerges. Takes great gulps of air. She looks around the forest and pulls her arms around herself. Her teeth chatter and goosebumps appear on her skin. Drips fall from her hair. She looks back into the water, but now there is nothing. No girl. Just the water, cold and clear.

PART TWO

11

Day Four

Jack

Jack listens to the rain on the windows. It runs down the lanes of Drumsuin. Little rivers in the ditches, mud and mulch soup, draining the mountains into the sea. Jack thinks about Saoirse, imagines her hiding somewhere all curled up in a ball, like a rabbit in a burrow he discovered once. When he thinks about that he feels sad. Freya has laid out the sandpit again, ready for him to tell stories with the figurines inside.

'Where do you think she could be?' Freya asks now, her expression serious.

Jack feels a pain in the back of his throat. *He was running. The wind was roaring. The game would not stop, and he could not get out fast enough.*

'I don't know, I can't remember … I wish …'

Jack stares into the sandpit again. He can see all of the plastic figurines are waiting to be moved by him.

He looks into Freya's eyes, as if for help. She turns her head away to stare at the paintings on the coffee table that Garda Morris has left. She picks one up with a concentrated look.

'Who is this?' she says, turning the picture to face him. It's the one of the little girl with the yellow dress, standing beside a river. He watches her face as she focuses on it again. 'And you've created something here, something – a figure behind the tree. What is that?'

The figure is brown and green with long arms, feet with roots. The paint looks flaky on the page. Jack remembers standing on a chair, pressing pins into the plaster, sticking the pictures up. Not this one, though – this one was only drying yesterday. The walls were like the inside of Jack's mind – the paintings were the memories he could not hold on to – but now they have been taken down. Now they have become clues for others to study. She puts the picture down and leans back on the wooden chair. It creaks. Freya smiles in a sad way.

'Sometimes when I am working with people who find it hard to remember things, I ask them to tell me the story as though it happened to someone else,' she says. 'Like, you might say *Once upon a time, there was a little boy called Jack ...*' She pauses. '*And Jack's sister went missing ... and he was scared.*'

Jack looks out of the window behind Freya, at the rain.

'Wilberry could play that game,' he says.

'He could?'

Jack nods Wilberry's head for him.

'Do you think you can help him play?'

Jack nods Wilberry's head again.

'Whenever you are ready,' Freya says.

There is a long silence, and then Jack takes a deep breath.

'Once upon a time, there was a boy called Jack,' he says. He reaches out and strokes Wilberry's head as he talks. He closes his eyes and tries to stop the din rising in himself. 'Jack lived with his mam and his two sisters ... and his dog Pearl and his fish Jack Dempsey, in Drumsuin, Ireland, The World. Jack was okay until the forest got angry with them.'

He opens his eyes.

'The forest?'

Jack thinks about Garda Morris's car on the day Saoirse went missing. Driving along through the trees in his Beetle. Jack had seen him from the side of the road. Where was Garda Morris going?

'What happened to the little boy next?' asks Freya.

'Things happened.'

'What kind of things?'

'Bad things.'

'Like what?' She stares at him calmly, her eyes steady, and lowers her voice to a whisper. 'Did Jack get hurt?'

He looks away and nods. He can feel the feelings tying a knot in his stomach. The sound of the wind outside seems to get louder.

'How was he hurt?'

'In his mind.'

'Is he better now?'

'No.'

'How can he be helped?'

'He can't.'

Freya searches his face. 'Are you sure?'

'Ye.'

Jack pulls his knees together and rubs his arms. He feels hollowed out on the inside. Wilberry watches Jack with a dim smile.

'This person you painted ...' she says, pointing to the girl in the yellow dress. 'Is she something to do with the game you mentioned yesterday?'

Jack nods. He wants to talk about the girl, but he's scared.

'Can you tell me more about the game?'

Jack shakes his head. 'I can't explain it.'

'I believe you can.'

Freya leaves time to pass.

'Do you still dream?'

Jack draws a breath and releases it. The ghosts are pulling at his stomach again. He thinks back to his dreams last night, and draws a tick sign on his leg.

'Bad ones?'

Jack draws another invisible tick. He feels the fear again. He is starting to remember.

'What are your dreams about?'

Jack opens his mouth, then closes it again. He sees pictures building, but swallows hard and pushes them away. He puts his hands around his cold toes and squeezes. The memory is almost there on the edge of his mind – Mr Fitzgerald, watching them from the butcher's shop window, with that strange smile on his face. Saoirse blushing and pulling Jack by the hand to hurry up and walk past.

But then it disappears. *Poof* – like smoke.

'I can't remember.'

There is silence.

'What *do* you know?' Freya asks. 'Just tell me that.'

'The forest ...' he says. Jack lowers his voice to a whisper. 'When it gets angry, bad things happen. That's why ...' He stops for a moment. 'That's why she's gone.'

'Because you made the forest angry?'

Jack nods.

'When the forest got angry, how did it take Saoirse?'

'That's the part I can't remember.'

Freya nods. She smiles, as though she has a new idea. 'Okay! How about ... if you get the pictures and put them together. Maybe that would give me a clue. Like a ... a storybook, or a comic?' She reaches out and picks up the pictures. 'You put them side by side, yes?'

Jack turns this over in his mind for a moment. He nods. Jack thinks about the people who are looking for Saoirse now, the lines of strangers stomping through the forest, calling her name, among the twisted branches, cut under the bow of the crumbling sky. The trees do not surrender easily – they will not shrink back to reveal his sister; they will stand solid as a wall. He thinks about Garda Morris and where he might be right now too. Searching for her, like a lighthouse scanning around with his one-eyed beam. That is, if Garda Morris is a good man, and not a baddie. Jack can't really tell. As Freya is picking up the artwork, he thinks to ask something he has been wondering for a while.

'Why does Garda Morris only have one eye?'

'I don't know,' Freya says. She chooses her words carefully. 'Sometimes people have accidents.'

Jack thinks about this. 'Did he tell you how it happened?'

Freya shakes her head, putting a picture on top of the pile. 'No, he didn't speak to me about it. Maybe he doesn't like to talk about it.'

Jack looks at Wilberry. He thinks for a moment.

'Maybe Garda Morris has a secret.'

12

Day Four

Freya

I tidy Jack's artwork away into a pile, and try to rid myself of the buzzing in my mind. This morning has felt strangely over-whelming. Voices emanate from the kitchen. I feel my curiosity pique, and steel myself to creep down the hallway.

As I open the door, two faces turn towards me – Kate, and someone else who I have not met before. Kate seems flustered, her normally pale face flushing red.

'Freya – all finished for the morning?'

'Yes, Jack is taking a break now,' I reply.

She looks from me to the woman opposite her.

'This is our Aunt Bronagh – she's back from the UK. Bronagh, this is Freya, Jack's therapist. I'm just going to check on Jack.'

With that, Kate leaves the room.

'Nice to meet you,' says Bronagh. She wheels towards me and holds out her hand. I shake it.

She has raven black hair, pulled back in a low plait, and looks to be a little younger than me, around forty. Her skin is lined in the way many Celtic people's tends to go when exposed to the elements, her cheekbones dotted with freckles, and she is thin-boned as a bird. It does not take away from her beauty: she has the look of a lost wildflower – a distant gaze, a mouth left open a little as though trying to remember something she has forgotten.

'I live across the road,' she says and turns her wheelchair. 'I feel so awful that I was away. I had a hospital appointment in London, for my legs.'

'You were hardly to know,' I say. 'These things often happen at the worst times.'

She gestures to her wheelchair. 'Tell me about it. I keep a second set of eyes on them, you know? When Kate isn't paying attention.'

'Does that happen often?' I ask, keeping my tone casual. 'Kate not paying attention, I mean?'

'Sort of. She is away with the fairies sometimes. She loves them, but then I go away, and this happens … I feel like it's my fault.'

'Honestly, I don't think it is,' I reply, trying to convey warmth in my tone.

There is a silence which feels thoughtful. I wonder whether to sit, but instead settle for standing near the window, casting my eyes over the garden.

'You're kind,' she notes. 'We need someone like you around here.'

'Oh really?'

Garda Morris had said something similar when I arrived. Perhaps many people in Drumsuin are in need of help.

'Yeah. The children could use a space to talk. Jack used to come over to my house and tell me things. Recently he's been quieter. I do wonder sometimes what he's not telling me, especially now.'

I glance over my shoulder to check Jack is not listening at the door, and I contemplate the pictures. A looming creature behind the trees. 'His pictures are certainly thought-provoking,' I reply.

'His imagination will get him into trouble one day,' she says. 'A few months ago, he stole some paints from the school and painted a crow all over the wall of the assembly hall. They had to hire people to decorate it white again. It was an embarrassing situation, and Jack was lucky not to be expelled. I think they could tell he was not deliberately trying to be bold, but they did say we should get him help back then … for whatever is going on in his head. I considered getting him help, but Kate was against it. She was worried it might draw attention to the family. Looking back, I should have insisted.'

She sighs, as if tiring of that topic. She takes a small T-shirt of Jack's from a mountain of crumpled dry laundry and places it on the top of a pile of folded clothes.

'They had helicopters out all last night. Did you hear them? It's all very overwhelming. I almost feel … detached. You know what I mean?'

I do know what she means. I have experienced it myself. *Loss.*

Bronagh abandons the laundry, moves to the drawer and takes out a knife.

'I barely caught two hours sleep last night. These past few days have been a living nightmare. I've been keeping myself busy since I got back from Dublin – shopping for food, washing Jack's and Kate's clothes, making sure Jack does some homework while he is off school. Trying to get this house in order, while I have the chance, feeding everyone … On that note, I was going to make some lunch, did you want something? A sandwich, maybe?'

Dublin? I thought she said she was in London. Perhaps she had meant back from Dublin airport. I feel my stomach rumble.

'A sandwich would be great,' I reply.

I sit heavily onto a nearby chair. Bronagh reaches up to the fridge, taking out the butter and cheese.

'The Gardaí are trying their best, I know they are, but it's not enough. They need to get national attention. Saoirse might have been spirited away by some tourist passing through. I have this necklace, see?'

She presents her necklace. I look closer to see the pendant encrusted with blue and purple gems. A butterfly.

'I keep touching it and saying "Come home, Saoirse", as though she can hear … Butterflies remind me of her you see, she has always been a free spirit. I think the necklace helps me feel connected to her.' Her eyes fill up with tears. 'We probably could have used you here sooner. There are mental health issues galore in this family, and so much secrecy. Don't get me wrong, Jack was always odd, but his energy before was different. Less … lost.'

She wipes a tear from her eye and sniffs.

'If you don't mind me asking, how was their mother behaving before she died?' I ask.

She coughs, clearing her throat. 'It's quite difficult to talk about – it's still so fresh. It only happened a few months ago.'

'I heard she jumped off a cliff?'

'Yes, it was awful – Kate thinks she may have fallen or been pushed, but she's just trying to cope.'

'I'm so sorry. Was she your sister?'

'Sister-in-law. My brother, Cahill, left and moved to Dublin prior to that. We had thought about it being him, but he was nowhere near Drumsuin the day Saoirse went missing. The forensics team searched his residence and there was no trace of her having been there.' Bronagh takes out the bread and begins to make the sandwiches. 'But don't get me started down that road of who might have taken her.'

I notice Bronagh has managed to avoid my question about Lucy, but at the same time, the last thing she has said piques my curiosity. 'Like who?'

'Father Maguire,' she says, her voice low and angry.

'The priest?'

'Yes – the man was moved from another parish. We all know why priests get moved around – they fiddle some child, people find out and then the church moves them on, instead of dealing with the problem. Anyway, I've told the Gardaí my suspicions.'

I think about what Jack said about Father Maguire and how I've had my suspicions about him too. It doesn't hurt to keep track of things. My hunches in the past had always been helpful to the cases I've worked on.

'And your brother and Lucy, how was their relationship?'

'Cahill found their mother a challenge, and I have to admit, God rest her soul, she was. He left before she died, somewhat abandoned the children, really. Though he occasionally sends back a cheque, he hasn't visited in about a year. He was a good father when he was here ... but his absence has been hurtful.'

I think sadly about what effect this may have had on Jack, but then I realise I need to stay on the topic of Lucy if I am to find out any more about her death.

'How do you think she died?'

'Personally, I think Lucy jumped off that cliff. The Gardaí couldn't rule out foul play when they found her. There would be no reason for anyone to kill her – no insurance policy on her life. But she was fighting her own demons every day. I think all the encounters she was having with men was affecting her mental health. Lucy's downfall was that she could be too friendly and too trusting – she let men into the house that she shouldn't have ...'

'Men?'

'They're being questioned by the Gardaí. The butcher, Mr Fitzgerald, and I believe the neighbour, Fergal Duffy – and a few other men down the village.' Bronagh slices the sandwiches in half. 'I just hope none of them have touched Saoirse.'

I try not to show shock at this comment, but my heart begins to thump nonetheless. 'You don't think they would?'

'I don't know ... Terrible things can happen in the world. Who knows if they'll happen on your doorstep.'

'Do you have children yourself?' I ask.

'No. Being an aunt is good enough for me.'

'Were you very close to Saoirse?'

She drops the knife suddenly with a clatter. It bounces across the floor, scattering crumbs and spinning, finally coming to a stop near my foot. She puts her face in her hands, letting out a gasp.

'Yes. My God, but what if she never comes home?'

I pick up the knife and place it on the table. I reach for something comforting to say but, in my haze of tiredness, I cannot think of anything. All I know is that, in reality, things are not always all right in the end. Bronagh's face is streaked with tears now. I pull out a packet of tissues from my bag and hand it to her.

'I'm sorry,' I say.

She sniffles. 'I just can't believe it, you know? She was there one minute, gone the next. It doesn't make sense.'

I observe the kitchen. There is a broken window covered by cling film. A hearth. While from the outside the property looks grand and desirable, from the inside the house looks a little neglected. As though they have been living here without someone who cares about the place for some time.

Bronagh wipes at one eye. 'Have you got children?' she asks.

I nod. 'Two.'

'What are their names?'

'Violet and Melody.'

'Where are they now?'

I look out at the garden.

Three images flash into my mind. The girls eating ice creams on holiday; Melody as a student waving goodbye at the train station with a rucksack on her back; and the third one: Violet falling into the pool. Something I never saw but have imagined a million times over. I picture her arms flailing around, the panic in her face as she tried to stay afloat. I imagine her calling out 'Mummy!' but no one coming and the terror and fear she must have felt as she realised no one was there to help. Ducking underwater and flailing, unable to breathe – lungs bursting for air and spots dancing before her eyes before she slipped into darkness. I remember Daniel's face, side-eyeing me at the funeral, stood to the other side of Melody who was next to me. We looked like a family unit, even though were no longer were. I remember him leaning in over Melody's head and whispering in my ear: *Have you been drinking?* I didn't reply, as I stared at her small, white coffin, just pressed my face into my handkerchief, tasting my own sour whiskey breath.

All of a sudden, Jack walks into the room.

'Someone is here!' he cries.

'Sorry,' Bronagh says. 'I'd better go get the door.'

She leaves the kitchen. I had changed the subject successfully again, but then so had Bronagh, it seems. Perhaps both of us have things to hide. I have a feeling this case is going to bring up more than I bargained for. A missing, potentially dead, child is hard to consider with my own history. I have only just arrived and already it's like Violet and my past are coming back to haunt me.

COUNTDOWN

Nine ...

Ten Months Ago

Saoirse

'Flower stems and legs,' says Kate, tilting her head and looking at the wild slashes of paint across the wall.

'Good. Now what do you see, Jack?' their mother demands, her expression intense, brow furrowed.

'A stork,' Jack replies.

Lucy's face lights up. 'There you are, a natural!'

Saoirse frowns. 'I don't see a stork ...'

She tilts her head and watches as her mother's face goes flat. She throws down the tattered cloth which she has been using to wipe paint off the brush with turps.

Saoirse thinks about earlier, running drenched through the forest in the rain. The pines had merged together, the ground had bounced under her feet. Flying along with the breeze. It was always futile to run against the wind, like arguing with her mother, though she still did.

'It's just streaks of paint. Did you even know what you were making?' Saoirse says.

Her mother pretends not to notice the spite. 'I work from the subconscious. It comes out and then it finds meaning.'

Saoirse steps back and looks at the paint all over the wall of the sitting room. The couch had been moved aside, and some bedsheets had been placed underneath the wall to soak up the splatters and footprints.

'I was creative. Don't you like it?'

'You could have just baked a cake,' Saoirse snaps, and turns to walk out.

Saoirse goes into the kitchen, snatches a piece of turf from the basket and throws it into the fireplace angrily. She winds a piece of newspaper into a tight bow, twisting once, twice, three times, drops it in, and lights a match, listening to the hiss. She throws the match onto the newspaper and watches as it licks, catching the turf. Hypnotic. Curling sparks of flame gaining a life of their own. She lets her tension out in a long breath. Then she feels guilty. Her mother was hardly hurting anyone by painting.

'Is there dinner?' a voice behind her asks. Jack.

'Ask Kate.'

'She's gone out.'

'Then no.'

Jack pushes a chair to the counter with a scrape, and jumps onto it. Saoirse watches him out of the corner of her eye as he pulls out a box of cereal. Her mother is singing in the other room.

'*My heart it gleams like broken glass ... for you ...*'

Then she stops singing and giggles aloud to herself. 'Bake a cake!' she scoffs.

'At least then we'd have something to eat,' Saoirse mutters under her breath. Her stomach yawns. She rubs it and leans back in the chair. It had been a long day at school. She could sit here a while and rest.

After an hour, Saoirse awakes to hear loud knocking. *Rat a tat tat*. She opens her eyes. The roaring fire has turned to glowing embers. Jack is gone. The knock goes again, more insistent this time. She stands and walks to the hallway, looking down towards the front door. Slowly she creeps forth barefoot, floorboards creaking. She can hear her mother's snoring from the sitting room.

She stands on her tiptoes and looks through the peephole. There is a man's face. Familiar from the village, but she doesn't know his name. He is shifting from foot to foot, agitated. His hair is grey. His expression is of someone who does not think he is being watched. He looks irritated waiting for someone to answer, glancing at his watch. Saoirse thinks about whether to open the door. Probably not, if her mother is not awake. But then, not opening it feels equally strange. What if the man is here to say something important? The man knocks again – louder this time.

'Lucy?' he calls. 'Open up!'

Saoirse's breath catches in her throat. She is about to creep away when she hears him again.

'I can hear you – one of those children? Open it!'

Saoirse freezes on the spot. She turns and looks at the door. She does not want to open the door to this man. Or to any one of her mother's 'friends' who come here. She should turn and go up the stairs – after all, what is he going to do? He would hardly break in. But another part of her questions: what if he has a reason to be here – a good reason? Or what if she gets her mother in trouble by not answering? The tension is too much. Not answering is almost worse than answering. Like not looking inside the wardrobe when you're afraid of a monster. Maybe if she answers it, she'll find there was nothing to worry about.

Swivelling on her toes, she creeps back to the door. She stands on her tiptoes and puts on the chain, unlocks the bolt and then opens the latch. She peers out through the gap – the chain stops her opening it more than a face's width. The man looks down on her. His lips pulled into half a smile, like a gurn, his eyes glittering.

'You not going to open it properly, then?'

Saoirse glares up at him. 'She isn't here.'

The man laughs. 'Don't be telling lies, now. She's only in one of two places, and she isn't in the pub, so she must be here.'

'She's asleep. Come back tomorrow.'

'But your mother made plans with me. Be a good girl and go and wake her.'

'No, I won't.'

He frowns. 'You'd have me coming here, wasting my time? That's not very nice.'

Saoirse looks sideways and down at the man's feet.

'Come back another day.'

'Or maybe *you* can help?' He leans forwards, peering in at her through the gap in the door. 'Fine slip of a girl ...' He leers, reaching out and trying to grab her. 'I'm sure you could pay her debt ...'

Before she can think about it, she slams the door on his hand. A loud yell emits into the air, then a series of curse words. She opens it again and the man pulls his hand out, then she slams it shut properly and locks it. The curse words continue to be called out into the night sky.

Saoirse watches through the window as the man walks away from the door, his gait wide as he clutches his arm with his non injured hand, shaking his fingers out. Then he swaggers out of the driveway.

After a while, she hears sobbing from the sitting room. The sobbing gets louder.

Bad ... bad ... didn't cook ... and look at the place now!

Her mother must have woken. Saoirse stands away from the window, dread in the pit of her stomach.

'Mam?'

Trepidation in her chest, she walks to the door of the sitting room. Her mother is lying on the floor, surrounded by paint pots. She is naked now, her flesh pale and exposed. Saoirse can see all her lines and wrinkles, her tree-like veins. Her breasts hang low and unceremoniously, her armpit hair showing as she reaches up. Half the wall has been repainted white.

'Why didn't you tell me?' she screams.

Saoirse runs towards her, grabbing a blanket from the couch and placing it around her mother's shoulders. Her mother's face contorts, water streaming down her cheeks.

'Why didn't you tell me?'

'Tell you what?'

'About the walls! And the twilight! You'll all grow up and leave me here, to die alone.'

'We won't leave you, Mam,' Saoirse says desperately.

'You will,' she says. 'You all will. You didn't warn me,' she sobs. 'That I'd be left alone in the end.'

Saoirse goes to fetch her clothes from the chair.

'Here, put this on.'

'No!'

She can smell it on her mother's breath now. Whiskey.

'I won't do as you tell me, you're just a child!'

'I'll get your dressing gown.'

'You'll never come back!' Lucy yells after her, accusingly.

Saoirse ascends the stairs. She can see Jack standing at the top. He follows her into the bedroom and as she gets her mother's dressing gown from the hook, there is a smash of glass from downstairs.

'Who was at the door?' Jack asks.

'No one.'

'I heard a man.'

'He's gone now. Go to bed,' she says. 'I'm just looking after Mam for a bit, she's having one of her turns.'

Jack stares back at her, wide-eyed and frightened in the gloom.

Saoirse goes back down the stairs. She feels nothing inside this time. Just a sense of duty. In her mind, all the trees in the forest float past her. She is running, not against the wind now, but through silence, towards the storm. To stop it blowing out of control. To tend to it, until it calms.

13

Day Four

Jack

They are inside, doing a different type of investigation now – an investigation into Jack's mind. Freya is trying to turn out his fears and the things he can't remember, as though his mind is made of pockets. Jack wonders what she will find in there.

She is leaning her chin on her hand, her eyelids heavy and tired. She watches Jack as he draws at the kitchen table. After he finishes, he counts the tips of the crayons and slots them back in order, from rainbow-bright to dark.

'Can I see?' she asks.

Freya takes the two pictures from him and turns them sideways. Jack runs his finger along the waxy surface of one of them. In it is Jack's treehouse, high up in the pines like a human bird's nest with a roof, partly hidden from the ground. In the other picture, there are more pines, towering and green, their roots curled and knotted like fingers. Each root has a name: Saoirse, Kate, Jack and Aunt Bronagh. Next to the trees, there is a little boy with yellow hair. He is standing beside a girl with fire-orange hair. There is a deep crater in the ground, and inside that there are many birds. Sparrows, pigeons, parakeets, and doves. At the other end of the picture, far away, there is the Creature which hides behind the trees. Jack has drawn a mossy tombstone in the middle next to the children. The crow sits on top of it.

'This is Saoirse and me,' he says, pointing to the forefront of the picture.

'What are you doing?'

Jack looks at the wax drawing of himself. Next to his head, he has drawn some numbers. 'Counting.'

'Why do you need to count?'

'We're playing the game.'

'And in the other picture, this treehouse ... where is it?'

Jack bites the inside of his mouth and thinks for a moment about his treehouse – the one everyone knows about, the one he is allowed to talk about.

'Near the entrance to the forest.'

'I see. Did you tell Garda Morris about it?'

Jack nods. 'Kate did.'

'And what is this?' Freya asks, pointing to the Creature in the other picture.

He takes the clay figurine from his jumper and hands it to her. 'The Creature.'

Freya turns it over in her fingers.

'Tell me about it,' says Freya.

Saoirse says the Creature cannot be burned or frozen, cannot be put in jail. The Creature can control time itself, and when it walks, it causes earthquakes and tornados. The ocean and the clouds, too, can be moved by the Creature. *We are just apple pips*, Saoirse had said. *Pinpricks of light in an endless blackness – the Creature could crush us with one toe, if it wanted to.* Jack runs his fingers over the black crayon lines of the Creature on the page.

'No one from the village wants to go into the forest, in case they see it too. Or in case they get haunted by the ghost of Mary Brady. Or disappear like the others.' Jack says. 'It's an awful size,' he whispers. 'It's dark, so it blends into the forest most of the time.'

'Do you think this "Creature" is real, Jack?'

Jack nods. 'Saoirse says we need to get away from it, as fast as we can. We need to finish the Counting Game to make it all STOP.'

Jack shouts the last word. He looks over to his fish tank. The fish is looking for food on the surface. He looks back at Freya, who does not seem to notice. All the adults are so worried about Saoirse, no one seems to care about anything like feeding pets. He feels sad again. He gets up from his chair, takes the flakes of fish food from the tin and sprinkles them through the top of the tank. Imagine caring so little that the fish just died? Imagine not having any food hour after hour, until your heart stopped beating? Sometimes people forget to give Jack food, but he can go to the cupboard and get it. It feels very unfair that the fish can't go and get himself any food and people might just *forget* to feed him. Jack almost feels like crying at the very thought of it. He watches as Jack Dempsey eats the food hungrily, gulping on the surface, inhaling the pieces of fish food quickly. Jack turns and goes back to sit down. When he does, Freya seems like she has a new idea up her sleeve. She smiles at him.

'Do you think we could try something?'

He nods.

'It's called Empty Chair.'

Jack nods again.

'All you have to do is to imagine Saoirse is sitting on that chair now,' Freya says and points to the empty chair near them. 'What would you say to her? What would she say back?'

Jack looks at the chair. He tries to picture it: Saoirse sitting there with her red hair in plaits. He can see her now. She appears on the chair in his mind. Her clothes look exactly like they did the last time he saw her, dungarees with mud at the bottom. Her coat is missing. What would she say if she was here now?

Saoirse moves her finger up to her mouth. *Shh, don't tell about the game*, she whispers. A drip of blood comes from her nose. She puts her hand up and wipes away the blood, frightened as she looks at the glistening red on her fingers.

'Saoirse,' he says, 'are you there?'

What happened to me? she asks, eyes wide.

Jack can feel the din rise inside himself again. The hot feeling creeps up behind his eyes.

'Remember that day Fergal Duffy Junior tried to take you?' he asks her. 'Did he try again?'

Jack cannot hear a reply.

'Are you still with me?' Freya asks. 'What do you mean Fergal Duffy Junior tried to take her?' Freya sounds panicky now.

'The farmer next door – he tried to take her before,' Jack replies. 'He tried to force her into his car one day when we were on his land. He had his hands around her but she kicked him and ran off. She never told anyone and I swore never to tell either, in case we got in trouble.'

Jack looks at Freya. He can't stay with her. He had sworn not to tell, but sometimes his fears are too big. He needs to push them down. He closes his eyes. *Erase.*

14

One Year Before Missing
Jack

'The spirits,' his mother reads, 'are like love. You cannot see them. They are invisible to the naked eye.' Jack's ear presses into the pillow, which feels so soft and comforting. He pulls the duvet up a little. He is warm now. 'But Little Dove said, *Why can I not see them? If I cannot see them, I don't believe they are there!*'

Mam always does all the voices. The voices of Little Dove and of Squirrel and of the Wicked Witch. Little Dove sounds high-pitched and funny, and Squirrel sounds like he has a sore throat.

'And then Squirrel said—'

'Mam?' he asks, interrupting the story. She lowers the book a little.

'Uh-hum?'

'What does hag-gard mean?'

'That wasn't in the story.'

'I know, but Kate said it. She said a person she said she saw in the forest, she said they looked hag-gard and smelly, like they lived in there?'

His mother thinks for a moment. 'I don't know how to describe it best, but it means you look very tired or worn out. For example, you are not haggard, you are like fresh roses. You're the opposite of haggard ...'

Jack rubs his toes together. His mother looks thoughtful a moment. She looks up at the clock on the wall. The light from the landing is coming through the door and his bedside light is on, but other than that it is gloomy.

'Is tomorrow Halloween?' Jack asks.

'It is,' his mother sighs.

'Are we going to go trick or treating? Everyone in my class said they are dressing up.'

'Where would we do that? We don't have any neighbours. We can bob for apples and have a party at home instead – just family.'

'What about Fergal Duffy Junior?'

'Can you imagine him putting up decorations? Dressing his animals up in costumes and handing out sweets?'

Jack begins to giggle.

She continues: 'Imagine – Fergal in a witch costume! His cows dressed like ghosts, with eye holes in the sheets, and his horses dressed like phantoms with headless riders!'

'Mam!' He squeals as she begins to tickle him. 'Not my feet!' He is laughing so hard now, his stomach hurts. He's laughing so much, he'll be sick. His mother wipes tears from her eyes, holding her stomach. Eventually, when they both stop laughing, Jack begins to hiccup.

'Can you tell me a story that you've made up?' he asks.

'Don't you like Biggly Squirrel any more?'

'I prefer your stories … the scary ones. Especially for Halloween.'

His mother nods. She puts down the book and nudges him over. She lies on top of the covers next to him.

'Once upon a time …'

'Do scary stories start once upon a time?'

'Yes, all stories do. Once upon a time … there was a little boy named Jack.'

'Was it Christmas?'

'No, silly!' she says, nudging him again. 'Be quiet. It was Halloween and Jack went into the forest to play, but then he saw something … a sort of monster.'

Jack holds his breath – he feels scared imagining it. 'What happened next?'

'Jack didn't tell anyone he saw the monster, because he was too scared to. He zipped up his lips. Later, he came home and he got Saoirse, his sister, and told her because she was his friend, and they went to investigate. But then something awful happened ...'

'What?' Jack asks, still breathless.

'Well of course, the aliens came. They snatched up one of the cows in the local fields and took their organs to make into alien hamburgers, and then made crop circles so everyone would be confused about what they were up to.'

'What did Jack do?'

'Jack decided he couldn't let the aliens get away with it – he was so brave that he went out there with his ... rocks, and he threw rocks at the spaceship and made a big hole and a dent in it. The aliens were so scared, they flew straight back to their own planet.'

'What about Saoirse?'

'She hid until it was all over.'

'Why did she hide?'

'She was scared ... but Jack wasn't scared, Jack was brave. You are brave, aren't you Jack?'

'I think so.'

His mother yawns.

'I'm tired myself now. Why don't you close your eyes. I'll tell you another story and by the time it is finished, you'll be asleep.'

Jack listens to his mother's voice, hardly paying attention to the words. He feels her get up as he's drifting off, and he looks up at her in the doorway, eyes half-open. She makes a heart shape out of her hands. 'Night Jack,' she whispers.

15

Day Four

Freya

Goosebumps rise on my skin as I listen to the silence. The toilet flushes somewhere upstairs. I glance down the hallway at the red and yellow filtered light, which comes through the stained glass.

'Fergal Duffy Junior? As in the farmer next door?' Garda Morris's voice echoes back through the receiver.

'That's right,' I reply. 'Jack saw him grab Saoirse and try to force her into his car!'

'When?'

'He couldn't remember exactly.'

I feel my heart speed up. What if Fergal has taken Saoirse?

'Thanks for letting me know. I'll bring him back in immediately for questioning.' With that, Garda Morris hangs up.

A breeze skirts around my ankles and I look at the statue of the Virgin Mary on the side table. I have an odd feeling, deep inside. I have felt it before, and I try to piece it together. A familiar feeling. Where from? Perhaps a house I had been to years ago. The floorboards of this house suddenly feel uneasy, as though something bad is about to happen. I listen to the hum of the radio in the distance. The newsreader's voice echoes out with local breaking news.

'The search continues for missing thirteen-year-old girl Saoirse Kellough, who has now been missing for almost a week from her home in Drumsuin ...'

Where is she? I look ahead of myself at the windproof jacket sleeve which sticks out from the edge of the understairs closet. Holding my breath a little, I pull at the sleeve. The door clicks open. I let go and it drops. There are some coats belonging to adults and children, scarves, clutter. Muddy boots on the ground, old toys, a fishing rod. I squat down and look inside, holding my breath, unsure what I am looking for. There is a space hopper, half-deflated, its smile lopsided. An Etch A Sketch. A box of tapes. A doll's house, little rabbit figurines inside.

I hear a noise and stand back up, closing the closet quickly. Footsteps, someone clearing their throat. I walk to the kitchen. Bronagh is there, making some food, and there are two others – one at the kitchen table, one looking out the window. The woman looking out the window is unfamiliar – she is willowy with an olive-skinned complexion, dark curly hair pulled back in a bun, little wisps escaping at the sides. She looks to be in her mid-fifties. She wears a slimline coat and jeans, and her outdoorsy appearance makes her look as though she has just come in from the search party. Then my heart catches in my throat. The woman at the table is familiar – I know her from the hotel. *Mary.*

I feel myself blush with embarrassment.

'Ah Freya, there you are,' says Bronagh, in a relieved voice. 'I was just telling Alice and Mary about you, how you've been a great help to have around.'

Mary's mouth drops open.

'I know you!' she says. 'You didn't say you were working on the case!'

'She was probably just trying to have some privacy, Mary!' the woman at the window jokes. 'She is staying in your hotel, she's not your daughter!'

I blush. Lying isn't something that comes easy to me, so it feels odd to be caught out.

'Alice,' the woman says, laughing a little and holding out a hand to shake. She puts one hand on my arm and rubs it in a maternal way. 'Christ, you're cold – come in here and get some warmth into your bones! Sit, sit.' She ushers me in. 'I was just making tea – you came at a good time.'

I take a seat.

'I'm Walter's girlfriend,' she explains. 'Though I feel a bit old for the word.' She smiles sheepishly. 'I'm a search volunteer on the case. I just came by with Mary to drop off some lasagne for the family, some extra food and flowers to brighten the place up. I'm a florist and we have plenty ...'

I glance over at the Tupperware on the counters, all of which have the name *Alice* scrawled on the side in black permanent marker. It is obvious she was a beauty in her time. She also seems down-to-earth, friendly. I can see Walter with her – they seem like a good match.

'That's very thoughtful of you,' I muster, realising as I say it how tired I am from the session with Jack.

'I can't take all the credit – Mary has helped – and we've been raising money down at the florist. So many people want to help and don't know how. They're happy to give what money they can ... It doesn't feel right, Saoirse being gone, does it? God knows it's all anyone can talk about down in the village.'

I glance at Mary. 'I-I was trying to keep it confidential,' I try to explain.

'Oh, don't worry, love! I'm not owed an explanation of why you are here.' But she shifts in her seat, looking disgruntled none-theless.

Alice glances at her watch, then picks up her handbag and slings it over her shoulder.

'Christ, look at the time. I'm sorry, Freya, I can't get that tea; I need to be back at the shop. Nice to meet you, anyway,' she says giving me a quick smile again. With that she hurries from the kitchen. It's silent in her wake.

'I'll get the tea,' I say, hoping to break the awkward atmosphere.

Bronagh looks to the door where Alice has just left.

'It's times like this I'm so glad to live in Drumsuin, with this community around me. They've been so helpful.'

'Indeed, she is a helpful one, that Alice,' Mary adds. 'In fact, last week – gosh, it must have actually been the day Saoirse went missing, now I think of it – she was helping me in the hotel. I needed a cleaner and she was able to take up the slack when I had to pop out for a few hours. She does great work. Had the place gleaming when I got back and she'd made friends with some of the tourists staying, giving people directions and all sorts. She was better than my usual lady, but I couldn't sack my regular after twenty years, now could I?'

I think about Dublin. The community spirit there was good too, but perhaps not as close-knit as this one.

'Do you know how they are getting on?' I ask. 'With the search, I mean?'

I was eager for morsels. I hoped I'd get the call any minute that Saoirse had been found and I could go home.

'Garda Morris said today they're investigating at a patch that sniffer dogs led them to? Digging around.'

My stomach drops.

'For a live person?'

She doesn't reply. There is no need for one. I know we are both thinking the same thing.

COUNTDOWN

Eight ...

Seven Months Ago

Saoirse

Saoirse can hear Jack climbing up a mound of hay bales. One bale atop the other, stacked together like eggs. It smells musty inside the barn. Hay and silo and dung. There are no horses, not any more, and the cattle are out in the fields. In the background, Saoirse can hear Fergal Duffy Junior's tractor outside. Jack is talking aloud, almost to himself.

'In twenty-five years, you'll be thirty-eight and I will be ...'

Jack counts on his fingers. Saoirse lies back and feels the prickle of the scratchy spines through her summer dress.

'Thirty-four.'

'What age is Mam?' he yells.

'*Shh!*'

Saoirse looks towards the closed barn door nervously. If Fergal Duffy Junior caught them in here, he would be furious. They'd get a giving out, or worse. One time Fergal even came around to their house and shouted at their mother for letting them in his fields. They never listened, anyway. The acres of land are too inviting, too full of things to do and places to play.

'Forty-nine or so.'

'Will she be dead soon?' Jack asks.

Saoirse looks up to the angular ceiling. Beams hang down, with cobwebs spun between each corner.

'No, not soon.'

Jack stands, arms out, wobbling. She looks over at him to make sure he is not about to fall off the bales. The last time he fell off, they ended up in the A & E. She notices the spiky pieces of metal machinery beneath.

'Careful,' she says, looking back up at the ceiling. She puts her hands behind her head.

'If Mam dies, who will take care of me?'

'Kate.'

'If Kate dies, who will take care of me?'

'Aunt Bronagh.'

Saoirse listens out for the tractor sounds.

'Hey, do you hear that?' she says, opening her eyes. 'I don't hear the tractor any more. Do you think he's coming back?'

Jack looks at the door. They listen for a moment, but there is nothing. Jack continues.

'If Aunt Bronagh dies, who will take care of me?'

She thinks about this for a while.

'Hellooo?' he says.

She snaps out of her thoughts, listens to her slightly faster heartbeat.

'No one,' she says. 'You'd have to go into care.'

'What's care?'

'Where they keep the children who are thrown away.'

His voice goes higher-pitched now, as though he is anxious. 'Why would someone throw away a child?'

'I don't know, but it happened to Vicki in my class. Her mam died and her dad lost it … and then she was taken into care.'

She lifts her arm and examines her snap-on bracelet. She pulls it off her wrist and extends it into a ruler, then snaps it back onto her wrist and watches how it immediately curls up back into shape, like magic.

'Weird Vicki?' he asks.

She remembers Vicki walking home ahead of them, in her oversized clothes and her Coke-bottle glasses, looking over her shoulder.

'Didn't Vicki get lost in the forest one time?' he asks.

Saoirse thinks back. It was true, Vicki had got lost, but she had escaped. She had been angry with the children who laughed at her. *Feck ye all who won't go in there, ye are scaredy-cats!*

Come to think about it, she hadn't been the same since. Maybe the forest had changed her that night, not just moving into care. A pigeon flaps from the rafters and Saoirse jumps a little. The tractor sounds start again in the distance. Saoirse breathes a sigh of relief.

'There is something I have to tell you, about Mam,' she announces.

Jack sits up. 'What?'

She pauses for a moment, remembering the other day. Mam's painting on the wall. Her breaking things. She had not been taking her pills. Now Kate was gone most of the time, it meant Saoirse was left looking after her.

'She's not well at all. She has an addiction problem.'

'*Ad-ick-shun?*'

'It means you can't stop. She's sick.'

Jack does not reply. Saoirse expects him to argue, but he doesn't.

She continues. 'I think we are going to have to either tell Dad, or ... run away.'

'Where to?'

'I don't know,' she sighs. 'But it seems like the only way sometimes ... the only way to make her realise she needs to get better.'

'Do you think Mam will die if she continues on like she is?'

'Yes, I do. And there is something else. I overheard Aunt Bronagh saying she was thinking she might want to take us away.'

'Take us ... away?'

'She was on the phone. She didn't think I was listening. I was at the top of the stairs, and she was downstairs, on the phone in the hallway.'

'What did she say?'

'I don't know who she was talking to, but she said, "I might take the children there …" Then she said, "I don't know how …" She was angry with the person on the other end. Then she said something that was strange. She said, "Not him, her – her first".'

They lie in silence a moment.

'I keep going over it in my mind. *Her first.* Was she talking about our dad or our mam? Or did she mean me and you? And if so, where is she taking me first? Where is she taking us at all? Why hasn't she asked us yet? Is she talking about a holiday, or somewhere she wants to take us forever?'

'Maybe she is thinking of bringing us to McDonald's.'

Saoirse sighs.

'I've never been to McDonald's,' Jack adds. 'Do you think we will ever go?'

'I don't know.'

'I don't want to run away. Unless we get to go to Dublin where there is McDonald's, then maybe I'd go.'

'Maybe it will just have to be me, then. Run away and make a point, make her realise how she is hurting us.'

'If you go, what about me?'

'I won't go forever, silly. Just for a short while. Just to make her see.'

'I don't want you to go like Kate. Don't leave me alone.'

Saoirse feels suddenly guilty. 'I won't leave you. Not yet, anyway.'

The sound of the tractor gets closer, then moves further away again.

'Do you think Fergal Duffy Junior would kill us if he found us in here?' Jack asks.

Saoirse shifts a little on the hay bale, trying to find a less scratchy position. 'He might.'

'How would he kill us?'

'He might run us over with his tractor,' she replies.

'He might stab us with his giant pitchfork,' Jack adds.

Saoirse lowers her voice. 'He might put you on a spike, roast you on a fire and then eat you.'

'Why me?'

'You're easier to eat.'

'What would happen to you?'

'He'd make me his mini-wife and I'd have to sleep in a bed with him every night.'

'Yuck.'

Saoirse begins to bite at the tips of her nails.

'He might bring us into the forest and leave us there without a map or a way out,' says Jack, in his ghost-story voice.

Saoirse feels her legs tingle and looks down. That's when she sees it, in the far corner of the barn. A black plastic bag, with something poking out of it – something that doesn't belong in a barn. It looks like a bright pink item of clothing.

Carefully, Saoirse climbs down and touches the bag. It's soft. Should she open it? A voice in her head says she should. But it's private – she knows she shouldn't. *Open it!* the voice insists. So, slowly, she unpicks the knot at the top of the bag.

'What are you doing?' Jack calls out. Saoirse doesn't reply, just holds her breath. Finally, she gets the knot open and she peers inside. The clothes belong to a teenage girl, Saoirse can tell. A pink top, a small pair of ripped, acid-wash jeans, some bracelets, a little jacket. There's also a Walkman, with a tape inside. Saoirse opens the tape and takes it out, examining it – *Kylie Minogue*, the tape says on the side. Inside the bag are also several old pages and cuttings, pulled out or cut from the original copies of the newspapers. Saoirse unfurls the first page.

CASE OF MISSING MAEVE MURPHY CONTINUES TO DEVASTATE COMMUNITY

Saoirse's eyes scan up to the top where the date is written: 11 November 1988.

> The community of Drumsuin continues to be devastated by the disappearance of local girl Maeve Murphy (17) exactly a month on from her disappearance. Maeve was last seen walking towards the forest area of Drumsuin at around 6.30 p.m. on Tuesday 11 October and has not been seen since. Local appeals from Gardaí have not yet yielded any results in the missing girl case, and ongoing searches have been unsuccessful in finding her. Gardaí are once again appealing for any witnesses to get in touch as soon as possible on the below number.

Saoirse looks through the other newspaper cuttings. All of them are about the same girl. Maeve Murphy. Saoirse has heard about her before – she was one of three girls from the village who went missing. All of the girls disappeared into thin air in the forest and were never found again. But why does Fergal Duffy Junior have what appears to be the clothes of a teenage girl and newspaper articles about Maeve Murphy's disappearance in a bag in his barn? Saoirse shivers, fear running up her spine. Quickly, she replaces the newspapers and ties the bag shut again, wishing all at once that she had not found it.

Saoirse looks at the entrance. A light wind blows at the wisps of hair around her face. She thinks she can see a long shadow under the door, but then it is gone. What if Fergal really is dangerous?

'I think we should go now,' she says urgently to Jack.

Jack climbs down the bale obediently. They creep to the door and peer out. The field is now just long lines of mud, turned over and under, like combed wet hair. There are a few birds on the ground, trying to eat the seeds, and there is a scarecrow in the middle of the field, but she can't see or hear anything else nearby.

Near the furthest fence, the red tractor is parked halfway along a ploughed line, but Fergal is no longer sitting in it. Saoirse scuttles around to grab her brother's hand, and they sprint towards home.

16

Day Five

Freya

I park outside a woollen shop named Quincy's, which borders a grubby, wood barrel-flanked pub called Hannigan's. It has shadowy windows, all the better for day drinkers to hide behind. No one seems to notice my car as I park except a steel cockerel atop a weathervane, which gazes down at me curiously from its perch as it spins uncertainly in the breeze.

I am here to drop off today's tape at the Garda station. I think about Jack as I get out. It has been hard to get the child's sad, terrified face out of my mind since I arrived here – his face has even crept into my dreams, waking me up in the small hours of the night, a sense of unease in the pit of my stomach.

I lock the door behind me. Next to where I have parked, there is a lopsided front-page stand outside the newsagent's:

MISSING GIRL SEARCH CONTINUES

Underneath are two other headlines:

FARMER'S ATTACKER ARRESTED

and

ADAMS AND BRUTON TO MEET AMID
PEACE PROCESS TALKS

A group of villagers stand around, near the corner. A woman sellotapes a 'Missing' poster of Saoirse to the shop window. She breaks away and approaches me. I look down at her mud-covered boots.

'You from around here?' she asks, tapping ash from her cigarette onto the ground. I pause, taking in her freckled face and her wide-set eyes.

'No ... I'm just visiting.'

'Have you seen we have a missing girl? You're welcome to join the volunteer search later – we need all the help we can get.'

I notice Alice, from earlier, stood in the centre of the group – she is pointing up towards the forest. In her hand is a bunch of missing-person posters.

'Sorry, I can't today – I'm helping in other ways, so not sure I'd be allowed.'

'No worries,' she says and begins to wander off.

'Hey, wait!' I call out, not wanting to waste an opportunity to get an insight into the thoughts of a local. She walks back to me, a small frown on her face. 'It's just ... so strange for her to go missing out of the blue, don't you think?' I offer.

She twists her mouth a little, as though thinking. 'You're not Gardaí?'

I shake my head. 'Definitely not.'

'Well, it's not that strange, considering all the odd men around here.'

'Odd men,' I reflect back. 'Like who?'

She looks towards the butcher's shop. I follow her gaze.

'Lucy was having relations with himself, over there, Mr Fitzgerald.'

Fitzgerald's, reads the shop sign.

'The butcher?'

'That's him,' she says. 'He was always lurking. He has a roaming eye – watches all the women and girls around here. He gives me the creeps,' she says, her face a picture of disgust.

'Do you think he could have something to do with it?'

'It's possible. I wish I didn't think it, I mean, the very idea of him … touching that poor young girl. But mark my words,' she adds. 'Saoirse was just a lamb, and there are many wolves around here who could have preyed upon her,' she says, wandering off back to the group. I look over to the butcher's shop: in investigating this case further, I realise there is no time like the present.

It is cold inside the butcher's shop. The fridges hum as the familiar unpleasant smell of raw meat reaches my nostrils. 'Afternoon,' a voice greets me. I look up at the red and white meat joints hanging from ceiling hooks. The man, who must be Mr Fitzgerald, is wearing butcher's overalls splattered with blood, and on top of it he wears a stripy apron. I put him at about sixty-ish. He has thinning white hair and is lean as a greyhound. Beneath the shiny glass counter, racks of lamb and burgers stare back at me.

'What can I get for you?'

I scan the meat options. I need something pre-cooked which I can eat in my hotel room. 'How about a few slices of that cooked ham? And a couple of sausage rolls, please,' I say, feeling suddenly nervous.

His smile seems frozen on and fake. A thin veneer of someone friendly. I feel uncomfortable immediately and I can see why the woman outside said he gives her the creeps.

'What has you around here?' he asks me as he reaches for the ham and begins to wrap it and weigh it.

I take a deep breath and decide to be honest.

'I'm supporting the Gardaí on the missing girl case. Dr Freya Hemmings,' I say, pointing to myself.

'Nice to meet you, Freya,' he says, his smile disappearing all of a sudden. 'I'm Barney Fitzgerald.' He observes me closely, his eyes narrowing as though trying to figure out the nature of my visit. I try to imagine him grabbing a young girl, dragging her away through the forest. Is he capable of that?

'Do you know Saoirse?' I ask.

He weighs the ham and prints out a sticker, pressing it on the side of the butcher paper.

'I do. Well, perhaps *know* is too strong a word ... but I knew their mother before she died. Many men around the village did, but for the wrong reasons, if you know what I'm saying.' He winks, and I feel another involuntary shiver. 'I was just a friend. Their mother used to come in weekly and buy her meat. She was nice too, despite seeming a little ... unhinged at times. She always wanted the cheap cuts of leftovers, for a stew, and she usually brought the boy with her. Nice lad, very intense; he'd always stare at you in a strange way. Sometimes she brought the girl too.' He looks into the distance as though remembering.

'What do you think happened?' I ask.

A grave expression crosses his face. 'If you want my honest opinion? I think someone has done a legger with her,' he says, jutting out his chin.

I think about the villagers' superstitions about this place – what Garda Morris had said regarding their beliefs about the forest. I wonder if Mr Fitzgerald is one of the people who subscribes to these beliefs.

'You don't think something supernatural has happened?'

He laughs, short and loud. 'No, no ... that's just something people make up. There are too many gombeens around here who believe in that kind of stuff. I'm a practical man. I don't think people go missing into thin air. I think someone has taken her.'

'Who would do that?'

He looks suddenly uncomfortable. 'You're asking me?'

'I just mean ... who do you think might do that?'

He lowers his voice. 'I think the family is responsible.'

I raise my eyebrows. I had not been expecting that, even though it is logical that the villagers might prefer to blame the family, rather than believe there is a kidnapper or a killer at large.

'What makes you think that?'

'Well for a start, that aunt of theirs … It's common knowledge in the village that she's been going to Dublin to get fertility treatment. She was so jealous of Lucy for having children. She wanted what Lucy had, and she was bitter she didn't have it. Nothing turns a woman mad like wanting a baby.'

He leans over and picks out a couple of sausage rolls with one rubber-gloved hand.

'You think Bronagh is responsible for Saoirse's disappearance?'

He glances up at me. 'Well, maybe it was her that pushed Lucy off that cliff – not that I can claim to know anything.'

Bronagh. Could she be responsible for Saoirse going missing? What if she hadn't been in London that day – is there any proof she had been there after all, or is it just her word?

I look into his eyes, which are staring at me in a way that makes me feel fearful.

'If you ask me, the reason girls go missing from Drumsuin is because people can get away with it. Up there in that forest, there are no cameras, no one for miles around. If I were the type of man who wanted to get away with something like that, I'd go up there, too.'

He finally blinks and looks away.

'They won't find her,' he says in a low voice. 'Mark my words, she'll never be found. She's probably buried somewhere already, in a shallow grave.'

I let out a breath.

'You here for long?' he says, placing the meat into a plastic bag.

'No, just for a few days,' I reply, shifting uncomfortably.

'Come back before you go and I'll give you some lovely burgers to cook back home,' he says, winking again. I nod and wave as I leave the shop. My immediate feelings on Mr Fitzgerald are that I don't trust him.

I cross the road and head over to the newsagent's. I would need some bread and mustard to go with the ham, if I was to make a lunch out of it. There are lots of notices outside sello-taped to the window: *Babysitter Available* and *Collie Puppies For Sale*. Another missing-person poster for Saoirse is on this door too, her solemn eyes staring out from the photograph. The door of the newsagent's makes a ringing sound as I enter. A woman is perched on a stool behind the till, knitting. I pick up a *Drumsuin Examiner* and fold it under my arm. She glances at me.

'Have you seen the crowds out there?' she asks. She is wearing a red woollen hat pulled low over a swathe of curls – it looks like something she has knitted herself. 'I haven't seen this many people in Drumsuin since the pope came to Ireland in '79.'

'I know, it is busy out there!' I reply.

I begin to search the shelves.

'Can I help?'

'Oh, I'm just looking for bread.'

'At the back there, love,' she replies. 'You're not from around here. Are you here on holiday?' she calls out.

I pause as I pick up a loaf. 'No, not really a holiday.'

'Are you here to work on the case?' she continues.

My eye catches on a shelf of souvenirs, and I pick up a little lighthouse ornament to examine it. It's wooden, painted blue and white. It reminds me of one I saw on holiday years ago with the girls, and I feel a tinge of hope and joy. I press the bottom, and a light turns on. Feeling emotional, I turn back towards her and walk to the till, carrying the souvenir, bread, and a jar of mustard.

I think about how I had been caught out hiding my real iden-tity from Mary and decide to be honest this time. 'Yes, I am working on the case.'

Her eyes spark with interest. She puts down her knitting.

'Poor girl. She's a strange one, though, so I can't say I'm surprised she's missing.'

'Do you know the family?'

'Sure, look, everyone knows everyone around here.' She stands up from her stool and stretches her arms into the air, as though they've lost their feeling. 'Their mother jumping off that cliff. Leaving children behind isn't fair.'

'So you know the children?'

'Yes, that girl Saoirse is always in this shop with her little brother. The pair of them, dressed like ragamuffins. Rarely buying anything, just looking at the sweets and acting the maggot. Looking and stealing, I might add. I don't think they have much money, that family, despite having that big ole kip of a house up there. After their mother died, I didn't have the heart to give out to them …'

She looks at the lighthouse, newspaper and the bread and mustard and types the amount into the cash register.

'That will be three fifty. I told them, don't be playing in that forest, but children don't listen. They go looking for danger. Anyway, we are all worried sick. Please God she turns up safe and in one piece.'

She sits back down after I've paid and goes back to her knitting. As I'm leaving the shop, a familiar red Beetle drives past and parks behind my own car. Garda Walter Morris gets out. He straightens his hat.

'I was just about to come over to the station,' I call out.

He nods at me, and points to the lighthouse I'm holding. 'Holiday memento?'

I press the button and turn on the light. 'It reminds me of holidays from the past … happy ones,' I say wistfully.

He grins. Then he looks down and his expression turns solemn as I put the ornament in my bag.

'Still no leads,' he says. 'Though we have Fergal Duffy in custody.'

'Has he said anything yet?'

'Claims he has an alibi that day. He was at a farming event, with witnesses to his attendance.'

'And the previous attempt to take Saoirse?'

'He says he was trying to get her off his land. That he was sick of them trespassing, that he was just trying to scare her, and had been planning to drive her home back to her front door.'

'Do you believe him?'

'I don't know.' He sighs. 'But we've no evidence on him yet. Officers are searching his property, so we'll see.'

I think about my conversation with Mr Fitzgerald and wonder whether to bring it up with Garda Morris. I don't want him to think I'm meddling. In my experience, Gardaí don't like you interfering unless you have proof, and hunches, hearsay, and village rumours aren't exactly evidence – but at the same time, I can't risk not saying it, for the sake of Saoirse.

'I spoke to Mr Fitzgerald today,' I say, scanning his expression as I do for any hint of irritation or derision, but there is none.

'Ah yes,' he says. 'The butcher, ex-boyfriend to Lucy. We have him under investigation. He has connections with the family, it would be silly of us not to look into his involvement.'

I sigh with relief. They are already looking into it – I don't need to worry.

'And the priest?' I ask. 'Jack mentioned he was having lunches with the kids?'

'Ah yes,' he replies. 'We heard about that too. We asked Maguire about the lunches he was having with the children and he seemed quite shocked they were an issue. However, we can't get any alibi for his whereabouts on the day Saoirse went missing, so we are continuing to investigate him as well.'

He removes his hat, scratches his head, and puts it back on again, looking down the street as though he might suddenly spot Saoirse. I feel the wind catch my hair and I zip up my coat. Walter puts his hands into his pockets, as if feeling the cold.

'We haven't ruled out all the locals yet, but we have to keep an open mind that it might have been an out-of-towner, someone who was staying the night locally.' He nods to the seafront. 'I'm going around the guest houses and hotels today – asking questions to the owners and staff. You're staying at Cois Fharraige, right?'

'I am. The owner, Mary, she's nice, isn't she?'

'She's fairly sharp, all right – no one could pull the wool over her eyes. She said no out-of-towner worth noting had been staying there when Saoirse went missing. Just families, a few regular workmen, sailors she's known for years. A few solo travellers.'

I think about how many suspects there could be. Even a well-known workman or sailor passing through. Who knows what they are capable of? I wonder about the villager I spoke to earlier and whether she might be as open with a Garda as she was with me.

'Are the villagers particularly secretive with the Gardaí here?' I ask.

'We are not included in their secrets and their rumour mill, if that's what you're asking. Nothing like walking into the pub and everyone turning silent to make you feel like an outsider in your own town!' Walter laughs. 'Though I do have one or two friends.'

'Speaking of which, I met your girlfriend today – Alice?'

He nods, blushing a little. 'Ah, you did?'

'Yes, she's lovely. She seems really …' I search for a word less trite than *sweet*. 'Caring?'

'She's great, isn't she?' Walter's face lights up. 'I've been dating her for around six months, ever since she moved here from Dublin. She's been such a help in every way. Especially lately – she has really jumped in with two feet since this all happened, dropped everything at work just to help look for Saoirse and support the family too.'

'Where does she work?' I ask, realising she already told me. *At the florist.*

He points down the road. 'A bit further up that way – at Drumsuin Posies. She wanted to escape the rat race. Many people retire to places like this when they've had enough of the city life.'

'This is a nice slower pace, I imagine.'

'It was, until this happened,' Walter says, his face turning grim. 'Did today go okay?' he asks, rubbing the back of his neck.

'As well as it could have,' I reply.

'Will you be coming over to the station now?'

I nod. 'Will do – I've just got to grab the tape from my car first.'

I watch him go and try to push down my sadness for Saoirse. I try not to think about what awful things could have befallen her since she went missing – and of all of the places she could be now, including, as Mr Fitzgerald had said, buried in a shallow grave. I hope with all my heart she is still alive. A part of me also hopes, for her sake, that if one of these awful men has taken her, that she is no longer alive. Looking at her photos, those haunting eyes peering out at me through the posters, I realise I couldn't bear the thought of that young girl suffering.

I return to my car, and that's when I see it. A neon yellow Post-it in the corner, under my windscreen wiper. Did someone put it there while I was in town? Surely, I would have noticed it if it had been there earlier? I scan the street, but everyone is minding their own business. The people around here have all been welcoming so far, despite what Walter said about them not liking the English. Maybe they're just friendly to people's face and then complain about them behind their backs.

Sliding the note out from under the windscreen wiper, I hold it up. *Back in five*, it reads. I frown. Perhaps someone mistook my car for someone else's. Nonetheless, feeling uneasy, I put the note in my pocket and hurriedly get into my car.

17

Day Six

Jack

Jack wakes up and peers out of the window, through the gap in the curtain. Today is Halloween. Usually on Halloween, he and Saoirse bob for apples, eat sweets and *báirín breac*, maybe even dress up like ghosts, but today Jack knows nothing like that will happen. He puts his fingers up to his eyes and looks through them. People are outside. They mill around the garden as though they live here. *Trick or treat*, Jack whispers. A man leans against their father's tractor in the garden and writes in a notebook, crossing one leg over the other. If Saoirse were here, Jack could imagine her calling out to them, or going to speak to them, hands behind her back, kicking at the dirt. He feels for a moment that he cannot breathe without his sister. An image swims into his mind of wooden beams held together with nails. Jack keeps thinking about his treehouse, the secret one near the Hollowing Place. Kate had told Garda Morris about the one that everyone knows about, but Jack has not told anyone about their secret treehouse – high up in the pines. He hasn't even told Freya. Saoirse had told Jack he could *never* tell anyone about it, that he had to keep it a secret; otherwise, they'd never have anywhere to escape to when they needed it, and one day they might need somewhere to hide. Jack wants to listen to Saoirse, because that's what brothers and sisters do – they keep secrets for each other.

People searching for Saoirse might not look up that high and helicopters might not find her there, hidden under the cloak of pine needles. Jack doesn't think Saoirse would hide up there for this many days, though. Not while hearing people call out her name. No, she would not hide from Jack for so long, not without telling him first. Unless she had been kidnapped by the Creature.

Jack turns away from the window and gets out of bed. He sprints downstairs and into the kitchen, straight to Aunt Bronagh's lap. He throws himself onto her in a bear hug and she makes a gulping sound. Kate is sitting with tea, her shoulders rounded, still in the dressing gown she has been wearing for days with the stain on the sleeve.

'There are people here,' Jack murmurs.

They don't reply, but keep talking between themselves.

He gets off Aunt Bronagh's lap and says it again, much louder.

'There are people here!'

'You don't need to shout,' says Kate.

'Who are they?' Jack asks, lowering his voice.

'They're from the *meedy-a*.'

'What?'

'Like the television, newspapers and radio.'

'Why?'

Kate doesn't answer, just takes another sip of tea.

Aunt Bronagh raises her eyebrows a little, as though she feels sorry for him. When she does that, she reminds Jack of his own father. Sometimes they look the same because they are brother and sister.

'They're going to spread the message further about your sister going missing. So that people all over the country can look out for her, and we can get her home safe.'

Aunt Bronagh wheels over to the window to look outside.

'If she's lost inside the forest, how will telling people who live far away help?' Jack asks.

No one replies.

*   *   *

Jack does not like visitors at all. Especially not men and especially not these ones. These visitors are not like the usual men who come to the house. They ask lots of questions but don't seem to pay attention to the answers. Jack pulls Wilberry closer and edges towards Kate. They are standing in the front garden, on a patch of grass nearest to the front door. Kate puts her hand around his shoulder and he rests his head on her side. Garda Morris is examining a piece of paper to read out for the visitors. Kate says it is a *stayt-ment*. This means it updates people on what has been going on. Kate says it just tells people they need to keep looking. Garda Morris clears his throat and calls out for the visitors to be ready. They all stop what they are doing and walk towards him. Jack zooms up in his mind and watches it from above like a crow might do. A big house, with little people all moving towards it. Jack and Kate are in the middle of it all. They roll the cameras and a red light goes on. Jack is standing behind Garda Morris, next to Kate. He is going to be on TV, which would usually be exciting, except now it is not, because Saoirse is not here. Garda Morris takes a deep breath and adjusts his glasses.

'Thirteen-year-old Saoirse Kellough went missing from the nearby forest a week ago, on the twenty-fourth of October. She was wearing blue jeans, a red jumper and a navy coat. She is five feet three inches in height, of slim build with shoulder-length red hair. The Gardaí have been searching for her twenty-four hours a day but, so far, she has not been located in this area. We are now extending our search nationwide.'

Jack can hear a sound. He looks up to see Kate sniffling into a tissue. He looks back at Garda Morris, who keeps reading.

'We are asking that anyone who has seen her, or may know of her whereabouts, please call Drumsuin police or the missing children helpline. Are there any questions?'

Some people raise their hand. Jack looks at all of the faces. They look worried.

Garda Morris points to a woman. She lowers her hand.

'Some people seem to think she was taken by an out-of-towner. Do you think this might the case?'

'Anything is possible. We don't know, is the honest truth.'

He points to another man, without a camera, holding a recording device.

'Wasn't the younger brother with her? Does he know anything?'

Jack feels Kate's fingers clench around his shoulders.

'Saoirse's younger brother is being very forthcoming with helping us in our investigation,' replies Garda Morris. 'As he is a minor, I would prefer not to comment on his involvement at this stage. Any other questions I can answer?'

A murmur goes through the crowd of reporters. Garda Morris points to a young woman near the front with a microphone.

'The forest is renowned locally as a place where people go missing. Do you think this is connected to other disappearances over the years?'

Garda Morris pauses.

'It is true that we have an unusual amount of missing persons cases here in Drumsuin. I cannot comment on that at this point, but I can say we are treating her disappearance as suspicious, which is why we urge anyone with any information at all to come forward as soon as possible, so we can get her home safely.'

There is a flurry of shouts. Garda Morris points to another reporter, this time a young man with a beard.

'I also spoke to many people in the village who seemed to think the place was haunted. Are you investigating any *para-nominal actif-itty*?'

Jack tightens his fingers around Wilberry.

'No,' replies Garda Morris in a flat tone of voice. He points at another person with a microphone.

'How much longer until you call off the search?'

'It's difficult to say. There is a limited timescale we can search like this, but we still hope to find her. The Gardaí remain optimistic.'

'Have you investigated all the local persons of interest?'

'We have been going through a thorough list of all local persons who may be connected to the case.'

Jack feels his thumb go into his mouth. He watches the faces of the visitors as they ask Garda Morris questions. Jack thinks back to Saoirse. *She looks over her shoulder at him as they are being chased. Fear in her eyes. Jack looks behind himself. Whoosh. It is heading towards them. Closer still.*

The words go around in Jack's head. Then, as suddenly as it starts, it is all over. Garda Morris turns around and tells them they can go back inside. The visitors are leaving just as fast as they had arrived, getting into cars, going off to other places. Jack feels weak and tired. Kate takes his hand.

'Let's get something to eat,' she says. 'That was a lot for one morning.' She turns to the Garda. 'Would you like to join us for some lunch?'

They sit in the kitchen, around the table again. Jack watches Garda Morris – he closes one eye as he does, so now he can see the way Garda Morris sees. He holds the number zero up to his face and peers through the gap in the hole of his finger and his thumb.

'Well done,' says Garda Morris, as Kate takes a seat. 'You dealt with that well. They're not easy, press conferences.' Garda Morris clears his throat. 'Are you sure you want me to stay? I can clear off and give you all time to rest?'

Kate shakes her head. 'No, I feel safer when you're here.'

Aunt Bronagh comes in. She wheels over and pats Jack on the shoulder. 'I'll fix us some lunch. You all relax.'

Jack watches as she goes and puts something that looks like a letter into the odd bits drawer. Then she opens the fridge door.

'Are you sure I'm not intruding?' Garda Morris asks again.

'No, don't be silly,' says Aunt Bronagh, taking out some cheese. 'Please stay.'

Garda Morris taps his fingers on the table. He whistles a tune and looks into the back garden. Towards where the chickens used to live, where now they have a vegetable patch. He looks at Jack, who quickly looks away.

'Fancy asking about *para-nominal actif-itty*,' he says then.

'What's *para-nominal actif-itty*?' Jack asks.

'Aliens and the like.'

'Green aliens?'

Garda Morris nods. 'We get some odd questions. But that one takes the biscuit.'

There is silence. Kate winds a strip of tissue around her finger and stares into space. 'I don't think it's odd.'

Jack feels the tension in the room rise a little, like a sound only a dog can hear. Aunt Bronagh moves to the fire and throws a log on it. It crackles and spits. Kate continues. 'Something other-worldly is happening in that forest. Everyone in the village knows there is a creature living in there – locals have seen it. Lots of them. Even Mary, the woman who owns the hotel. She said she saw it too! How can everyone be wrong?'

Aunt Bronagh unfurls the wrapper around the cheese and begins to cut slices of it. She interrupts before Garda Morris can reply.

'Nonsense. The place is like anywhere else. That "creature" is just in people's imagination. Having a burial ground and a few missing people on a piece of land doesn't change it; the fear is just in people's minds. It's superstition at best. Sure, if you didn't know the history, you'd never think anything of it!'

Garda Morris nods in agreement with Aunt Bronagh.

'I don't believe in that creature myself,' replies Garda Morris shifting in his seat. 'I think it's in people's imaginations.'

There is another silence.

Kate has a sad expression. Jack draws the number seven with his finger. Saoirse has been missing for exactly seven days. Maybe she'll return today. Seven is lucky. Also, it has been a week. A week is a good amount of time. Things change in a week.

'You wouldn't believe it if you didn't see it, I suppose,' Kate replies. 'I've seen it many times – we all have. Just ask Jack.'

Jack doesn't want to be asked any more questions, not today, and especially not about the Creature. Garda Morris sighs.

'If it's a creature, I can't help you … but if it's a person who has taken her, I'll try and find them for you. I want to get her home, your sister. That's the main thing, *para-nominal actif-itty* or not.'

Kate pinches the bridge of her nose with two fingers. Aunt Bronagh puts the cheese sandwiches onto some plates and glides over, placing them on the table.

'Here we go,' she says in a comforting voice. She rolls up next to Jack and squeezes his arm.

They all eat in silence. The sound of the radio buzzes in the background. Faraway voices and music. Jack looks over to Jack Dempsey fish as he swims around in his tank, under the rocks and out again. Jack fed him again this morning because if you don't feed pets, they die. Pearl taps into the room and comes over to Jack, licks his hand and then goes to bed. From his bed he stares at Jack, his tail curled around his body, ears down and nose twitching. Jack looks between the adults and feels calm for the first time in a week. He will be okay. Saoirse will be okay. All the adults are helping to find her. Jack sits up straight and draws the number eight three times on the table in invisible ink. Eight is for infinity. Forever. Saoirse will come back as they are friends forever. She said so.

18

Day Six

Jack

Things start and things end. When things start they are usually happy, and when they end they are usually sad. One is for start, ten is for end. When you reach ten, the game is over. Jack painting a scene from one of his dreams. A face pokes around the door. It is Garda Morris. He takes off his hat and pulls up a chair at the kitchen table, clearing his throat.

'The six o'clock news is on.'

'Will we be on it?'

'I expect so.'

Jack nods and continues to paint. 'I don't want to see myself.'

'That's understandable. I don't like watching myself on screen either,' replies Garda Morris. His face slack, he rubs his face with his hand and seems to wake up. 'What are you painting now?'

Jack considers it for a moment. He isn't sure how much to tell Garda Morris, though he is finding it easier to talk now, both to Garda Morris and to Freya. He doesn't know how many words exactly he has said, but he has gone from probably ten or twenty words a day right up to a few hundred now. He doesn't feel so afraid of words as he was at the start, like on the first day when they came looking to speak to him. That day the words had seemed to crawl all over him like bugs, out of his mouth, and inside his ears.

'A car,' Jack says.

Garda leans in closer to look. Jack can smell the scent of the Garda – soil and trees, mixed with cigarette smoke.

'Who is inside the car?'

Jack smiles a little. He points to the head in the front seat. 'You.'

Garda Morris yawns a little. 'Me? Gosh, you're drawing me now, are ye? Well, I'm very honoured, so I am.'

Jack nods. 'This is your red Beetle, and you are driving, and here is the road.'

Garda Morris looks at it, frowning. 'Where am I going?'

Jack shows his palms and shrugs. 'Not sure. Probably to the forest.'

Jack stops and looks up. Aunt Bronagh has come in and is giving a wan smile at Jack. She moves to the fridge, where she picks out the butter, examining the date on the side. She sucks her cheeks in as she throws it into the pedal bin, then takes out some jam.

'Continue, Jack,' Garda Morris says, pressing his lips together. He looks closer at the painting.

'Never mind,' Jack says. Aunt Bronagh is snooping again. She has been doing that a lot lately – hanging around when Jack is talking. It's like she wants to know what he's saying to the Gardaí.

Aunt Bronagh looks over her shoulder and side-eyes them. 'Everything okay?'

'Jack was painting me,' says Garda Morris.

Jack can feel a flutter in his stomach, a sour taste in his mouth.

'He certainly loves to paint,' Aunt Bronagh says, 'and to tell tall stories.'

Jack dips his paintbrush into the red and continues to paint in the lines of the car.

'The stories are not tall if they are true,' mutters Jack.

Garda Morris pushes his glasses up on his nose, then scratches at his neck.

Aunt Bronagh turns from her place at the sink, a plate of jam and bread in hand.

'He comes over and tells me all sorts, don't you.' She appears behind him. Jack feels her ruffle his hair affectionately. Like a bug crawling over his scalp. 'About that forest, the creatures inside. He has a *big* imagination,' she says. 'Whether he's a reliable source, I'm not so sure ...' she trails off.

Jack continues to paint the car, the black wheels now.

'This must be a difficult time for you all. I hope you feel we're doing enough to support?' Garda Morris asks.

Aunt Bronagh nods. 'I didn't feel it until today, that you were all doing enough, but I am satisfied now. Soon, the whole country will know.'

Garda Morris nods.

Jack watches Aunt Bronagh leave the room. He washes his brush, then paints green on the trees around Garda Morris's car and takes a deep breath. Perhaps, now Aunt Bronagh is gone, he can write something down, then Garda Morris might be able to help.

Jack puts down his paintbrush. He takes a pen with one palm, damp with sweat. He holds it close to the paper and begins to move it.

All of a sudden, the phone rings in the hallway, loud and shrill. Jack jumps.

'Sorry, Jack,' Garda Morris says. 'I'll be back in a moment.' Garda Morris leaves the room.

Jack stops writing, his hand frozen on the pen, and he listens. Now he can hear voices in the hallway. His sister Kate on the phone, the phone being passed to Garda Morris. The quiet, deep voice of Garda Morris as he speaks to the person on the other side. Jack hears Garda Morris hang up the phone and speak to Kate in the same calm voice as though he is soothing her. Then there is a scream and a wail. It is Kate. Jack drops the pen and jumps away from the table. The wailing turn into cries.

No, he hears Kate yell. *No!*

Things start and things end. When things start they are usually happy, and when they end they are usually sad. One is for start, ten is for end. When you reach ten, the game is over.

PART THREE

COUNTDOWN

Seven ...

Nine Months Ago

Saoirse

If the world is a canvas, today something different is painted on it. Two children and a mam on a cold winter's day down at the beach. At a quarter to ten, which is a strange time not to be sat in Mrs Clarke's geography lesson. They had been walking to school when the diversion happened.

'I won't give you one,' Saoirse had snapped at Jack.

'Please,' he had replied, staring at her rucksack.

'No.'

'Why not?'

'Because.'

'Because what?'

'Because they're mine!'

Lucy, who was walking with them, had finally turned to them. 'Stop arguing over sweets! Christ, I'm so bored listening to you both. There is enough war going on in Northern Ireland. Saoirse, share your jelly babies, for God's sake.'

'They're in my bag; I'm not giving him one now because he ate all of his own already.'

'I didn't ask for one now.'

'You did.'

'Didn't.'

'Did.'

'Didn't.'

'Did!'

They had walked in silence a while. No one said a word.

'Is there a ceasefire?' Lucy asked eventually, letting a breath out.

'What's a *see-fire*?' Jack asked.

'When people say *I'll put down my guns, and you do too, and neither of us will fight.*'

'How does it work?'

'It often doesn't. Someone always wants the last word.'

It was at that moment that Lucy had looked down to the beach and announced they needed a day out instead of school. That perhaps their souls were lacking and that was why they were arguing. Not because they were both hungry, which they were, because last night they had no dinner again.

Now they are down here, shivering in their school uniforms, the sea seeming to unfurl like a tongue, licking the shore. Lucy stands and watches the sea. She takes a deep breath, in through her nose and out through her mouth.

'Look at that. Why go to school, when you have the Atlantic Ocean right here?'

'I have a test,' Saoirse replies in a flat voice.

'What is the point of a test?' Lucy replies.

'Does that mean I don't need to do my homework?' Jack asks.

Lucy shakes her head. 'They never tell you none of it matters, not really.'

Saoirse wonders if she is talking about Northern Ireland again. Her mother always gets upset about it. Probably because it's always there, on the telly. The men in green uniforms and people throwing milk bottles that explode when they land. The frightened people running, just trying to get their kids to school. No ceasefire in sight. Jack always asks: *how many miles away is that?* Their mother always replies: *a few hours' drive*. Saoirse thinks it looks like a different world. A whole different place on the other side of the planet. Or maybe it just feels safer to pretend it isn't just a few hours' drive away.

Suddenly, Lucy rips off her top and takes off her long skirt, stripping down to her underwear and socks.

'What are you doing?' Saoirse asks, frowning.

'Swimming,' she says. 'Come join me!' she yells as she runs towards the water. Saoirse watches her legs wobbling a little as she runs. Lucy squeals as her feet touch the frozen tide. She sounds happy, alive. Saoirse looks at Jack, and Jack looks at Saoirse. Neither of them speak because a look is enough to say everything.

'Come in, it's beautiful!' Lucy calls back to them. 'So icy fresh!'

She is waist deep now. She ducks down and screams. 'Oof!'

The water is rolling, thrashing almost. It is not a good day for a dip. The red flag is out, whipping in the wind. Saoirse eyes the lifebuoy nearby, waiting ominously by the wall. No one is supposed to swim today. In fact, the more Saoirse looks, the crazier the canvas seems. A woman in the sea, practically naked on a freezing day. Two of the woman's children watching her. It doesn't feel normal. Saoirse is starting to wonder if anyone else's mother behaves like this.

Once, Saoirse's geography class came down here and threw oranges into the sea, timing how long it took for them to travel along sideways. Saoirse had watched them bob along in the water, out of place, floating in the tide. Her hands had been so cold that day, and as she had hooked them inside her woollen jumper, she had thought what a waste of time it all was. Who cared how long the orange took to get further along the beach? Who cared about longshore drift, and whether the sea wanted to move the sand over hundreds of years?

'Come out,' Saoirse demands.

'No! I'm only getting started!'

Lucy begins to swim out further. Now just the back of her head is visible, like a seal's.

'So fabulous out here!' she shouts.

'Will she be all right?' Jack asks.

'I think so,' Saoirse says. 'She just needs to get it out of her system, then we can go to school.'

The ceasefire has happened naturally by creating a common enemy: Mam.

'Come and join me!' Lucy shouts again, but this time her voice sounds shivery, weaker, less sure. Saoirse looks up and down the empty beach. A long strand of stones and sand in both directions. Her mother swims around in circles now. Bobbing to stay afloat. It seems she is caught in a rip current, about thirty feet out from the shore. Not too far out, but not close enough for comfort either. Every so often she is carried in or out a little further. Now her mother is the orange bobbing along. She is getting carried sideways and out to sea, ever so slightly by the second.

'I can't touch the ground!' Lucy yells all of a sudden. 'I'm too cold! I can't feel my arms!'

When Saoirse thinks of her mother, she thinks of a storm. You cannot control the wind when it comes. You can only take in the washing and batten down the hatches. The storm does what it wants. She recognises the shift in her mother. From excitement to the moment when she realises her plan might not be so good after all. It usually happens in a split-second.

'I can't swim to come get you!' Saoirse calls out. 'Swim back in here to us.'

She and Jack walk down to the edge of the water.

'I can't! I can't feel my legs either!' Lucy's voice sounds panicky now. 'It wants me to go out to sea, but I don't want to go! The devil is trying to take me, even now – it hates me!'

Saoirse looks at Jack. He bites his lip.

'Mam, come back in!' he says, stepping forwards too close to the tide and getting his shoes wet.

'Jack, get back,' Saoirse says urgently.

'I'm trying to swim but the current's too strong!' Lucy shouts, her voice vibrating with frustration.

Saoirse can feel her heart begin to race now. An out-of-control, out-of-body experience. Helplessness settling in under her bones. She looks around the beach desperately. It started so simply, and now they are here.

'Mam, I'm going to come in!'

Saoirse takes off her jumper and her skirt but keeps on her shirt and knickers. She knows she will need dry clothes to put on when she gets out. There are no witnesses. No boats. Not even a flock of seagulls coming to help. She steps into the water. The icy temperature takes her breath away. It is almost painful on her skin.

She is afraid of the sea. No one ever talks about what is underneath, all the many creatures. The sea is even more frightening than the forest. So unknown and full of monsters. She tries not to think about how it feels to hover so high up above a dense nothingness, not even able to see the ground. It's like standing on the edge of the cliff and staring into the fog.

She takes a breath and wades in to knee level.

'It should have been fox dust! Mankind! Wake up, mankind!' her mother calls out, pausing when the sea splashes her face. 'Stop letting the devil-speak overcome your starry petals, your sky-face!'

Saoirse looks desperately behind her at the lifebuoy but decides against it. Running to get it would waste time and she has to be quick. She pushes herself into the water all at once. It pushes the air from her lungs. Like hitting concrete, hard. She takes a moment to let herself adjust. It is ice. *One, two, three*, she counts to herself. *Bilgewater, blackwater, firewater, greywater. Breathe in. Breath out.*

'I am drenched in colours!' Lucy calls out. 'Carry me home, Atlantic!'

'I'm coming now, Mam,' Saoirse yells, coughing as some seawater gets into her mouth. She swims one breaststroke towards her mother, then another. So slow, like moving through tar. 'Stay there!' she gasps. Saoirse is not a great swimmer but she is slightly better than her mother. As long as she doesn't get caught in the rip current too.

Her mother is looking up at the grey sky, moving less now.

'The devil forgets what I've done for him!'

'Stay there!' Saoirse repeats. She kicks forwards. A wave rocks her sideways and pushes her back. The sea is mighty, she remembers. It is so much stronger than it seems.

Suddenly she hears a person. A man's voice.

'Oi! Are you okay out there?'

Saoirse doggy-paddles around, spitting salty water out. She tries to wave to the man. He is tall and wiry, around sixty-ish, with a black and white collie on a lead. She recognises him. It is the local butcher, Mr Fitzgerald.

'No!' Saoirse shouts back. 'I need help!'

'Are you able to swim back in?' he calls to Lucy.

Lucy does not reply but her head goes under the water. She is gone for a moment, then she pops back up, her face pale and confused.

Mr Fitzgerald drops the dog lead. He doesn't even stop to take off his clothes, just wades in and begins to swim. Despite his age, he seems strong – spending all his days lifting dead meat might do that for a person. Saoirse watches, treading water. Lucy disappears under again.

'Mam!' Saoirse yells.

Her mother waves her arms, no longer screaming – she looks like she can barely breathe.

'Mam!' Jack cries.

Mr Fitzgerald slices through the water. His lined face is reddened by the cold, his hair plastered to his head.

'Come here! Let me help!'

There is a splash as he reaches their mother, grabs her. She seems to pull away from him.

'I'm trying to help you!' Mr Fitzgerald shouts, sounding furious now. 'Stop struggling!'

Saoirse begins to swim back towards the shore. Counting the seconds. Pushing against the waves.

'Grab the lifebuoy!' Mr Fitzgerald shouts to Jack.

'Jack!' Saoirse screams from the water as she swims. 'Get it!'

Saoirse puts down her feet onto the rough sandy floor, wincing at the sharp shells and stones and trying not to think about what else might be down there. Jellyfish? Crabs? She feels the slimy seaweed on a smooth boulder beneath her toes and recoils. She looks to the left and sees Jack sprint the fifty feet or so back to the beach wall and grab the orange circle from its post.

Jack returns with the lifebuoy as Saoirse stumbles out of the waves, feeling the pull of gravity and the tide arguing with one another over her legs. She drags herself to the shoreline, then collapses onto the sand. Trembling she crawls over and picks up her jumper and skirt and tugs them on. She watches Mr Fitzgerald as he puts his hand around Lucy.

'Get off me!' she pants, getting her breath back.

'Your mam's not letting me help her – throw it to me!' he gasps of the orange lifebuoy.

Jack stands close to the shore and throws it out to the butcher. It lands a few metres away. He reaches out, unable to grab it.

'Come on …' Saoirse mutters. Lucy looks as though she is trying to swim in the other direction – away from Mr Fitzgerald. He takes the lifebuoy, swims after Lucy and grabs her by the shoulder.

'Let me go!' she screams.

'I'm trying to help you!' Mr Fitzgerald shouts again, his eyes wild.

He puts Lucy's arms around the buoy. Finally, she relents and hangs on.

'Grab the rope!' Mr Fitzgerald yells. 'Help pull her in!'

Saoirse jumps up and tugs on the end of the rope. She and Jack yank it as hard as they can as the butcher pulls Lucy and swims at the same time.

'Oh, the devil works in vain!' Lucy shouts. 'He failed today!' she cackles. 'Try harder next time, Devil!'

Mr Fitzgerald staggers in with their mother, dragging her along. Saoirse grabs her mother's clothes and hands them to her. Lucy looks white and lilac-lipped now. Her hands shake. Saoirse helps her put her jumper on and then her skirt.

'What happened?' she asks suddenly. 'How did I get here? Who are you?' she asks, turning to the butcher she speaks to every week, someone she should recognise.

Mr Fitzgerald, whose clothes and hair are dripping wet, looks confused.

'I'm Barney Fitzgerald – you know me, Lucy! I think you were getting hypothermia out there – you wouldn't let me save you.'

'I wouldn't?'

Lucy looks confused.

Mr Fitzgerald gives Saoirse a questioning look.

'Don't ask,' Saoirse replies.

He frowns and gestures to his wet jeans and shirt.

'I have to get back and change myself, before I catch my death. Can you get her home okay?'

Saoirse nods. 'We'll bring her home straight away.'

'You sure?' he asks.

Saoirse nods.

'Right,' Mr Fitzgerald says, nodding to them both. He retrieves the lead of his dog, who is sniffing excitedly at everyone's heels, darting about on the shale with the occasional bark.

'Thank you,' Saoirse says, meaning it with all her heart.

Jack goes and hugs his wet mother as Mr Fitzgerald walks off.

'Why are you not in school?' Lucy asks in a cross voice. 'It must be almost midday! Why are we on the beach?'

'Let's go home now,' Saoirse says.

Lucy looks dazed but she lets them lead her back towards their home. Saoirse links her arm with her mother on one side and takes Jack's hand on the other. She feels heavy with unspoken worry as she walks back up the hill. She glances at Jack's face, which is far away now. He is whispering to himself under his breath – counting again, perhaps. These kinds of incidents are not good for her or her brother. She has tried not to worry about the future, but her mother's behaviour is getting worse by the week, and now Saoirse needs to know: how will this all end?

19

Day Six

Jack

Jack stands at the doorway and watches Kate slump on the sofa. The TV is on and Jack can see a journalist talking to the camera. Behind the journalist, there is a river. Spacemen in white suits pick their way among the branches, which have been tied with yellow tape.

'*It is not clear whether the body that has been discovered this morning belongs to that of missing teen Saoirse Kellough …*'

Kate is wailing like a banshee Jack once saw in a play in school. A *bean sí* is a fairy woman who tells you when a family member is about to die. Jack hopes it is not true that Kate has been taken over by a *bean sí* but the sound coming from her mouth is the same. The *bean sí* from the play had danced around with a painted face and wild white hair. Kate's hair is sticking out the very same.

Jack looks over Kate's shoulder to the TV set. He feels a sick feeling rise inside himself. A loud buzzing, like thousands of bees, splitting his head in half so he cannot think. He goes over and slips his hand under Kate's arm. He rests his head against her face, feeling her tears against his own skin. They sit there for a moment, rocking back and forth. Kate sniffles as they both watch the screen. Jack's eyes drift up to the mantelpiece with the photo of his mother. He tightens his fingers around Kate's arm, trying not to think about the unthinkable: that the body they found might be Saoirse's.

20

Day Six

Freya

I turn off the sloshing tap. The silence is almost louder now as I put one foot into the bathtub and wait for the temperature to become bearable. I listen to the water swishing, echoing off the tiles, then lower myself in, wincing at the heat. My heart quickens in my chest, trying desperately to cool me down.

I sink back and inhale, running through the list of names in my mind. Who took Saoirse? Father Maguire, Mr Fitzgerald, or could it even be someone in the family, like Bronagh? Fergal Duffy? Father Maguire is still a suspect, of course, but more interesting to me are the family. The things Mr Fitzgerald said about Bronagh being jealous of Lucy were harsh, but what if they were true? And then there is Kate. Could Saoirse's older sister be responsible for her disappearance? I know from experience that the perpetrators often turn out to be related to the victims.

I suddenly hear my ex-husband Daniel's voice in my mind. *Just focus on your own life! If you weren't so obsessed with fixing other people's problems, you might have been focused on the right things that day. Like your child playing next to a pool. Instead, you were on the phone inside the villa, trying to help a friend with a problem they could have solved themselves.*

Last night I dreamed of Violet again, as I have done every night since I arrived in Drumsuin. She was walking ahead of me,

135

through the forest, weaving in and out of the pines, her hair around her shoulders. It was a new dream. I had never seen her in a forest before. I could not catch her. I called her name, but she did not seem to hear me. There was someone else there in the forest too. A presence behind me. A voice. There were whimpers of mirth, a dragging sound. A shovel slicing through dirt, a man's heavy breath. Did I see the person? No. I close my eyes a moment. Fear runs through me. I look down at my arms, lifting one from the hot water. My skin has goosebumps on it, despite the heat. I can feel my heart begin to speed up.

What is it about *this* case that's messing with my head?

I need to stop thinking about this dream, and about the past. I can't afford to let thoughts of Violet spiral and overtake me again.

A sudden thought enters my mind. I could leave the hotel right now and go and explore that forest. Get this dream and the associations with Violet and that forest out of my system once and for all. That might help. There are areas the volunteers have finished with – areas where no people will be, where I could go and look for myself – reassure myself Violet was not connected to the forest at all. What's stopping me? Am I secretly afraid what the villagers say is true? That the forest is haunted, a creature lurking inside?

I hear a loud shrill sound. It takes a moment to process what it is. It is the hotel phone. Distinct and ringing. I stand up and jump from the water, grabbing a towel.

'Hello?' I say, pulling the soft, white towel closer around me, my hair dripping onto the carpet.

I look towards the curtains, which are ajar. It is evening, but there is still a gloomy light outside.

'Hello?' I say again.

A slight buzzing sound. Faraway white noise.

'Mary?' I ask, imagining the receptionist on the other end. There are sounds in the distance. Quiet ones. Almost like the wind.

'I don't know who this is, but I can't hear you,' I say.

No reply. More sounds of wind, and waves crashing.

Finally, there is a voice. It's Walter.

'Sorry, Freya! It's a terrible line. Can you hear me?'

'Yes,' I say, relieved it is just Walter.

'Sorry to bother you so late. There's been a development. Superintendent Ridgeway told me to call you.'

'What about?' I perch on the edge of the bed.

'A body has been found.'

I put my hand to my mouth. I remember what Alice had said about the sniffer dogs.

'It's not … ?' I say, a question in my voice.

'We don't know yet.'

I feel my eyes well up with tears. Surely this isn't how it ends for Saoirse?

'And I'd like to ask your professional opinion on something …'

I nod, waiting.

'The boy, Jack. You don't think he could have it in him to, you know … have hurt his sister in any way, do you?'

I feel as though I have been slapped. Is there something about the body they've found that has led Walter to this question? I think about Jack, his vulnerability and his sadness, those eyes, staring at me as though he was trying to decide if I could really help him, or if I was going to hurt him. I think of his strange drawings, of the way he spoke about missing his mother.

'No,' I reply confidently.

'Fine. Just thought I'd ask. See you tomorrow,' he says.

I put down the receiver. Why would Walter ask me that question now, over the phone – a question he could ask me anytime? I hope to God that I'm right, and Jack didn't hurt Saoirse. Walking to the window, I look out at the sea rolling in the harbour. My eyes suddenly fill with tears. I need to get a handle on my feelings. Otherwise, this case might just drag me back to a dark place I cannot return from.

21

Day Seven

Freya

As I approach the house the next morning, I see Jack running around the front garden. He stops and raises his arms and, for a moment, I think he is alone. As I pull into the driveway, I notice another figure of a middle-aged woman. I smile and wave at Jack. The woman tosses a pink frisbee into the air and Jack chases it, energetically. It is Alice, the search volunteer – Walter's girlfriend. I get out of the car and Jack stops and stares then throws the frisbee towards me. It lands near my feet on the grass. I go and pick it up, turning it over in my hands. It's like something you'd buy at the seaside, and for a moment, I am transported back to days on the beach with my own children. As I toss it back to Jack it soars wide, landing over near the large oak tree.

'Sorry!' I call out. 'I've terrible aim!' Jack turns and sprints off to fetch it. I amble over to Alice, the cold air making goosebumps rise underneath my coat.

'Any news?' she asks.

'Well, just what you've probably already heard about the body they found.'

She nods, her eyebrows knitted together in worry. She lowers her voice to a whisper. 'I heard it was a child.'

'You did?'

She looks over her shoulder at the house as if to check no one is listening.

'Yeah, but not sure if it was Saoirse – it could be one of the missing ones from years back.' She pauses and tilts her head. 'You're really helping him, you know,' she says, nodding to Jack. 'He told me he felt better because you are here. He said you listen to him, and no one has done that since his mam.'

A rare compliment. I feel pride well up in my chest.

'I'm probably going to have to borrow him now, if you don't mind,' I say.

'Sure.' She looks at her watch. 'I need to get on anyway – get back to work. You know, I really hope the body isn't Saoirse's. The villagers are devastated. They're desperate to get her back alive, even if the family are not—'

She puts her hand up to her mouth as though she has said too much.

'What do you mean?' I ask.

She looks over her shoulder again, and lowers her voice.

'Well, they're quite detached about it, don't you think? Especially Kate.'

I think about this – it's true that she has seemed a little bit detached, but this could be a normal reaction.

'Perhaps she's in shock?'

'Well, I'm no psychologist, but it doesn't take a shrink to real-ise maybe they didn't want her found because they're involved somehow?'

I tilt my head and look at Alice.

'Do you really believe that?' I ask.

She breathes out heavily, looking torn about whether to keep talking or whether to stop.

'Sorry. I've probably said too much. It's not my place to cast aspersions on them. Don't tell anyone I said this, will you? Perhaps it's all in my imagination.'

'Of course not.'

'See you later,' she says. 'Bye, Jack,' she calls out.

But it's strange – something about what Alice said has slotted things together in my mind. *Aunt Bronagh and Kate.* Until now, Kate's behaviour has seemed to me consistent with someone genuinely in shock, a grieving relative. But in most of the cases I've worked on, it's been someone known to the child who committed the crime. Could her behaviour be more aligned with a guilty conscience? She had burst into tears when we first met, but subsequently she's seemed more detached – immediately ducking out to check on Jack after his sessions. Is she worried Jack may have told me too much? Something tells me not to discount Alice's words.

I look over to Jack running towards me, his face a picture of hope and trust. Hearing what Alice has said about me helping Jack makes me feel even more motivated to move forwards and figure out what happened. I need to start listening more closely to everyone in this house, not just Jack. I need to figure out what happened to Saoirse – to try and get to the bottom of this case once and for all.

22

Day Seven

Jack

Jack is a puzzle. A puzzle with pieces. Some pieces are big and some are small. Jack is scared of what he might see once the pieces have fit together to become a picture. Freya says she'd like to talk to Kate and Jack together. She has followed him up the stairs and climbed through the crawl space. Now Freya lowers herself onto the ground cross-legged and Kate settles on the beanbag. Jack sits on his little chair and focuses on the skylight. Pearl the dog lies on his side and dozes quietly, his white fur calm, his eyes half-open. A gentle rain taps on the glass. A grey light fills the room. Up above, the clouds hang low over the house. There is a musty smell in here of paint drying, white spirits and old boots. Freya puts in a tape and turns on the clunky recording device. She places it between them in the middle of the floor. Jack watches the tape turn, recording what they are saying.

'Are you happy here, Jack?' Freya asks.

Jack nods. He had asked if they could all go to the attic room today to talk. Jack likes the attic room, it feels safe, there is only one way in and out. People can't creep up on you in the attic, or walk in uninvited.

'I don't know what I'll do if that body is hers,' says Kate. 'But how can it be anyone else's? I mean, what are the chances it is?'

'It might not be hers,' Freya says gently. 'There were other people who went missing in there, remember?'

There is a long silence. Kate keeps her eyes down and Freya watches carefully.

'When should you find out?' Freya asks.

'Later today, they said they will be in touch very soon. They might need me to identify it if they think ...' She stops and bites her lip. 'I can't think about it being her.'

Freya narrows her eyes and stares at Kate for a long moment. Then she shifts in her chair looking between them both.

'Is there anything you want to talk about today – either of you?'

Kate shakes her head. Jack shakes his head, copying Kate.

'I know what you are thinking about us,' says Kate eventually.

'What?' Freya asks. 'What am I thinking about you?' she says, her voice curious.

'You're thinking we're mad. But he's not mad and neither am I,' she says gesturing to Jack. 'These supernatural things ... they're happening. It's worse for Jack. I go to sleep and turn off from it. He goes to sleep and gets awful dreams. He never escapes it.'

'Do you still have bad dreams, Jack?' Freya asks, turning to him.

Jack nods.

'What about?' Freya shifts a little, changing her tone of voice. She clears her throat. 'What do you dream about, Jack?'

'Scary things. Kate gets angry. She thinks I'm pretending about them. She thinks I'm bad.'

Kate looks down. 'I don't think that, Jack. I just told Freya that I believe you.' She runs her hand through her hair and lets out a breath.

'I'm not making it up,' Jack says. He puts his arms around himself in a hug and begins to rock back and forth. 'Kate gets angry with me.'

'I don't ... get angry,' she says through gritted teeth.

'You do, you are doing it now!'

'I am not!' she snaps back. 'That's not why I was angry! I was angry with the situation because we couldn't stop any of it from happening.'

'Couldn't stop what?' Freya asks.

'The game,' Jack says in a small voice.

'This game – Kate, can you explain it?'

'It's just some hide-and-seek rubbish our mother taught them. People in the village all know about it too – someone made it up years ago and it's become like … folklore. It's messed with their heads. They believe it's true – but it isn't, of course.'

'You said you believed in the game,' Jack murmurs. 'You said we needed to stop it, that it was real.'

'That was until your sister went missing,' Kate hisses back. 'Now, I don't believe in it any more! How can some made-up creature take a real-life girl? It doesn't make sense,' Kate says angrily.

'Sounds like you don't want to believe in it any more?' Freya says.

Kate nods slightly.

'And how does this game work?' Freya asks.

Kate sighs.

'The purpose of the game is to protect the forest – people play the game to sort of … appease the forest.'

'To appease it?'

'People … are afraid of the forest. It has a power. A mind of its own. The game is a test. To figure out if the players have been good to the forest. If they haven't, the hidden player won't be found.'

Freya looks at them both.

'Your mother taught you this game? Before she died.'

Kate looks down at her hands and nods.

'I'm very sorry for your loss,' says Freya. 'It must have been a lot for you to process and such a lot for you to take on. And with the circumstances of her death too …' says Freya.

'I don't want to talk about it,' Kate says in a tight voice, her leg jittering.

Freya leans over and turns off the tape recorder with a click. She picks it up and removes the batteries and places them on the floor. Jack watches them roll a little across the wood.

'Is there anything you feel you would like to share confidentially, off the record?' asks Freya.

'No.'

'Are you sure?'

Freya looks at Kate as though she is wondering something. As though she is trying to get her to tell her secrets out loud.

'So now you are there for Jack,' Freya says softly. 'Now that your mother is sadly gone.'

'Yes,' says Kate.

'How has that been lately, between both of you? How is your relationship right now?'

Kate pauses, side-eyeing Jack.

'Fine.'

'Fine?'

She breathes out heavily.

'Mostly fine. Look, I don't want to get him into trouble … He is my brother, after all.' She moves her eyes as if conveying something she cannot say. 'I think he knows more about Saoirse than he will tell,' she says. 'In terms of what happened to her. In all likelihood, *he* knows what happened but he won't tell anyone.'

She stops and looks at Jack. Freya shifts a little on the floor and looks at him directly.

'Jack, what happened?' she asks in a calm tone.

There is a long silence. Jack feels for the Creature figurine and rubs the edges of it. He can feel the outline of the roots with his thumb.

He doesn't reply for a moment. 'No one has looked there …' he says eventually.

'Looked where?'

He draws a T on his leg. Thinks back to climbing up those thin branches, to the hidden treehouse in the pines. Jack looks at

Freya. She appears to be studying him as though he were an animal in a zoo. She narrows her eyes for a moment.

'T-r-e-e-h-o-u-s-e,' he spells out softly.

'Treehouse?'

Jack nods.

'I thought you said you told Garda Morris about that already.'

'I didn't tell him about our secret one,' Jack shrugs. 'Saoirse told me not to tell anyone about that one, ever.'

'Christ, Jack,' whispers Kate. 'How could you not tell us this for a whole week?'

'I'm sorry,' says Jack in a small voice.

'Where is it?'

'A hundred steps from the Hollowing Place. High up in the pines – high, high – you can't see it from the ground.'

'But the body …' Kate says desperately. 'What if they have given up looking for her alive now?'

'They won't have given up, not yet,' says Freya. 'You don't know that body belongs to Saoirse.'

'I'll go call the Gardaí,' Kate says standing up. 'I'll get them to go and search there. If they can't find it, Jack will have to show them where it is.'

Jack keeps his eyes down. What if Saoirse is stuck there with the Creature and he didn't help her? He needs to help her, so she can come home safe and this will all be over.

COUNTDOWN

Six ...

Nine Months Ago

Saoirse

The towel feels rough on her skin as she looks in the steamed mirror. It had taken a long time for the heat to get back into her bones after the icy water. It already feels like years ago, like a distant nightmare. What if Mr Fitzgerald had never shown up? Would her mother have drowned?

Opening the cabinet, she peers inside at the bottles, examining them one by one. *Clozapine*, the third bottle reads. She picks it up and fingers the plastic cap of the bottle, reading the instructions on the label: *For the treatment of mood disorders*. She had seen her mother take a few tablets out and knock them back with juice at the breakfast table a few weeks back. She shakes it a little to hear the rattle, then places it back on the shelf, turning it to its original position and closing the cupboard.

Before her mother started taking the pills, the yelling was frightening. Jack can hardly recall it, but she can. Since their dad left a few months earlier there have been no arguments like that any more. No more plates smashed against the walls. Everything is fine and peaceful when Mam takes the pills.

For the past two weeks, though, she's seemed far away in her head. When she goes that way, Jack says she's on planet Saturn. She stares into the distance, ignoring everyone around her, or starts saying things that don't make sense. Sometimes after dinner, Saoirse picks up the plates and takes them away to wash and their Mam is still watching the wall.

Saoirse dresses quickly into dry clothes. A pair of linen trousers, a jumper and woollen socks that are thick, like slippers. She goes downstairs.

'Where's Mam?' she asks Jack.

She ties up her damp hair with a scrunchie. Jack doesn't look up from his painting. His long eyelashes are cast down as he examines a circle he is making with the brush.

'Bed,' he says. 'I'm hungry.'

Saoirse goes to the cupboard and gets crackers, puts them on a plate and brings it to Jack, then sits opposite him at the table.

'What are you painting?'

'The girl – the one from the river. The one I play with.'

Saoirse tilts her head to see it. A figure with a yellow dress, a cardigan and long dark hair. It is the same girl she had seen herself in the river, just recently. She feels the hairs on her arm rise.

Jack looks up as she tries to hide the fear from her face.

'It's good. All your paintings are good.'

Saoirse squeezes her fingers, still pale from the cold. They sometimes go like this – like there's no blood in them, and they belong to a vampire. She rubs them together and coughs, feeling the salt water in her lungs, then gets up from the table and walks to the fireplace. She'll light it to warm up.

'I've been thinking, and I think we should call Dad,' Jack says to her back.

Saoirse kneels by the hearth. 'What should we tell him?'

'That Mam has stopped taking her pills and he needs to come back and help us.'

'Shouldn't we tell Aunt Bronagh first?'

'No,' Jack says.

'Why?'

'Because I don't think she should know about Mam. She might tell someone and it might get Mam in trouble.'

'That's true. Do you have Dad's phone number?'

Jack shakes his head. Saoirse drums her fingers against her lips for a moment, thinking. 'It might be in Mam's notebook, the one she keeps in her handbag.'

'How would we get it?'

'Wait until she is out of the house. Or there is always plan B.'

'Plan B?'

'I run away to Dublin and try and find him myself. I have his address, the one he sent me a few months ago, it was on the back of the envelope.'

'Or *we* could post a letter?'

'That might be easier,' Saoirse agrees. 'If we write to him, he might come and save us.'

Jack is silent for a while.

'Do you think the forest really is haunted?'

Saoirse lights a match and doesn't reply.

'Do you think our house is?' Jack asks.

Saoirse frowns.

'Aunt Bronagh told me ghosts are just secrets of the family hanging around. That bad feelings turn into ghosts. People who think their houses have ghosts really just have bad feelings and *tra-au-ma*.'

'What does that mean?'

'I don't know,' Saoirse replies.

'Do you think people in the village would go to the forest if it wasn't haunted?'

'I think they want to forget about that forest. That's what Aunt Bronagh said.'

'Why?'

'Because when bad things happen, people want to forget about them. Things happened in that forest years ago. People have decided it is haunted, never mind if it really is.'

'But we've seen it,' Jack says.

That's true, Saoirse thinks – they have seen it. Seen it, heard it and felt it. That thing in the distance. The Creature. Or was it all in their imagination?

'You know,' she says, taking a calming breath, 'Mam loves us, even when she doesn't take her pills.'

The fire is taking hold, so she gets up and sits back onto a rocking chair. Jack doesn't reply. Saoirse considers what she has just said. She thinks about her mam, when she is on other planets, and she wonders if it is true. Can someone on Saturn love you? Or are they just gone? Either way, Saoirse has to look after Jack and keep it all together. One day at a time. At least until their mother returns from Saturn, or their dad comes home.

23

Day Seven

Freya

The boards creak underfoot as I ascend the stairs. We have taken a break to eat, and I've decided to return to the attic, while it is empty. I want to have another look at Jack's paintings on my own. At the painting room hatch, I stand still. I cannot hear anything. Seizing my opportunity, I bend and crawl into the attic space.

Around me, paintings cover every inch of wall and ceiling. They are all offbeat and marvellous, but also surreal, peculiar. I stop and focus on a picture of a black cloud with a face coming out over a river. Next to the cloud is the figure of a little girl and a little boy, clearly meant to be Jack and Saoirse. Was this a dream, or something he had seen?

I look around at the items in the room. No furniture apart from a few child-sized chairs, a beanbag and a short, antique chest of drawers which would just about fit through the crawl space entrance; some statues and children's toys sit on top of the chest of drawers. There is also a drying table for Jack's paintings and a ladder. I pick up a stuffed toy and sniff it, holding it close for a moment before gently putting it down and tiptoeing over to the closet. I click the string to turn on the light. Inside, there is an oak bedside table and a pile of books. A white tip of paper pokes out of the drawer. I bend down and pull the metal handle. It creaks open. The scent of old wood and dust rises up. I glance over my shoulder and listen for a second. I lift the paper carefully out of the drawer and unfold it. On the page is writing, scrawled in crayon.

Dear Kate, Please don't be angr-ee wit me. I will try hard-r to stop the game. Jack.

I remember what Jack and Kate spoke about. Kate said she didn't want to believe in the game since Saoirse went missing, but she had believed in it before. How often have they played this game, and has Kate really been up to something she shouldn't – hiding things like Alice suspected?

I hear footsteps up the stairs. I shove the paper back into the drawer, and close it hastily.

My heart speeds up as I listen to the rattling of the hatch. Someone is coming in. I move closer to it as the hatch opens and a blonde head appears. Kate. She is wearing day clothes for the first time since I have met her. A jumper, a skirt, and woollen tights.

'Oh, you're in here …' she mumbles, looking crestfallen and, it seems, a little like she has been caught in the act.

She stands up and faces me, her pale cheeks reddening a little.

'I didn't mean to intrude,' I explain. 'I was just taking another look at Jack's drawings.'

'He's just like our mother,' she says with a bitter laugh. 'She would have drawn things like this.'

Kate flops down onto the nearby beanbag. I look at her long eyelashes, her button nose. She is almost a mirror image of Jack, with badly cut blonde hair, pale translucent skin, in contrast to Saoirse's red hair and freckles. This is a good opportunity to talk to Kate properly. To suss out if what Alice said about her might be true. Could her mother Lucy be the way in?

'Your mother, was she difficult to get along with?' I ask.

'Yes …' she sighs. 'Not for want of trying.'

She cranes her neck back and peers at the skylight.

'I see,' I reply. 'It's an awful thing that happened to her. It must have been a shock.'

'She didn't jump,' she says in a tight voice. 'People say she did, but it's not true. Our Mam wouldn't have abandoned us like that.'

I am silent. I don't want to argue with her, but another part of me wants to elicit the truth. It does feel like Kate has something to hide – something in her body language and tone of voice. Years of listening to people in the therapy room has given me a radar for deception. It's just hard to know what exactly she is hiding and whether or not it pertains to Saoirse's disappearance.

'Was she unwell?' I try.

'She was, but she didn't kill herself,' she insists.

I lower myself slowly onto the floor and cross my legs, so as to be at her level.

'Do you think she was … alone … that day, your mother?'

She stares at her fingers. 'I don't want to talk about it right now. It's bad enough with the Gardaí asking me questions every two seconds. I came here for a bit of peace.' Her jaw tightens as though she is trying to contain her emotion, but I can detect her lips are quivering.

'Sorry. You're right. How have you been the past day or two?' I ask. 'It must be an awful strain, the not knowing …' I don't want to say it aloud, the thing we are both thinking. That the body they found might be Saoirse's. 'I don't know how I would cope if it were me,' I add. Or perhaps I do know. The answer is that I wouldn't be able to cope. God knows, I haven't in the past.

I study her sickly complexion. She doesn't look as though she has slept.

'I can't relax, I can't eat or sleep until I know if it's hers … the body. I still blame myself for letting them play out in the forest … and …' She pauses. 'And there is something no one knows.'

'Oh?'

'The day Saoirse went missing …' She stops.

'What?'

153

She watches me for a moment, as if assessing if she can trust me. 'If there is something you need to say, now would be a good time,' I say.

She nods. 'The day she went missing we had … a-an argument.'

Shame hangs in the air like a cloud. There is a silence. I need to tread carefully now.

'What about?' I ask.

'We argued about our mother. I said something … I shouldn't have. I can't repeat it.'

'People argue. It happens,' I reply.

'I know, but I feel so guilty that we argued and then she disappeared … I never got to apologise.'

There is a question on my tongue, but I am worried she will shut down if I say it. Nevertheless, I need to.

'Have you told the Gardaí?'

'No.'

'Is there … any reason for that?'

'I feel so much regret about it. I was worried they might judge me. I suppose a part of me also didn't want to say it aloud or admit it to myself.'

'What was the argument about?' I ask.

'It's complicated.'

'Family arguments always are.'

'It goes back a long way.'

'That's common too. How were things in your family before your mother died?'

She thinks for a moment.

'Everything was bad. Our father left and then our mother was so sick … mentally, I mean. And since she died, it's like Jack, it's like he's lost his mind or something. Like he has taken on her madness. He is behaving the way she did. Like he is possessed.'

'From my conversations with him, it seems to me that's his way of coping.'

But she isn't listening. She averts her gaze, her eyes filling with tears.

'I was only able to help my mother so much, and then ... I couldn't help any more.' She puts her face between her fingers and sobs. 'Sometimes I really want to ...'

'What?'

'You know ... not be around any more.' She sniffles. 'Sometimes I just wish it was all over. All of this. Our mam being gone, me having to mind the children, this whole thing with Saoirse. Then I remember it can't be over. I'm stuck in this mess, and it makes me just want to turn off the switch. You know?'

'You mean like end things?'

'Yes.'

'Do you have plans to do anything?'

She hesitates, then shakes her head.

'If you need to talk, I'm here. Do you have my hotel phone number?'

She shakes her head again. I take out a pen and scribble on my pocket notebook.

'Here,' I say, passing her the hotel's name and number. 'Call the reception and ask to be put through to room twenty-three. Whenever I'm not here, I'll likely be there. If not, call Garda Morris. You have his number?'

She nods. 'Thank you,' she says.

I stand up. 'I'll let you have some time to yourself.'

I want to ask her one more question before I leave. 'Kate, you rang the Gardaí about the treehouse, right?'

'Yes. They said they were on their way up there now. They said they'll come get Jack if they can't find it, but they should be able to with those directions. There's only so many places it can be, a hundred steps in any direction from the Hollowing Place.'

'Good. You know, I might go up there myself too later, have a look around.'

But as I say it, I feel dread in my chest. Part of me is reluctant to set foot in there. Something must be stopping me or I would have gone already. Would it be mad to go into that forest after everything I've heard about the place?

She looks up at me, her face wary.

'Just be careful,' she says softly. 'People think the rumours about that forest are a joke, but they're not. The forest knows how to punish people who don't respect it.'

I nod, then lower myself into the hatch and climb out. Perhaps I will find the courage to go looking in the forest tonight.

At the end of the hallway in one direction is an overflowing laundry basket. Socks, arms of sweaters and a muddy trouser leg all hang out. I scan the walls. A painting of Jack's is hung up here in a frame. It depicts the whole family, including the dog. I lean up to look closer. The father is drawn stood apart, near the tractor. Lucy is next to Jack. In the middle is Kate, and on the other side, Saoirse. I continue to two bedrooms opposite one another. The name on the right-hand door in messy paint reads *Jack*.

I wonder if I'll find anything in Jack's room to give me a clue as to what is happening in his mind. I listen out, but now I can hear Kate's voice downstairs, talking to him. The coast is clear.

I push the door and poke my head inside to see a striped duvet on a single bed, a poster of some superheroes and a box of toys. A cup of juice sits on the side, and there is a lamp and a wardrobe, a line of figurines across one shelf. I edge closer to inspect the figurines. They are twisted and grotesque, clearly made with a child's hand, but imbued with character nonetheless. Stretched eyes, oblong mouths, licking tongues, mischievous and devilish expressions. They are different things: a dog with the head of a bird, and a cat's head on the body of a horse. Some are mixes of animals and inanimate objects: a giraffe head on the shape of an ironing board. They look to be handmade with clay then painted.

I want to look around more, but can feel an urgency and a tightness in my stomach now. I have been welcome to potter about the public spaces in the house like the attic and the sitting room, but the bedrooms so far have been off bounds, under-standably. There is no reason for me to be in here alone. My ears are alert for the sound of Kate. If she decides to come out, she might find me. At the same time, I feel I cannot help myself. Any clue could help. I leave Jack's room and swiftly cross the hall to the master bedroom. All is silent.

A musty scent hits my nostrils. There is a double bed, unmade, the duvet rumpled up on one side. On the walls are photos – one of Jack, Saoirse, and Kate together, others of Kate and her friends – all of them taken several years ago. She looks like an ordinary teenager in the pictures. There is light in her eyes, no pinched look about her face. This Kate is not as worried or frightened as the Kate I have just spoken to, the girl on the brink of wanting to end things. I listen for a moment again, but there is no sound.

I walk to the bedside drawer and carefully open it. There are some crystals of different colours, a bunch of sage which looks as though it has been half-burned, and a dreamcatcher. I close the drawer.

Flitting to the other side, I pull at the opposite bedside table drawer, but this one will not open. The drawer is locked. I curse, and wonder if the Gardaí have already looked here. Perhaps they felt there was no need, with no reason to suspect her.

Something stirs in me – a need to know what is inside. I know what I am doing is extreme, a gross invasion of privacy and something I would never usually do, but I am suspicious of Kate now. Not just from what Alice said, but from her own actions – the strange way she has behaved, the guilt she has repeatedly expressed, and Jack's note to her about stopping the game. If she had anything to do with Saoirse's disappearance, or the body they have found, surely it is worth violating this privacy on the chance it might yield some answers.

I grab a nearby nail file and jam it into the drawer, rattling and twisting it for a moment until it springs open. Inside, there is a notebook. I pull it out and open it. *Saoirse's Diary*, it reads on the first page. Why does Kate have Saoirse's diary? Did she take it after Saoirse went missing or before? Why has she not given it to the Gardaí as evidence?

Suddenly, I hear a sound. Kate on the stairs. I shove the diary back into the drawer and close it. I run to the bedroom door, and creep back out. Quietly, I slide into the main bathroom and listen to her humming a tune as she passes.

I drive past crowds of volunteers who are congregating before a prayer service for Saoirse. *Kate, Bronagh, Mr Fitzgerald and Father Maguire.* These are the people I feel suspicious of and have not discounted in my own mind yet. I have a hunch that Kate is withholding something else from the Gardaí, and Bronagh gives me the same feeling – like there is something she isn't disclosing. I feel like I'm missing something – pieces of a puzzle that the people of this town are hiding.

Walter paces outside the Garda station. He is wearing a neon yellow tabard over his navy coat this afternoon and he wears just one glove. With his non-gloved hand he holds a cigarette. He taps at the end of it, takes one last drag, then extinguishes it on the wall. His forehead is furrowed, as though he is deep in thought. I park in a nearby space. The wind catches in my hair as I walk towards him, and for some reason, I remember Jack's drawing of his car, driving through the forest.

'Here she is,' he says. 'The lighthouse keeper herself.'

'Very funny.'

'You're a bit late,' he replies, a slight sharpness to his tone which confuses me.

'Am I?'

He glances at his watch. 'Were you held up?'

'Sort of. I was speaking with Kate.'

'Right,' he says tersely.

'Listen … I wanted to talk to you about something,' I say.

'Yes?' he looks concerned for a moment.

'Did you … ever think the family might be involved themselves?'

'Why, is it something Jack or Kate said?'

I think about the diary. Should I tell him about this find? I'll have to admit to snooping, and I don't know how kindly Walter would take that. What if I lose his trust? Or worse, get sent home and taken off the case? I decide against it for now. Though perhaps I'll tell him about my conversation with Kate, and frame my suspicion that way.

'Yes, Kate did tell me some things today.'

'What did she tell you?'

'She said she had an argument with Saoirse the day she went missing.'

'Did she say what about?'

'No.'

'She hid it from us?'

'It would seem so.'

'Christ,' Walter says under his breath.

'She also mentioned wanting to end things, feeling suicidal. She didn't say she had any plans to do anything, but she seems very low. I've told her to contact me if she ever needs to. I just feel ... Kate is hiding something. And their Aunt Bronagh too, I mean, who knows where she was the day Saoirse went missing?'

Walter rubs his face. 'Freya ...' He sighs.

'What?'

'With all due respect, don't get drawn into ... trying to figure out who has done this. You're not a detective. Leave that aspect to us. Just speak to Jack, concentrate on getting as much out of him as you can, and pass that information on to us. I don't mean to be rude, but it's just about staying in your own lane. I know the temptation is there to try to figure it out, but ... it might distract you from your task.'

I feel shame rise up my neck and burn at my cheeks. It is classic me, I realise. Getting side-tracked from my real responsibility. Focusing on the wrong thing.

'No, of course. You're completely right – I'll stay out of that side of things.'

I pause and try to think of something to say to change the subject, to clear the awkwardness in the air.

'Did you go to the treehouse?' I ask.

'Ah, you heard about that, did you?'

'Jack told me and Kate together,' I reply.

'Well yes, we found it, thanks to those directions. It's quite high up – not very visible from the ground or the air, but it's a big enough structure for a few people to sleep inside. They've cordoned it off now to do a search of it. There were no live girls or dead bodies, by all accounts. Though one of the forensics did radio down to say there was an item of clothing, so we will be investigating that as soon as they bring it down. Do you want to come inside?' he offers.

I nod and follow him into the station. We enter an interrogation room.

'Any more updates on Fergal Duffy?' I ask, almost afraid to ask now, in case it's outside my remit.

He doesn't look at me, instead moves things around on the desk.

'Aye. We had to release him without charge – there was no hard evidence at all, not to mention the fact that we spoke to multiple alibi witnesses who confirmed he was indeed at a farming event that day. Unless he was in two places at once, he's not our guy. We did find out something interesting though – Fergal Duffy is Maeve Murphy's uncle.'

'The missing Maeve Murphy?'

He looks at me now, as if wondering why he is telling me. As if weighing up if I should know this information now, seeing as I couldn't 'stay in my lane'.

'That's right. He was devastated about his niece's disappearance, even keeping some of her belongings. This whole thing has brought it all back for him; he was really upset when we interviewed him and was very cooperative with us. He just wants Saoirse found. He said the day he tried to bring Saoirse home, he had been annoyed about her being on his property, but also worried about her going into that forest after what happened to his niece.'

'Right. And what happened with the body you found?' I ask. 'Do you know who it belongs to yet?'

I hold my breath a moment and cross my fingers under the table, hoping that it isn't her.

'Specialist searchers and members from the dog unit came and alerted us to a patch, which seemed significant. When we started digging, that was when we found it … the child.'

I feel myself inhale sharply. He makes the sign of the cross. I feel sick, and I put my hand to my mouth. 'Did you identify them?'

'The body was badly deteriorated. The pathologist had to use dental records.' He paused. 'It wasn't Saoirse,' he says.

I let out a sigh of relief.

'Oh, thank God.' But then my mind immediately resumes its searching. 'Who was it, then?'

The look on his face is the same he had when we were stood outside. I have pushed too far.

'I can't say. The next of kin haven't been informed yet. But every effort is being made to locate them, as well as enlisting the assistance of the HSE …' He trails off, shuffling together some papers. 'Probably time for me to get back to work now. Are you okay to extend your contract with the Gardaí?'

I hesitate, and it hits me that I can say no. I could go right now if I wanted to. But then … what about Saoirse and Jack?

'I'll stay another week,' I agree, wondering immediately if it's the right decision.

He slides the contract over to me. I sign it and pass it back.

Then he stops, just like that, and stares at me. The feeling that passed between us before – when I first arrived – passes through again, of many things unspoken, and it leaves me feeling awkward. I don't say anything and wait for him to speak, except he doesn't. Finally, he looks away.

'I didn't think you would want to stay another week,' he admits.

161

'Well, I do. I want to help that family.'

'To the detriment of yourself,' he reflects.

I turn this over in my mind. I suppose he is right, perhaps it is a little bit to the detriment of myself. Why *do* I want to stay so much?

Walter suddenly looks confused, and a little thoughtful.

'You are strange,' he says eventually. 'I knew you had to be.'

'What makes you think that?'

'I just sense it in your way of being. We don't get many people like you around here.'

'How so?'

'Do you answer every question with a question?' he asks.

'Do you treat every visitor like this?'

'How?'

'Like they're a clue in your puzzle?'

'No. Just you. You've got a strange way about you. You're familiar or something … Have you ever bumped into an old friend in the middle of a city somewhere, where neither of you should be? You know that feeling?'

'You mean a strange coincidence?' I reply, my gut churning, trying to keep a calm demeanour.

I'm not sure what's going on here. Am I imagining things or is there an attraction here?

'Yes. That's the feeling I get around you too,' I admit.

I feel suddenly embarrassed. Then exhausted. I lower my chin and put my hands in my pockets, thinking back to Saoirse. That is what matters – not whatever is happening here with the Garda officer. The Garda officer who has a girlfriend who lives in the village, I remind myself.

'I'd better be going,' I say, pushing my chair back.

The female Garda who I saw at the reception on the first day enters the room.

'Walter?' she says. 'Someone is here to talk to you about Mr Fitzgerald – it's a woman.'

My ears prick up. Mr Fitzgerald?

'Be right there,' he says to her.

I walk to the door.

'And remember – just stick to speaking to Jack,' Walter says. 'Otherwise, your mind will be full of too many other things. I've learned the hard way to try and do one thing at a time.'

I nod, but as I stand up I realise I won't be able to do that. If Walter wants me to stay out of it, I'll just have to investigate on my own.

'I understand,' I say. 'I'll try.'

But I know as I say it.

I am lying.

COUNTDOWN

Five ...

Nine Months Ago

Saoirse

Night stretches out in surrender to the frozen dawn. The room is bright. She must have fallen asleep with the curtains open again last night. From her bed, Saoirse can see shadows of cloud ripple across the front yard. She feels like a bee caught in a spider web, paralysed and heavy. A stiff chill up her spine, her skin prickling with heat. Pain blooms in her ears, high-pitched and shrill. It is a shock to awake like this, after going asleep feeling fine.

Her dream last night had been so strange. She had been caught in the middle of a storm. *I need to get help*, the girl had said. The girl had been wearing a Girl Guides uniform, pointing at her map. Ashling McGill. Saoirse had known her name in the dream somehow. She was a missing person from the forest. *Where are we on this?* Ashling had asked desperately. She was carrying a hiking stick and a rucksack, and wearing glasses flecked with glimmering rain that reflected the green pines in that dim limestone light. Her Girl Guides tie around her neck was in two shades of blue, a leather knot clasped around it in the centre. She had squinted through the storm, her features in a terrified grimace, tears and rain running down her face. *Can you get help? I'll pay you ... anything ... please. You're scared, I understand. I'll write you a note, see? Just give the note to the first person you see* ... Now Saoirse remembers the end of the dream. Ashling was lying on the ground, in a pool of rain and blood. It was difficult to tell from where the blood was seeping. Her eyes were wide and staring. Dead.

Saoirse tries to erase the dream from her memory as she loosens her fingers which had been clamped tight around the duvet and calls out, her voice coming as if from underwater. There is a long wait, footsteps up the creaking stairs and finally, appearing in the doorway, Mam, up and dressed. It would seem the day has been turning for hours already. Her mam comes and sits on the side of her bed, lays the cold back of her hand against Saoirse's forehead.

'You've taken a fever ... it must have been from swimming in the cold yesterday.'

Saoirse shifts her arms of lead. She tries to roll the covers underneath herself.

'You almost caught your death in that sea, and it's all my fault. I'm sorry,' Mam says, casting her gaze down.

Her mam must have taken her pills this morning. She is normal for the first time in a while. Saoirse looks at the eaves outside the window, moss and stone. She tries now to forget the trees that clawed at her in her dreams and the underwater girl. She tries to forget how she'd felt in the night, when she'd woken from the dream. Her brother had been standing at the end of her bed, his face expressionless and strange, unlike himself. Sleepwalking again. For the third time this week. She had felt scared when she saw him. Hardly able to drift back to sleep after she had guided him back to his bed.

Now as she lies here, she remembers the lake a few miles from the house, near the cemetery, where they had found the old brown boat. The lake had been full of darkness, so many ghosts that seemed to float inside it. Ivory hands caressing the surface and turning into plants as they rowed closer. She remembers the tall trees of the forest and the pines with their angular branches. Triangles waving in the wind, hiding people and memories.

'I'll try to keep taking my pills,' Lucy says, her eyes changing from calm to fearful. 'I know I need to take them. I'm worried I'll lose you both if I don't. They'll take you away … So I'll be better from now on. I promise.'

Saoirse has heard it before, but hopes this time it is true.

She returns to the reels of her memories, to last week: Jack sitting on the edge of the brown boat as she rowed, him staring straight at the horizon, searching for the girl in the yellow dress. The water pulsing at the oar and sloshing at the sides. The smell of salt and trees, and their ship, its shadow long in the evening light.

24

Day Eight

Jack

The grassy knoll is damp with morning dew, next to the black gate, which creaks in the wind. Rain drips off the edges of the drainpipes and from the tips of the trees. Puddles reflect the cloudy sky. Jack and Freya are outside in the garden beside the vegetable patch and near the collapsed shed. They have come out for a walk around the yard. The ground smells earthy beneath them, like wet-penny rain. The tree stump marks its years with circles, surrounded by wooden boxes with holes in them.

'What's this?' Freya asks.

'My snail farm,' replies Jack. He squats down and picks up one of the boxes, holding it aloft. He has many memories of being with his snail farm. Like the day he saw the person speaking to Saoirse at the gate. It had been sunny that day. Jack had been kneeling in the mud, picking up snails. All under his nails was squidgy muck. He had heard a sound, looked up and saw a woman talking to Saoirse. He had stood up and shuffled closer. Saoirse was watching the woman, not moving much as though she was a little startled or afraid. Jack could not see the woman's face, but her hair was dark. Saoirse was shaking her head and leaning back a little away from the woman, as if denying something she had done.

'Jack,' says Freya, bringing him back to the present. 'Are you okay? That conversation we had the other day with Kate – you said she knew about the game, that she was scared of it too? Is that true?'

Jack nods quickly. 'Kate is scared of the game. Maybe she is scared to tell you the truth.'

Jack bends down again and opens the box with holes in its lid. Snails crawl all over one another. Grey slimy tails and eyes on stalks. Corded necks, which stretch out as though they are trying to see into the future. Some are long, some are squat, some curl into the corners, others climb up the sides. Half-blind snails. Angling towards the light. There is a big hole at the side, which means they could escape if they wanted, but most never do. Jack begins to count under his breath. Freya watches him as he does.

'And your mother? Did she have any visitors to the house when she was alive?'

Jack thinks back.

'Ye.'

'And the visitors … what kind of people were they?'

'Friends.'

'Girlfriends?'

'Men friends.'

'What would happen when they came?'

'They would stay upstairs.'

'How often did this happen?'

'Most days.'

'And did the men ever speak to you?'

'Not really. Sometimes they spoke to Saoirse. I don't like visitors.'

Jack looks at Freya's purple shoes. They look out of place in the mud. She squats down next to Jack as he runs his fingers across the edge of the snail house, lowers her voice.

'Here, take my hand,' she whispers.

'Why?' Jack replies.

'Trust me.'

He puts down the box and brushes the dirt off his fingers. He reaches out. Freya's hand is warm. She closes her eyes. Jack does too.

'We're wake-dreaming,' she says.

'Where are we going?' he asks, keeping his eyes closed.

'Wherever you want.'

Jack tries to follow where his mind takes him.

'What can you see?' she asks.

He imagines flying over the forest and looking down. From above, he can see lots, like he is a crow, flying along. Crows are clever, they see everything.

'The forest,' he replies.

Jack takes a breath of air in and out. He can hear the whooshing of wind in his ears.

'Can you see your sister?'

Jack looks down. He can see all of the places under the thick of the trees, the rutting trails, through the pines and the redwoods; his treehouse, the ravine, leading up to the Hollowing Place. He looks down and sees her running.

'Yes.'

'What is she doing?'

'Running,' he replies.

'Where?'

'She's trying to hide because I am counting ... And there is someone else.'

'Who can you see?'

Jack sees Saoirse disappear into a thicket of trees, being followed by the Creature. At least, he thinks it is the Creature. It is hard to tell.

Suddenly, there is the sound of a car. Jack starts and comes back to the now, opening his eyes. He turns his head to see a red car come down the driveway. A Beetle with its searching eyes. Jack wonders if he is imagining it. He can see it: Garda Morris's car, driving through the forest roads. The day Saoirse had gone missing. Where had he been going? Jack stands up, he rubs his eyes and looks again. But he is not imagining it, Garda Morris's car is still there, right in front of him.

'Where did she go, Jack?' Freya asks urgently. 'Where did she disappear to?'

Jack turns his head to look at Garda Morris as he gets out of the car.

'I … I couldn't see anything else,' he says.

Freya looks over Jack's head at Garda Morris, who is walking towards the house. He is carrying a clear bag with a piece of clothing inside.

25

Day Eight
Jack

Garda Morris has found a clue inside the secret treehouse. At least that's what he says. It has sleeves and buttons and it is made of sheep wool, but the type they knit and dye in factories, not the type you buy in the local Aran shops. Garda Morris has put it into a clear plastic bag. He carries it into the kitchen and Pearl growls at him, baring his teeth.

'You okay, doggo?' Garda Morris asks, but Pearl growls all the louder.

Garda Morris sits, and Kate sits too. This time she does not tend to the fire or make the tea; she just stares into the distance, her shoulders slumped, her hair unwashed, wearing her flannel pyjamas. She has not bothered to get dressed today. Aunt Bronagh busies herself getting tea for everyone, offering reassuring words. She pats Jack on the shoulder every so often, trying to soothe him. The clear plastic bag sits at the centre of the table. If it could talk, it would be screaming out for people to notice it.

Kate looks over at Aunt Bronagh. She looks at Garda Morris, and he looks at Jack. No one wants to look at the bag. The cardigan is stained with old blood. Jack knows it is blood because it is brown and stiff, how blood goes when it is a scab. Sometimes Jack has a scabby knee, and it is the very same. Jack looks at the bag closely, narrowing his eyes at the stitching. There are little flowers on the cardigan, daisies, all stitched around the neck. The buttons are red. They gleam in the light. He looks up at Garda Morris, with his one eye trained on Jack. He looks tired today, like he has not slept at all, and his wisps of comb-over hair are sticking up.

'Could this belong to Saoirse?' Garda Morris asks.

Kate is sniffling into a tissue now. She moves her mouth from behind the tissue.

'No, she doesn't own anything like that.'

She continues to sob. Aunt Bronagh puts her arm around Kate's heaving back and shoulders. Jack turns his head and looks at the fire that licks away in the corner, letting out little sparks once in a while.

'Why would there be so much blood?' Aunt Bronagh asks.

Garda Morris shakes his head and rubs his nose.

'Where did you find it?' asks Kate in a groggy voice.

'In the treehouse. I cannot say more than that – we have to keep parts of the investigation confidential.'

Aunt Bronagh laughs as though something is a joke, but it is not funny because her eyes are raging fires.

'We are her family!'

Garda Morris lowers his chin and scratches his forehead. Aunt Bronagh takes Kate's hand and holds it on the table.

'It's nothing personal. It's just the usual protocol,' says Garda Morris.

Aunt Bronagh clears her throat in a frustrated manner.

'Should I be worried … I mean should I be packing a bag for Jack – are you planning on taking him away?' she says.

Jack thinks about being taken away. About adoption and being fostered. Aunt Bronagh sometimes says she wants to foster Jack and Saoirse. Jack once asked Kate why she wanted to foster them and not adopt them, and Kate said it was about money – you got paid to foster, but not adopt. Still, it doesn't make any sense to Jack. Surely adoption would mean Jack and Saoirse would be safer?

'Now, now … no need to jump to conclusions. No one is taking Jack away.'

Kate covers her eyes with her hands.

'What if the blood belongs to Saoirse?' Aunt Bronagh asks. She turns her head. 'Jack, what were you doing in that treehouse? Why would Saoirse have gone there?'

Jack feels his eyes widen. 'I don't know … we used-ed to … to hide up there. Sometimes.'

Garda Morris sighs.

'Look, there are these new tests they do in Dublin. *Deenay tests*. They can identify people using blood, saliva, and other bodily samples. They take a few weeks to come back but we can identify if it is Saoirse's blood. I just wanted to know if you recognised the cardigan first.'

Jack imagines what the *deenay* might look like. A sharp-toothed monster as high as a house, with red fur, who has taken his sister in its great jaws. Last night he had watched out for it from the window of the house, as the mad moths had flapped against the glass.

Garda Morris takes the plastic bag away from the middle of the table.

Jack has a sudden memory.

Saoirse lay on her stomach, peering over the edge of the cliff.

Garda Morris interrupts. 'Are you sure there's nothing you can tell us about this cardigan, Jack?' Garda Morris asks.

Jack pulls Wilberry closer to himself. 'There is,' he says eventually.

'What is it?' asks Garda Morris.

Kate looks at him sharply, and so does Aunt Bronagh.

'Something you can tell me?' Garda Morris repeats.

Jack nods. 'The cardigan,' he says. 'It belongs to Ellie.'

'Who is Ellie?' Aunt Bronagh whispers.

Jack looks at the cardigan. He has seen it before. On the little girl with the yellow dress who played in the forest with him.

Garda Morris clears his throat and then speaks. 'Ellie is the girl whose body we just found.'

Jack wonders if Ellie was trying to escape the forest too. *The forest knows*, he remembers Saoirse saying. *The forest knows but it refuses to tell.*

PART FOUR

26

Day Eight

Freya

I stare out of the phone box. *Please pick up*, I pray. Rain batters against the panes and rolls down it in rivulets. The phone box near the local pub seems like a convenient place to call Melody, rather than going back to the hotel before dinner.

It rings out.

Finally, the line crackles as the familiar voice comes over the line. My daughter. I feel relief at hearing her voice.

'Mum? You caught me just on my way out ...' She sounds breathless.

'I can call back another day?'

'No, let's talk for five. It's just a college social thing ... Where are you?'

'Still working on that missing girl case.'

I had let her know I was going to Drumsuin, but I haven't been able to contact her directly until now. I hear her zipping up her coat. The sound of a radio or faint music in the background, laughter.

Her voice is strained. 'I tried to call you at home yesterday. I thought you might be back. Can I have your hotel phone number?'

'Of course.'

I hear her search in her handbag. 'Can't you get a pager or mobile phone or something?' she asks.

'A pager? I'm hardly a lawyer working in the city.'

'Most of the doctors in the hospital have them, two or three even have mobile phones too … and it's better than me worrying you're lying dead in ditch somewhere.'

'You didn't really think that, did you?'

'Only for a minute. Didn't you used to worry about your mum?' That's a good point. I did, especially towards the end. 'I don't have a pen,' she says eventually, sighing.

I stare out at the blackness and rain as it runs down the phone box's glass door. A frozen breeze blows at my ankles, making me shiver.

'How is the case?' she asks.

'Awful.'

'Better or worse than the Boland case?'

'Worse. The girl who's missing is only thirteen. I don't know if it will have made the news over in the UK?'

'Not yet.'

'How is everything with you?' I ask, changing the subject. I want to think about something other than work for a few minutes.

'Good. I have a date tonight, sort of, at the social.'

'Exciting, who is he?'

'I can't say his name.'

'Why not?'

'Because it's an awful name … and I'm embarrassed by it.'

'Go on.'

'Honestly, I can't say it aloud.'

'How will you marry him if you can't even tell people his name?'

'It probably won't last that long, Mum.' She giggles. 'He's generous enough … but he has got weird dress sense.'

'Remind me why you're going on the date?'

'He's clever and kind – a junior doctor, actually. I met him at the hospital.'

'Are student nurses allowed to date the junior doctors?'

'Not particularly …' she says, sounding like she's been caught out. 'But it's fine, I've only got another few weeks there and then I'm moving on and it won't be frowned upon any more. I just ignore him when I'm at work.' I can't lecture her. I'm so proud of her, pursuing her dream. 'Oh … sorry Mum, someone else is trying to call – it might be my date! Give me your hotel name so I can find you if I need to.'

'Cois Fharraige,' I say. I spell the name for her then we bid goodbye and hang up. I look through the glass out into the darkness of the street and I see a figure moving in the shadows. My heart almost stops for a moment in fear. Who is hanging around so close? Were they trying to listen in on my conversation? If so, what do they want from me? I open the door to the phone box, trying to see who it is through the darkness and rain, but the figure disappears.

I know I am dreaming because I've had this dream before. Lifting my neck, I look down. All I can see is the bathwater, the ridge of the tub, the silver taps and the round, black holes which stop the water from overflowing. Spider legs keep protruding from the holes. A spider trapped inside the drain. The water jets into the bath, frothing at the plughole. I am paralysed – it's always the same way in this dream. The water in the tap turns bloody. I open my mouth to call out but no sound comes from my throat. Crimson water continues to rise until it is at my ears, then my face and lips. It seeps into the opening of my nostrils. I feel more and more helpless by the second. As the water reaches my eyes, a shadow falls and the bathroom door creaks ajar. The person in the doorway is always someone different, and it always brings momentary relief: someone who might be able to help. This time, Jack enters. Wet footsteps trudge across the floor and his face appears above the bath. Solemn and staring. I feel some relief for a moment, but then he leans over, puts his hands into the water and pushes me down. I sink under, staring into the bloody water in panic. I try but it is no use, I cannot move to struggle.

Eventually, I cannot hold my breath any longer and I breathe in, inhaling water into my lungs. The dream ends the same way every time. I awake with a gasp, soaked in sweat. Tonight, I click on the light and look around the hotel room. All is quiet, but my heart is racing.

27

Day Nine

Jack

Villagers keep coming to the house. Bringing food, asking nosy questions. Walking past and staring at the gate. Kate said some villagers don't believe his sister is missing. Some think it is Jack's family who have done away with Saoirse, who have hidden her or even killed her. Jack isn't sure why the villagers would think that. How could anyone think they'd want Saoirse gone?

Finally, Freya arrives mid-morning, like a waving bluebell in the distance, floating down the lane and through the gate. Late today. Freya is ready to turn out Jack's mind with her bag of tools. Maybe she will hold him by his ankles and shake him until his thoughts fall onto the floor. Or maybe she will shine a light in his ear to see inside. A scared Jack, running through the deep woods with his sister, a sad Jack by the flat pond in the back garden all alone. Maybe there are figures inside Jack's head who will speak for him. She'll excavate them and lay them out on the table, like slimy, dead sea creatures with dissected squirmy guts. Maybe she won't do anything and the words will fall out of Jack's nose when he sneezes. He won't be able to grab them back.

But Freya does not want to ask Jack questions today. When she arrives, she suggests, instead, they play a game.

'What kind of game?' Jack asks.

'I was thinking perhaps you and I could play hide-and-seek together.'

'In the forest?'

Jack feels his heart begin to *thud thud*.

'No, not in the forest. Right here, in the house.'

Jack thinks for a moment. He watches Freya. She raises an eyebrow and smiles.

'What do you think?'

'What for?' he asks.

'For fun, silly. You are still allowed to laugh sometimes, you know,' she teases.

Jack thinks about this. He'd like to have fun, but he has questions. Is fun allowed when Saoirse is missing? Then again, perhaps it would be a good thing.

Jack nods and balls up his fists.

'Okay.'

'You sure?'

Jack nods.

'Would you like to hide or should I?'

'I will hide,' Jack says. Before he can change his mind, Jack runs out of the room and up the stairs. He can feel excitement in his veins. It feels like the good times, playing the Counting Game with Saoirse. The same thrill of being chased. He almost laughs. Almost, until he remembers Saoirse is gone. He holds his breath and looks both ways. One way is Kate's bedroom and she is in there, so that's out. Another way is Saoirse's bedroom. Maybe he could hide in there. He opens the door and looks inside. All is still. Saoirse's posters of Boyzone and Take That stare back at him. Jack backs out of the room and runs to the closet near Saoirse's bedroom. The airing cupboard.

He closes the door and shuts it behind himself. Inside, it is dark. Heated too, where the towels live. He listens to the hum of the pipes and the glug of the water. It feels peaceful in here, so peaceful he could fall asleep.

184

Jack hears a sound. Freya calling out numbers. *Seven … Eight.* He holds inside a giggle.

Nine … Her voice sounds playful. He hears her opening doors.

'Where is Jack? Where could he be?' she asks aloud. Jack covers his hand with his mouth, holding in his laughter. He waits for a while.

Suddenly he hears the airing cupboard door creak open. The light beams in and two hands come for him. They tickle him under his arms. Jack cannot hold it in any more. The tickles are unbearable. He squeals and collapses on the floor. Freya shrieks. Jack rolls away from her grip and runs down all the hall. Freya chases him, laughing so hard she looks like she cannot breathe, her eyes shiny and her cheeks rosy.

'Come back here!' she yells.

'No!' Jack replies.

Jack runs down the stairs, joy flowing through him. For a short few minutes, he forgets everything – his mother, his sister, all the troubles, everything – and just plays again.

28

Day Nine
Jack

G arda Morris's foot goes *tap tap tap*. He takes out his half-moon glasses and a magnifying glass. He perches the glasses on his nose, writes something, then he leans back and surveys the sitting room. Jack looks back at the paintings. *Red, yellow, blue, green.* And thinks about the numbers, *five, six, seven, eight.* Mam used to say one picture equals a thousand words. So how many words are here now? Too many to count.

Playing was fun, but now they need to understand Jack's mind again. Freya starts to lay out the paintings all across the floor and table. The fire crackles. Outside, the clouds continue to hang low. Aunt Bronagh sits near Jack. She has a new dress on today, like she is trying to look special for the visitors. Jack remembers this morning when she took a parcel from the postman who knocked on the door. She had hidden it in the closet. What was in the parcel? Kate had gone upstairs saying she might like to sleep a few hours before nightfall came again. At night she doesn't sleep. Instead, she paces around the house like a ghost, watching out the window and waiting for Saoirse to come home.

Aunt Bronagh fixes Jack with her grey eyes, which are like Jack's father's eyes. She runs a hand through her dark hair, which is also like his father's, picks up a biscuit, and takes a bite with her chin pointed. From here, Jack can see her gold wristwatch – the one their grandfather had given to her before he passed. He cannot remember Aunt Bronagh being able to walk, though he knows she used to. Kate said she had a car accident when she was younger. She still drives, though Jack wonders why she is not too scared to drive now. Jack runs a finger down Wilberry's zip and smiles to himself. A smile because only *he* knows how much fun he had earlier, playing with Freya. All the adults are boring, but not Freya. She is almost as fun as Saoirse. It helped him not miss Saoirse for a few minutes.

'The villagers are talking,' says Aunt Bronagh eventually. 'They think we have something to do with Saoirse's disappearance. The very idea ...' she says angrily. 'Why would *we* want to hurt Saoirse? I had some oul wan woman throwing rotten fruit at my car window the other day ... and another yelled *murderer* at me when I was down at SuperValue. *You don't seem upset*, she said. Don't *seem* upset? How am I meant to behave? Cry all day and not take care of Jack?'

'I wouldn't take any notice of them,' Garda Morris says as he leans forwards and peers through his magnifying glass at the picture.

Jack's eyes rest on the painting of the cliff for a moment, then move away. He looks over his shoulder towards the forest, imagining he might see the crows but now there is nothing, only a dense fog. When Jack closes his eyes the days flick backwards in his mind, like on a film. He feels a tight feeling winding around his head now, so he rubs the middle of his forehead with one finger. How many days has Saoirse been gone now?

'Tell me about this one,' says Freya, pointing to a new painting Jack did a few days ago.

Jack stares at the painting and tries to remember what is going on in it. He and Saoirse are running and behind them, there is the Creature.

'Is that the Creature again?' she asks.

'Ye.'

'What is happening?'

'It's chasing us.'

'Why?'

Jack looks at her. 'Because that is what it does … it chases. You go into the forest and it finds you. But only when—'

'Only when what?'

'Only when … the numbers say so.' Jack looks down. 'And you can't upset it, or bad things happen.'

Freya frowns a little and moves on to the next painting. She looks at Aunt Bronagh, who turns to the window. Aunt Bronagh doesn't believe him, Jack knows that. She thinks this whole thing is silly and crazy. Though she has put on make-up today, so maybe she is worried that people will think *she* is too crazy to look after Jack.

'How do you upset the Creature?' asks Freya.

'Lots of ways.'

'Like?'

'Going into the forest when you are not welcome there … Damaging things.'

Aunt Bronagh rolls her eyes. 'Why are you telling them this nonsense?'

'Because it's true!'

'We've talked about this,' she says in a weary voice.

'You don't know,' says Jack. 'You weren't there. My mam was there. She knows. Kate knows.'

Garda Morris writes down some notes.

'You believe this stuff is true, boyo?'

'We need to understand him through pictures. Bear with us,' explains Freya to Aunt Bronagh.

Aunt Bronagh leans forwards, her eyes open wide.

'But what we need to know, Jack, is: where is your sister?' she says. 'Isn't that right?' She looks at Freya and Garda Morris, her palms out. Closer up, Jack can see there are pictures on her dress – pictures of birds.

'Where is Saoirse?' Aunt Bronagh snaps.

Jack feels the memory coming up now, like a million of Fergal Duffy Junior's bees are raging in his mind and the hum is so loud he wants to cover his ears. The memory is too scary. He swallows it down. *Erase.*

Jack pulls his knees up in front of himself and glares at Aunt Bronagh. She has turned. He feels afraid of her because she has the same sharp gaze as their father used to when he misbehaved.

'Now, now,' says Garda Morris. 'We're doing this slowly, the right way.'

Aunt Bronagh rolls herself to the window and raises her voice a little. 'And how is that going to help Saoirse? She could be hidden in some pervert's garage and we're playing picture book. Jack, where is your goddam sister?'

'I don't know.'

'That. Is. A. LIE!' she yells.

There is silence for a moment.

Jack looks at Garda Morris's missing eye. He looks at Wilberry and closes his own eye again to see how it feels to have only one. After a while, his eye gets tired of doing all the work. He can feel a headache coming on.

'You're getting upset,' Garda Morris says to Aunt Bronagh. 'Come with me.' She follows him out of the room. Jack hears them talking from the kitchen – her voice high-pitched and fast, and his low and slow.

'What about this painting?' Freya says in a soft voice, pointing to the next picture.

Jack looks. It is he and Saoirse standing near the ravine. Standing near a girl, the one in the cardigan. Who was she? A girl from his dreams or a real person? He remembers the rough bark under his fingertips. Sweat on his spine. The summer air. His head was hidden between the branches of pine as he counted and waited.

'I don't remember,' he says. His brain is all jumbled. The past and the present mixed together like a flipbook going backwards.

Where is Kate now? Asleep. Hiding from what is happening

while people question him. Jack feels alone all of a sudden. Saoirse is gone and Kate is asleep. His mam is gone too. It is just Jack now. Is he such a bad boy that he deserves all of this? Jack looks out the window into the back garden, to the tall oak tree.

The door creaks open and Pearl comes tapping in, his claws loud on the wooden floor. He lays something down in front of Jack. Freya leans over and picks it up. It is a piece of crumpled paper. She smooths it out, wiping her hands on her black jeans after she does. Pearl must have found it inside Kate's dressing gown pocket when he was sniffing for treats.

Jack cannot breathe. He feels a wave coming over him, which he tries to push away, but it is no use. It is a tidal wave, like in the wild Atlantic Ocean. He might be drowning. Freya holds up the note. Jack squints to read it. '*Don't … tell … them … anything.*'

'Know anything about this?'

Jack shakes his head. He doesn't know about that note. He wonders when Kate wrote it and if it had been meant for Jack. And if so, if it means she doesn't want him to talk.

29

Day Nine

Jack

'Don't tell them anything?' Garda Morris says.

Kate keeps her eyes down. They had woken her up and she has come downstairs to answer questions. She strokes Pearl's head, trying to calm the restless dog. Jack makes a low whistling sound.

'Do you know who might have written this?' Garda Morris asks.

Jack tip-taps his fingers on his knees, then moves Wilberry from one knee to the other.

'How would *I* know?' Kate asks.

'Well, it's in your house.'

Kate takes her hand off Pearl's head and he trots to an empty chair. He jumps up, curling around himself as he settles down. Kate walks to the window and looks out towards the trees.

'A girl is missing out there – my sister,' she says in a trembling voice. 'And you care about a *note*?'

Jack watches Garda Morris as he watches Kate, her gaze concerned.

'It's relevant to the case if you've told Jack to hide things,' Garda Morris says gently.

'Back off,' Kate snaps. 'I wasn't hiding anything.'

Garda Morris's eyebrows raise in surprise, and he lifts his hands in surrender.

'Now, now,' says Garda Morris. 'We're just asking questions here, no one is judging you.'

Kate folds her arms and mutters to herself.

Garda Morris puts the note on the coffee table. It has Kate's scrawled handwriting, Jack can tell.

Sometimes rooms can trap you, a locked door and a key. Other times you are trapped in a mirror maze with no way out. You are dizzy from turning around and around and do not know which way to go. Sometimes not looking where you're going is easier in a mirror maze; that's what Jack does know. *Sometimes the dark is safer than the light.* He closes his eyes now and begins to count. *One, two, three, four, five, six …*

'It was nothing …' Kate says impatiently.

'Nothing?' Garda Morris asks.

'I wrote the note, but it's not what you think.'

'When did you write it?' Garda Morris asks.

'A few days ago. I can't remember which day … They have all blended into one since Saoirse went missing.'

She walks over and bends her knees, leans down to face Jack. She looks into his eyes, searching for something. She puts her hot hands on Jack's cold ones.

'I was asking him not to talk about our mother. I didn't want Jack to talk too much about that. I thought it might distract from Saoirse, make us seem like we couldn't cope. I was worried you might take him away from me. Put him in care. But I didn't give the note to him in the end – I realised it wasn't fair to ask him not to talk, and that it might stop him talking openly about Saoirse's disappearance, so I wrote it and then I just put it in my pocket and never gave it to him. Isn't that right, Jack?'

Jack nods. He had not seen the note before.

'Jack, have you been keeping anything else from the Gardaí that could help find Saoirse?' asks Freya, watching him closely.

'I can't remember,' says Jack, tears of frustration filling his eyes.

Kate stands up, letting go of Jack's hands. She laughs in a way that shows she doesn't actually think it is funny.

192

'You think he would keep all of this a secret on purpose? Or conceal some perfect clue that might lead to her? Jack wants his sister home as much as all of us! If he was hiding something on purpose, he would have told us by now!'

Garda Morris takes out another note and puts it on the coffee table, next to the first one. Kate looks surprised.

'How about the note Jack wrote to you about stopping the game?'

'Where did you get that?'

'Freya found it.'

Kate shakes her head. 'Jack takes the game seriously but it's just a silly game. It has nothing to do with Saoirse going missing.'

'Technically, they were playing the game when she went missing, so it does have something to do with her disappearance,' Garda Morris replies.

'Yes, but …' Kate says impatiently. 'That's where it ends. They were playing the game and then Saoirse was kidnapped. Whether by a human or something non-human … I don't know any more.'

Jack feels as though he is back in the mirror maze again, spinning around with no way out.

'Why would Jack write a note saying he'd try to stop the game for you?' Garda Morris continues.

Kate throws out her hands.

'You said it yourself – you don't believe in that kind of thing. You even laughed those journalists away who asked about the paranormal! Why should I bother to explain it all if you're sceptical of anything supernatural?'

Garda Morris appears speechless for a moment.

Kate's voice lowers to a calm level. 'Everything in that forest is linked,' she says softly. 'Everyone in the village knows the forest makes people pay for disrespecting it. The evil forces in that forest stem from the Magdalene Laundry and the horrors back then – the forest felt desecrated by these atrocities – so that's why we don't mistreat the forest now. You mess with that forest and you'll end up involved.'

'Involved ... how so?'

'Through birds, through crows, through the things that live inside there. Your worst fears are realised. The game ... it's not just a game, it's a curse you can't escape.'

Jack tightens his knuckles until they turn white, then he speaks aloud:

'The crow looks after the Creature, and the Creature looks after the crow.'

Garda Morris looks fed up.

Jack feels the buzzing sound rise inside himself again. He stands up. 'I've had enough of this!' he yells.

Everyone looks at Jack.

'I just want my mam!'

With that, Jack feels himself running from the room. All he wants to do is hide. He runs up the stairs and into his mother's old bedroom. He gets inside the wardrobe and closes it, hiding in between her old dresses.

'The crow looks after the Creature, and the Creature looks after the crow,' Freya says, into the wardrobe. 'What does it mean?'

Jack can only see her shoes. Freya doesn't hide important things. Not like everyone in his family.

'I don't want to talk any more.'

'Well, how about just to me?'

'No.'

'Fine, I'll sit here until you do.'

There is a long stretch where neither of them speak. Jack listens to the silence. He can hear a clock ticking. The sounds of voices downstairs. He thinks about his mam and what she might say to all of this. *Jack, tell the lady. She's trying to help.*

'The crows know everything that goes on inside the forest,' says Jack softly. He keeps his head between the dresses, inhaling the comforting familiar scent. 'Crows are clever birds. They care for people and they protect people too.'

'Oh, yes? And how does the crow look after the Creature?' Freya asks in a curious voice.

On his leg, Jack draws an imaginary circle with a bird inside it.

'By telling it things that happen in there. Sometimes crows protect me, other times they protect the Creature.'

Next, he creates a shadow of a monster on the back of the wardrobe where a slit of light beams in. He pulls his hand away from the wall to make the shadow bigger.

'Is there anything you are really worried about right now, Jack, apart from Saoirse?'

Jack is worried about a lot of things, but right now he is worried about Kate. No one else knows how sad she is, and how she won't eat sometimes. How Jack worries one day he'll find her trying to hurt herself again, like the time before, when he found her in the bathroom with the razor. But Jack doesn't tell Freya that, because he knows Freya might try to take Jack away from Kate – put him in a strange home, where they throw away children.

'Lots of things,' he replies, instead.

Freya seems to accept this answer. She slides a book into the wardrobe. Jack looks down at the cover. *101 Birds of the Forest.*

'I found this in your bedroom,' she says. 'Which is your favourite bird?'

Jack feels suddenly nervous. What if he picks another bird and the crows are angry with him? 'I like a lot of them.'

'Any in particular?'

He leans over and pulls the book towards him carefully.

'Parakeet,' he says.

Jack thinks about the parakeets flapping around the trees last summer. Greens, blues, and whites, speckled blacks. Lovebirds, fluttering around in the sky. In his memory, Jack was spinning, looking upwards. Dizzy and surrounded by trees. Twirling until he fell over onto the ground.

'What is it about the parakeet you like?'

He opens the book and flicks to the right page, then glances down at the picture of the two green birds with red beaks, sitting on a branch together.

'They don't like to be alone.'

'Like you?'

Saoirse ran away from the cliff, pulling Jack by the hand behind her.

Jack turns the pages for a while then stops on another picture – a penguin with spiky yellow hair, waddling along, with white stripes over its eyes and an orange beak.

'I like the rockhopper penguin too ... They care about their babies. Keep them safe. Like my mam used to,' he says quietly.

'It must be hard, your mam being gone. Who keeps you safe now?'

Jack can feel a storm rising in his gut, thrashing waves on the sharp rocks. He feels like he could be out in the sea himself, in a dinghy, all alone, being tossed around in the water like the fishermen he sometimes sees from the beach. He doesn't like to think about his mam being gone and doesn't like how things don't feel safe at all any more. He puts his thumb into his mouth and hugs himself, pushing the book aside.

'Does Saoirse know all the names of the birds too?' Freya asks.

He keeps his thumb where it is.

'I grew up in the city, so I don't know these things,' she continues. 'Tell me, what might a child need to know around here?'

Jack takes his thumb from his mouth to talk. 'Apart from about the Creature?'

'Yes.'

'Weather ... Storms ... Birds, fish, cows, rivers, trees ...' Jack lists them off on his fingers.

'Saoirse ... she'd know what to eat and what to do if she was lost outside?'

'Maybe,' he says. 'Or maybe she would not be able to do things if she was stuck.'

'Stuck?'

'The game keeps you stuck sometimes, frozen. You can't call out or move. The Creature steals your voice box.'

'Oh,' says Freya. 'That sounds scary.'

They sit in silence for a while. Eventually Freya speaks.

'Garda Morris brought home a cardigan, but your sister Kate said it didn't belong to Saoirse. You said you thought it belonged to someone called Ellie? How do you know Ellie?'

'We play together in the forest sometimes. She has a yellow dress.'

Jack thinks back to the dream he had last night. It feels more like a memory now than a dream. He is sure it was true. The dreams he has never feel like they are imaginary; they feel more like doors. Doors that open into lost parts of time, where Jack has not been, but where real things happen.

'Garda Morris had an accident. I saw it.'

'What do you mean?'

Jack points to his eye, closing it and poking his finger onto his eyelid.

'I saw it in my dream,' says Jack.

'What did you see?'

He draws a zip across his mouth.

'What did you see?' Freya repeats.

Jack shakes his head. Locks the key at the side of his mouth and throws it away.

'Whisper it to me?'

Freya pops her head into the wardrobe. He can see her ear now. She is wearing a dangling yellow earring of a bird in a cage. Hard to know what kind of a bird – a canary, perhaps. Her ears are soft-looking and she smells of perfume.

'I saw what happened to him,' Jack whispers.

'What do you mean?' she whispers back.

The letters and words catch in the wisps of her curls.

'The accident,' he says. 'I saw how he lost his eye.'

30

Day Nine

Jack

'You saw how he lost his eye?' Freya asks. 'Hang on, Jack.'
Her feet disappear, and there is the sound of footsteps moving to the door of the bedroom. She is gone for a few moments. There is the creak of a door closing. Then the footsteps return. He can hear her sit down and her shiny purple shoes reappear.

'Okay, tell me what happened in the dream.'

Jack takes a deep breath.

'In my dream ... I was sitting in the Beetle with Garda Morris. He was driving. We crashed into a tree and he lost his eye. There was lots of blood. I was okay, though. I climbed out the window.'

'That sounds frightening.'

'It was.'

Freya makes a humming sound. 'Dreams can be strange things,' she says with a sigh. 'They're how we make sense of things we see or hear during the daytime. Things we fear and things we want ... or just things we don't understand. Sometimes I think they mean something, and sometimes I think they don't.'

'Do you know how Garda Morris lost his eye in real life?' he asks. His voice sounds small and scared now.

'No, I don't, Jack.'

Jack can hear his own heartbeat in his ears.

'Do you ever dream about Saoirse?' Freya asks.

'Ye. I see her with the Creature on that day she went missing … but I can't see where the Creature took her, just that he did.'

He can see Freya close her notebook on her lap and put it down next to her.

'Am I in trouble for shouting at people?' he asks.

'No … no, Jack, not at all. Everyone understands you're upset. And thank you for telling me about your dreams. It's always good to talk about things that scare us.'

Jack nods. 'Will you speak to Garda Morris about it? Are you going to tell him about his car accident?'

'Probably not, unless you want me to. We don't have to tell people about our dreams if we don't want to.'

Jack thinks about all the things he hasn't told people, things he's forgotten or tried to forget. It's easier that way sometimes. Just close your eyes and swallow it down into your stomach. Then get the top of your pencil and: *Erase.*

31

Day Ten
Freya

Hope's Café perches at the end of a length of seafront shops. I push open the door and scan the restaurant for a familiar face. Bronagh sits in the corner, staring out of the floor-to-ceiling windows. I pull out a bright yellow chair and sit down opposite her.

Bronagh had cornered me yesterday on my way out of the house. She suggested we meet somewhere neutral rather than at the house. But what would she speak to me about? What Mr Fitzgerald said had piqued my interest in the aunt who was always around. She is a strange character in some ways – spending a lot of time at the Kellough's house. She often takes care of Jack, but isn't his official guardian. Is this just out of compassion, care, and familial duty? Or is it true about her jealousy towards Lucy having children when she could not have any? Does she have a motive to kidnap her own niece? Or might she know something about someone who has?

The café is rustic-looking, with sanded-down benches and beechwood ceilings, a skylight, a wooden floor, and yellow lamp-shades that cast a sunrise glow. Enya's dulcet tones emit from a nearby speaker. I focus on a framed inspirational quote opposite the table. *If it doesn't open, it's not your door.* I wipe my hands nervously on my skirt. A pink-haired waitress with tattoos and a lip ring gives me a nod as I sit, then recommences slicing a sandwich. A gruff-looking man in the corner with a long beard gives me a suspicious side-eyed glance from over his cup. Before I can start, Bronagh speaks.

'Thank you for meeting me here,' she says. 'I'm becoming frustrated with the search. I need your help.'

'How so?'

'I can't go to that forest …' She gestures to her wheelchair. 'Most of it is trails and trees, uneven ground. Do you think you could go for me?'

'Into the forest?' I feel my stomach knot in fear as I reflect on this. Something is drawing me to that forest, but something powerful is also stopping me. It comes up every time I drive to the Kellough house. I want to keep driving towards those trees but my hands always turn the steering wheel into their driveway. Every time I've considered going to the forest, there has been another excuse, another better thing to do. Deep down, I know that if I go in there, I'll have to face my own past, face my nightmares of Violet.

'Yes. I know it has been scoured already, but they've scaled back their search in the forest in favour of focusing on other areas now, places that haven't been searched. I know Saoirse is likely gone from the forest, but what if there are clues that have been missed? I have a feeling there might be signs in there of where she has gone, it's just a hunch that won't leave me alone … Maybe I'm mad, but I can't stop thinking about it.' She stares at me intently.

Unsure what to say in response, I begin to fiddle with the blue vase of baby's breath in the centre of the table.

'I guess I could go … But it has been searched quite thoroughly already.'

The pink-haired waitress comes over with a tray and places two cups of tea onto the table, along with a jug of milk and a sugar bowl with a spoon.

'Thanks, Fionnuala,' Bronagh says. 'I assumed you'd want tea?' she adds, glancing at me.

'Thanks.' I pour some milk in and stir.

'If I could go with you, I would,' she says.

She seems desperate. A feeling rises up in me: mother's guilt. If it were my child or niece, I would want people to keep searching, wouldn't I? But then similarly, why would Bronagh want to send a psychotherapist to the forest alone to search for Saoirse when hundreds of people and Gardaí had already looked there? Unless she wanted that psychotherapist to look in a different direction for a while, perhaps away from Jack and the house? Is this all a ruse, a distraction? Mr Fitzgerald hinted there might be another side to Bronagh. I need to understand more about her and about the family.

'Fine,' I agree, sighing. 'But you've got to be honest with me.' So much seems to be hidden. 'Is there anything you're not telling me?' I ask, searching her face for clues.

Bronagh raises her eyebrows. 'Like what?' she says, crossing her arms.

'Well, there's you ... and Kate. You said you were away in London when Saoirse went missing. Were you really there?'

She looks startled. 'Hang on a minute – are you accusing me of kidnapping my own niece?'

'When we first met, you mentioned returning from Dublin ... Do you have proof you were in London?' I try to sound confident, though my stomach churns.

A blush creeps up her neck. 'I was talking about Dublin airport! And yes, I have proof I was in London. Not that it's any of your business, but I was getting a number of procedures done over there, including an egg retrieval last week. I've been doing IVF – the only thing I didn't tell people was *why* I was there. It's private. I'm forty-one years old, single and in a wheelchair. People have always judged me for wanting a baby, but ...' Her eyes lower and fill with tears. 'I ... I can't help that I just want a child of my own.'

I feel myself soften. I shouldn't have opened up this wound. If this is why Bronagh was lying about wanting children of her own and the reason she didn't tell people why she was in London on the day Saoirse went missing, it is understandable.

'I'm sorry, Bronagh, I didn't mean to pry—'

'You should stay out of business that isn't yours,' she says, wiping away a tear. 'This past week has been hard enough without being accused of something unthinkable.'

'Again, I'm so sorry,' I say.

She sniffles for a moment. 'Anyhow, I can prove I was there – I was with multiple doctors that day, under sedation. Anyone can contact the clinic to confirm – it is called Women's New Hope – call them yourself right now if you like. And … and' – she reaches into her handbag – 'I can show you my printouts of my appointments and results. The Gardaí can have them too – I really do have nothing to hide.' She brandishes some pages from her handbag and passes them over to me. I unfold them and read her name and date on the top. The right-hand corner has a logo on it: *Women's New Hope IVF*. On the page are the details of her egg retrieval. Lots of medical terminology I don't understand, but I can see a signature of a doctor at the bottom, and I can see the handwritten date next to that: 25 October 1995 – the exact date Saoirse went missing. Bronagh was in another country at the time. Additionally, she was undergoing treatment that made her extremely vulnerable – the last thing on her mind would have been kidnapping her niece.

'You know it wasn't Cahill either,' she says. 'The Gardaí have ruled him out. As much as I don't always like him – for instance, I thought it unconscionable that he walked out on Lucy and the children, hence Kate and I started hiding his letters and parcels to the children more recently – but I know he wouldn't do something like this.'

'Do you suspect anyone else of taking her?'

'Is there anyone I don't?' She scoffs. 'Sometimes I think it's Mr Fitzgerald, the butcher.'

My ears prick up at his name. I've been thinking of him since our conversation in the butcher's shop, mulling over how strange he had been.

'Oh, I spoke to him,' I admit.

'You did?'

'Yeah, about Saoirse and the case – he said some odd things ...'

'Like what?' she says in an urgent tone. She leans towards me now, rapt.

'Just about how if he was to kidnap or kill someone, the forest would be the place to do it.'

'He used to date Lucy,' Bronagh says. 'He was at the house *a lot*.'

'He didn't mention that to me, about dating Lucy. In fact, he said he didn't know her that well ...'

'Well, he did. Jack once said Mr Fitzgerald watched him and Saoirse in the forest on his walks. I did mention it to the Gardaí.'

I think back to my conversation with the butcher again. How he had made me shiver.

Bronagh scratches her head. 'But then again, I'm starting to doubt people who I have no reason to suspect, like the Gardaí themselves. At one point, I didn't even trust Kate. I'm completely paranoid.'

I know how she's feeling – I've felt the same. I think about the hidden diary, concealed in Kate's drawer. I feel a sudden sense of dread and doom, and wonder if it was the right decision not to tell the Gardaí about it. What if Kate had something sinister to hide in relation to her sister's disappearance?

'That said,' she continues, 'I really don't think Kate would hurt Saoirse – not really. I think about the priest, Father Maguire, as I mentioned to you before. Saoirse was often an altar girl at the church. But then, he knows all the neighbourhood children ... so perhaps that doesn't add up. And there was ...' She stares into the distance. 'Now I am thinking aloud, I'm only just remembering something else ... There was this woman.'

'Woman?'

'I don't know who she was, or even what she looked like ... She was wearing a coat, with the hood up. We were leaving Mass, last Christmas Day. Jack and Saoirse were playing by the end of the churchyard in the snow and I was gossiping to someone, as you do, when I saw a woman – or it looked like a woman, anyway – standing there, just staring at them. She was stock-still, looking at them so intensely it made the hairs on the back of my arms stand up. I called them back ... I never forgot it, because it scared me so.'

'Christmas Day?'

'Yes ... almost a year ago now. The woman, as soon as she saw me, she turned and got into a car and drove away. I don't know why it got to me; nothing happened. But it was more a feeling. Something wasn't right, especially when people are usually with their families or friends on Christmas Day, not just stood alone in a car park.'

I take a deep breath. 'Did you not tell the Gardaí this?'

'No. Like I said, I'm only remembering it now. You asking me these questions, us talking about this, it has jogged my memory. I'll tell them later today.'

'Maybe the Gardaí should be questioning you more, having these kinds of conversations with you, not me. I think you should tell them about this woman.'

'Okay ...' she says, but she sounds reluctant. 'I can tell them if you think I should.'

'I do,' I say.

'It's just, I trust you more than them. I don't know why.'

I scribble down my hotel phone number and my room number. 'Here. Call me if you need me. Anything, don't hesitate to call.'

'Thank you,' she says, seeming sincere.

I tilt my head and analyse Bronagh a moment. She seems to be telling the truth, but something in me can't discount her yet. I shiver as I think about her request for me to visit the forest. Can I face finally going in there?

32

Day Ten

Freya

I'm on the pier in Drumsuin. Kate balances on the end, facing out to the sea, her toes almost off the edge of the stone slabs, her hair blowing in the wind. She is wearing similar clothes as the other day – tights, a skirt, a jumper – but they are all different colours now, more retro, like she has just walked out of art college. The waves crash against the concrete, rolling and writhing. The tumult of the sea seems to encroach upon me, and the breeze whips my face as I sprint down the pier. I am dreaming again. I know it because I still have a daughter called Violet who is alive. I don't have to see her in the dream to know that; it's a feeling. A feeling of wholeness in my heart, of oneness with the world. Like I have been pieced back together.

'Kate!' I call as I draw near. She looks over at me, then back towards the skyline.

I don't say anything, but I slow my pace. I approach her now, slower so as not to startle her. She squints.

'It's freezing here. Why don't we go grab a cup of tea nearby?' I offer.

She shakes her head.

'You've got Jack to think about now,' I remind her.

'Jack doesn't need me any more.'

I walk up next to her and look into her eyes. They're a piercing shade of blue, like two whole worlds with the horizon reflected in their glassy surface. They suddenly turn brown, like Violet's eyes.

'He's only nine. Of course he needs you,' I reply. I reach out and take her hand. She clings on to me, tightly. 'I know you're frightened.'

She doesn't respond, just squeezes my hand so hard it hurts.

'You're so scared that you might have let her die … that she might never come home.'

Tears drip down her cheeks. She lets go of me and places her hands over her face, beginning to sob – deep, abysmal cries. She roars violently then, towards the sea. An anguished sound. I had let out a similar sound many years ago, when I lost Violet. She takes one step forwards and falls like a stone. As I look down, it is not Kate in the waves. It is Violet.

'Help, Mummy!' she calls out, her little voice high-pitched. Her arms wave desperately as she is submerged in the sea, once, twice. She pops up, her hair wet, gasping for breath. Without a thought, I dive headfirst into the water and try to swim. I dig my arms forth, but no matter how hard I try, I cannot reach her.

33

Day Eleven

Jack

Jack can feel it. The house is quiet but awake. Its eyes are closed, but it is still listening for the call from the forest. Perhaps the house knows something is about to happen, because it blows its curtains open wildly and jolts Jack out of his sleep. The dawn light streams in through the windows, through the petal-shifting drapes that flutter on their fixtures. They could never fly away fully; they are only bird-like because of the wind.

How long has Saoirse been missing now? Ten days or eleven? Jack counts on his fingers, but he gets confused. He sits up and closes the window with a bang. He pulls the curtains to one side until they have settled, flat and lifeless. He realises he's still wearing his clothes from last night.

As Jack moves into the hallway, he catches sight of her head. Her chopped hair spills off the edge of the bathmat. The bathroom door is open a crack, revealing just a sliver of the other side. At first, he thinks she is sleeping. Jack moves closer, holding his breath and counting. His eyes flick to the still life oil painting of the framed flowers on the landing and the patterned carpet beneath. Jack takes another shaky breath. Now he feels as though he is floating body-less in the hallway. He takes another step and pushes open the bathroom door at last.

The bright blood startles him. It trickles slowly from one wrist and soaks into the bathmat below. Next to her open hand, on the floor, lies the kitchen knife, rusty red at the edges. Next to it is Saoirse's diary. Kate is pale but she is alive, awake. She turns her head towards him, not moving from the bathmat. He kneels next to her and puts his face close to hers.

'Big sister Kate,' he whispers. 'Don't die.'

Kate's eyes close. She swallows, keeping her head and neck very still.

'I'm sorry … I just got so tired of it all,' she whispers. 'I can't protect you.'

Kate was trying to control things, trying to end the game, but it wouldn't work. Jack runs downstairs to the phone in the hallway. His fingers shaking, he dials Aunt Bronagh's number because he knows that by heart. He listens to it ring, once, then twice, then three times. He knows she is the best person to call because Kate would say she is. Not the ambulance. The ambulance would lead to the police, and the police would lead to being put into care. She answers with a worried voice.

'Hello?'

'Kate is hurt.'

'What's happened?' Aunt Bronagh's voice is low on the other end.

'She's bleeding.'

'How much?'

'A lot – she's cut herself again.'

Aunt Bronagh says some curse words then tells him to go and be with his sister, to keep Kate talking and to keep her awake. She tells him to try and stop the blood with towels. She says help will be there soon. She tells him he is a brave boy.

Jack puts down the phone. The sight of the blood seems to have taken the breath from his lungs.

As he runs back up the stairs, he tries counting the steps and the number of seconds passing. He fetches towels and lays one gently under Kate's head as though he's tending to an injured bird in the garden, helps her to wrap another around her wrist, and they wait until they hear the sirens. Aunt Bronagh must have sent them. The ambulance. Jack feels as though he might become fear itself. Kate stares at the ceiling until the ambulance people bang down the door and run up the stairs, calling out their names.

34

Day Eleven

Freya

'Is Walter here?' I ask the slack-jawed Garda behind the counter. He chews on some gum. 'I think he's having a fag out the back, hang on. Morris!'

I wait, reading the posters on the waiting room wall, once again. Eventually, Walter comes through the double doors into reception. I gesture to the hordes of Gardaí out in the street.

'What's going on?'

On arriving in the village my first horrible thought was that they had found Saoirse dead. But the energy in the place does not seem morose – it's more positive, frenetic.

'There has been a progression,' he says. 'We've been in the incident room having a conference. I tried to call you, but you must have left your hotel already.'

I nod. I had gone for an early walk around the coast, needing some fresh air, before heading into town.

He gestures for me to take a seat. I lower myself onto one of the nearby plastic chairs. Sitting down next to me, he looks over his shoulder and lowers his voice.

'Kate self-harmed early this morning.' My stomach drops. 'She is going to be okay – she's in hospital,' he adds.

I breathe a sigh of relief. For a moment, the dream from last night flashes into my mind. Kate standing on the edge of the pier, ready to jump, tears dripping down her cheeks. Concern and fear fills my stomach. Had I subconsciously known this was going to happen, and if so, could I have stopped it? The dream had almost been prophetic. Poor Kate.

'Should I go to the Kellough house today?'

'Yes. Jack will need someone to talk to.'

'Of course,' I reply, lowering my eyes.

Around us, Gardaí swarm and bustle.

'Don't tell any of them if they ask you,' he says nodding outside to the journalists. 'We don't need them reporting on what Kate has done – the family have enough to contend with. I'll just call their father, Cahill, and let him know.'

'Of course,' I reply.

'And there is another thing. We think Saoirse might still be alive.'

Alive? I feel dizzy all of a sudden. I lean forwards and put my head between my legs. There is a faraway voice as if underwater.

Freya. Freya?

Finally, the world comes back. I sit up and Walter is gazing at me, looking alarmed.

'What just happened?'

I look down and see his hand on my arm. 'Hey, Derek! Grab me a water, will ya?' he calls out.

I feel the lucidity swim back to my head as Walter lets go of my arm.

'I don't know what happened – it was just shock, I think … We thought she was—'

'Dead, I know, so did I. But a local woman called Aoife Brennan – she lives half a mile from here – contacted us. In the middle of the night. She was turning the dial on her baby monitor because the thing was playing up, and she heard a voice. A girl's voice. It said, "My name is Saoirse Kellough, please help, I've been taken. A woman took me, I couldn't see her face … I don't know who she is." Those baby monitors have only a one-way signal, so Aoife couldn't reply to her. The voice – Saoirse's voice, we assume – just repeated the same sort of things again and again. If it was really Saoirse, whoever has her might not be keeping tabs on her at certain times. Like in the middle of the night.'

Imagining Saoirse tied up, held captive somewhere by some sick individual makes my skin craw. How is she feeling now? Having been away so long from her family – how is she coping?

He continues.

'As it is now suspected foul play or kidnapping, the National Bureau of Investigation have been notified. We've also brought in a technical analyst – they work with CCTV and phones and that kind of thing, so we can understand a bit more about what this means, how far away she could be. Naturally, that means we are really amping up our search today. We're starting closest to Aoife Brennan's house near the village. Though we can't be sure, these devices don't tend to have a long range. Apparently, they said it might be a walkie-talkie that her captor could be using to keep tabs on her.'

'Can you search every house in the area?'

'No. It's difficult because we can't just search every property willy-nilly. We need to quietly ask around, try and gauge if there are any properties that are suspicious, with any strange residents or people who have been acting odd. Then we need to apply for a search warrant. Search warrants specific to the property to be searched have to be obtained from a district judge.'

'What a nightmare.'

He nods. 'Nightmare is right. And we cannot let this information out to the press. It might compromise the investigation, so please don't say anything to anyone.'

'Of course not.'

'Also, I was meaning to talk to you today.'

'Yes?'

He fidgets nervously.

'About your letter … Listen, I think you're lovely. Really, I do, and I'm flattered. A woman like you … liking someone like me? I never thought you would, but I'm seeing Alice, so …'

As I look at him, I can't muster any words. An awful sense of confusion comes over me. Walter stares back at me, a flush creeping into his cheeks.

'The letter you left in … an envelope, under my windscreen wiper? You typed your name at the end.'

I shake my head. He puts his hand to his head.

'Christ …' he curses. 'I knew it was strange you'd be confessing your feelings for me in a letter while all this was going on.'

'A letter?' I frown.

'Either one of the other officers is playing a joke on me or …'

'Or what?'

'Well, someone wanted me to think you were interested in a relationship with me.'

'Who would want to do that?'

'I don't know. I'll send the letter to forensics. There might be fingerprints on it.'

'Can I see it?'

He nods, and goes to a filing cabinet. He brings it over to me and holds it out.

'Don't touch it …'

I look at the letter.

Dear Walter,

I wish I was your date. Do you feel the same? If so, meet me at the bar opposite the Garda station tonight at eight.

Freya

In black and white, there it is: supposedly, me expressing my feelings for Walter.

I cringe internally, a flush rising up my neck. 'I didn't send this to you,' I say, embarrassed.

Who could have done this? Perhaps someone who wanted to distract Walter or myself from the case? What other reason would anyone have for making Walter believe I had feelings for him?

He folds the letter carefully and places it back in the envelope and in the filing cabinet once again. Then he stands up and begins to pace, running his fingers along his jaw.

'I'd better get back. The clock is against us. This person might not plan to keep Saoirse alive for much longer. Another strange thing was that the ambulance men found a diary next to Kate. It appears to be Saoirse's – one of the officers is reading through it as we speak, analysing it for clues.'

The embarrassed flush on my neck turns to a cold sweat. They had found the diary after all, no thanks to my silence on the subject. And it seems it is considered important evidence. How could I have failed to give it to them? What if something in that diary reveals a crucial clue to where Saoirse is? I lower my eyes guiltily.

'Go be with Jack,' he says. 'He might give us clues today about the person who has taken her. Because the radio range suggests she's local, the likelihood is Jack and Saoirse already knew this person before they took her.'

I stand up to leave. Suddenly I feel a weight on my chest. Saoirse is still alive and somewhere local; the pressure is now on to find out who took her. Before whoever has her makes sure she is silenced forever.

35

Day Eleven

Jack

The rain begins to fall outside the window where Jack sits and watches out. A Garda car is outside the house, with four officers inside. They hold walkie-talkies close to their mouths from time to time. Other times they eat sandwiches and drink from flasks. He sees Freya get out of her car, which is parked near the officers, dust off her coat and pick out her briefcase. Aunt Bronagh lets her into the house and then Freya's reflection appears in the sitting room window.

'Jack?' she says. He does not turn but continues to count softly under his breath.

Six, seven, eight, nine.

In the reflection, he sees her take off her coat and sit in her usual seat, putting down her briefcase and papers on the floor beside her. Once the room is silent and still, Jack turns. Freya's face is not as relaxed as the other days. He feels a tight feeling in his chest, picks up Wilberry and sits him on his knee.

'I'm concerned,' says Freya.

'What does that mean?'

'Worried, in a caring way.'

Jack nods and looks down. 'Me too. Wilberry is sad.'

'Is he?'

Jack examines the stuffed toy, fixing one of its buttons. 'Ye. He's scared Kate is never coming home from *host-able*.'

Jack looks at Freya then back at Wilberry. They sit for a while and he examines the pattern on Freya's skirt, her pink shirt, and her gold watch. He doesn't know where she came from or where she goes at night. Freya has purple shoes and yellow canary earrings. Freya wears lemon-scented perfume and listens to sad people like Jack. Maybe she goes home and forgets all about Jack.

'What happened?' Freya asks.

Jack feels a knot in his chest, and tears fill his eyes. He wishes she was his new mother. Freya, with her soft eyes and patient stare. Jack could sit in the calm with her forever. If Freya knew he was bad, she might not like him any more. That idea scares him. It makes him want to tell even less.

'I noticed you were counting again. Does that mean you're scared, like Wilberry?'

Jack closes his eyes and tips his head back on the chair, letting it loll.

'Come on, Jack. You were talking so much, so well. Don't disappear on me,' says Freya gently.

Jack raises his head and looks at the painting above the mantel-piece. A woman is leading geese to market. The geese are wearing little bonnets and the lady is calling them to come. Where will the geese end up – as pets, or on a dinner plate? He doesn't feel like talking again today – like how he felt at the start, when Saoirse went missing. He *is* scared.

'Garda Morris said you found Kate in the bathroom. That she hurt herself quite badly.'

Jack remembers the blood and feels fear run through him.

'She wanted to end the game, I think ...' he says.

He bites at his fingernails, which taste like apple slices.

'Has she done this before?'

Jack nods slowly, wiping his nose on the back of his hand. He sees it now: Saoirse crouching on the floor, holding Kate's wrists as his mother called an ambulance. He remembers the time he found her passed out next to the toilet too. He'd had to call his mother. Kate had needed hot tea with sugar to bring her back to life. *Not eating enough*, he remembers his mother saying. She's still thin, but she eats now. She hadn't done anything like that in years. This was the same, but a bit different too. This was part of the game. Kate wanted to control it.

He hears bees humming in his head again.

'Who will mind me now?' he had asked Aunt Bronagh this morning.

'I will,' she had said.

Was that true?

As though Freya can read his mind, she says: 'Your Aunt Bronagh said she would look after you, Jack, while Kate is in hospital. You believe her, don't you?'

'Maybe.'

'Remember when we did wake-dreaming in the garden?'

'Ye.'

'Who was with you and Saoirse in the forest that day?'

Jack thinks about it now. The last time he had told Freya something, he had felt better. Maybe he could tell her a little bit. A little bit wouldn't hurt. Maybe she could even help.

'Would you like to wake-dream again?'

Jack nods.

He closes his eyes. Freya comes and sits next to him and holds his hand. He goes back to the forest.

Saoirse is running and someone is behind her. He goes closer to her, as if floating above like a ghost. He can see it now. It is the Creature.

'The Creature,' he says.

'Can you look closer at it?'

'No.'

'Please Jack, this is important.'

Jack concentrates. His heart thumps as he tries to concentrate on the image of what he saw. His foot begins to tap. He can focus in on the Creature now; he is safe. There are branches and leaves, feathers – it is bigger than Saoirse. That is all he can remember.

Jack thinks about this a moment, then frowns. He gets up and walks to the chest of drawers and sits down, opening the bottom drawer. He takes it out: the picture he had painted of him and Saoirse with a broken bird's nest, near a cliff. He stands up and brings it over to Freya to show her.

'See?'

Freya examines it closely. Next to the nest there is a Creature holding Saoirse in its arms.

'The Creature took Saoirse. The same one that hurt my mam. Can I bring Mam back?'

Freya sighs. 'No, Jack, I'm sorry – no one can do that.'

Jack thinks about Kate now, in the hospital. She had been trying to end the game, he knows that, but she hasn't succeeded. He's glad she didn't. If she had, she might never come back. He remembers his mam and the day she went. They had been playing the game that day too. Every time they play the game, someone goes missing, it always happens. Jack closes his eyes and tries to forget, because it all feels too big. *Erase.*

36

Day Eleven

Freya

After I had spoken to Jack today, I crept back into the attic room. Once he had shown me the painting of the Creature carrying Saoirse away, I was certain there had to be a clue in something Jack had painted.

There was so much artwork on those walls. I had looked hard at some of them, which were filled with ghosts and ghouls. If they depict what Jack sees in his nightmares, there's no wonder he's so quiet all the time. Some paintings seemed obvious in their meaning, others abstract. There was one of a little boy rowing a boat down a river and another with numbers all over it. A third was strange – it had images but also what looked like lettering. The painting depicted a little girl near a train track. The writing ran sideways down the page. I took the picture off the wall and spelled out the letters: I-A-M-L-I-A-R.

I am liar?

I brought the painting closer to my face, feeling the paint under my fingertips.

Then I rotated it, and the letters, so childlike and poorly crafted, suddenly took on a different slant.

R-A-I ... L ... W ... A ... I. Railway, spelled slightly wrong.

Railway. On the map of Drumsuin which I have in my car, there is a new railway that brings people to and from Dublin, and a disused one, which runs through parts of the forest. The lines Walter had said transported the old stones from the quarry to the seafront when the village was first being built. Was that what Jack meant?

Perhaps this is my sign that it is time to visit the forest, as Bronagh asked me to. Maybe this is also my chance to heal my demons regarding Violet. The dreams have been directing me to this forest for many nights now, linking my past to the present. Maybe now it is time to go and face my fears.

The sun begins to dip behind the distant mountains as I approach the disused train tracks at the edge of the forest. Perhaps nightfall is not the best time to visit this place, but now I have decided to go, I realise I cannot wait another night. The light dissipates into shards, bathing the tracks in an orange glow. Of course, it's just a few days past Samhain now. A murky time of year, which marks the end of the harvest season and the beginning of winter. People in Ireland historically believed the barriers between the physical and the spirit world broke down during Samhain – the veil separating the living and the dead was at its thinnest – which allowed for crossover of spirits and souls from the afterlife. The thought makes me shiver a little as I pull in and park the car. I cast my gaze across the lake beneath. The water reflects the shadows of hundreds of trees lining the lake and mountainside. In this light, it looks ethereal but also isolated. The Kellough children should never have been here alone.

I think about the creepy things people have told me about this place. About the Creature Jack talks about and the beliefs the villagers have about this forest. I shiver for a moment. I don't believe in yetis or the Loch Ness monster or anything similar. Surely there must be a reason for the disappearances in this area, a graph that could prove why they went missing. Quicksand, a freak weather issue or simply, as Barney Fitzgerald the butcher said, a remoteness that makes women vulnerable to attack. I get out of the car, grab my torch and, digging my cold

221

hands into my jacket pockets, stroll down to the abandoned tracks.

I keep my vision on the ground for signs anyone has been here. The old line runs down the perimeter of an old, overgrown cemetery with sunken headstones, past a broken chapel without a roof and across the boundary of the lake, through a patch of the forest, then down to the old quarry.

As I head down the railway line, carpeted with sharp rocks, the wind blows across from the lake. Anxiety rises in me as I watch the cumulous clouds form in a bulging mass in the distance above the forest. It will rain again soon.

Still, a strange force pulls me onwards, towards the quarry. The trees stretch into the gap where the train used to run – years of not being cut back once the trains stopped. Entering the forest, I slow down. I steel myself to continue, trying not to think about my nightmares from the past few nights. I try not to think about the things Jack has said about the forest and what it 'knows'.

I check around myself every few moments, keeping a lookout for glimpses of anything unusual. It is silent, apart from the odd bird call. Almost eerie in how quiet it is, apart from the endless blowing gale. I breathe out and talk to myself, softly.

See? Violet, your dead daughter, is not in here. There is nothing to be afraid of.

My skin comes out in goosebumps as I stop and look through the trees. I have the feeling of being watched. As though a set of eyes exists beyond the shadows. I edge along further, scanning above me. Suddenly a black flapping creature threads through the air and I jump. As it flies off, I stare up. A crow. My heart thumps in my chest from the shock. I take a deep breath in and out. *Just a bird*, I remind myself. *I am alone, and everything is okay.* As I turn, looking up at where the bird flew off to, I see it: a glint of gold attached to a branch. I advance on the pine tree in question. It appears to be a necklace. I reach out and turn it around to look at it. I've seen something like this before – on Kate. A heart-shaped locket. I remove it and open the clasp gently. Inside, there are two photographs. The first is of Jack and the second is of Lucy. The locket is broken and was wound around the branch, as though it had snapped off someone who was moving past. It must have been missed by the volunteers.

I look through the clearing. If the necklace belonged to Saoirse, she would have run this way. I turn on my torch and shine it into the gap in the trees. It is opaque and gloomy at the front, but pitch-black further down where the pines are spun closer together, interlocking. Then I shine my torch down and I see it, on the ground near where I found the locket. It is unmistakable, made from black leather. I've seen Walter wearing just one recently. I pick it up and hold it to the light, and sure enough there are the letters sewn on the cuff: WM. The question is: what is Walter's glove doing here, right next to Saoirse's locket?

My hand shakes as I put my seatbelt back on and start the car, turning on the windscreen wipers on account of the rain that has just started. I feel like I am about to cry, though I am unsure why. This is all so much – the locket, the glove, and everything to do with Violet. I didn't find my daughter's ghost in that forest. I thought it might help me to heal, somehow, going in there, but it's only raised more questions about what happened to Saoirse. I realise the only place I want to go is back to Jack, to speak to him again. Then I can bring the locket to the Gardaí. I don't know yet what I will do with the glove. If I bring the glove to Walter, then he might hide the evidence, if he has got something to hide, but if I bring it to another Garda, Walter will realise I no longer trust him.

I start down the road back to the house, jabbing at the radio buttons, but it will not tune in. White noise and high-pitched sounds fill the air. I turn it off, my mind whirring around all the possibilities as to how the locket got there. Had Saoirse gone there of her own free will or had she been chased or coerced there?

My mind is on Walter now – the locket next to his glove – does he have something to hide? I think about how easily he could conceal evidence, what with being a member of the Gardaí. But could he hide a live girl? Which leads me to think about Kate and Bronagh.

So far, Bronagh's alibi for being at the IVF clinic seems watertight; she would also physically find it almost impossible to capture Saoirse in the forest, but she could have hired someone to do it. That said, she seems to love her family, so I'm not sure I really believe she'd do this. Then there is Kate. She was at home the night Saoirse disappeared, but she would have still have had time to take Saoirse and pretend to be asleep before Jack got home. Kate has confessed they'd had an argument, and she has attempted suicide since – could this be a sign of guilt? Add to that the hidden diary, and perhaps Kate can't be discounted just yet. I am lost in my thoughts completely until I turn the final corner to the Kellough house. I slam on the brakes. Standing in the middle of the road is a figure. The car skids on the wet tarmac and comes to a sharp halt. I brace as I'm thrown forwards in my seat. Trembling, I look out through the rivulets of water on the windscreen. Jack stands there alone, in the half-light of evening, his back to the car. I cannot see his face.

'Jack?' I call as I get out. Jack turns around, holding up a water-logged picture he has drawn.

'Are you okay?' I ask. 'What are you doing out here?'

Jack's chin is tilted down, his hair soaked. He looks up at me and lowers the wet paper.

'Forest,' he says sadly.

'Oh, Jack, you weren't trying to go back in there, were you?'

He nods, his tears mixing with rainwater.

'Come out of the rain!'

He hesitates, then advances slowly. I take the paper from him. It has been destroyed by the rain, the colours all blending in together.

'Why were you going there?'

'To try and find her,' he says, his voice high-pitched.

'Jack, it's not safe for you to go alone.'

'I need to find her.'

'I know,' I say softly. 'It's okay.'

I open the back door of my car, and Jack climbs in. I close the door behind him, then throw the wet drawing into the boot – it's only good for the bin. I get in the front and start the car again, my hands still trembling, my legs jelly-like. I glance in the mirror as I do. Jack is staring out of the window, his lips moving slightly. It looks as though he is counting.

37

Day Eleven

Jack

Jack runs inside from the garden where Freya had dropped him off home. She had picked him up in her car. Jack's clothes are wet. He runs fast. Up the stairs. The hallway swallows him like a mouth, a throat. The door of Saoirse's bedroom creaks as he opens it. The first thing that hits Jack is the musky scent of dried mud. The pillows lie askew in the opaque light. Jack takes a step forwards, his toes falling soft on the floorboards. He can feel the fear rise in him as he does, a snaky greyness. He swallows it down. *Erase.*

It was the dream that had directed him into her room the night before. Jack pulls the wardrobe door open and takes out the bird's nest with the broken eggs inside. He feels fear when he looks at it. Fear and sadness. Every time he looks at the nest now, he thinks of the things he has hidden, the things all of them in the family have hidden. The nest represents to Jack the game. Especially after that fateful day. The sound of Aunt Bronagh's voice rises through the house.

'Jack? Are you up there?'

Jack puts the bird's nest back inside and tiptoes out of Saoirse's open door and looks down the stairs over the bannisters. Aunt Bronagh is sitting at the bottom of the stairs. She looks up at Jack, but she cannot climb up to him.

'Jack?' she calls again, squinting into the darkness.
Jack does not reply. Instead, he watches her from the shadows.

38

Day Eleven

Freya

I am busy drying off in the hotel. I've showered after returning from my trip out, but the cold from the rain still feels like it is in my bones.

After dropping off Jack, I decided to go to the station to speak to Walter. I came clean about the glove – albeit in front of another Garda officer so someone else knew about it. I remember his reaction.

'What is this about, Freya?' he said, seeming surprised.

'Sit down,' I said, and took out the glove, placing it on the table between us. His face was a mixture of confusion and surprise.

'It was in the forest, right next to this,' I said, placing the locket belonging to Saoirse next to the glove on the table. The female officer had frowned and leaned forwards, taking the locket carefully in her hands. 'Does this belong to missing Saoirse?' she asked, opening the locket.

I nodded.

'I've been looking everywhere for that glove,' Walter exclaimed. 'The last place I saw it was in my car a week ago!'

I think about Walter's reaction again and again. Confusion and surprise – there had been no fear or guilt.

I feel lonely all of a sudden. It's tough having these thoughts and no one to discuss them with. I scan the room, my eyes catching on the TV. *Crimeline* will be on soon – they are showing Saoirse's case tonight. Should I call Melody first? I pick up the phone. Melody sounds sleepy when she answers.

'We stayed out all night,' she yawns. 'Didn't get home until six in the morning. I was just napping.'

'Sorry to wake you,' I reply.

'It's okay. How is the missing child investigation going?' she asks.

'She's still not been found,' I sigh.

'Oh … That must be stressful. Who do you think took her?'

'That's what I'm trying to figure out. There's something strange going on here. They think there is a monster or a haunting in the local forest.' My laugh comes out as hollow.

'Looking for monsters in forests – just your average day at the office,' Melody replies dryly.

She is silent a moment. 'Oh, by the way,' she says, in a voice that sounds rehearsed. 'Dad is moving house.'

My mind casts back to the house we raised the children in. The house he kept when we divorced.

Another awkward silence. I'm sad to hear he is leaving that house behind for good. I know she is trying to be kind in how she delivers the news. A blush of shame rises up my neck. It isn't her responsibility to rescue me from this discomfort.

'Okay,' I reply casually, as though we are talking about a distant cousin, not the man who broke my heart and, for a time, left me with children to raise alone. 'Where to?'

She hesitates. 'Cornwall.'

Of course. Sunny Cornwall. Where we used to holiday together.

'He's moving in with Amy.'

'Amy?' I echo, trying to keep my voice light, distant, disconnected.

'New girlfriend. They've been together a year or so, that's what he says. The one who teaches yoga.'

'Uh-huh, cool, great …' I say. 'Have you met her, is she … cool?'

'You don't have to pretend to be okay with it all, Mum.'

'Thank God,' I breathe out. 'Is she awful?'

'No, she's annoyingly nice.'

I curse inwardly. There's a pause.

'But she's not as cool as you. She's not out there helping people battle monsters in forests.'

'Oh good,' I chuckle, feeling relieved.

We talk a bit longer and then Melody tells me her take-away has arrived and she has to go. I grin as I put down the phone.

But it is not long before my mind is back with Saoirse. What more can I do to help her?

I shove some shop-bought popcorn into my mouth and chew, sitting cross-legged on my hotel bed. The fuzzy television screen comes to life with a flick of the remote, and the theme music for *Crimeline* blares. Just in time.

A female presenter with a sharp blonde bob appears, and she begins to explain the case of missing Saoirse Kellough in a sombre tone. A photo of Saoirse flashes onto the screen, the same photo the media use every time. Saoirse standing on the beach, her red hair down by her shoulders, staring into the camera, unsmiling. The presenter begins to talk about the where, the when, and the how of Saoirse's disappearance. The televisions all around Drumsuin will be lit up now, the villagers watching, whispering, gossiping in their sitting rooms. Walter had said those villagers would not tell even if they did have information. They wouldn't talk about their neighbours or the things that happened in that forest unless pressured to. The best the crime team could hope for, he said, was an anonymous tip-off.

The hotel room phone rings out all of a sudden. I put down my bag of popcorn and stare at the receiver, frozen for a second, feeling almost nervous, before picking it up.

'There is a woman for you. Are you okay to take it?' Mary says on the other end.

It must be Melody, calling back. Perhaps she forgot to tell me something.

'Sure.'

There is a silence and a click. Then the voice speaks.

'Are you watching?' says the female voice. It is not Melody.

'Who is this?'

'Bronagh,' the voice replies.

'Oh,' I smile, feeling a little silly. I should have recognised her voice.

I watch the screen. There is a crude reconstruction of a red-haired girl walking into a forest. This woman in particular looks around twenty-five, not thirteen.

'I'm watching *Crimeline*,' Bronagh says. 'It made me think – you said to call if I ever wanted to talk. Have you been to visit the forest yet like we discussed?'

I pull at my socks and wiggle my aching toes. My feet are tired from the rough terrain earlier.

'Yes, I went earlier, and I found something – Saoirse's locket on a tree.'

'What? Where?'

'Near the old abandoned railway line. I passed it on to Walter. It seems like she was running from something. The jewellery must have gotten caught. And another thing,' I say.

I tell her about Walter's glove.

'Did you believe he didn't have a clue how it got there?' Bronagh asks.

'I think so,' I reply.

Bronagh finally seems to get the courage to speak. 'You know when we spoke before, about people we suspected of taking Saoirse?'

My heart skips a beat at the mention of it. 'Yes.'

'I'm starting to feel suspicious of Kate again – that she might be involved somehow.'

'What makes you think that?' I ask cautiously.

'It's just a few things she's said, and then the note … Why was she trying to keep Jack from talking? And why hide the diary, what was her motive for this? The Gardaí said the ambulance men found it next to Kate when they came the other day. I know she's my niece, but I don't trust that she knows nothing. Then she goes and tries to take her own life – why do this if she is not guilty or doesn't have something to hide? It makes me worry – if she took Saoirse and locked her up somewhere, who is caring for Saoirse now? But then surely Saoirse would have mentioned over the radio if the woman who took her was Kate? I am just left thinking Kate has something to hide – but I'm not sure what.'

'I don't know, Bronagh – do you really think she could be capable of being involved?'

'Trust me, she has resented having to take care of those children ever since their mother died. I think she's been pushed too far. So yes, I think she's capable of it – I think she's capable of anything at this stage.'

'Are you going to tell Garda Morris?' I ask.

'Not yet. Can you promise you won't either?'

'Okay,' I agree. Besides, a hunch from Bronagh is unlikely to help the investigation move forwards – it is hardly something I could take to Walter.

I sigh. The *Crimeline* anchor is now showing clips from Walter's last press conference. The reconstruction is over.

'You know, I sometimes regret not trying to have children sooner,' says Bronagh. 'The IVF is a nightmare, but after this, I wonder if it might be more difficult to have children than to never have them at all. This has all been so emotionally difficult.'

I think about how to word it delicately, but there is no decent way. Is Bronagh the right person to open up to? Can I trust her? Perhaps if I am open with her, it will inspire her to open up more in return?

'My first child died,' I confess.

'Oh, I'm so sorry,' she replies softly. 'What happened?'

I take a deep breath. We have come this far – I realise I may as well explain.

'She drowned. We were on holiday as a family. I went and left her next to the pool. I told her I'd be right back, to wait for me. But when I came back, it was too late.' There is a silence. 'The phone rang,' I say, as if by explanation, though the explanation always sounds futile, even to my own ears. 'I was gone five minutes. Too long for a child who has fallen under the water.'

'Oh my gosh, that must have been so ... horrific.'

Bronagh sounds full of empathy now. I feel a weight off, having told someone about it.

'Yes. It was ... a momentary lapse. A mistake. Something I paid so very dearly for.'

'A momentary lapse,' she echoes. 'I can understand completely how it would happen.'

There is the sound of Jack's voice in the background, calling her name.

'Sorry, I've got to go – Jack needs me. Speak soon?' she says in the same kind voice.

'Yes,' I reply.

The line goes dead.

The presenter talks directly to camera.

'*Anyone with information on Saoirse Kellough's disappearance should contact Crimeline on 555-1800.*'

I turn down the volume and sit, looking at the screen. I wonder if there will be any calls tonight from *Crimeline*, or whether this will be another dead-end. Another child who will never grow up. Another child whose story will go untold for far too long, because her loved ones are too ashamed to tell it.

39

Day Twelve

Freya

I approach the Hollowing Place. No one else is around, but still, I grip the knife just in case. I pull myself through the clearing and finally come out at the wide circle of trees. Nothing now. It is empty. The treehouse is not far from here. I catch sight of it in the distance, but that's when I stop. It's like something from a nightmare. The closer I get, the more of them I can see. They have the place surrounded. Crows. Hundreds of them, perched on every branch, every surface of the treehouse. My heart begins to race. A mocking voice rises in me. *You're going to let a few birds stop you finding her? From saving a little girl? What a joke you are. No wonder your child died. You're just a coward.* Suddenly there's a wild sound of wings – birds taking off, others circling. I don't need to think any more. It's not a choice. I turn and begin to sprint away through the trees. Breathless. Faster and faster. I trip and fall into a heap on the hard dirt. Gasping, I roll downhill for a second, then grab a tree root to stop myself rolling any further. With that, I jolt – waking up, in a cold sweat.

Kate has the air of a martyr or a hunger striker. Her skin is pallid and her arm on one side is swathed in a bandage from the fingers to the elbow. Her lips are turned down at the edges. The private hospital room is stark with a bite of disinfectant. Powdery walls and Victorian radiators. The smell. That's what has always got me about hospitals. I can stomach the rest of it: the sights of ill people, the clatter of steel on steel. It's the chemical scent, clean but malignant, that I hate most. Sanitiser mixed with the faint smell of decaying flesh, of blood. An almost undetectable reminder of the frailty of human life. Once you leave, you can get the whiff out of your nose, but you can never forget it. I focus on the flowers next to her bed, trying to breathe in their scent instead. White lilies. They hang their chins low as if in mourning. Kate's eyes are shut, her lashes fluttering a little. She lies stiff, hair splayed across the pillow.

'Kate,' I say. 'It's Freya.'

She opens her eyes momentarily and looks at me. 'You didn't call,' I say gently. 'Remember I told you that if you needed help, I was here anytime?'

'I wanted it to work,' she replies in a hoarse voice.

There is silence except for the regular bleep of the heart monitor beside her. 'What do you want from me?' she asks.

'I want to talk to you about the diary – the one you concealed from the Gardaí? What made you hide it from them?'

'I've already spoken to the Gardaí about the diary. It's none of your business.'

I look out the window at the uninspiring hospital car park, car bonnets glittering in the cold November light. My stomach sinks a little. I don't like to force a sick person to talk, especially a vulnerable woman like Kate, but it's necessary.

'I just need to know – are you hiding something? Why hide a diary that could help the investigation?'

'The diary wouldn't have helped, trust me. There are things that are bigger than you in that forest – I don't know why it's taking you so long to understand that. The rest of the villagers do. The Creature, the game – they keep well away from it all. But you think you're too good for it, that the rules don't apply to you.'

I don't know how to tell Kate that I do believe her, that I am all too aware how the forest can affect a person. I feel sad and frustrated for a moment. She doesn't want to open up about the diary.

I'm unsure how to say this next part, but I also know it might be the only way to get her to talk. 'Kate, I want you to consider this. We now know Saoirse is still alive. As it stands, you won't be her guardian again. You weren't coping. There was neglect, and now you've tried to … to end your own life. You won't be caring for them alone after this. Knowing that you cannot save things, can you please think about talking? If you know something, whatever it is, you need to tell me or the Gardaí. If something has happened to Saoirse and you're not telling the Gardaí everything, that makes you complicit in her disappearance.'

'I don't know where she is,' she whispers. 'I've told you that a million times. I want her home as much as everyone else.'

A tear rolls down her cheek.

'Look, your Aunt Bronagh has offered to take Jack and Saoirse. They'll still be with family, and you can work on getting your life together. Perhaps you can even go back to studying.'

There is a pause, then she speaks.

'Fine,' she sighs. 'You're right.'

'About what?'

Kate pushes herself up a little in the bed. She leans over and takes a sip of water, then puts the glass down shakily.

'I didn't hurt her – despite what half the village would have you think.'

I take a seat on a visitor's chair. 'What is it, then?'

Kate looks out the window as though remembering. 'On the day she ran away, Saoirse and I argued about our mother. That was how it started. She blamed me for our mother's death, saying our mother got worse because I was not around, and was always staying at friends' houses. I got upset and yelled at her. I said she was ungrateful … that I'd be in college if it weren't for her. That she was lucky I was caring for her at all, wasting my own life to mind her and Jack …

'She said, "Leave then, if that's how you feel," and I said, "Why don't *you* leave? Go live with Dad! Let him take responsibility for you." I know I never should have said that. After a while, she and Jack said they were going to the forest to play. I let them go.'

I can feel her guilt, palpable in the air. For a moment I sympathise with her. How awful to say these things then have your sister go missing, with no time to apologise. That is, if she is telling the truth.

'And there's another thing …'

'What?'

'After she left with Jack and headed off to the forest, I decided to try and follow them. I wanted to apologise to Saoirse properly before going to work. I only had twenty minutes to spare, so I went off in their direction.'

'I saw a woman – she was talking to someone who looked like Fergal Duffy Junior. I couldn't see her face, but she was talking to him through the window of his car, which was stopped on the road. I realised I wasn't going to catch them, and I went home. I keep thinking about that woman – what was she doing around here? Was she a tourist or a friend of his? Why was she talking to him? I didn't think anything of it until this morning, after it sank in that Saoirse was taken by a woman.'

'What did she look like?'

'I really couldn't see her properly. She had dark hair, but I couldn't tell more than that. A lot of women around Drumsuin have dark hair, so it doesn't narrow it down much.'

The woman Bronagh said she had seen on Christmas Day also had dark hair, didn't she?

'Why not tell the whole truth and let the Gardaí decide?'

'I was so ashamed.' It's all coming out now. 'How could I have let this happen?' She breaks into sobs. 'I'm her big sister. I should have protected her …'

'It's okay,' I say. 'You are as much of a victim in all this as Saoirse.'

237

She shudders. 'Ellie,' she said, sniffing and wiping at her cheek. She points to the TV screen, where they are showing the news. 'That little girl whose body they found. Jack says he sees her. It creeps me out. I don't understand what is happening, whether we're haunted or whether we're all mad ...'

'Trauma has different ways of manifesting,' I say. 'Perhaps in some way, all the things that happened around here have affected you, even those Magdalene homes all those years ago.'

I stand up and pick up the phone next to her bed. I dial the police station number and hand her the receiver. 'Please tell whoever answers everything you've just told me.'

'Now?'

'Right now,' I say. 'There is no time to lose.'

She takes the phone. I sit down next to her and listen in as she tells them the full truth at last.

40

Day Twelve

Freya

We are sitting on a bench at the end of the beach, sheltered behind a wall from the worst of the wind coming in from the bay. A fishing trawler sits nearby in the ocean, waiting for its catch. The tide laps in and out and I can taste the salty air on my tongue. Walter pulls his zip up under his chin.

'That blustery Atlantic wind would cut you in two,' he says, swallowing the last of his corned beef sandwich with mustard. He wipes his mouth. 'Thanks for agreeing to the chat,' he adds. 'I know you're busy with Jack.'

'No problem,' I reply. 'I could manage on my lunch break. And thanks for the sandwich,' I crumple the greaseproof paper from my sandwich into a ball. 'Anyhow, you're busy too.'

'I am indeed,' he says with a sigh. 'I've just come from another interview.'

'With who?'

'Oh, a woman who claims she was with Mr Fitzgerald the day and night Saoirse went missing. We've been interviewing her over the past few days on and off. He didn't have an alibi until now. She said they're having an affair and she was scared to tell anyone in case her husband found out. Once she realised how serious this all was … well, she wanted to help rule him out for us. She said she couldn't live with knowing we might be wasting time on someone who didn't do it. For Saoirse's sake, more than anything.'

'Did you believe her?'

'Yes. She has proof. They were staying in a hotel just outside Drumsuin and there are multiple witnesses to that – I drove up there with a photo of him to confirm it. So, as much as the man might like to sleep around with women in the village, he doesn't appear to be a kidnapper.'

It is strange to think Mr Fitzgerald has been ruled out. That his creepy way of being is only that: a creepy way of being. He hadn't hurt Saoirse, despite all of the odd things he said to me. I almost feel guilty for suspecting him. What if he had been arrested and accused of something he had not done? Then another thought occurs to me. Now Saoirse has said she's been taken by a woman, is there any need for male suspects at all?

'How about what Saoirse said about being taken by a woman?' I ask.

'Unfortunately, we cannot rule out anyone based on her words alone. How do we know what Saoirse is saying is true? She could have been coerced into saying those words. Or, it could be a couple who have taken her together, a woman *and* a man – a team.'

I nod. I hadn't considered that Saoirse might have been coerced into saying a woman had taken her. The thought is frightening.

'What did you want to speak to me about?' I ask, looking down at the sand, at the glistening array of stones and shells by my feet.

'Listen, I wanted to reassure you about that glove you found. I didn't lose it in the forest – I don't know where I lost it, but it wasn't there.'

I nod. 'Sure,' I say.

'I know it seems weird, but I don't know where I lost it.'

I nod again.

'Do you believe me?'

'Yes, I believe you,' I reply. It's uncomfortable for a moment. I do believe him but at the same time, who knows what things are being hidden from me in Drumsuin.

'I also wanted to talk to you about Jack's memory. Do you think it's normal for the boy not to remember things?'

'It depends ... It's not uncommon for children and adults to subconsciously block out traumatic memories, if that's what you are asking.'

'Yes, that's what I'm asking. How does it happen?'

'You want the explanation?'

'Humour me.'

'Okay, well ... a region in the brain called the hippocampus stores time, events and place. The hippocampus can be affected by stress and can effectively shut down during traumatic events, thus not encoding the memory properly.' I check to see if Walter is following, and he nods. 'Memory is not a single process, it's a complex system involving multiple brain regions. When the trauma is happening, the body can get overwhelmed. People can experience memory loss and blackouts to certain events. I think Jack has the memories, but he was overwhelmed when they happened so he can't consciously recall them. Yet, much like many people with PTSD, he gets flashbacks and nightmares. I think that's why he might be able to access more memories through drawing and being creative. In my experience, I can access more memories with clients when they're working creatively with me.'

Walter wipes his hands on a paper napkin, then fiddles with a gold wedding band, which is not on his wedding finger.

'It does seem the drawings are the key to understanding Jack.'

I nod. I feel suddenly curious about Walter. He seems more emotionally aware than I first gave him credit for – keen to understand Jack and the whole family, rather than just judge them. 'Hey, something I've wanted to ask you since we met ... How did you become a detective?'

He looks out to sea. 'I started at twenty. It was different when I was stationed in Dublin; you just had to do what you were told.

I started off with small jobs – guard duty, patrolling, arresting drunks. I always wanted more ...'

'How did you get more?'

'I suppose I watched, learned. Eventually I was put forward as a plain-clothes junior member, known as a *buckshee* in the force. For a while, I was just that, an eager buckshee trying to prove my worth. I'll never forget my first murder case ...' He looks out to sea. 'The suspect had an alibi, but I knew it from the moment I met him that he'd done it. We got him in the end. He's away now, still there, rotting in prison.'

'Do you enjoy doing what you do?'

He looks over. 'Why do you ask?'

I shrug. I am genuinely curious about Walter and, if I am honest, I want to know more about him.

'Well, I've seen things that would turn your stomach, seen more than my fair share of dead bodies when I worked back in Dublin too. But it's never boring, and it can be rewarding, like when you help a family. Still, there are things I'm not familiar with,' he admits. 'Things I have yet to learn.'

Something seems to be bothering him. 'I have to admit,' he continues, 'it makes me feel powerless knowing Saoirse is still alive, but I can't track her down. Technology is one of those things I don't understand. It frustrates me. I wish I understood where she was with this baby monitor business, but that's when I have to pass it on to people more expert than me in that field.'

I want to say something comforting, but I realise I don't have the words.

'How about you?' he asks. 'How does one end up doing your sort of a job?'

I think about Violet. My daughter, and how she died. The journey to my own therapy, and then wondering if I could sit in the opposite chair and help others too. I give him a half-truth.

'I think I was always just drawn to it. I notice things other people don't notice – shifts in mood, body language, that kind of thing.'

He nods. 'I can see that about you. And you've always done this?'

'No, I used to be a journalist, and I used to sing in a choir too, semi-professionally.'

'What made you stop?'

Where do I start with that answer? Perhaps I didn't believe I deserved to sing any more. Not the way I used to. Singing in the shower doesn't count. I look over at him, taking in his profile.

'Walter ... what happened to your eye?'

He has a stoic expression now, his jaw tight. I immediately feel guilty for asking him. He looks at his watch. I should have known. I don't like talking about the death of my child and here I am, making Walter talk about his past.

'It was a car accident,' he says eventually, and then clears his throat. 'My wife was killed in the same accident ... so I got away lightly.'

'I'm so sorry for your loss,' I say. 'I didn't know you had been married.'

I feel a pang of sympathy. Walter was a widower – and it had been a car accident, just like in Jack's dream. How had Jack known that was how Walter lost his eye? Perhaps he had overheard his aunt or sister talking about it. Perhaps it was common knowledge in the village. Something like that couldn't happen in a close-knit town without people knowing about it.

Walter looks over at me. 'Meeting Alice gave me hope.'

'Hope?'

'That I might not be alone forever. That there is life after losing someone.'

We sit in silence and listen to the waves. Where could Saoirse be? I look over at the forest on the cliff edge.

'Do you ever think about all the missing children in the world?' I ask. 'All the millions of places they could be kept ... I suppose it's every mother's worst nightmare,' I add, almost to myself.

'Yes. That's what keeps me going, through the horrible mortuary visits, through the dead bodies and the crime scenes and the sad days and the lack of sleep ... The families. Justice.' He pauses. 'There is a motto you learn in the Gardaí, when you are training ... Do fuck all, but whatever you do, do it well.'

'And do you?' I ask.

He stands up slowly.

'I try to,' he says. 'On that note, it's time to get back, wouldn't you agree?'

PART FIVE

41

Day Twelve

Jack

There is a loud bang. Gasping, Jack opens his eyes and stares at the ceiling. He listens carefully to what is happening. The banging continues, louder now, and the front door clicks open. A familiar man's voice speaks in a low tone. A quiet voice, a woman's, replies.

Jack sits up in bed.

'Why did no one tell me?' the first voice demands.

'Don't get upset.'

'I'm not upset! Let me in. You're my sister, for Christ's sake,' the man hisses.

Jack looks out the window to see a red car. Different to Garda Morris's – this one is longer and flatter, like one of Jack's toys. There is a familiar sticker on the window. Jack squints. He's seen the sticker before – a yellow shield with red and green in it. The county's hurling team logo. Aunt Bronagh sounds cross now.

'You can't just come here … Things change.'

The deep voice speaks again. 'I found out about my daughter going missing from the Gardaí banging down my door in the middle of the night.'

Jack swings his legs out of bed, opens his bedroom door and pads to the top of the stairs, peeking down over the bannister. He can see boots on the doorstep. Men's boots. Aunt Bronagh has her hand on the doorframe. Now Jack can hear them clearer.

'They thought I took her. My own daughter – can you imagine?'

Jack walks down a few steps. Now he can see his dad's face. His hair is shaggier than before. He has a moustache, and his eyes have dark rings around them. His face is red, his moustache looks almost ready to leap off his face and run away.

'They were questioning me for days on end! Until they realised I had a dozen alibis, and there were cameras proving I couldn't have left Dublin for long enough to do anything of the sort! I had to miss work to speak to the Gardaí. If I'd come down here any sooner, I'd have got the sack!'

He looks up and spots Jack.

'Daddy!'

'Jack!' His dad sounds sadder than Jack remembers. 'Jack!' he exclaims, again, holding out his arms.

Jack suddenly feels shy. He wants to run to his dad, but he is also embarrassed to.

'You're frightening him,' snaps Aunt Bronagh.

'How could he be frightened? I'm his father!'

'He hasn't seen you for a whole year. That's a very long time for a little boy.'

Jack takes a step downwards.

'Where is Katherine?' his dad asks.

'In hospital.'

'What's wrong with her?'

Jack takes another step down. It feels like there is an invisible barrier in the way between him and his father.

'She was upset, she tried to hurt herself again.'

'Christ. And no one tells me my other daughter is in hospital now? I sent letters and a few parcels. Did they never receive them?' He looks at Aunt Bronagh in an accusing way. 'Were my letters and parcels being hidden from them?'

'We didn't want to upset them, Cahill.'

'Oh, that's lovely! Just hide the post from my children so they think I don't care! Why did no one call *me*?'

'You can't just pick and choose when you contact them.'

Then the words come out of Jack's mouth, like an explosion.

'I wanted to call you! We didn't have your number,' Jack yells. 'Mam wouldn't let us talk to you, and then Kate hid your number and Saoirse wanted to run away and find you!'

Aunt Bronagh turns and stares at Jack in shock. 'Run away?'

'She wanted to come looking for me,' Jack's father mutters. 'See, it's your fault she's missing. If you hadn't kept her away from me, this wouldn't have happened.'

Jack's father tries to get past, but Aunt Bronagh manoeuvres her wheelchair in the way and wedges herself in the doorway.

'Get back,' she hisses.

Jack feels tears running down his face – he wants to talk to his father, but everything feels out of control. Aunt Bronagh looks angry and now his dad seems lost too, like he has forgotten about Jack. His face changes to a different expression, eyes wide, lips downturned.

'You'd turn away your own brother?'

'I will if you come barrelling in here at a time like this. The children have had enough stress. You didn't come back when their mother died, so why now?'

'Now is as good a time as any. Saoirse is missing!'

'Six months ago, when they were practically orphaned, would have been a lot better.'

'I couldn't leave my job. What use would I be to them without money to send back for the bills?'

'You didn't even visit on the weekends!'

Jack's dad falls quiet. 'I thought Kate was coping,' he says after a few moments. 'Clearly, she wasn't.'

'Well, it's too little, too late.' Aunt Bronagh glances up at Jack, then back at his dad. 'Please, just go,' she hisses.

Aunt Bronagh tries to shut the door. He puts his foot in the gap.

'I'm not going,' he says firmly. 'I'm their father.'

Another voice comes from behind him, a deep, familiar voice.

'Why don't you come and have a chat with me instead?'

Jack sees Garda Morris standing behind him. Garda Morris puts his hand on Cahill's shoulder, as though they are friends.

'It's my daughter that is missing, and the other one in hospital!' Cahill exclaims. 'Can't you talk sense into my sister – tell her to let me in?'

'First, let us get into my car and have a chat together. You can come back and speak to Aunt Bronagh and Jack another day. When everyone is not so upset.'

Cahill turns and gives Jack one more sad look. His shoulders drop as he walks away with Garda Morris.

Jack watches as Aunt Bronagh closes the door.

'She wanted to run away?' asks Aunt Bronagh softly. 'Did she have a plan?'

Jack nods. He hadn't told anyone about the plan. The one Saoirse had to go to their father's, steal some money, and get the boat to England where no one could upset her any more.

COUNTDOWN

Four ...

Six Months Ago

Saoirse

The wind is picking up outside. Everything is blowing around in the garden – leaves, branches, washing. The swing set creaks madly. One of the corrugated metal panels has blown right off the shed.

They are having a cooked breakfast this morning. Their mother went to the butcher specially and bought plenty of food. Or maybe the butcher had come to them. Mr Fitzgerald has been visiting the house a lot, ever since the incident in the sea. One morning, Saoirse had woken up to find him standing in the hallway, staring at her bedroom door. He had looked as though he had been caught out, and ran off into the bathroom quickly, head down and ears burning red. Luckily, today he was not here, for once.

'More toast?' Lucy offers.

Jack puts up his hand. 'Me!'

Lucy smiles indulgently and puts more bread under the grill. She sits down in a nearby chair for a minute, keeping half an eye on the toast so it doesn't burn.

'Mr Fitzgerald brought flowers as well as the meat yesterday,' she says coyly. 'Early daffodils.'

Lucy takes a pill, puts it in her mouth with one shaking hand and swallows it with water. Saoirse pushes her rasher across the plate and picks up a forkful of beans. She takes a bite, watching

Jack as he eats. She guesses Mr Fitzgerald is the new boyfriend to replace the last one, who Saoirse hasn't seen for a few weeks. She wants to ask if this is the case but she doesn't want the answer to be that he is.

'Where is Kate?' Saoirse asks instead.

Lucy rolls her eyes. 'Apparently, she's too good for us nowadays. She's been staying with the Byrnes.'

Saoirse says nothing. She can understand why Kate doesn't want to be here any more.

'We have to do a project for homework this weekend – my family tree,' says Saoirse, changing the subject. 'I need photographs.'

Lucy chuckles. '*My family tree?* Did you tell them your family was bananas?'

Saoirse spears a piece of mushroom. Lucy continues. 'Speaking of family, your father rang the other night.'

Saoirse feels a desperation rise in her, an awful feeling of having missed out on something important.

'He's too nosy,' Lucy says, grabbing her napkin and dabbing at her mouth. 'I don't want him getting involved. He jumps to conclusions. I don't want him coming down here again, threatening to take you away.'

Saoirse wants to ask her mother what her father had said on the phone, but she does not dare. Her mother is only more difficult when she gets defensive.

'We just want to speak to him – we won't tell him anything bad,' Saoirse says.

Lucy gives a short, sharp laugh. 'You'll soon learn in life not to bother wasting your time missing people who leave you.'

Saoirse feels something boiling inside her. Then she finally says it, all the things she has been holding in for weeks.

'He only left us because he was sick of you!'

'Excuse me?'

'And you've left us often enough before!'

Lucy frowns. 'I've never left you.'

'You have,' Saoirse replies. She picks up her half-empty plate and pushes her chair back. 'Every time you forget to take your pills, every time you drink, every time you disappear into your room with a man – you're not here. We're used to it.'

Lucy frowns. 'I suppose I'm just the worst mother there is?'

Saoirse scrapes the remaining food off her plate, rinses it and puts it on the draining board. 'Maybe one of these days the answer will be yes.'

She leaves the kitchen and stomps up the stairs, a hot stone of anger in her chest. She is angry at her mam for making her miss her father's call and she is angry at herself for missing the other version of her mother, the one who tells stories and jokes, who makes sure they have dinner and do their homework. She is also angry at how her mam makes everything about her. For once, couldn't it have been about *Saoirse's* pain, not Lucy's?

The next morning her mam is gone again. Her body is here, but her mind is elsewhere. She lies in the foetal position next to the toilet and an empty bottle of prescription tablets, snoring loudly. The tablets have been flushed down, but three or four still float on the top of the water. Her mother sometimes does this when she decides she doesn't want to take her medication any more. A half-full vodka bottle is in her mother's hands. Saoirse cannot deal with this, not on a school day. As if on autopilot, she goes back to her bedroom and dresses in her uniform.

None of it seems to matter. It doesn't matter that Aunt Bronagh mentioned their father is on the brink of calling social services. Or that Jack is having nightmares and sleepwalking every night, or that Saoirse nearly drowned and caught a fever trying to rescue their mother from the sea. It doesn't matter that they are both frightened and not themselves, or that they can't focus in school, or that Kate hasn't been home for a week, and doesn't speak to anyone when she is here.

The disease or addiction or whatever it's called is so insidious that it doesn't care. It comes back with a vengeance every time things are good for a week or two. Lucy always eventually stops taking her pills, the alcohol comes back, and then real Mam goes to Saturn.

Saoirse, still in her bedroom, hears a stir and a curse and then the sound of her mother vomiting. She winces and puts on her school jumper, then goes into Jack's room to wake him.

'Get dressed,' she says flatly. He mumbles and sits up, looking at her as though he barely recognises her.

She leaves the room and goes downstairs. Sets the breakfast table for them both, takes out the cereal and milk and bread and butter and jam, clicks on the kettle for tea.

As the kettle boils, she stares out into the back garden. It is a mess from the storm yesterday. A sapling lies on its side. The wind has dropped now and all is still.

In the reflection of the window, she sees her mother enter the kitchen. Saoirse turns. Lucy is dressed now. She has washed her face. She looks remorseful. Half-sane. Like a spacewoman who has just returned home. She sits at the table and straightens her shoulders.

'I'll walk you both to school.'

'No.'

'I want to. Let me.'

Saoirse takes a seat opposite her.

They sit in silence for a while and eventually her mother speaks.

'I'm sorry … You were right, what you said yesterday. I keep abandoning you both. This back and forth is so unfair on you. I *am* a bad mother.'

'You're not when you're here. You're brilliant, but then when you don't take those pills – when you descend …'

'Where did you learn that word, *descend*? You're only thirteen.'

'I read it in a book.'

Lucy sighs. She rubs her eyes.

'Let's go on a walk today.'

'We have—'

'I know. You have school, but it's Friday. Let's have a family day. You, me, and Jack. The last one. After this, no more missed days from school. I'll go back to the doctor again. I'll get help.'

Saoirse hesitates. This is what she has needed to hear for so long.

'Promise?'

'Yes. I'll tell Bronagh and your dad. I can't keep putting you through this. You and Jack, you deserve better.' Lucy smiles. 'I don't want to descend … again.'

Saoirse puts out her hand and sticks out her little finger. Lucy puts her hand out and hooks her little finger in hers. As Saoirse looks into her mother's eyes she feels hopeful for the first time in a long time. Hopeful that her mother might get better, that she might return from Saturn for good.

COUNTDOWN

Three ...

Six Months Ago

Saoirse

They are exploring the forest, the three of them. Their mother calls out into the trees.

'With a monstrous body ... and the talons! You've never seen anything like it.'

'What about its teeth?'

'They're huge. As large as boulders, but they look like the burned ends of a cigarette. When it roars it sounds like fifty bombs going off, but it has the wind strength of ten hurricanes!'

'How does it know people are there?' Jack asks, his voice excited.

'It can smell you,' their mother says.

'What, like in *The Witches* by Roald Dahl?' Saoirse asks. She got that book from the library a few weeks ago.

'Yes, exactly like that.'

They have lost where they are going now, Saoirse can tell. Their mother is weaving a strange route; they never usually go this way. The forest is like a maze at this point, where the fog rises and the mountain sweeps up towards the cliffs. The cliff edge is off limits for Jack and Saoirse. It has never been fenced off, much to the annoyance of the locals.

Saoirse can smell damp earth and pines. They are in the thick of the forest, where it's calm and eerily quiet. Sounds from the outside are filtered and deadened by so many trees. Their mother's voice is louder now, against the stillness.

'Have you ever seen it?' Jack asks.

'The Creature?' their mother replies. 'Of course.'

She digs her walking stick into the ground, gouging into the earth with every step. Saoirse watches her fragile frame, her calf-length skirt, her orange coat. Her dark blonde hair hangs wild and free today, wavy around her shoulders.

'I've seen it too,' Jack replies.

'Have you?' Mam asks, in a voice that sounds like she doesn't really believe him.

'Yep.'

Saoirse smiles to herself. 'Tell us again how the game started?'

Saoirse can see her mother's shoulders tense a little, as though she doesn't want to talk about it today. Her mother had seemed quite well this morning before they left for their walk, but is she okay now?

'You don't want to know that old story,' she says, without looking back. Saoirse's stomach turns in knots. Her mother's behaviour is shifting, just like that day on the beach.

'We do, we do!' Jack yells, not picking up on their mother's change in mood.

'You know it already.'

'Tell us again,' Jack shouts.

Their mother huffs and turns around, her face almost angry, contorted. 'It's simple, really,' she snaps. 'The game started here not long after the Magdalene home was knocked down, to keep the evil spirits away. We play it so the forest doesn't hurt people or disappear them. I don't know *who* exactly started it ...'

'What about the part ...' Jack starts, sounding frustrated.

'What part?' their mother challenges.

'The part' – Jack lowers his voice almost to a whisper – 'where you did something bad?'

Their mother laughs with her lips together, but it is not a happy laugh. Her eyes glisten with tears. She looks away again and begins to stomp up the hill, stabbing her walking stick into the mud. Saoirse gives him a look. *Why did you say that?*

Their mother used to talk about it. The thing she had done inside the forest that was so bad the forest turned against them. Not just them, but the whole extended family. *The forest has a memory*, she remembers her mother saying as she threw a log on the fire. *Nothing you do is ever forgotten – that's why we play the game, to keep us safe.* She has never told them the bad thing she did, but Kate said it was something to do with a bonfire she had not put out properly around Samhain, which killed a whole section of trees. Apparently, after that their mother had become obsessed with playing the game. A fire is one of the worst things you could do to hurt a forest. Wildfires destroy them whole sometimes. Saoirse has seen it on TV.

Saoirse hears a caw and a flapping of wings above, and all of a sudden, something thumps on the ground at her feet. She jumps. It had missed her face by a few inches.

'Oh!'

'What now?' her mam snaps.

'Something almost hit me!' Saoirse gasps. 'It's a ... dead bird,' she says, bending over to peer at the glassy stare of the crow, lying unmoving on the dried-out pine needles. Its neck is bent at a strange angle, its wings are fanned out as though nailed to an invisible cross. The silence of the forest throbs in her ears.

'Leave it!' her mother shouts. 'Don't touch it!' She stalks back towards Saoirse. 'Come ... this way.'

Her mother's face is thunderous now. Jack's expression is bewildered. 'Why did it die?'

Lucy looks around the forest, her pupils darting from side to side. Saoirse can see the whites of her eyes. 'It's listening to me,' Lucy says. 'The Creature, it thinks I'm mocking it. The crow ... it's a symbol.'

'The crow?' Saoirse echoes.

'Yes ... The forest,' their mam adds. 'It knows.' She looks at them both, as if a realisation is dawning on her. 'We need to play the game. To show respect to the forest.'

'Now?' Saoirse asks. She is suddenly uneasy, goosebumps on her arms.

'Yes. Let's go up here to the top of the hill, near the cliff edge and we can play. You can both count.' With a wide-eyed look, she says: 'Today, *I* will hide.'

Saoirse closes her eyes and begins to count slowly. *One potato, two potato* ... She listens as her mother's footsteps get further and further away. *Three potato, four* ... Slower now. Her mother will need time to hide. Eventually there is complete silence apart from the whisper of Jack counting next to her. *Eight potato, nine potato, ten* ... As she opens her eyes, the forest looks blotchy at first, then her gaze sharpens. Overhead, a bird trills.

'Which way shall we search?' Jack asks.

Saoirse glances to where the trees end at the cliff edge.

'I'll go this way, towards the cliff. Why don't you try looking for her that way? Remember to count as you walk and shout out the numbers.'

'What if we don't find her by ten?'

'Count to ten again. Keep counting to ten. We have to find her. Otherwise ...'

Saoirse does not finish, unable to speak the worst thing aloud. She is about to walk off when there is a loud crack.

'What was that?' Saoirse whispers. She turns and looks up. Above is a branch, half-snapped and ready to fall. It looks as though it might have been damaged in the storm. On the end of the branch is a bird's nest. It is tilted and only just hanging on. The tree has a wide trunk, but there are some grooves on which to climb.

'If we let that nest fall,' she says, 'we will have wilfully let something bad happen to the forest.'

'What does wilfully mean?'

'On purpose.'

'But we didn't break it.'

'You don't understand,' she replies. 'If we just let it fall, we may as well have done it on purpose. That's worse for us than taking slightly longer to find Mam.'

Grabbing the bottom branch, she begins to ascend. Slowly at first, and then faster, pulling herself up. Pine needles graze her skin, and it takes a surprising effort. Breathless, she reaches the broken branch. She can see the eggs in the nest now. They are beige and blue. Speckled and tiny. Around them, tufts of feathers, sticks and other bits of foliage as well as the odd piece of fabric are all woven into a perfect circle.

'Don't worry, little eggs,' Saoirse whispers.

She holds her breath and firmly grips the tree. All she has to do is lean forwards, being careful not to put her weight on the broken branch, and pick up the nest. She could place it higher and leave it there for when the mother returns. She won't touch the eggs directly – she knows her scent might scare off the mother – but she has to try and save the nest.

'Quickly!' Jack calls up.

'I'm trying,' she gasps.

Saoirse reaches out. She is one inch from the nest, her fingers almost ready to clasp around it, when she hears the noise above her, and screams as the wings of a bird beat against her head. The mother must have returned. She almost lets go of the branch above and falls, but instead, instinctively she stands on the broken branch. The mother bird flaps away. The nest, already at a steep angle, slides down the soft pine needles.

The nest falls, the eggs spilling out. They smash on the ground with a light crack. Saoirse looks down now to see the upturned nest with the eggs scattered around it.

Saoirse is silent, her mouth open in shock. Shaking, she pulls herself down, a heaviness in her heart. She jumps to the ground and inspects the mess. There is a glob of a boneless hatchling protruding from one of the shells. She feels a pang of guilt in the pit of her stomach; tears sting her eyes.

'What should we do?' Jack asks.

Saoirse stands still, frozen, for a moment. She knows she isn't meant to touch them, but here they will certainly be eaten. Carefully, she leans over and picks up the broken eggs, including one which has fallen unscathed, and places them into the soft nest. She arranges the nest on a low branch of a pine tree nearby as if preparing a corpse for a viewing. The poor mother bird will find the nest here. Trembling, she takes a deep breath, realising the time.

'We need to find Mam. For now, you go that way into the trees, I'll go down along the cliff this way.'

'Five … six … seven …' Jack calls out.

As Saoirse walks away, Jack's voice begins to disappear. The wind whips at her face and ears, tousling her hair. She tries to focus on looking for her mother but all she can think about is the bird's nest. Apart from the sadness of the bird losing its babies, there is also the worrying fact of the forest to think about now. Like Mam said, the forest doesn't like to be disrespected.

Out here on the cliff edge, she observes the green peninsula and the rolling sea, dots of white horses on the surface of the Atlantic Ocean. She looks at the straw-like grass and inhales the salty air, then wanders one direction for a while, peering back into the trees every so often, looking for a hint of colour or movement.

The gale almost pushes her sideways as she presses on, a fearful feeling in her gut, as though something very bad is about to happen. Reality is dawning on her at a bovine pace. The cliff edge is only around ten seconds away from where they had counted. Where else could her mother have disappeared to so fast?

Suddenly, all worries of the bird's nest vanish from her mind and a new horrific fear replaces it. A fear so deep and painful she almost collapses to her knees then and there. Her legs weaken and a feeling of confusion swims into her mind as she turns back in the opposite direction to where she had been looking and stares back along the cliff. That is when she sees it – a movement out of the corner of her eye, fast and bright. Now, her eyes focus clearly. Jack. He is parallel to where they counted, but at the cliff edge. Too close. He is staring down. Saoirse sprints towards him.

'Jack, no! Get down Jack, don't stand so close!'

He turns his head and stares right through her, as though he is waking from a dream.

Saoirse throws herself down on the long grass behind him. She reaches up and grabs the bottom of Jack's jumper and pulls sharply. He stumbles backward and sits down hard next to her.

'What are you doing?' she hisses. His expression is blank. He stares into the far-off distance – miles away, the whites of his eyes visible like their mother's were earlier.

Saoirse crawls and peers over the edge. As soon as she does, her vision turns blurry.

The image would be burned into her mind forever. The splayed legs, the orange coat, the skirt ruched up and the blonde hair half across her face, arms at an odd angle, like the crow's neck from less than an hour earlier. The blood all pooled under her, like the missing girl from her dream. The face lifeless – her eyes from afar look open and staring, but it is hard to tell.

Saoirse lies there on the cliff edge, unable to speak. It is as if the Creature really has stolen her voice box. She crawls back and grabs Jack again, pulling him close, hugging him as though their lives depend on it. Unable to cry. They stay like this for a while, a tangled mess. That is when they hear it. The rumbling in the distance. Saoirse listens. The rumbling gets closer.

Behind Jack, the sunlight splits and blinds her. They run down the steep hill towards home and away from the thing that is chasing them. Saoirse's body gathers momentum. Her legs unfold underneath, as if by their own accord. Gravity pulls her down, causing her to trip over twigs and silt, as she ducks under branches. She glances over her shoulder. The Creature sucks up everything in its path. Tornado-like. An embolism. Like the forest is haemorrhaging from the insides.

Her lungs ache. They reach the place where the pines begin to thin, calcify. The sea air looks hazy. Old sycamores and oaks bend like burned corpses on a stake.

Saoirse's breath burns. Duck. Dive. Swerve. Her feet hit the ground again and again. Crunch, crunch, crack. Breaking the soft marrow ground. Her footsteps are more careless now. Desperate. Flowers, bugs, and new buds all trampled. The squirrels run away as they approach. A sharp branch scrapes her arm. She curses as she grips the broken skin, legs still moving forwards.

It is closer now, hovering like a shroud. She looks ahead again. The edge of the forest where the seagulls glide on the currents. The tributary. The bridge. All of a sudden there is a thud. She halts. Looks back. Jack is crouched, cradling his ankle. She jogs back and pulls him up, but he stumbles. It is gaining on them now. Closer through the pines. It will not stop. *Jump on my back*, she yells. She takes his legs, hooks them over her hips. She begins to run again, slower now. Her little brother's arms are clasped around her neck. He weighs more than she had imagined.

COUNTDOWN

Two ...

Six Months Ago

Saoirse

Saoirse hangs up the phone after calling the emergency services. Her brother's face is muddy, his eyes are red from crying. He is only nine. Imagine no longer having a mother at that age. Saoirse feels as though she is drowning. Aunt Bronagh, will she be home? Jack searches her face for answers.

'Why have we stopped counting?'

Saoirse thinks about their mother, lying at the bottom of the cliff, like a broken egg. Will the emergency services get to her soon? Before the tide comes in and takes her away?

'I don't like this game any more!' Jack shouts. He sounds close to flying into a rage.

Saoirse puts her arm around him and pulls him into another hug. 'Stop counting,' she orders.

He pushes her away. 'I won't ... not until she comes home!' he screams.

Saoirse rubs the bridge of her nose. 'She won't come back now.'

'She will!' he yells at the top of his lungs.

'You saw her yourself. How can you think she's coming home?'

'I don't believe you.' Jack gets off his chair. 'You're horrible to make that up!' he screams, his voice even higher and his face even redder. His whole body is upset now, in a tantrum. His muscles tense, his fingers outstretched. Saoirse looks at her brother, wild-eyed and emotional. He continues to shout. 'When she gets home, I'll tell her what you said!'

With that, he storms from the room, slamming the door behind him.

Saoirse sits in silence a moment, wishing it all could be different. Maybe it was a bad dream, or a mistake. Maybe her mam will walk in any moment and ask them why they had given up on the game.

The kind, calm woman on the phone had asked her for exact directions to where their mother was. Deep down, Saoirse knows they cannot save her. The cliff was too high for someone to survive the fall. Then there is another fear. What will happen to her and Jack now? She can hardly comprehend what it will mean if her mother never comes home. Will their father come back to care for them? Will they go and live with Aunt Bronagh, or could Kate take care of them? Will they be put into care?

It's strange how she's thinking so logically, but somehow, she is. She cannot feel any of it properly. Not really. How can she process her mother is dead when she saw her only a few hours ago, walking around the house? They had linked pinkie fingers together. How can it be that just hours after that promise, she is gone?

Kate. Saoirse realises she needs to call her. Mam's pocketbook has a list of Kate's friends' numbers in there, in case Mam wanted to check where she was. Saoirse gets up. She will call around and find Kate, get her home. They can figure out a plan. A plan to keep them all together.

42

Six Months Ago

Jack

Mothers are born and mothers die; this is all Jack knows any more. The morning light has been sucked out from the sea and tossed under the blood-red sun. The car trundles. The rain on glass is the only thing to intrude on the silence. Kate's hands on the steering wheel are clasped in a tremble. Saoirse, her loose red curls collected in a braid, sits in the front seat. Jack cannot read her expression from here.

A fat ladybird climbs across Jack's finger. He watches it. Puts his other finger out and the ladybird continues walking as though it were the same path. Ladybirds don't know what is underneath them. They cannot tell flesh from bone nor skin from tree bark. Ladybirds don't have mothers, and if they do, they've already flown away.

The villagers never liked their mother. Kate had said as much over breakfast. She was a blow-in, not of the Drumsuin kind, not like Jack's father or grandfather, men with Irish blood. They didn't like women much either – women were to be housewives, meant for carrying babies. Or women could be trophies, beautiful things for men to look at and do other things with also, which Jack is too young to understand about – thank God, Kate had said. After breakfast, she had held out Jack's white shirt and told him to put it on. He had slid his arms in. Watched his sister's face as she did up the buttons for him. She had kept her eyes down, her jaw firm and tight, lips in a thin line. She said she hoped Jack would not grow up to be a man like that.

Drumsuin tries hard to keep outsiders out but it never works. Gradually more and more people from the outside have come in, visiting the forest and getting lost, or moving into nearby houses and getting jobs. The villagers don't like this, but even worse, Jack knows the forest does not like it. The Creature especially does not agree. As they drive Jack remembers walking hand in hand with his grandfather through the streets and everyone saying hello, then walking with his mother and no one saying hello. In some ways, it will be easier now that Mam is gone, Kate had said as she got into the car this morning. Because she was just a woman, and just an outsider. But Jack cannot see how in any way life could be easier without his mother. Without the everything of her.

They drive until they're at the cemetery, near the forest. Jack looks out the window into the tall pines, whose shadows claw at them. He thinks of the sea, and how trees can be just the same. You can drown inside them. So, he asks, 'Did Mam drown?' and Kate replies, 'Yes,' and that is how it all starts. Jack pretending in his head their mam had drowned accidentally in the sea. That is easier to think about than what really happened.

That's how it had started, the lies.

Many lies start like a little seed and grow into a great Norwegian pine, as high as the sky and just as powerful. But never mind the lies. The worst of it is no more mornings in bed with Mam's musky scent. No more Mam's nightgown as she walks to the toilet in the night, barefoot on bare floorboards. No more smiles and encouraging words after school.

Jack watches as the men lower his mam's coffin. He watches them throw the dirt down in handfuls. His mam. Jack had blown the ladybird off his finger. It had spread its wings and taken off. Like one little lie, flying away.

A crow descends to watch from its spot atop the tree nearby, for crows attend all funerals. A holy bird in all its black-heartedness. Jack's own heart kneels and dives right down there into the hole with her. And even though he is only a young boy, a part of him knows he will stay here forever. Buried too, underneath the dirt.

43

Day Thirteen

Jack

Garda Morris is seated in front of Jack in the sitting room now. Freya is next to him.

'Bronagh tells me your sister had a plan to run away to Dublin?'

Jack nods. He stares at Garda Morris's empty eye and then at his good one.

'What was the plan?'

Jack swallows a lump in his throat.

'She was going to call our da, but she couldn't find his phone number because Kate hid it.' Jack sniffs. All these new questions are making him cry. He wipes away a tear with the back of his hand.

'And then what?'

'She found h-his address ... She said she wanted to try-y and find him. She wanted to ... to take some money from him and then get the boat to Wales. Where no one could upset her any more.'

'Are you saying Saoirse wanted to get the boat to Holyhead from Dublin port?'

Jack nods.

'Yes.'

He does a big sniff and wipes his nose on his sleeve.

Freya leans over and grabs a tissue and hands it to him. 'Was there anyone else involved in this plan? Did she plan to hitch a lift, for example?' Freya asks.

Jack nods. 'She didn't have money for the train so she said she might try and get a lift to Dublin in a car with a stranger. She said everyone does it, that it's safe as long as you pick someone who looks okay, especially a car with a woman inside.'

Freya looks very worried now, her brow knitting together.

'But she didn't have her bags packed,' Jack continues. 'She s-said maybe she would do it after … if Da didn't come home to see us for C-Christmas …'

'Could it be that she decided to go sooner and not tell you?'

Jack thinks about this and begins to cry again.

'I don't know … there were strange things happening …'

'What kind of things?' Freya asks quickly. 'Do you remember anything new?'

Jack racks his brains.

Freya whispers something in Garda Morris's ear. Jack cannot hear properly but he just hears a few words.

Better one-to-one …

Garda Morris nods and says in a quiet voice, 'Right you are, indeed.' Then he turns to Jack. 'I'm going now, can you keep talking to Freya? Tell Freya what you saw on the day, and don't leave anything out this time.'

Jack nods. He wants to tell the truth, he really does.

44

Day Thirteen

Jack

'I believe you can remember the day Saoirse went missing, Jack, if you try hard enough.'

If memories are like things you collect, sometimes they are also like items you've lost. Things that you can't find. This memory is a very valuable one, but it definitely doesn't want to be found.

Freya looks into his eyes.

'Let your mind drift back. Don't push it away. Like wake-dreaming.'

Mam said when you couldn't find things the best thing to do was to retrace your steps. Maybe that could work now. Jack thinks hard. He tries to remember from the very beginning. That morning he had got out of bed. He did some painting first. Then he heard Kate and Saoirse argue – their voices louder and louder. Angry. After that, Saoirse had come upstairs to where he was painting and said why didn't they go and play in the forest. She had looked as though she had been crying. She wouldn't talk about the argument. They had left the house.

After playing for a while in the fields, they had gone into the forest. It had been about lunchtime at that point, or early afternoon. Jack was not sure as he did not have a watch.

Jack had closed his eyes and counted, next to a tree they called the Sea Tree, because it had wavy branches like seaweed.

'So, you were in the forest?' says Freya, interrupting his thoughts.

Jack closes his eyes now and tries to remember.

He had closed his eyes and counted *one potato, two* ... Saoirse had been the one to hide.

'And Saoirse hid?'

Jack nods.

'What happened when you opened your eyes?'

Jack thinks back. He had heard an awful scream. He had opened his eyes and looked around. There had been light rain, drizzle. It had been a dull, grey afternoon. They were near the river, close enough to hear it, but not so close he could see it. He'd had a bad feeling. Like being watched. He had run in the direction Saoirse had gone. Jack can remember the terror he had felt now, looking around at the black gaps in the trees.

'I had a feeling ...'

'What kind of a feeling?'

'Like when I have bad dreams.'

'Like fear?'

Jack nods.

'Then what?' Freya asks. She leans forwards in her chair.

Jack had tried to play the game, had walked forwards counting aloud. *Four potato, five potato, six* ... Then there had been a sound, like a voice of a person. Not Saoirse, but in the distance. The sound of hushed conversation between people. Jack closes his eyes and he is back there now, among the trees.

'Saoirse?' he'd whispered. 'Are you here? Come out, I don't like the game any more.'

She had not come out. The trees had stared back at him. So many branches. He'd looked hard into the shadows.

'Saoirse? Stop playing now!'

He opens his eyes and looks at Freya.

'You're there, aren't you?'

Jack nods.

'Don't leave your memories. I know you're scared but you need to stay there, another minute. You're safe here with me. What happened next?'

Jack closes his eyes again. He looks around in his memory. That was when he had seen it. He had screamed. He had turned and run, his heart beating out of his chest.

'Don't leave,' Freya repeats.

Jack remembers now. Before he had run away, he saw it. The Creature. It had its back to Jack with Saoirse in its arms, but then it had turned and Jack had seen a flash of something from underneath the branches, feathers, and leaves. A human face? As he looks closer, he can see something else. Feet. Wearing boots? They didn't seem so Creature-like now he's focused on them.

'It has feet with boots and it is carrying a rope.' Jack frowns. He opens his eyes. 'That's all I can see.'

'Jack – considering the feet with boots … could it have been a *person*, someone dressed up as a creature?' Freya murmurs.

He opens his eyes again now and feels they're full of tears. 'It's my fault!' He begins to sob.

Freya leans forwards. 'No, Jack. It's not your fault. I promise.'

He cries openly now.

'It wasn't the Creature, it was a person. They took her!'

Jack continues to sob, uncontrollably. Freya comes and sits next to him and puts her arm around him like a mother. 'None of this is your fault. If Saoirse was taken, they are the person at fault, not you … Now, can you describe the person to me?'

Jack feels terror rise in himself. He had only glimpsed them. That wasn't much use, but he would try.

45

Day Thirteen
Freya

'Excuse my appearance,' I say, gesturing to the bathrobe I am wearing. I lift the laundry bag and pass it to Mary at reception, who leans over and takes it, giving me a smile. She is printing out some documents, and in the background, the printer makes a grinding, masticating sound.

'Oh Freya, while I have you – just to let you know, the Gardaí were around here asking me questions the other day, about my guests?' My ears prick up. 'They wanted to know if I'd seen anything strange. Anyway, they said they needed the registration numbers of the cars belonging to everyone here. I had to pass yours on with the others, hope that's okay – I assumed it wouldn't be a problem, considering you're working on the case and all.'

'Okay by me.'

'Thanks,' she says. 'I know it's peculiar but we're all suspects, being around here at the moment, you know?'

I nod thoughtfully. Mary is possibly one of the only people I haven't suspected so far. It's a stretch to imagine the older lady would have any reason to take Saoirse, other than perhaps her strong resentment to the forest and people who trespass in there. That said, who knows any more?

As I head back towards my room, I hear a noise. Stopping in the hotel hallway, I listen carefully. I can hear the wind and sea.

There is a car alarm going off somewhere. I have a sense that something is wrong. The hairs on my arms rise, and I rub them through my robe. I continue walking to my room, slower now. I place the key in the lock and turn it with trepidation, then push open the door and feel the breeze. The window is wide open – not how I left it ten minutes ago – and the curtains blow wildly. The drawers have all been opened. My belongings are all scattered around. The framed photo of me and Violet is propped up on its backboard in the middle of the floor. I edge into the room.

'Hello?'

I can feel my heart in my chest. Then I see it and I almost get sick. In the middle of the bed, there is a dead crow, its eyes glassy. I back out of the room and run. Adrenaline courses through my veins. I reach reception and Mary is gone. I press the bell insistently. She saunters out.

'Everything all right, love?'

'Someone has been in my room!'

'What, just now?'

'Yes.' I am shaking.

'How do you know?' she asks with what feels like exaggerated slowness.

'Everything is all over the place, the window is open and … and there is a dead crow on the bed. They must have got in through the window,' I gabble. 'They could be still hiding …'

Mary picks up the phone and dials a number. I walk in a daze to the couch in the waiting area and sit down. I drift off somewhere. Frozen in time. Mary's voice on the phone sounds very far away.

'… *Break in … come by immediately … okay …*'

Then I hear my name.

'Freya? Freya?'

Mary is handing me a sugary tea.

'I think you're in shock,' she says gently. 'Drink this.'

We both stare at the doors, waiting for the Gardaí.

'A crow,' I say softly. 'How could it be?'

There is a pause.

'You haven't gone near that forest in the past few days, have you?'

I don't reply, but I can see what Mary is alluding to – if the two things are linked, Jack, Kate, Mary, and the villagers might be right about that forest.

COUNTDOWN

One ...

Day Thirteen

Saoirse

Dark clouds whisk the sun away into the night. Through a slit of window, a flash of lightning illuminates the treetops. She tries to think of anything. Spring and lilies. Blizzard-white mornings. The scent of burning peat. The curlews hidden beneath the conifers nearby, waiting for dawn to sing their chipping call. It is torture to be laid so still. Bone-cold and feathered in stone, held together with tightened string. Yet she remains optimistic. After all, you are not gone until you are gone. *Drip drip drip*. Rain seethes through the roof like acid. A maddening song clamours from the bucket. Constant and rhythmic. Her heart mirrors it, hummingbird-slow.

After the thunder dies, a numbness settles. The morning yawns and stretches. Fragments. A meadow pipit lands on the windowsill. *Anthus pratensis*. Rare around here. It hops with delicate feet along the edge of the rough timber. Perches with four toes. It stays with her for a long spell. Tilts its head to one side as though it thinks it's strange for her to be here. After a while, it flies off into the colourless morning. As it disappears, she calls after it in a whisper. *Please. Don't go. Don't leave me.*

46

Day Thirteen

Freya

The village square is full of locals. They stare into the horizon, a fiery amber glow, as twilight takes hold. A swathe of flowers and teddies have been arranged in a vigil outside the steel pointed gates of the school. Ironic, it seems, that it takes a girl to go missing for people to care about her. When she was not missing, she was just a penniless child of a mother with an addiction issue who had died by suicide and a father who had fled. Now she is national news.

There is a desperate feeling in the air as I approach, edging past the people at the back of the throng. Father Maguire stands at the top of the vigil, holding his rosary beads aloft. His eyes are closed and his lips move in silent prayer. I can hear the faint echoes of Hail Marys whispering throughout the crowd. Saoirse has been missing almost a fortnight now.

Hail, Mary, full of grace, the Lord is with thee … Blessed art thou amongst women and blessed is the fruit of thy womb, Jesus …

I move on to the perimeter of the flowers and flickering candles, reading some of the scrawled messages. *Come home, Saoirse. Please come home safe!* I place down a stuffed bear I bought in the local shop for Saoirse and cast my eyes across the people who have gathered. Gardaí hang around nearby. Some rock on their heels and scan the crowd. Others are deep in conversation with each other, but their conversation looks strained.

The choir on the steps, dressed in white robes, begin to sing and I close my eyes, listening as their voices lift into the air. Their song is well-formed and melodic – they are talented for a local choir. I remember myself, singing for an audience, back in the Dublin Gospel Choir. The memory is quickly replaced with another image, of Violet and me singing in the kitchen, Violet clapping her hands along to the music. I turn my head. It is at that moment that I catch sight of a man, standing separate from the crowd. He is not much older than a boy. Eighteen or nineteen, I guess, with his hood pulled up over his head. As we meet eyes, he looks away. I go back to reading the cards and notes but when I look up a second time, he is watching me, more intently now. His eyes flash with something. Judgement? Fear?

I move around the crowd and when I see a space near the back, I stand sidelong to the teddies and flowers. I look out to the sea, which is where the crowd is facing, as if the Gods of the Atlantic Ocean could lure Saoirse back. The choir continue to sing, their voices almost joyous, despite the occasion. As though their song might spirit her home.

Next, they break into the gospel number 'Oh Happy Day'. As they do, I notice a shadow moving towards the flowers where I have just been. The young man who had been watching me now reads the cards for Saoirse. He approaches the teddy that I've left among the other items. I watch as he bends and picks it up. He darts a glance over his shoulder and shoves it inside his hoody. The choir begin to clap and some of the audience join in.

'Hey!' I yell. He looks over, then he turns and runs away up the street. People are too busy watching the choir to notice what is happening.

I sprint after him. In the distance, I can see the man's hood as he skips between people. Where the crowd thins, he pivots down a side street which runs straight down to the harbour. I push past people, but I am not fast enough. At the end of the narrow sloping street, he turns a sharp corner and disappears. I follow him downhill with difficulty, my low heels clicking on the stones, and when I turn the corner, he is no longer there. Gasping for breath and sweating, I curse and scan the beach, then the harbour, but it's no good. He is gone.

PART SIX

47

Day Thirteen

Saoirse

The night will eventually peel away to reveal the orange mouth of morning. She opens her eyes to see the walkie-talkie next to her face. She reaches out and touches it, pressing the button. '*Hello?*' she whispers, her voice shaking, but there is no answer – just an occasional hissing. The frozen air is stark on her skin. It needles through the bug crawl damp. Black shapes hollow against the ochre sky. The light sketches dark green lines. Stretching to where the silver birch lines up next to purple moor-grass. The tattered trail to the forest, where she hoped the search parties would come, lights in hand. Broad-shouldered strangers with foghorn voices, pooling about the forest, calling her name. She could almost picture it now. Almost hear their voices through the silence. She waits for the rattle of metal and blows into her hands continuously. Rubs her feet together to gather a sliver of feeling other than cold. Cheek to wood, the bucket in her eye line. Sometimes the walkie-talkie speaks – the voice of the person keeping her here calling out. Checking she is still alive. Sometimes she calls out to her captor too, pleading that they come – sometimes they reply, other times they do not.

As she drifts back to sleep, huddled under the blanket, she tries to count the days to herself, but she lost track of the hours a long time ago. She tries to picture the views around her home as she closes her eyes. Ravens taking off against a clear blue sky. The shape of the mountain, covered in the peaks of endless trees. A chimney somewhere releasing the smoke from a peat fire, which keeps a family warm.

It is cold today. Autumn has come in fast. She was a baby born of autumn herself. With hair as red as a crab apple tree. But she is also as hardy, as willing to shed her leaves as long as they will grow back in spring. Jack is different. She worries for her little brother. For memories slip away through the avenues of time, leaving only foggy glimpses in the mind. The moon churns over the Atlantic nightly, erasing things. Leaving only spindle trails, silver and white like milkweed. Her brother, little seedling. How easy it might be for him to forget his sister. His roots pulled up from the ground, his memory erased by the people who would replace her in time.

48

Two Months Before Missing

Jack

Aunt Bronagh's back garden is full of wildflowers in bloom. Snapdragons and birds of paradise and wild purple lilies. Jack presses himself against the cool window, his breath steaming up the glass in front of him.

'Yesterday I painted a flower like that one,' Jack says, pressing his finger on the glass.

Aunt Bronagh opens the cupboards. Her kitchen is made for wheelchairs. It is much easier than when she tries to use Jack's kitchen to make things.

'I like painting,' Jack adds quietly to himself. Jack can hear Aunt Bronagh opening a packet. He turns around and watches as she puts some yellow lumps of something in a pan and pours in some water from the tap. She places it on the cooker, takes out a green jar from the cupboard. It is comforting to watch her cooking as his mother had done.

'What do you usually eat for lunch?' Aunt Bronagh asks.

Jack shrugs. He sits upon a leather chair, his bare legs sticking to the seat as he tries to make himself comfortable. Aunt Bronagh lays down the juice in front of Jack. He takes a long gulp, finishing it in one go. He burps.

'Would you like some more?'

Jack nods quickly.

Aunt Bronagh pours another glass.

Jack draws a shape on the wooden table.

'There is a Creature in the forest that not many people know about,' he says. 'We saw it today.'

Aunt Bronagh turns and hands the glass to Jack, who takes it with two hands. 'Is that so?'

Jack nods and takes another long gulp. 'Saoirse said "*Run!*"'

Aunt Bronagh's eyes narrow and she purses her lips.

Jack continues. 'Whenever I go to the forest I see it. It's usually far away, but today it came much closer.'

Aunt Bronagh straightens up and stares at him, then she rolls her eyes. 'I think I know the one you mean.'

'You do?' Jack asks, his eyes widening.

Aunt Bronagh nods again. 'Yes, remind me, what does it look like?'

Jack makes his lips disappear, scrunches up his eyes, then waves his arms around wildly.

'Ah yes, that one. I see it all the time,' she says, sounding bored.

Jack gasps. 'You've seen it too?'

'Yep. In fact, I was going to invite it around for dinner tomorrow.'

'No!'

'I was … I was … and I was going to feed it … roast children!'

Jack giggles as Aunt Bronagh tickles him.

Then he remembers another thing.

'And then after we saw the Creature today … we saw a man.'

'What man?'

'The one that works in the butcher's shop who used to stay in our house. He was watching us. Saoirse said "Don't look back", but there he was, and I did look back and then we ran. Ran away as he watched us. We have seen him near the forest before. He goes walking in there all the time by himself.'

'Mr Fitzgerald?'

Jack nods.

Aunt Bronagh pauses, searching his eyes. She is not laughing any more. She looks very serious. 'If he ever tries to talk to you again and it feels weird, just run away and tell me. Okay?'

Jack nods again.

'Is everything okay at home at the moment, everything with Kate and Saoirse?'

Jack looks down.

'You would tell me if it wasn't?' Aunt Bronagh adds. 'Anything at all. You can tell me. I won't tell Kate. Promise.'

'Okay but … can I … have a bath?' he asks.

Jack sits in the bath. Aunt Bronagh sits outside the door. She had poured all sorts of potions inside and it smells like lavender fields and rosemary from the garden. Jack picks up the bubbles in his hands. He stretches out his legs in the warm water of the long tub and surveys the mountains of bubbles, which look like the mountains from the picture books of Tír na nÓg. He builds a castle of foam and swishes the hot water between his toes, and swims the duck across the water around the moat of the castle.

'Where is my dad now?' Jack asks, his voice echoing on the tiles.

'You know this.' Aunt Bronagh's voice is slightly muffled.

'Tell me again.'

She sighs. 'Your father Cahill is in Dublin, working on the building sites.'

'Why does he never visit?'

'I don't know.'

'Why didn't he come back when Mam died?'

'I don't know Jack, I'm sorry.'

'Are you angry with my dad?'

'Sometimes sisters and brothers do get angry, but I still love him. He's always my brother, no matter what he does wrong.'

Jack is quiet for a moment. He lies back in the warm water. 'Are there monsters and creatures and forests in Dublin?' Jack asks tiredly. He yawns.

'Jack! Stay awake. You can't fall asleep in the bath.'

Jack shifts up a little, splashing the suds. 'I'm awake.'

'Good. But to answer your question, no, I don't think there are monsters or creatures in Dublin. Not many, anyway.'

'I might move there, then. Is there an ocean?'

'There is the Irish Sea. It's calmer, less deep, with fewer waves.'

'Sounds nice. The Atlantic can be too wild,' he adds.

Aunt Bronagh chuckles. 'You do say strange things sometimes, for a little boy.'

'I am not a little boy, I'm a monster!'

Jack roars and then is quiet for a while.

'Do you have many friends?'

'Some,' replies Aunt Bronagh.

'Are they nice?'

'They're okay. You've met some of them, they live in the village. There is Molly and Aoife. You remember them?'

'Not really.'

'Do you have friends?'

'No.'

'What about at school?'

'They call me smelly at school,' replies Jack.

Aunt Bronagh hums. 'That's not very kind. What do you say back?'

'I tell them they stink worse.'

'Good answer. It's the summer holidays, so I guess you've not seen them for a while?'

'Yep,' replies Jack, making the duck swim on the moat again. 'Only Saoirse and the Creature are my friends now.'

Aunt Bronagh is silent for a moment.

'Jack, you know the Creature is not real,' she says. 'If you continue to tell stories like that, they might come true.'

'They're not just stories,' he says. Jack reaches for the towel and climbs out, wrapping the fluffy warm cloth around himself. He looks in the long mirror, at the boy looking back with a clean, wet face: a coward, a monster. A Creature.

49

Day Thirteen

Freya

As I enter the church, the first thing I am aware of is the scent, so familiar from my childhood. There is a certain smell you only get in Mass – a mixture of polish and incense, of dust and marble. A feeling of peace washes over me and I wonder why I don't come back more often. Despite not having the faith myself, there is something about the quietude, the calm, the coolness of the church that feels like a sanctuary.

I wander up the aisle, past the confessional box and effigies, to the carpeted altar with a marble table, adorned with gold and green woven cloths. A statue of Jesus on the cross sits high above, below the stained-glass windows. The statue looks down in quiet judgement.

'Hello, can I help?' Father Maguire says, appearing from a door beside the altar. He is a balding man with wisps of a grey comb-over – neck and shoulders bent forwards. He has removed his flowing gown and is just wearing his black shirt and trousers with his clerical collar.

'I was wondering if I could have a chat with you about Saoirse?'

'Of course.' He nods, an air of calm in his voice.

He picks up a figurine from a mahogany table and I follow him into a side door. It leads into another room, lit up by florescent strip lights. I glance up at a painting of the Virgin Mary, cradling her baby in her arms. Father Maguire offers me a seat. He holds the figurine in the air and places it on another table.

'Saint Anthony,' he says. 'Do you know who he is?'

'No,' I reply. I sit down uneasily and watch as he takes a seat opposite me at the wooden table.

'Patron saint of lost things.' He digs out something from underneath his collar and shows me the gold medal, engraved with a figure. 'I've been wearing this every day since she's been gone. Praying to St Anthony to bring her home.'

His face is haggard and tired-looking. A weak chin and a furrowed brow. A nose that is flared at the nostrils. He looks like he has seen so much in his life – horror, sadness, and pain. He tucks the medal back under his collar. His pale blue gaze seems to dart off occasionally. He looks at his watch, then interlinks his fingers together on the table, like the ceiling of the church itself. I wonder if the rumours about him are true.

'Thanks for agreeing to chat to me,' I start.

'Of course,' he replies.

'It's not just to do with Saoirse … but also the Kellough family, and that forest.'

He raises his bushy white eyebrows, as though he had been expecting this. Am I imagining it or does he look worried, almost frightened at the mention of the Kellough family?

'How can I be of help?' he asks carefully, one deep furrow forming in his brow.

'Well, Kate mentioned you went to their house a few months ago? She said you said you thought they were … haunted.'

He winces, as though in pain at the memory.

'Perhaps they misunderstood … I didn't mean *they* were haunted, I meant, it is as though they were holding on to the haunting of that forest themselves and it is ruining their lives, does that make sense? They are not in touch with the Holy Spirit of our Lord Jesus Christ.'

He begins to cough, banging on his chest with the palm of his hand.

'Excuse me, I am getting over a chest infection, the damp has been particularly bad lately.' He pauses. 'To say they are troubled would be an understatement. Their mother was … She had many men around to the house. I personally would not be surprised if one of those men … took Saoirse.'

He looks over my shoulder towards the back door as though someone might be listening. He leans forwards and begins to whisper.

'I take confession and I'm bound to secrecy. I have never been told anything outright, but some men have alluded to things in confession – not enough to be considered as evidence to the Gardaí, but enough to make me think it could have been one of those men seeing her mother that took Saoirse. If you operate a brothel in your own home, what do you expect?' He grimaces. 'I'm all for women's rights and liberation, but it simply was not safe for those children. Lucy was taking prescription drugs, she was drinking and their father had left, leaving them all vulnerable. The church would have helped her financially and with food. I told her that many times. She wouldn't accept help, too proud to accept charity, but it would have been better for her and her children all round if she had.'

We sit in silence a while. I think about Father Maguire himself, having children over to the house. As if suspecting what I am thinking, he continues.

'Look, I know what people say about me, but it's not true. I only held a couple of lunches for the children from disadvantaged backgrounds – Saoirse and Jack were among those children. My housekeeper, Brenda, was there the entire time in the room with us; it was just a feast of good food for them. It was to help them,' he says firmly. 'I'd never hurt a child. I don't have it in me to hurt anyone …' He looks almost ashamed of this admittance. 'The amount of people who have taken advantage of me in my life because I'm too … soft,' he adds, looking sad. 'The world is made of all sorts of people. Some of us are too soft, and some don't have any conscience at all, it would seem.'

He looks into my eyes for a long moment. I believe him, I realise. It's in his tone – and as I look at his face, I can see there is nothing there other than concern, sadness, and worry for Saoirse.

I decide to ask him the other thing I wanted to ask, before our time is up.

'Can you tell me about the forest?' I ask. 'Everyone I talk to tells me the same thing, that it's haunted and to stay away. Is that true, in your opinion?'

He looks into my eyes with a serious expression.

'That forest is not safe,' he says in a matter-of-fact voice. 'That is true.'

'Why?'

'There is probably no time to go into it now—'

'Please,' I say. 'It's important.'

He relents, glancing at the clock. 'Fine, well, it's just that … women and children were killed there in awful ways. You've probably heard about the Magdalene Laundry?'

I nod.

'It was a big house in the middle of that forest. The building was since destroyed, but things won't grow on the space where the building was before. People call it the Hollowing Place.'

I remember. I feel a chill run over my skin.

'Have you seen anything yourself?' I ask.

'Multiple things. Things that would make your skin crawl. People think a … a "creature" lives in there.' He thinks for a moment. 'People think the forest was desecrated by the atrocities in there, so they are afraid to mistreat it, afraid to litter, afraid to cause any damage at all to the place. It's my belief that, if there is something there, it's the spirits of the bad people who hurt those women that haunt that forest.'

'The nuns?'

He nods. 'The nuns, and whoever else was there harming the women.'

I rub my temples, thinking over the last few weeks. I can see what Father Maguire is saying. It is the human evils that have caused such fear and rumours to linger over time. That's what is really 'haunting' the forest – human evil, not the supernatural evil that people think.

'Listen,' Father Maguire says. 'I know you haven't asked for my advice on this but if I were you, I'd leave this place and go home as soon as you're able to.'

'What makes you say that?' I ask.

'If I know anything about this place, about that forest, I know it can get under people's skin – give you bad dreams, mess with your head. You seem stressed. Best to get out now.'

I want to argue but he's right about the bad dreams, and right about the stress. And I've thought about leaving – my contract is due for renewal again soon. I think about Jack and Saoirse and the family. I imagine leaving, going home and forgetting it all. Guilt has told me it would be wrong. Is that healthy guilt or does it belong elsewhere? It is so difficult to know.

Father Maguire clears his throat. He leans back and looks at the clock.

'Sorry to rush you off, but there are other people who want to speak to me tonight. This whole thing with Saoirse has really opened up a can of worms here in Drumsuin. If you can't leave, my advice is to go back to wherever you are staying and get a good night's sleep.'

'Right,' I say. 'Thank you.'

He meets my eyes with a look of concern and sadness.

'No problem. Good luck,' he says, as if genuinely meaning it. With that, he stands and leads me to the door.

Though it's pitch dark outside, and I'm in a new room on the third floor – different view, different layout – I check, for the umpteenth time, that the window is locked. Not that anyone is likely to climb up this high – they'd be seriously injured if they fell – but who knows?

I glance nervously around at the walls. *You're safe.* I remind myself, rubbing my own forearm. I was thankful Mary had given me a new room. That said, I have already peered under the bed in a childlike fashion, investigated the wardrobe and snapped back the shower curtain like I was in a horror movie. I hum to myself to try to cheer my spirits, a song the choir had sang earlier at the vigil. The phone calls out, piercing the silence. I jolt and pick up the receiver from the bedside table.

'Hello?'

Walter's voice comes through the receiver. 'How are you after earlier?' he asks. The gleaming mirror across from the bed reflects the moonlight coming in from the bay.

'As good as I can be,' I reply.

'Yes, it must have been a shock,' he says, thoughtfully. 'Any updates on the case?' he adds.

'Nothing on my side,' I say, looking at my watch. It is almost time for bed. 'Except,' I say, thinking of the young man I saw before I went to Father Maguire's. 'I saw someone strange at the vigil this evening. He stole a teddy I had left among the flowers. I chased him, but he disappeared.'

'What did he look like?'

'I didn't get a good look. He was wearing a hoody, and it was getting dark.'

'Okay,' he murmurs. 'I'll get someone to go down and check the cameras around there around the time it happened. What time was it, roughly?'

'Around five thirty, five forty-five, I think?'

'Okay, thanks for letting me know.' There is a pause. 'I've been meaning to ask, are you okay to renew your contract for a third week?'

This is my moment to say if I want to leave. I realise I can't.

'Sure,' I reply letting out a breath.

'Sorry it's not being resolved as quickly we expected. With all the new things going on, like the body being found … I can't imagine you leaving would help matters, especially with Jack.'

297

I feel a warm glow. At least Walter thinks my presence useful. 'By the way, our technical forensics team think Saoirse might have been communicating on a walkie-talkie.'

'A walkie-talkie? But I thought a baby monitor picked up her voice?'

'Apparently baby monitors are known to interfere with cordless phones, radios, police scanners – that kind of thing.'

'So, the baby monitor picked up the walkie-talkie?'

'Yes. According to our tech guy, it's not unusual for them to cross paths because of the way wireless signals tend to operate. He also said the monitor can be affected by the weather and the time of year. Some parts of the atmosphere are more charged in winter than in summer, which means they can pick up on radio waves from more faraway locations. So she might be within a few miles, but she also might be further away than we thought.'

I reflect on what this means. Even a few miles increases the volume of buildings and other places the Gardaí will have to search, which means finding her could take longer. Walter sounds dejected, fed up. This is not good news for the case, or for Saoirse.

'Additionally, as I'm obliged to keep victims of crimes informed and updated, I was calling to let you know the progress on the break-in.' My eyes land on the framed photograph of Violet and I on the hotel table. 'As you probably know, we've had the forensics team down to the hotel. According to forensics, there was no sign of forced entry or of anyone climbing in through the window. No footprints or scuffles or dirt or fibres from clothing caught in the window catch. It's as if it was a ghost.'

I feel goosebumps rise on my skin at this last observation, then look around the room, a feeling of frustration in my muscles. I can feel my jaw tighten.

'The drawers were all wide open. There was a dead crow on the bed,' I remind him.

'I know it is strange, but one conclusion is that it might be the bird who caused the mess. Your windows were open, it flew in – crows are notorious for being scavengers.'

'But what if someone broke in?'

'Mary said no one strange was seen coming in the front entrance at that time – it's unlikely someone got in another way.'

'What about another guest?'

'They'd have to have had a key. I suppose it's possible but we don't have any evidence of that. Sorry, Freya. Wild birds have been known to lift things with their claws. Most likely the bird flew in panicked, and then it died on your bed.'

I put my hand to my forehead and stare in the mirror at myself. My hair looks dishevelled. I try to channel my frustration into getting through to him.

'Really, Walter?' I say, trying to appeal to him as a human, not just as a detective.

'You don't think it's more than that? What about CCTV?' I ask.

He sighs, as if sounding disappointed for me. 'I'm sorry,' he says quietly. 'We've checked the CCTV. There is no sign of any person entering the building.'

'What about the camera further down the seafront ... outside the newsagent's?'

'MacCauley's said the footage was wiped. Sorry, we've tried all we can,' he continues. 'Thanks for understanding.'

'Sure, thanks anyway,' I say, feeling disappointed.

'Really, I am genuinely sorry,' he repeats, sounding like he is. 'Let's catch up again tomorrow,' he adds, his tone gentle.

We bid goodbye and I hang up the phone. I look around the room and wonder if it really was a bird, and if so, is the forest haunting me too?

50

Day Fourteen

Jack

Jack counts on his fingers. When it gets to ten, he needs to stop and start again. He counts to ten over and over. *One potato, two potato, three potato, four ... eight potato, nine potato, ten.* He and Freya are in the sitting room, in the same place they were on the first day. Freya's sleeves are rolled up to her elbow, and her pen makes a scratching sound across the page. Jack draws a shape with his toe on the sofa. He can feel something in the air. A thick, damp feeling, as though the Creature is nearby. He looks out the window and watches the rain, listens to the tick of the clock. Jack thinks of all the meals he has eaten since the first day Saoirse went missing. Sandwiches, cereal, stew. What if Saoirse has not eaten since then?

'Jack?'

He looks up.

'You told me about a woman before.'

Jack is silent.

'Can you tell me more about her?'

Jack does not reply.

'Perhaps we could do a creative exercise now?' Freya asks.

Freya lays out Jack's paintings all around the room. Everywhere, covering all the tables and chairs. Jack is going to tell a story, not with words but with pictures.

He stands up and steps around the room one by one, careful to avoid the cracks in the floorboards because that is bad luck sometimes. He peers down at the paintings. Oblong circles and stripes, splotches, dots, and planets. Stick figures and monsters with pointed teeth. Jagged, ready to bite. Frosty branches, rocks, and roads. A painting of a little boy. He hands it to Freya.

Jack keeps going around and he finds the next one. Then the next, then the next. He hands them all to Freya and she places them in a careful line. Jack feels a tightness in his chest now; a dizzying fear. He finds a picture he is looking for. She takes it from him and puts it down next to the rest. He finds a few more. As he does, he thinks back and remembers. *Saoirse hides. Jack counts.*

There is only one painting left now. Freya goes over to it. The picture is of a person standing near the edge of the forest.

'Who is this?' she asks. 'Is this the person dressed up as the Creature that you saw take Saoirse?'

Jack nods, pinching the skin between his finger and thumb, then pinching the other side too, so it is even. Jack looks at the painting of the figure.

There is the sound of an engine now. Car lights shine into the window. Freya looks out and Jack follows her. It is Aunt Bronagh's car. Freya looks at the last painting again and puts it down at the end of the line. Now there is a whole line of paintings on the floor, which tell Jack's story. Once secrets are out, they feel smaller. Their mouths close and they stop eating you alive. Jack stops counting. Takes a deep breath and looks out of the window, watching as Aunt Bronagh pushes her wheelchair towards the house.

51

Day Fourteen

Freya

'Come through,' Walter says, his face grave as he gestures to the double doors. I can smell the sandwiches from the incident room. As I pass, I look in to see Gardaí milling around in there, sipping on cups of coffee and tea.

I sit down opposite him. There are dark rings under his eyes, which are bloodshot. I wonder about him for a moment – his house, how he lives with his wife gone. Or perhaps he lives with Alice now – I can't remember if he said they lived together. Their relationship was fairly new at six months, so it was likely they did not. Does he look after himself with full dinners or does he live on convenience food and sandwiches at the station? I imagine you have to be tough to be a member of the Gardaí. I think about how the men are in the local pubs in Ireland. How they all stare up at the TV screens and sip on their pints in between talk of the weather, the hurling, the GAA. There is no space to talk about their feelings. Instinctively, I feel a glimmer of sympathy for him. Empathy. I cannot let it grow, though. There is too much going on for me to let it cloud my judgement.

'Jack has drawn something. I think you need to have a look at it. It's a woman … dressed up as the Creature. He says he saw this woman carry Saoirse away.'

'What?'

302

'Yes,' I say, and pass him the painting. 'He finally remembered.'

'Right,' he says, nodding thoughtfully. 'So this, together with what Saoirse said over the baby monitor, is fairly convincing evidence that it *is* a woman who took her.'

He examines the picture. There is a sliver of mid-length dark hair poking out from the side of the feathers and branches. Two feet with boots on underneath the costume. It is unmistakably a woman, even drawn with Jack's childish hand.

'Who is this?'

'He doesn't know and he can't say if she is familiar to him, but this is crucial. We need to find out who this is.'

He nods. 'We do. Women don't usually commit these kinds of crimes, especially ones involving other women ... I mean, it's less likely to happen, but it would seem it really is a woman we need to be looking for now.'

I think back over all the women who have gone missing in the forest over the past twenty years.

'That reminds me ... something that's been bothering me,' I say. 'How was Ellie's body only just found now?'

Walter looks guilty, almost ashamed. I know a girl or young woman has gone missing every six or seven years in the forest. Why is it only now they have been searching properly?

'Cadaver dogs ...' He seems to search for how to explain it. 'They weren't commonly used by the Gardaí in Ireland in the 1970s. Not when Ellie first went missing in 1975, twenty years ago, and especially not in this area. Until Saoirse went missing and it caused a media storm, we never searched the forest as thoroughly as we have done in the past few days, not with dogs and not with such intensity.'

'But what about the other missing girls – Maeve Murphy and Ashling McGill?'

'We are now trying to connect the dots between Saoirse and these other missing girls. I do think they might be connected somehow. The time gap between the disappearances could be a coincidence, of course, but it also might not be. Simultaneously, we've been looking high and low for Ellie's mother so we can deliver the body to her, help her lay her daughter to rest. The HSE and Gardaí in Dublin have been trying to track her down, but with no luck. As you know, we released the information about Ellie O'Connor's body being found, and that should have made the national news now. Gardaí in Dublin have been to her mother's house, but there is no sign of her, and none of her relatives have been able to contact her. We've got a lot on our plate with finding Saoirse right now, we're stretched so thin … but it's like Celia O'Connor has fallen off the face of the earth. It's the strangest thing.

'Anyhow, thank you for this drawing. It's very helpful.'

I think about the people who could, to my mind, have taken Saoirse. Every single one of them, apart from the young man in the hoody, has now been ruled out – and he no longer fits the suspect profile now we think she was taken by a woman. Maybe a woman none of us had ever met before was responsible. An outsider, as the locals would say.

Either way, something in me has been ignited since I came here and I couldn't stay away from this case – not to save my life.

I leave the Garda station and that's when I glimpse him again, watching me from outside the café across the street. His hood is pulled up and he looks jumpy, apprehensive. It is the same person as the other night – same snub nose, same boyish features. When he sees me, he turns and moves away, almost as though he is expecting I will follow and make chase.

'Hey!'

Refusing to let him get away this time, I sprint after him. He jogs up a lane and I call out again. He swivels his head to see me, but keeps on running. It feels as though he is half-trying to get away, but also wants me to catch up – though I have no idea why. He looks over his shoulder at me a second time, then trips over a kerb. It gives me enough time to catch up. He stumbles and continues to run but I am already at his heels. I grab a fistful of his hoody.

'Get off!' he shouts. His eyes flash with anger. I let go. He glares at me, breathless.

Now I am closer I can see how young the man looks. Stubbly, blue-eyed. Shaved head underneath the hood. He is just a teenager, perhaps seventeen or eighteen.

'You stole that gift from the vigil,' I accuse.

'So?' he shoots back. 'And what?'

I catch my breath. 'Why would you do that?'

He pulls a face. 'What's it to you?'

I edge closer.

'It was meant for Saoirse.'

'If it was hers to start with, it was hardly a gift,' he replies defiantly.

Hers to start with? What does he mean by that?

Through my work, I have met many children with many issues, a whole range of disorders. Something that is true of most children, and of most people, is that they don't do things without reason – whether that be for attention or because it means something to them. The first option is out, because he had not meant to be seen. Though he did seem to want to be chased. I decide to hedge my bets and try for the other option: the teddy means something to him.

'What do you mean it was hers? Do you know something about where she is?'

He shakes his head, but his expression is guilty. He bites his lip.

'What is it?' I ask.

He stares at me.

'Saoirse used to go to school with my little brother Paddy. They were friends. Well, she was his girlfriend.'

His eyes begin to shine. There is more, something he is not telling me.

'What is it?' I demand. 'Tell me or I'll tell the Gardaí about you. You'll be arrested for withholding vital information on a missing person investigation.'

He looks worried all of a sudden. 'I did see her,' he admits.

He casts his head over his shoulder, as though someone might be coming for him.

'When and where?' I ask. I take a step closer to him. My voice echoes a little in the cobblestone laneway, and I'm suddenly aware someone might be listening. I glance up at the windows of the surrounding houses, but no one seems to be there.

'I saw Saoirse the day she went missing.' He looks over his shoulder again. 'Near the forest.'

'Have you told the Gardaí? They've been appealing for information – it was even on *Crimeline*. Did you call in?'

He shakes his head.

'Why not?'

I edge closer still. I feel strange now. Dissociated, as though I'm watching myself from a windowsill up above where we are stood.

'The pigs – they don't do anything around here,' he says. 'They just accuse you – they accused my little brother, he's only fourteen and they came around trying to terrify him. He did nothing wrong.'

'Surely you'd just be helping Saoirse if you say something.'

His face reddens. He looks as though he is ready to cry. 'The teddy, it was the same one she had.'

'I bought it, in the local shop.'

'No. Paddy gave it to her, as a present.'

'Could there be more than one of the same teddy?'

He stares at me, his chin lowered, his eyelid twitching, his lips begin to quiver. 'I suppose.'

'So why did you assume it was the same one?'

He frowns.

'I'm not going to hurt you,' I hear myself whisper, and take a guess. 'Just tell me who you saw her with, if you saw her with anyone at all.'

He puts his face in his hands. 'It was a woman.'

A woman again.

'What did this woman look like? Did you know her from the village?' I ask, taking another step towards him. He looks over his fingers. Then he stretches his finger out and I realise he is pointing. I look over my shoulder expecting to see someone behind me but there is no one.

'Who?'

'She looked like you,' he whispers.

The boy had thought the woman he'd seen with Saoirse was me. Who is this woman? My mind spins as I jog up the hotel stairs. I slide my key in and push the door. I sit on the bed for a moment, deep in thought. I need to tell Walter. The brother of Saoirse's boyfriend had seen Saoirse with a woman that very day she went missing. Someone who looked like me. He might be able to help investigators draw the woman to publicise her image, or even point to a photograph of her.

Before I pick up the phone to call Walter, I have another strange feeling.

I grab my briefcase. I haven't checked inside it since my room was broken into. I open it. My notebook where I jotted down thoughts and hunches on the case is gone.

I sit back on the bed and put my face in my hands. How could I have missed that the notebook had been taken? Perhaps it was the fact that I hadn't looked properly since the break-in; I had been too frightened, and then too busy, to notice.

I take out the manila folder. The one I keep Jack's notes in. Holding my breath slightly, I open it and realise the most important item of all is missing: Jack's counselling notes. I only carried my most recent session notes with me back to the house each time to pick up on the previous session, so I hadn't realised until now. All of his counselling notes from the last two weeks are missing. Someone wanted to know what was going on in Jack's mind and what he was revealing to me – and I had a feeling that someone, had something to do with Saoirse's disappearance.

* * *

I curse. Fear and confusion swim through me. This was not a theft motivated by money. I pace for a moment, trying to decide what to do. I glance up at the picture on the wall. It is of the sea, a local image, snapped, late at night. The Atlantic Ocean is calm and up above it sits a full moon, shimmering across the water. *Think*, I urge myself.

I look down at the *Drumsuin Examiner* which I bought this morning, and every morning since I arrived here almost two weeks ago. I open up the newspaper and look at the front page. Saoirse is in the headlines again. Today the headline reads:

HOPE IN CASE OF MISSING SAOIRSE

Regretfully, someone had leaked the baby monitor story to the press, and now it was in the news that she was possibly still alive. This means whoever kidnapped her has the upper hand on the Gardaí's searches.

Every day of the past two weeks the *Drumsuin Examiner*'s headlines and main stories have all been about Saoirse – apart from the two days they reported on Ellie O'Connor's body being found. Still, the second and third pages on those days still had updates on Saoirse's case, and mentions of her in connection to Ellie's case, wondering if the same person had committed both crimes. Speculating whether there was a serial killer in the area, after all the missing girls in the forest.

I look at the front cover, at the black-and-white photograph. It's of the volunteers yesterday, combing the local farmlands. They had a warrant to search several sheds and barns which, rumour had it, seemed suspicious. In the background of the photo, I notice a familiar face. It catches my eye because all the volunteers in the photograph are looking at the ground for clues but this person is looking directly at the photographer. At the camera. From behind a bunch of volunteers you could almost miss it. Her face looks guilty and hollow, unsmiling and not like

308

the other times we had met. It is as though the camera could see right through her. *Alice.*

I go and get the other newspapers. Something in my gut tells me she will be in other photographs and I am right. One by one, I rifle through each paper. There she is on day one, day three, day five, day seven, day eight, day eleven … she is in so many of the photographs. Almost every time looking at the camera.

The hairs on my arm prickle. I can't tell Walter, not yet. He might not believe me. Or worse, he might be involved too. *Stay in your lane,* he warned me, and while that might have been a genuine attempt to keep me on track with Jack, what if he has something to hide? Hurriedly, I pick up the phone and dial reception.

'Mary, can you look up an address for me in the phone book please?'

She pauses a moment. 'Sure. What's the name?'

I glance at one of the close-up photographs of Alice with two other volunteers. Underneath, the newspaper had written their names alongside the photo, in left to right order.

'Alice … Alice Brown.'

PART SEVEN

52

Day Fourteen

Freya

Alice's house sits adjacent to a row of six houses which border the forest, further up the mountain. It is silent up here, apart from some distant birds calling out. The house itself is covered in ivy, obscured by bushes. A neighbour, a man in his sixties, is digging in the garden next door.

'Are you okay?' he calls to me as I get out from my car.

'Hi. I'm just here to see Alice,' I say. 'Do you know if she's at home?'

'The new woman who moved in a few months ago? No, I believe she's out.'

There is a pause. He has a full beard and is a short man, wiry, with upright shoulders that look like they could carry a weight if they wanted to. He is standing tall, solid, studying me as though I am a potential threat.

'I'm a friend of hers,' I explain. 'I couldn't reach her by phone so I decided to come over and check she's okay.'

He crosses his arms. 'She might be at work.'

'I might go knock anyway, just to check,' I say. 'Maybe if she hears my voice?'

He frowns and watches me intently as I approach the house.

I open the gate and head up the narrow footpath. Scattered autumn leaves have formed a mulch on the path. The landscape is overgrown and doesn't seem to have been tended to in years. Weeds and wildflowers have overtaken any manicured garden that may have been here before. A murky green pond that looks as though it had formerly housed fish now only buzzes with flies.

I rap on the door and wait a minute, looking over my shoulder. The neighbour is still watching me. I avert my gaze. Nervously, I peer through the glass, but there is no movement. A coat hangs on the bannisters, and a child's bucket and spade are below the window beside a line of shoes. I stroll around and peep in through another window. There is a sofa and chairs, a bookshelf.

Without looking back at the neighbour, I enter through the creaky side gate and turn down the side of the house. The back garden is wide and lustrous, but rather overgrown, with a greenhouse at the back.

I carefully step through the long grass to the greenhouse and peek in. There are gardening gloves, a spade, herbs, and lots of pots. It is sparse in there, perhaps due to the time of year or the lack of recent care, and there are plenty of dead plants. I nosy around for a bit, then all of a sudden something catches my eye. A piece of paper whips into the air and lands in the hedge nearby. It is florescent yellow. A Post-it note. I go over and pluck it from between some twigs. On it is scrawled a shopping list. It has to be recent, as the paper is not wet. *Butter, milk, tomatoes, cereal, crackers, bread* – it reads. I tuck it in my pocket. Looking around, I feel a little disappointed. I don't know what I had hoped to find. I feel uneasy all of a sudden. There is nothing here, but now I am an intruder – lurking in Alice's back garden, alone. I realise I should go.

When I get back around the front, I pretend to scribble a note and pop it in the letterbox. I amble back down the path.

'No luck?' he calls out.

I shake my head. I turn and head back to my car.

'I'd stay away,' he calls after me.

I turn around.

'Excuse me?'

'You'll become like them if you spend too much time with them.'

'Who?'

'The Gardaí, the pigs. Awful people – professional snitches the lot of them, and corrupt to boot. That is who you're working for, isn't it?'

'No,' I reply, sharply. 'Like I say, I'm just a friend of Alice's.'

I take one last look at Alice's house before I get back into my car and slam the door.

53

One Week Before Missing

Jack

Everything starts with sin and ends in a confession. This place is familiar, from most weeks attending with his mother, and then with Kate. He goes to Mass when they draw spots on people's foreheads with ash and when there is a crooked nativity with the stable and Mary – the cattle surrounding the crib with the three wise men. He goes to Mass when it is raining and when it is snowing, even when it is sunny.

The church in the early morning feels like an umbrella for the rain. When you die you go to church, and when you are born you take a name at its altar. Jack cannot remember taking a name. But here he is with a name, inside the sanctuary of its clove smell. Near the watchful statues.

He views himself from the altar. From up there he can see a little boy standing in the middle of the empty church, a boy who has just eaten a tangerine and has the peel in his pockets. The boy who stands in between the rows of pews with his hands by his sides and who casts a shadow much longer than himself.

Jack comes back into his own eyes. Scans the stained glass above. A scene with the Virgin Mary and the baby Jesus. A mam and her baby. Jack looks at the top of the church near the altar where he once made his Holy Communion.

As he walks up the aisle Jack can hear his echoing footsteps. There is a flash of soundless light waves from outside. The rain hammers like rice on the windows far up above and he touches each pew as he counts the seconds. *One, two, three, four, five.* Then comes the roar from the sky and the rumble. The storm is five miles away. The green light is on at the top of the confessional box which means it is empty. The name on the door reads *Father Maguire*. He knocks. There is a pause.

'Enter,' the priest's voice says.

Jack opens the door and steps inside the box that smells like wood and varnish. He sits up onto the red cushion. There is a scraping sound, and a glimmer of light appears. The priest opens the slat. Jack's head barely reaches the bottom of the gap. He can see the diamond shapes of the holes in between. Through it, he sees the shadows of a person with tufts of white hair. Jack feels his mouth dry up. He feels nervous sitting there with the priest waiting for him to talk.

'I can't remember what to say.'

'Bless yourself.'

Jack puts his hand to his head and then to each shoulder.

'How long has it been since your last confession?'

'Crocuses were coming up through the frost.'

'Oh yes, it has certainly been a while, then.' He hears Father Maguire chuckle a little. 'What brings you here today, dear boy?'

'I'm worried I've done something wrong.'

Jack looks at the pool of water which has formed below his feet, dripping from his boots after coming in from the rain.

'Go on,' the voice says.

'It's my mam. I have been wishing for her to come back. I'm worried it is my fault she's gone.'

The priest sighs. 'She is gone away?'

Jack nods, and then remembers he can't be seen. 'She is dead.'

'Oh, I'm very sorry.'

There is silence.

'And the sin?'

317

'I keep wishing for her to come back. I know you're not meant to wish people back from Heaven, where they are happy with God.'

'You cannot bring people back from the dead in any way at all. Though it is not a sin to wish for it.'

Jack nods.

'Now I have a question for you,' says the priest. Jack waits, wondering what it might be. 'What are you worried about? Why do you think it's your fault she's gone?'

Jack looks at the diamond gaps.

'I don't know, but I am scared that they will put me in prison.'

'What, a little boy like you?'

'Ye.'

There is a long silence.

'Are you there?' the voice says.

Jack opens the door. He walks quickly down the aisle and looks back. The green light is still on. The priest does not come out to look at the little boy who had visited. Instead, he just lets him go.

54

Day Fourteen

Freya

There she is. I breathe out a sigh of relief as I approach the Garda station to see Alice outside. She bends low over something feathery. On the ground next to her is a bunch of bright flowers. As I approach, she looks up at me. I search her eyes a moment, as though I might find an answer there.

'There's a bird, it fell down here,' she says, her eyes full of tears. 'From the sky.'

She points up. She has wrapped her cardigan around it. The pigeon has its eyes half-open, as though it is close to death, as though it is suffering. Its breathing is laboured – heavy and slow.

I kneel down next to her.

'Do you know if I can bring it somewhere?' she asks me. 'A local vet, or anything?'

'I'm not sure. I think I saw a vet on the high street, you might be able to try there?'

She nods.

I look at her. A tear tips over her lower eyelid and she rubs it away.

'Gosh, I'm sorry. I don't know what has come over me.'

'Are you all right?'

'It's just this case … everything. It's so tiring, I haven't stopped. Walter hasn't stopped. And I'm so worried we won't find her, you know?'

I feel guilty all of a sudden. This woman in front of me clearly is not the type of person to kidnap a child. On the contrary, she seems kind and compassionate. She seems exhausted by the case and I know how she feels. I feel this way too – almost depressed about the whole thing. It feels futile knowing Saoirse is alive and we still can't find her.

Concern is now etched onto Alice's face. 'You seem upset too,' she notes.

I look down. 'Yes, I am upset,' I admit. 'It's tough, this case, and it brings up my own stuff too … past stuff,' I explain.

'Walter told me, you know. Sorry, he wasn't gossiping, but he told me about your daughter. I am so … so sorry. I can't imagine losing a child. Trying to get Jack to open up. It must bring all of it back up for you. Your own daughter?'

'Sort of,' I admit, sadness rising in my chest. I want to cry – to lean on Alice and sob, to tell her about the past paranoid few hours. I want to apologise for suspecting her.

'Is there anyone you think it is?' she asks me in a low voice. I think about my hunches. There is no one left. Nobody I think could have done it. All I know now is that it's a woman.

'No,' I say softly.

'Me neither. I'm all out of ideas. I think it must be someone from out of town.' She looks down at the pigeon. 'Oh, this poor bird. I'd better get a cardboard box from the station for this little one. I'll try that vet on the high street, they might know what to do.'

She stands and picks up the bunch of dahlia roses, chrysanthemums, daisies, intertwined with red berries she dropped. I glance at the whites, reds, and oranges. Something in the orange of the flowers makes me think of Saoirse. I stand up too.

'Hopefully it recovers and I can set it free,' she says sadly, as though she knows it will probably perish. 'I hate seeing animals die,' she adds.

'Where is Walter?' I ask.

'Oh, he's off interviewing witnesses right now.' She nods to the flowers. 'I have to give these flowers to the butcher, Mr Fitzgerald. He gave me free meat the other day for the Kellough family, and meat for me and Walter, so this is a thank you.'

'I hope you have a nice day,' I say sincerely.

As I walk back to the hotel, I feel embarrassment and disappointment mixed with frustration. If it isn't Alice, then who is it – and will we ever get closer to finding out who took Saoirse?

My room feels cold. I stare out of the window at the sea, with its white horses dancing on the surface. I have showered and tidied the room, and I have turned up the radiator, but I am still shivering. What am I still doing here? Had the haunting of the forest spread onto me too? After all, they couldn't find any evidence a person had broken into my room, but yet a dead crow had ended up on my bed.

I pace for a while, wondering who I can talk to. I don't want to worry my daughter, and I somehow don't feel like I want to talk to anyone else involved in the investigation, like Garda Morris.

Decisively, I grab my key and head down to the reception area.

'Yes, love?' Mary asks, looking up from the desk. I look around me. Thankfully, the reception is empty of any other guests.

'I need your help with something. I've been into the forest. I think – this is going to sound mad – but I think it is haunting me.'

Mary nods. I feel relief. I can tell she understands.

'Take a seat,' she says, pointing to the couch in the small lobby. She comes around the desk and sits down opposite me.

'What's been going on?' she asks.

'I don't know but it feels like it is haunting me. And another thing, I also think someone, a human, wants me to leave.'

I think back to the last few days. There was the young man Paddy's brother – the one who thought he had seen me with Saoirse. I don't think he had anything to do with it, but it had still shaken me. There had also been the letter to Walter, pretending to be me. As I am mulling it over, I look across the table at a piece of hotel paper with handwriting on.

'Wait, hang on, one second.'

I lean down and zip open my bag. I rummage around and then I find it and pull it out – the shopping list I found in Alice's back garden. I keep digging in my bag and find the other thing I've kept – the Post-it that was left on my car windscreen not long after I arrived here. *Back in Five.* I place them down, side by side on the table.

'Would you say they look like the same handwriting?'

Mary leans forwards, pulling her reading glasses up again.

'Yes, they do. The loops and spaces, the roundness of the letters.'

'I have to go,' I say, standing up.

'You're going home now?'

'No, I need to check something.'

'You're not doing anything stupid, are you?'

'Not really,' I lie.

She thinks for a moment.

'How about I come with you? I know this place better than you. Whatever you are doing, it will be easier to have me with you.'

That is probably true.

'But you might not agree with what I am about to do,' I say hesitantly.

'Try me.'

'It's Alice ... your friend. How close are you?'

'She's more like an acquaintance. She hasn't lived here long – I've been friendly to her because she's helped out at the hotel. She seems keener than me on being friends, if that makes any sense?'

'It does. What if I told you I thought she might have something to do with Saoirse ... with her going missing?'

She is thoughtful a moment.

'I'd say I have no idea if you're right, but then, I've no idea if you're wrong. She's a blow-in, I don't know her too well ...' Mary looks thoughtful. 'What makes you think she's involved?'

'This handwriting, it's the same. She left a note on my car, and there's been some other things. It's just a hunch, but will you come with me?'

'Where?'

'To her house.'

Mary thinks a moment.

'Okay,' she says. 'You're going to try and speak to her?'

'Well, perhaps ... But ideally, I want Alice *not* to be there. I went there but I might have missed something. It's just a hunch, but I just feel like there is something inside that house – whether it is clues or Saoirse herself. I need to look inside.'

I am unsure whether revealing my full plan to Mary is the right thing to do, but it is better for her to know before she comes with me.

'Fine,' she says decisively. 'I'll come. I just hope you're right,' she says, giving me a withering look.

We walk to the door.

'What about the hotel?'

'I'll close the front desk. We are not expecting anyone in or out for the next few hours.'

'Okay,' I say. My heart is beating fast now. I can't figure out if it is nerves, or excitement.

As we glide past the edge of the forest in my car, shadows flick over our faces. I might be about to humiliate myself. I could be completely wrong about Alice – the helpful volunteer, treasure of the community. What if I get in trouble with the Gardaí for getting involved without permission? And what if Alice is there, or shows up as I'm searching?

I fret, running through the evidence in my mind. There is the handwriting, for a start. She had clearly left that note on my car. Then there are the photographs of Alice in the newspaper, her odd expression staring at the camera, and the young man who thought someone who looked like me was with Saoirse on the very day she disappeared. Alice could look a lot like me from a distance. We are the same height and roughly the same age – we also have a similar lean build, and the same hair colour and skin tone. She knows where the master keys are kept in the hotel from her time working there, and she knows enough about the case to have taken my counselling notes if she thought Jack was leading me towards her. Who else would think to do that? Jack had seen a woman in the forest – *a woman*, not a man. Didn't so many perpetrators hide in plain sight? Helping out with cases like this – appearing to search for clues? While she did *seem* compassionate and caring as a person, the matching handwriting made me wonder if my instincts had been right after all.

As my own mind races, Mary sits in the tense silence, taking in the view out the window.

'Have you ever believed something and people thought you were mad?' I ask Mary.

We enter another patch of dense forest.

'Many times,' she says keeping her gaze on the trees. 'No one ever believed me about the things that I've seen in there. But I don't lie.'

'What have you seen?' I ask.

She continues to look out as if staring into the past.

'You know that creature they all talk about?'

I nod.

'Well, I saw it. It is a real thing. It chased me out of there. I was absolutely petrified.'

'How did it look?'

'Dark, tree-like … covered in leaves and branches and roots. But it could move – it sort of seemed to hover.'

'Strange,' I reply.

'Yes, it was. I told a few people who asked me what I expected going in there. A few others thought I was making it up, so I kept it to myself after that. I was embarrassed people might think I was mad or attention-seeking. Whether it was real or my eyes playing tricks on me, though, I never went back in there again after that.'

Most people don't believe in monsters – not fictional ones, anyway. Monsters are usually humans. But Mary and the people in this village seem to be the exception – they do believe.

'When did that happen?' I ask, keeping my focus on the road ahead of me. You can't take your eyes off it around here – it is too perilous. One wrong move and you could be staring head-long into the beam of another car or a truck.

'A good six or seven years ago now.'

I try to think about how that would be, to live so close to a place that had left you so terror-stricken.

'Do you know where Alice's house is?' she asks suddenly, changing the subject.

'Yes, I came up here earlier. Can I ask you a favour?'

'Sure,' Mary replies.

'When we get to her house, I just need you to stay in the car and keep watch for me. If anyone comes to the house while I'm in there, or you see the neighbour, you try and distract them from going in.'

'How will I warn you?'

'Beep the horn. I'll hear it and come out as soon as I can.'

Mary nods. The fields flit by as we leave a patch of forest and head into the hinterland again. Brush the colour of burnished copper is woven into green and grey rocks. The road becomes bumpier again, then I see Alice's house in the distance now, rising on the hill. Anticipation churns in my gut. I want to get to the bottom of this. I want Saoirse to be found – and to be found alive.

Alice's house feels even more ominous today, shrouded by its trees and shrubbery. I park outside. Her car is not nearby, so I guess she is still in the village. There is no stir in the opaque window of the neighbour's house, no twitching curtains. The gate creaks as I open it. Pausing for a moment halfway down the path, I listen for the murmur of voices but there is nothing. This time, instead of approaching the front door as normal, I creep to the window. I peer in, but there is no one sitting in the shadows of the room. Items have been moved around since I was last here. A book is wide open on the coffee table now, face down. I tilt my head and try to read the title. *101 Birds of the Forest.* Isn't that the same book that Jack has?

I go back to the door, conscious of the neighbour's upstairs window, and rap hard on the knocker, then ring the bell. It rings out insistently, a shrill sound. There is no movement. My heart begins to race and my palms are clammy with sweat. I glance over my shoulder, and from here I can see my car. Mary's profile stares into the distance. All is still.

In every moment that passes I feel more relief but also fear building. What if the neighbour sees me and calls the Gardaí? What if I am completely wrong about Alice?

I wait an extra two minutes for good measure, then creep around the side of the house. Once in the side passage, hidden from view, I can stand up straight. I pull open the gate. In the back garden, I search under the mat outside the door. A beetle scuttles away. Surveying the garden, I lift a few flowerpots, but there is nothing. Finally, I catch sight of a stone statue of a bird near the end of the garden. I glance around nervously as I approach it, then lift it. There it is, glinting in the late afternoon light – the spare key. I pick it up and slide the statue back into position.

If I think about it too long, I'll change my mind. So I quickly slide the key into the lock, and the back door clicks open. I listen for a sound, but all is still. The kitchen is as mundane as they come, no less ordinary than any kitchen around this area, with wooden work surfaces and a rustic farmyard feel. There is nothing unusual here, except I can see signs of a child. Pinned to the fridge with a magnet is a drawing in crayon of an oblong-bodied man, chestnut-haired woman, and a little girl. On the counter too, there is a photograph of a small child at a petting zoo. She holds a tawny, twitching-nosed rabbit in her grasp. She has dark hair and olive skin and looks around three years old. She looks vaguely familiar. Holding my breath, I slowly make my way down the hallway, almost expecting someone to emerge at any moment, screaming blue murder at finding an intruder in their house. But no one comes.

I enter the sitting room at the front of the house now. It is more cluttered in here, as though Alice has been through cycles of being tidy and then manic. An art project lies half-finished on the coffee table. Pieces of fabric rest by a sewing machine, and a pile of crumpled clothing is waiting patiently to be ironed. The bookshelf contains a mixture of adult and children's books. It is strange – it's as though she has a child living here, one younger than Saoirse, though neither Alice nor Walter have mentioned a child before.

I find a basket by the fireplace and open it to find glassy-eyed dolls and bloated bears staring back. Closing the lid, I catch sight of a framed photograph of a younger Alice on the mantlepiece, with the same little girl sitting on her lap. In the little girl's grasp there is a stuffed toy that is so familiar it takes me a moment to realise where I have seen it before. It could have been a different toy from the same batch, but something tells me it is not. The toy looks worn and battered, exactly like Jack's version, but this one has two eyes. Yes, it is definitely Wilberry.

Alice is beaming from ear to ear, like she really loves the person behind the camera. The photo looks dated and faded, possibly from the 1970s, and it looks as though it had been taken on a day out. It's the same photo that has been circulating in the newspaper in the past week in black and white. The woman in the photo looks very different to how she does now. It is Celia and Ellie O'Connor. Tragic child and tragic mother who lost her. Of course, that's not the name I know connected to that face. Her hair is much different in this picture, a different colour and style

327

– and she has aged: crow's feet and time, exposure to harsh weather and conditions, have rendered her almost, but not quite, unrecognisable compared to the happy-go-lucky, fresh-faced woman in the photograph. The person I've talked to several times, the woman who claims to be a florist, Garda Morris's girl-friend. The woman who told me her name was Alice.

My vision blurs a little as I try to slot the pieces together. Alice is Celia – the mother of Ellie who died in 1975, and whose body was found this week. I blink and stare closer at the photograph. That's why the locals would never have recognised her – when Ellie had gone missing, she was holidaying here for a short time, long ago, before Garda Morris was working here. Was that why no one had noticed it was her? Without knowing it was Alice, the photo wouldn't give her away in any case.

Hastily, I leave the room. Could Saoirse be here? There has to be a reason Alice is lying about her identity – a reason she wants to drive me out of town. The house is deathly silent, the lighting funereal. I hold my breath. Any moment I expect Alice to jump out, but there is no movement or sound. I ascend the stairs slowly, watching for shadows at the top. Shapes stretch across the wall – a hung jacket briefly becomes a person and then changes back to a jacket in a ripple of light, as my heart skips a beat. At the top, I switch on the landing light and push down the door handle to the room in front of me.

The lighting in here is brighter, with a lamp left on. It is a child's room, looking like it belongs to a little girl. Ellie's bedroom. I swallow hard. Alice has only been here six months. This isn't a bedroom; it's a shrine.

A doll is tucked under the covers, painted-on face benign and expectant, as if awaiting the girl's return. Childlike artwork depicting a forest is framed and hung by the bed. It looks like one of Jack's pieces.

I go into the hallway, passing a large closet or airing cupboard. I open it and peer inside but it is empty apart from a vacuum cleaner and a broom. I close the closet and continue to the next bedroom. This is clearly the master bedroom. A double bed, wooden floors, built-in wardrobes, plenty of space. On the bedside table, there is a framed photo of Ellie, next to a half-full glass of water. It looks fresh. I am not sure what I am looking for. Clues? Signs of Saoirse?

Heart thudding in my chest, I open the door and peer inside the ensuite bathroom, but there is no one there. I listen intently for sounds as I tiptoe back into the bedroom. Gently, I open the wardrobe. My mouth drops open. There, in all its glory, is a large costume – brown, orange, and green in colour. Sewn into the netting are feathers and autumn foliage – leaves of deciduous yellow and red, mixed with branches of evergreen firs. Magpie and crow feathers have been spun into the mix. I reach out one hand as I hold my breath, barely wanting to touch it. It feels surreal as I do, the sensation of the leaves, the feathers, and twigs under my fingertips. Cut into the middle of it is a hole big enough for a face, big enough for someone to see and breathe, but from a distance you would hardly be able to discern it from a human or some sort of monster. Some sort of creature.

My heart quickens. Alice is more insane than I could have imagined. I will have to be quick with my investigation. Bending down, I pull out a box and open it to find printed papers – plans, maps, tickets. Two tickets for the train and the boat to the UK – then two more tickets for the boat from the UK to France. One adult and one child. The train ticket from Drumsuin is for tomorrow's date. I feel my heart speed up with hope. If there is a child ticket, that only means one thing – if Alice has Saoirse, she's likely still alive.

Below that is another piece of paper. Someone's sketching letters into different orders. *Celia. Laiec. Aliec.* Alice. Of course – Alice is an anagram of Celia.

Peering underneath the paper, I find something else even more disturbing. Polaroid photos. Photos of me pulling into the Kellough's house, me looking over my shoulder coming out of the hotel, me at the vigil, my ransacked hotel room. There's one of the framed photo of Violet and me, placed in the middle of the floor of the hotel room. I feel sick as I look at the final one: a photograph of Saoirse and Jack from a distance in the forest, playing together. It had clearly been taken from behind a tree or bush, perhaps when she was dressed in her costume. Haunting that forest as a 'creature'. Those poor children never stood a chance.

Suddenly, the car horn beeps. Loud. Once, then again, urgently. Desperately, I look around for somewhere to hide. I hear the sound of the front door being unlocked, and with a click it opens.

I creep back into Ellie's bedroom, sliding myself under the bed. It is dusty underneath, and I feel a sneeze coming on. Gripping my nose as though my life depends on it, I wait, barely breathing. From here I spy some dainty pink shoes and a trinket box with a painted ballerina on the front. I listen carefully. There are sounds of keys being thrown down and heavy footsteps up the stairs. The footsteps pace around as my heart speeds up, and I watch a shadow flit across the floor. There is a long, pregnant silence as the shadow does not move. It hovers there, appearing to wait. Eventually she speaks. A hollow voice.

'I know you're here. Your car is outside.' I don't move. Her voice sounds taunting. 'The game is over, or do you need me to count to ten?' She laughs a little, a bright, sarcastic sound, and bends down. A hand comes towards me and brushes my hair.

'Wait!' My voice comes out hoarse and weak.

The hand disappears. I am trapped under here. There is only one way forward. Nervously, I slither out from under the bed and stumble to a stand. I stare at her. She looks different now, more menacing. She sneers as she leans against the doorway, still wearing her coat from outside – there are flecks of glistening rainwater on it.

'Breaking and entering now, are we? Add that to your list of misdemeanours.' She holds out her fingers and counts on them.

'So that's manslaughter, trespassing ... anything else?' She pushes her hands into her pockets.

'Well, hats off to you, Alice – or Celia, whoever you are. You've had everyone fooled, even the Gardaí themselves,' I say, my voice shaking.

Her eyes fill with tears, and I cannot tell if they are fake or real.

'Trust me, Freya, I didn't want to fool people.'

'Then why did you?'

I glance down and try to see if she is carrying a weapon. Her hands are now hidden in her pockets and I imagine she might be concealing something – perhaps a knife?

She sighs. 'I thought you of all people would understand things in life are not always ... plain and simple.'

'Explain to me, then,' I say, trying to buy time. I think about Mary. Would she go to a neighbour to call for help, or would she drive my car and go and get someone? Might she even risk coming inside?

'I lost a daughter too,' she whispers. 'Back in 1975.'

'I know,' I reply. I try to keep my voice calm. It is clear right in this moment Alice – Celia – is not thinking logically. I need to pretend to be on her level for as long as possible. 'What happened?' I ask.

She gazes into the distance.

'She was just playing on her holiday picnic. I didn't know how close she was to the river. I thought she was safe. Turns out when you're near water, you're never really safe.' She shifts her gaze and looks into my eyes. 'You understand that just as well as me.' There is a pause. 'It's sad we can't be friends,' she says. 'We're so similar ... both of us have lost our little girls; both of them drowned. I couldn't believe we had so much in common. In a different life, maybe we could have been friends.'

Back in Five. The note she had left on my car makes sense now. She knew about my daughter and how she died. That I'd only stepped away from that pool for five minutes.

'How did you know?'

'Well, first Walter told me you had a child that died, and then it's amazing what information you can glean from grief support groups. I had a few friends just a phone call away who were only too happy to share the details of your terrible tragedy – all the way through to how you turned your life around – quit drinking, trained to be a psychotherapist and even got a doctorate degree. They do say Dublin is like a big village sometimes.'

I feel intruded upon and betrayed. Alice had rang around trying to get information on me from kind people who had lost their children too, people who would have told her that information in good faith. God knows what lies she told them to get them to talk.

But those are not feelings for now. I have bigger things to take care of. I glance around the room at the shrine to Ellie.

'You saw what happened to Ellie?' I ask.

'Sort of. She drowned while playing but we had another child nearby. Our son. He was meant to be keeping an eye on her but he was young, too. He left her alone. I couldn't risk the agony of a court case or having him taken away. I panicked ... my husband and I panicked. We took her back to the holiday home, and when it was clear that she was dead and couldn't be revived, we buried her the next day. We pretended she had been kidnapped.'

'She was never taken at all?'

She shakes her head.

'The Gardaí back then, they weren't great – nothing like now. They looked for her but they didn't have the technology they have today. There was an article in the news a few times, but then she was largely forgotten. At least that's how it felt. But now I'm back here, I can see they didn't forget. She is among the names never forgotten in this village.'

'What made you take Saoirse?' I say, keeping my tone light and non-confrontational. 'And why now?'

Her eyes narrow. 'I help children who need a new start ...'

Children plural. Did that mean there are more?

I think back. One every six or seven years. Was Alice responsible for those other young women too?

'No one noticed it was twenty years exactly ...' She trails off. 'Since my darling, poor Ellie ...' She covers her eyes. 'I wanted to start afresh, give him a better life. Just like I did for Ashling and Maeve.'

'You were responsible for Ashling McGill and Maeve Murphy's disappearances?'

She looks down. 'I didn't plan to hurt them. It was an accident. They tried too hard to escape. I thought he would be different – easier.'

My mind is spinning with her confession, but the thing that jars me the most is her use of the male pronoun.

'He?' I echo.

'Jack! I never meant to take Saoirse ... it was Jack I wanted,' she says, seeming frustrated. 'But I couldn't get close to him, not properly. Saoirse was always around, preventing me from getting too close. The wrong child was better than none, so when she was finally alone, I took my opportunity. It was easy to drug her, carry her sleeping to that high-up, hidden treehouse – she's not heavy. But they didn't leave the forest alone, the Gardaí wouldn't let it drop. I had to move her out of the forest eventually. The only time it was possible was when I went there with Garda Morris. I waited until the volunteers and Gardaí were safely at the other side of the forest, then I managed to slip away and move her out of there in the boot of Garda Morris's own car when he wasn't looking ...'

I frown.

'You may think I'm a monster, but I was only trying to help.'

My mind is spinning. She had taken Ashling and Maeve too. She was the one waiting in the forest dressed as a creature at intervals over the years. Is *she* what Mary saw that day, years ago? The Creature Jack has been seeing?'

'People aren't looking for things they don't want to see ... except for you. I knew you were perceptive as soon as I met you.

That was why I wanted you to leave. I know I shouldn't have tried to get you to leave … but you were going to ruin my plan. And here you are, I was right. You even found the glove—'

'Walter's glove?'

She nods. 'I wanted to direct your attention away … I thought perhaps his glove turning up in a strange location might do that. That you might think Walter had something to do with it.'

I nod, thinking she had been right. It had thrown me off and put my attention onto Walter briefly. Alice had been threatened by me, that much was clear. My mouth feels dry. I am aware of how she has me backed into a corner.

'I know what you're thinking, Freya. I'm a bad person and a bad mother, but I'm not.' I shake my head, listening out for Mary. 'And I know you won't believe me, so I can't let you go, I'm afraid.'

My heart quickens. *Keep her talking.*

'Help me understand,' I say in my best, empathic therapist voice. 'Why … Jack. Did you really think he was suffering?'

She looks suspicious, then she nods. 'Yes. Jack and Saoirse were both suffering – with their mother dead, their sister neglecting them … playing in that forest with no supervision. They need someone to care for them. Someone like me.'

I nod, knowingly. 'See, I completely understand that, and I think the Gardaí will too, as long as you let her go.'

She narrows her eyes again.

'That's not going to happen, Freya,' she says in a flat voice.

'And what about the other two?' I ask quickly. 'Why did you take them?'

'Maeve was in an abusive relationship. Ashling was being abused too – but no one knew about it. I knew because she told a friend when I was listening to her talking in the forest. They both needed an escape.'

'What did you … do with them?'

'Like I say, I never *meant* to harm them,' she says sadly. 'But they were too … unwilling to go along with things. They both survived a few months with me, but ultimately, they kept trying to escape and it was impossible to start a new life with them, to help them. I had to stop them escaping and telling people about me. It was easier for them to go for an … eternal sleep.'

My stomach churns as these words sink in. She is dangerous – very dangerous. I feel a shiver up my spine.

I realise Alice or Celia and I are similar but we are also opposites. I turned my tragedy into something good, constructed a career out of helping traumatised children. She has let her past pain turn her into some madwoman who hides in the forest dressed like a creature. A woman who kidnaps people, who scares people, who ultimately kills people.

Suddenly, I hear a noise above me – a thumping followed by a muffled moan, like someone trying to call out through a gag. Without hesitation, I lunge towards Celia and try to grab her hair, but she clutches at my wrists. She is wiry, much stronger than I expected. The moment of her vulnerability is over. She is back to anger and fear.

'What are you doing?' She hisses, pinning me on the floor by my wrists.

'I'm trying to get help for Saoirse!'

'She doesn't need help. I'm her mother now,' she says. 'A new life for Saoirse and a new start in France for us both – me as the mother whose child grows up this time.'

'Kidnapper isn't the same as mother,' I gasp, struggling to breathe.

'She'll learn to love me when we start our new life. After all, every child deserves a second chance.'

She pulls me up and before I know it, I'm flying backwards into a closet. I slam against the wall and the door shuts, leaving me in darkness. I rest against the wall wincing, my shoulder in agony. All I can see is a sliver of light under the door, and apart from that it's just inky blackness. A damp, musty smell fills my nostrils. I hear the closet lock. Immediately a feeling of panic and claustrophobia rises in me. I kick the door.

'Let me out!'

I hear her muffled voice from outside.

'Your Garda friends won't come looking for you here.'

I realise she is right, but then remember Mary with relief. Thank God I brought her with me. At least she knows I am here – unless Celia has already intercepted her? I can't let that idea into my head. Instead, I try to focus on my breathing and think about the information I've just learned. Alice is Celia. Her daughter had not been kidnapped – she had drowned accidentally. Celia was the Creature, Celia killed the other missing girls and now she has Saoirse too. She has clearly lost her mind in the process of trying to atone for her daughter's death, lost her grip on reality. How did she think she would get away with it forever?

I listen to the sound of my own heart beating in my ears. Is Alice gone? After a few minutes, there is a bang from downstairs, which sounds like the back door slamming, and I hear someone call out my name. *Mary*. Then I hear a noise on the stairs. I call out. 'Help! I'm in here!'

I hear Mary's voice, but it is not directed at me, 'Christ, Alice, what are you doing!'

Alice must not be gone. My stomach turns. What if she hurts Mary? Then I'd have no chance of getting out of here. I hear a scuffle for a moment and there are three dramatic sounds in quick succession: half a scream, a smash, followed by a thud. I hear Mary cursing loudly.

I call out again.

'Mary, are you okay?'

Footsteps come to the door. The door rattles a moment.

'Freya?'

'Yes, thank God! What happened?'

'She tried to hit me but I got there first!' Mary sounds breathless. 'There's no key …' she says.

'Try her pocket?' I reply, desperately.

More footsteps as I hold my breath. There is a long silence.

'Mary?'

'Got it!'

Finally, the closet unlocks and light and air floods in. I almost faint with relief. Adrenaline courses through my veins as I crawl out. I look down at my hands – my wrists are red and burned from where Celia grabbed them. Slowly, I turn my head and stare down the hallway. I hardly dare look.

Celia is lying in a pool of blood surrounded by a broken ceramic vase, her arms tied behind her back with phone cord. Her head is bleeding. She is still.

'We had better call an ambulance,' Mary whispers. 'I don't want to go to prison for murder.'

A sound comes from downstairs, a man's voice.

'Alice?'

Walter?

I hear him climb the stairs. When he sees Alice, he looks shocked.

'Alice!' he exclaims. 'What have you done to her?'

Walter radios for backup, for more Gardaí and an ambulance.

Celia groans, trying to speak. Walter unties her hands and puts her into the recovery position. He ties a scarf around her head to stem the bleeding.

'Walter, she has Saoirse …' I explain. 'We were protecting ourselves from her. She locked me in the closet, but Mary got me out.'

'What are you talking about?'

'Alice has Saoirse … she's not who you think.'

I cough, holding my chest and wincing.

Confusion crosses Walter's face, as though he's processing that the person in front of him is not who he thought. There is the sound again. Scraping up above.

'I'm going to check the attic,' I gasp, expecting Walter to stop me, but he doesn't. He just nods, his expression sombre. 'I'll stay with her,' he says nodding to Celia.

I search for the attic and locate the panel, then grab the pole which hangs nearby on the wall. I pull down the hatch. A ladder extends down automatically, and tentatively, I begin to climb up. I wince as pain shoots through my shoulder. When I get to the top, I grasp on to the ladder with my injured arm, and push up the hatch with my fit arm. It is difficult to balance. I feel dizziness swirl around me but I won't give up now.

Finally, the attic hatch shifts to one side. I climb up further and stick my head into the darkness. It smells musty in here. I peer around, unable to see much. It is almost impossible to pull myself up with one arm, so I climb to the very top of the ladder and lean in, rolling onto the wooden beams until I'm inside. I wince as pain shoots down my side and I gasp for air. I feel for a switch or string until I find it on the floor. I press it down and the attic illuminates around me. Beams above and boxes stacked everywhere around. The first thing I notice is the walkie-talkie and next to it, two small bare feet. Saoirse.

I crane my neck to look behind the boxes, and that is when I catch sight of her in a corner in the gloom of the attic. Wrists and feet tied. She is wearing the clothes she was reported missing in – blue jeans and a red jumper, the only thing missing is her shoes and socks. Her pallid face is pulled taut with a gag.

'Oh my gosh,' I murmur. Tears come to my eyes at the sight of her. She whimpers through the gag and tears glisten in her eyes too. I shift myself across the beams.

'Don't worry, you're safe now,' I whisper. 'I'm Freya,' I explain. 'I've been helping your family this past couple of weeks. I'm going to take off your gag, okay?'

She nods, tears streaming down her cheeks. With that, I reach over and untie and pull down the gag.

'Thank you,' she whispers.

I feel tears well up in my eyes. Finally, a child I could save. Saoirse is not going to be the child that never grew up – she is going to go home.

55

Day Fourteen

Freya

I stare at the beige wall of the hospital corridor. Perhaps I am in shock? It's not normal to go through all of this in the space of a fortnight. Another part of my mind just keeps repeating the words over and over. *She's alive. She's going to be okay.* A gentle nurse had wrapped my arm in a sling and it hangs now, awkwardly, at the front of my body. Every time I take a deep breath, pain presses sharply at my lungs. My shoulders feel dense and sore. Walter sits down next to me. I avoid his eyes.

'I hope they have you on plenty of pain meds?'

'Not enough,' I reply, thinking about the mental pain.

'Freya, I'm so sorry for not realising all of this sooner. I feel so stupid ... and I can't believe what was right under my nose with Celia.' He shakes his head. 'She was so believable. I thought I was a reasonably good judge of character.'

'You couldn't have known,' I murmur, trying to comfort him.

'But I should have. I'm finding it hard to come to terms with everything – the lies, the promises she made to me, the nights she spent at my house over the past six months ... none of it was real. I mean, right from the start, I thought she was just a blow-in who needed my help. I thought she was genuinely attracted to me. Now I see she was just using me so she could kidnap a child without being found out. I understand now why she never invited me

339

over. There's the embarrassment, too. My colleagues. What are they going to think of me? How could I have been so close with someone like that?' He puts his head in his hands and leans on his knees. 'What if Saoirse was missing for so long because Ali—, I mean, Celia was getting clues from me about the Gardaí's plans and whether we were on her trail? I trusted her. And for you to find her before I did – it makes me feel so … bad at my job.'

'She was working at the hotel that day,' I say, the realisation dawning on me. 'Mary said so. That was the thing – she even had an alibi. I never suspected her until I saw the photographs of her in the newspaper. She looked so suspicious.'

'I never noticed …' Walter says, shaking his head again.

'How would you? You were in love.'

He nods and sighs, then he scratches his head.

'If she was at the hotel that day, how did she take Saoirse?'

'I suppose cleaning rooms is a solitary activity – it would be possible to sneak out and then come back, as though she had never left. I've since realised she was the person who disturbed my hotel room that day and left the dead crow on my bed.'

Walter nods slowly, as though the realisation is dawning on him.

I could tell this was going to be harder to come to terms with for Walter than it was for me. I look down at the beige lino floor of the hospital. There is a burned patch. I wonder where it came from. This hospital with all its stories and dramas. In some part of it, Kate is still here. I look up as a nurse passes us, glancing at her watch. She disappears around a corner, her shoes squeaking.

'What made you come to the house when you did?' I ask Walter.

'Alice dropped her driving licence outside the Garda station … It had the name Celia O'Connor on it. I realised something was wrong, but I didn't understand the magnitude at that point, didn't understand she had kidnapped Saoirse … and I didn't know you or Mary would be there. I thought I would arrive and confront her myself, ask her about Ellie, nothing more.'

I shift in my seat and wince.

'What's the damage?' he asks, nodding to my arm.

'Dislocated shoulder, bruised ribs, luckily no fractures or breaks.'

Walter nods. A trolley goes past. A wizened old man with gaunt cheeks observes me from the stretcher, his eyes far away. He looks away, up at the ceiling, as if accepting his fate. It makes me feel grateful I can walk out of here now.

'By the way, Saoirse is stable, according to the doctor I just spoke to,' Walter says. 'Shock and dehydration only. She is slightly malnourished too. Apparently, she was being left without food and water for long periods of time. Luckily the doctor said she would be fine and that she would have no long-term damage.'

I shudder, thinking back to the crazed look in Celia's eyes. The irony of her wanting to be a perfect mother and leaving Saoirse without even basic sustenance. Saoirse must have been so frightened.

'What will you do now, head back to Dublin?' he asks.

'I suppose so. There will be other cases to work on – other children to help.'

Walter nods, thoughtfully. 'I've one more question today for you before I leave you to rest.'

'Yes?'

'When are you going to stop?'

'What?'

'Sacrificing yourself for a mistake you made fifteen years ago. Ironic, isn't it? Doctor, heal thyself.'

I look down at my bruised fingers.

He stands up. 'I think the squad have a celebration planned for you,' he says. 'When you're out of hospital, let me know. You're the new talk of the town. The new big hero.'

He grins at me and tips his hat. He strides off, down the corridor. I watch his tall figure disappear into the distance. I try to imagine Walter before his accident. Full of even more confidence, a young buckshee, as he called it. He must have been a positive

341

energy to be around. A reassuring presence, as he still is now. I listen to the sounds of the hospital as ward staff bustle past. I sit and close my eyes. I have plenty of time to talk, plenty of time to think about what has happened. I have the rest of my life to process it. Thankfully, Saoirse does too.

56

Day Sixteen

Saoirse

S aoirse sits next to the fire, listening to the flames crackle and
spit. She is relieved to finally be home, grateful the hospital
had only kept her in for two nights for observation.

She watches as Jack comes in balancing a tray between both
palms, walking as though he is on a tightrope. A cup of tea, some
pink wafers on a plate. He puts the tray on the table and then
runs over to Saoirse. His thin arms pull her into a close hug. She
feels his clammy fingers on her arm and his hot breath in her ear.

'I'm so glad you're home. Don't go away again?'

'Of course not, silly,' she replies patting his back. 'Now go
away,' she giggles, pushing him off her.

Jack runs back to the couch and jumps up, tucking his feet
underneath himself. Saoirse remembers Kate at the hospital. How
they had embraced. Kate had apologised for their argument.

I never meant what I said, she had whispered, tears running
down her cheeks.

I know, Saoirse had replied. She knew Kate loved her really.
Sisters argued all the time – it didn't mean they didn't love one
another.

Saoirse runs her finger along the raised mark on her neck,
where her locket had broken off and cut her. She looks around
the room and begins to notice things – fat logs in a basket next to

the hearth and a set of gold pokers with birds etched onto the sides. There are things about this room she has never examined before, like the silver frame on the mantlepiece, a photograph of Kate as a child. The brown and navy threads in the throw on the sofa, the old sewing machine that belonged to her mother. The broken piano, covered in dust that never gets played anymore. She pulls her knees closer to herself and looks out the window to see the journalists pacing around outside. They are hanging around, waiting for her to come out. She feels trapped all over again.

Aunt Bronagh comes into the room. 'I wish they'd give us peace,' she snaps, sticking her middle finger up at someone outside, then yanking the curtains closed. 'They've been here long enough now,' she adds. Aunt Bronagh moves her wheelchair to the couch, then transfers herself over onto the cushions. Jack snuggles up to Aunt Bronagh. She puts her arm around him like a wing, and pulls him close. They sit in semi-darkness now with only the light from the fire.

Saoirse stares into the flames and summons the courage to ask the question she has wanted to ask since they checked her over in the hospital. Since they photographed her cuts, asked her hundreds of questions which she answered in a monotone voice. Since she had come home and had a hot bath, her wrists and ankles stinging.

'If Kate is still in the hospital, what will happen to us?' she asks. 'Will we go into care?'

They all listen to the flames crackle. Jack lays his head on Aunt Bronagh, who looks thoughtful for a moment.

'How could I let that happen when I've three spare rooms in my bungalow?'

Saoirse looks into the flames and feels something dissipate – a tired, fearful feeling. She closes her eyes, feeling the warmth on her skin. She breathes out and lets the worry leave her.

Day Sixteen

Freya

A smattering of applause erupts as I enter the incident room flanked by Walter. There is a crudely pinned plastic banner on the beige wall that reads *Well Done*. Walter offers me a plastic cup of wine but I shake my head. I can't help notice everyone's eyes on me, which is an unnerving feeling. It's times like these I wish I could still drink.

Officers openly stare, but when I look at them, they either nod or glance away awkwardly. I hang around in the corner, hoping the staring will stop. Gardaí sip beer and wine and others sip on coke – there has to be some sober Gardaí available in case something kicks off locally. Though hopefully the crime in the area will return to normal now – the odd tractor theft or an occasional vandalism report. On the nearby table there is an array of pizza slices and piles of fat chips from the local chipper.

Derek, one of the ruddy-faced, plump officers, approaches holding the *Drumsuin Examiner*. 'Have you seen the front page from a few days ago? I kept a copy for ya!' I glance over it. There is a photo of me next to one of Saoirse with the headline:

HERO PRAISED AS MISSING SAOIRSE FOUND

He thrusts the newspaper at me. I take it with my good arm and scan through the first few lines:

> Missing local girl Saoirse Kellough (13) was rescued from the clutches of her kidnapper yesterday in a dramatic intervention. A Dublin psychotherapist, Freya Hemmings, has been hailed a hero by her colleagues as she traced clues to where Saoirse was being kept hostage. Celia O'Connor, who was posing as a search volunteer on the case, has been detained and questioned pending formal investigation for kidnapping and withholding information from the Gardaí. The body of her missing daughter, Ellie O'Connor, had been recovered just a week earlier in the local forest, and it is now believed the woman withheld information regarding her daughter's death in 1975. Celia O'Connor is also now being investigated in relation to the other cases of missing girls in the area.

I lower the paper and pass it back to Derek.

'No, that copy is yours, keep it!' he says, earnestly. He wanders away and back over to a crowd of Gardaí. I put the newspaper down next to my handbag and look at Walter, who's grabbed a slice of pizza from the table behind us.

'How's it going?'

He nods, taking a bite of pizza.

'Grand,' he replies, in a flat voice.

'All blown over regarding Celia?'

He shrugs. 'Sort of. Everyone was quite sympathetic about it. I think they just feel sorry for me. Superintendent Ridgeway gave me a stern questioning about how I didn't notice anything, but I think she understood. It's not like people walk around suspecting their girlfriend or boyfriend is that type of a character. Besides, we found Saoirse alive *and* have closed three

346

unsolved missing persons cases in the past fortnight, so she's not too upset.'

'Are you upset about Celia?' I ask, feeling angry just thinking about her. My shoulder twinges as I think of her face when she sent me hurling into that closet.

'I'm getting there. I keep having flashbacks to things she said and did that were kind. I just feel so stupid.'

'That's understandable. I can't imagine it would be easy to move on.'

He nods, and looks away from me awkwardly. 'Should have known someone like her would never be interested in someone like me.'

'Now, now – I don't want to hear any of that feeling sorry for yourself stuff. You'll find someone else.'

He laughs. 'I knew I wouldn't get much sympathy from you!'

'Well, it's just nonsense – you've a lot going for yourself. At least with this breakup you know your ex is actually going to be behind bars, so there's no chance of them ever turning up with their new partner in the restaurant you're in one day,' I say, trying to make him laugh.

'Good point,' he says dryly, but the corner of his mouth twitches. He puts his shoulders back a bit and stands straighter.

'What's happening with Ellie O'Connor's case?' I ask.

'It hasn't been formally disclosed yet, but it has been like pulling at a piece of wool and having the whole jumper unravel. The cardigan we found turned out to be Ellie's when we tested it for DNA. It seems as though a bird must have brought it up to the treehouse when the body was uncovered.'

I shiver, thinking about the dead crow that had been left in my hotel room.

'We managed to get a full confession from Celia for witnessing her daughter's accidental death,' he continues. 'And a confession for the kidnaps and killings of Ashling McGill and Maeve Murphy. She has told us where they are buried; we just have to find the bodies now based on the map she has drawn and confirm everything. She'll likely be charged with their murders and withholding vital information about Ellie's disappearance. She may get away with being put in a psychiatric institution, though – she seems completely nuts.'

'She does seem …' I search for a word. 'Mentally unstable,' I finish. 'Has she been evaluated yet?'

'Apparently, a psychiatrist who saw her yesterday seems to think she's lucid and fine to go through a trial, but we shall see. The way she had the house like a mausoleum to her daughter – that was very strange.'

'It was, wasn't it?'

I understand grief and not letting go. I understand keeping your child's things after they have passed. But it was the way she had it set out. A new room for her in a new house – a room Ellie had never stayed in.

'Apparently, after Ellie's death, her husband left her, taking her son with him and emigrating abroad. That was what pushed her over the edge. She became a recluse and started returning to the forest in Drumsuin every six or seven years, in some sort of strange homage to Ellie. She began dressing like the Creature and waiting in the forest for young women to take. I suppose she was playing some skewed counting game of her own.'

I try to imagine what it would take to push someone that far. It did sound like a psychiatric institution might be where she would end up.

'As regards to the Saoirse case, Celia was an open book – she told us everything. She was keeping her in the forest initially, in that treehouse, until we got too close to where she was being hidden and almost found her. Then she moved her. After that, she brought her to the attic of her rental property to keep her close by. She was using walkie-talkies to communicate with her until she found out about the baby monitor picking up the signal, so she took that away and gagged the poor girl … I guess she had the advantage of dating me and knowing where the Gardaí were going to be at all times.'

It was what Celia had told me herself.

'Everything is solved, it seems,' I say.

'Pretty much,' he replies.

The room begins to stir and everyone looks towards Superintendent Ridgeway, who is standing by the banner. She taps her glass with a fork.

'Hello everyone, thanks for coming. We are obviously here to just say thank you to Dr Freya Hemmings for her amazing input on this case and for eventually catching our culprit and saving Saoirse from being an unsolved mystery case forever. For getting her home to her family and friends.'

There is a smattering of applause.

'This is also a moment for us to recognise that we have finally been able to resolve Ellie O'Connor's case as well as understand what happened to Ashling McGill and Maeve Murphy. Getting closure for their families is of paramount importance.' A hush falls over the room. 'Let's not forget that they never got to live their lives. Ellie didn't live past her ninth birthday. Ashling and Maeve never got to go to university or have families of their own. All these years, they have been without justice. They have never had a voice. Now we can hopefully lay them all to rest, knowing we have solved their cases and justice has been served. I'd like to thank everyone who helped with finding Ellie's body – the sniffer dog team, and to our volunteers and officers who helped guard her body. To everyone involved, you've been excellent. We've raised a glass to Freya, and I'd just like to propose one more toast. To Ellie, Ashling, and Maeve – you won't be forgotten by this village, and you are the reason we all do this work. Thank you.'

Tears well up in my eyes. They are tears of pride, and of sadness, but also of hope. Those poor girls, all buried by Celia in unmarked graves, can now be laid to rest properly. Walter looks over at me, he nods solemnly and raises his glass at me.

I feel myself relax for the first time in weeks. A strange sense of pride wells in my chest – it is over. The stress of coming to

Drumsuin, all those nightmares and the uncertainty of the forest and facing my own demons too. It has all been worth it.

58

Found

Jack

The Treehouse is made of devilled wood. Hung above twisted conifers. It sits like a screw loose with green moss clinging to its edges, as though it has grown sick over time. A blackened and water-logged shell with a gaping mouth. Among the pines it stoops, like a mother gathering her child in its arms.

Freya looks at the painting Jack is staring at.

'That one is important, huh?' she says, folding her legs together, perched on the beanbag. They are in the painting room. It is his last session with Freya before they say goodbye.

'You were a brave little boy, throughout this whole thing, weren't you?' Freya says.

Jack is not so sure. Brave little boys didn't hide what happened to their mother. They didn't fear a thousand trees on a hill, so black they sucked the night into them and spit the dark out again. Brave boys would tell what they did wrong.

Jack looks at his fingers and does not meet her gaze. He gets up and goes to the cupboard, pulls the light and bends down, feeling around for the toy chest. After a moment, he retrieves the diary. He knows Kate had hidden it there. He turns it over in his fingers. Then he walks back to Freya and holds it out. She has a bruise on her left eye from her fight to save Saoirse.

'What is this?' she asks.

Jack can hear the rain start outside. It patters on the skylight. 'Saoirse's diary,' he whispers.

Freya shakes her head, but Jack pushes it closer to her. The important page has been marked – folded over with one corner, so it is easy for Freya to find. The day when their mother died. Saoirse had written it all down so no one could forget. Kate had read it on the day she was cutting Jack's hair. She had not wanted anyone to see the diary – didn't want anyone to know what Jack had done. She didn't even want to admit it to herself, that's what she had said. *I don't even want to admit it to myself.* We just need to forget it, put it behind us like a storm or a bad dream. That was how memories disappear, Jack took his eraser and went *Erase*, and then it was gone.

As he waits for Freya to read, Jack looks at his knees. He draws the shape of a tree on his skin with his finger, the branches and roots included. He does not feel brave right now, waiting for Freya to know the truth. Saoirse had whispered into his ear at night that she would never tell. That he was her brother, so she would always keep that secret for him, as good families do. But Jack knows, afraid or not, he must show Freya. For if he does not, he might be eaten by the *tra-au-ma* forever. He can feel a tear creep out from the side of his eye as he waits for her to hate him. *If they never reached ten it could never end. They kept going around in circles. Trapped forever in the game.*

'Jack,' whispers Freya eventually. 'Jack is this really what happened, the day your mother died?'

Jack nods. His chest hurts with pain.

Freya nods, calmly. She closes the diary.

'I understand now,' she says softly. After a long pause she says, 'I have an idea. Do you remember the Empty Chair work we did with Saoirse a few weeks ago?'

Jack nods.

'I'd like to do it again now, with your mam. Would that be all right?'

Jack thinks about it for a moment, then nods again.

'Okay,' says Freya. 'That little seat over there, see it? Your mam is sitting there now. I want you to imagine her.'

Jack watches as his mother comes into view. She is hunched on the chair, her hands folded across her lap, wearing a long skirt and a white blouse. She has the same wide beaming grin she always had when she saw Jack coming towards her in the distance. She nods at him to talk.

'Is she there now?'

Jack looks at his mother.

'Speak to her, Jack, tell her just what you would like to say about what happened that day. You've never told her before, so you can tell her now.'

Jack feels the hot feeling in the back of his eyes as he looks at his mother. He feels a lump rise in his throat.

'I'm sorry, Mam,' he whispers. 'I didn't mean to.'

'Didn't mean to?' his mother replies.

'I didn't mean to scare you.'

Jack thinks back to the beach, the day he had been there with Saoirse. He looks at the painting of the forest and remembers.

'You were looking at the sea.'

Jack thinks back to his mother stood near the edge of the cliff. Her shirt and skirt were dancing in the wild wind. She had been still. Like a statue or a soldier, with her arms rigid by her side. Fingers bound tightly into fists. Her hair ruffling and quavering about too; it was as if everything moved except her. She was frozen in a moving picture.

'You had gone to Saturn again.'

His mother's face stops smiling now and she looks sad, staring at Jack from the chair.

'I wanted to get your attention. Step back from the edge, Mam, I said that to you … step back, you're too close.'

His mother tilts her head, puzzled.

'You didn't see me. You got a fright. I watched you … fall.'

I'll never tell, Jack. I know it was an accident. That's what Saoirse had said. An accident, that was true.

'I'm sorry, Mam,' Jack says. He starts to cry. Big heaving sobs from deep within. His face is hot with tears now. His mam looks sad, but like she understands. She always understands. *She* knows Jack is not bad. Finally, she holds up her two hands like she always used to do, in the shape of a heart. She puts her hands to her own heart then mouths, *I love you.*

With that, she disappears and there is just an empty chair.

Jack dissolves into tears. He could cry a whole ocean now. He heaves sob after sob, maybe he will never stop. What if he can't? He misses his mother so much. He'd do anything to have her back for just a day.

'It's okay, let it out,' Freya says.

Jack nods, his bottom lip sticking out and the tears all over his face now. He wipes all his tears away from his face with his sleeve.

Freya continues to speak.

'We all make mistakes. You didn't intend to hurt her, and you can't carry that blame forever.' Freya comes over now and cradles him. She strokes his hair. 'I can't explain why, but I understand accidents. How a few short minutes can change your entire life. You didn't mean to do it.'

Jack realises Freya is crying too. It feels comforting being hugged by her. Safe. Like how he had felt when his own mam had hugged him. Jack thinks back to Kate's thin, pale face yesterday as they left her room in the hospital. As soon as she is well enough, she will be allowed to leave hospital and move in with Aunt Bronagh too. He thinks about his dream last night. In the dream, Kate was better, and they were all living together. Alice had arrived at their house. She was furious because she was trying to run from the Counting Game. Aunt Bronagh had bellowed at her to leave. He had woken up feeling confused.

This is his last session with Freya. What would he do without her? Who would he talk to? He wonders where Freya will go next.

'Will you help other boys and girls when you leave?' Jack whispers.

Freya nods and sniffs. She lets go of Jack. 'Gosh, look at me getting sentimental … Yes, I will. And you will be okay without me. I know you will.'

Freya takes out a tissue and dabs her eyes. Then she reaches into her other pocket. 'I wanted to give you something,' she says. She takes out a toy and hands it to Jack. He takes it and examines it. A plastic penguin with shiny eyes.

'It's just a small thing, from McDonalds,' she says. 'But it made me think of you.'

Like the rockhopper penguin. *A rockhopper penguin minds its eggs.* Freya had minded him, at least for a short while.

Freya looks sad.

'Time for me to go, then, I suppose,' she says ruffling his hair.

Jack feels fear all of a sudden. Maybe he might never see Freya again. What if he didn't? It is as if Freya can read his mind.

'We might never meet again, but I'll always remember you,' she says. 'Every time I see a penguin,' she says with a watery smile.

Jack nods.

'I'll remember you most of the days. When I'm a grown-up I'll call you and say "Hi, it's Jack. I'm okay …"'

'That would be nice, I'd really like that,' she says. Her eyes shine with tears for a moment. She stands up and turns. Jack watches as she crawls from the painting room. She turns back one more time to look at Jack, then she disappears.

59

Day Twenty

Freya

I give Mary a grateful hug goodbye outside the hotel. She smells comforting and familiar, yet her body feels frail. Not too weak to overpower Celia, though. I chuckle to myself at the idea of it. As if hearing my thoughts she says dryly, 'I didn't think I had it in me … you know, to knock someone out.' She lets go and looks at me with a warning look. 'I've had my fill of drama for a lifetime now.'

I laugh. It's so hard to believe it's been almost a week since everything happened. I was told to rest my shoulder for at least seven days before driving home. Mary has let me stay for free for the remaining nights, but now I really do have to get back to Dublin, to my apartment, my safe space. Then it will be time to sort my own head out and work through my own grief once and for all.

'What will you do next?' Mary asks.

'I've decided to go back into private practice. You know? Help children long-term for as long as I need to. Leaving Jack was so difficult this time. It made me realise I want to go back to long-term work, to be able to support children and not have to leave them as soon as the case ends.'

'It's amazing what you do,' Mary replies.

'I just do what needs to be done,' I reply with a shrug.

'Go on, then,' Mary says. 'You've a long drive ahead. Don't come back. I don't have the energy for it.'

I laugh as I stride off, pulling my wheely case behind. It clacks along loudly. I stop and pull up my zip, narrow my eyes into the coarse wind. Down the path, I turn. Mary gives me one last wave and walks back into the hotel.

The day is strangely bright for November. The clouds have lifted and there is a high, bright blue sky. I pull my scarf tighter up around my chin and shiver. I hear Walter's voice in my head. *That blustery Atlantic wind would cut you in two.* I get into my car and hold my frozen fingers to the heater until the air turns warm.

As I am driving away, I cast my eyes over the quaint shops. Colourful facades and little chimney pots, all clustered together in a terraced line. One thing that could be said for this place was that it was beautiful and picturesque. Not that I'd ever want to return. My car groans as I ascend the hill out of the village which leads towards the forest. I follow the route, through some fields on either side, where sheep graze.

It is strange now, to drive alone through this place. I feel goose-bumps rise on my arms. The radio turns to white noise again and I switch it off. I keep my eyes ahead. Just a few more minutes and I will be out of here forever. I'll never have to come back to Drumsuin again. Not as long as I live.

I think about Jack. It is funny – all along I had thought Jack reminded me of Violet, but now I can see that he reminds me of myself. He is a troubled soul, and we both share something – a deep grief and loss at our core. We have both lost people very close to us. When Jack spoke about the forest and 'the Creature', he had been speaking about himself and his own psyche all along.

Then there is Kate and the diary – she presumably didn't want Jack to get in trouble, or for them to waste time investigating their mother's death. But now, I reflect, perhaps hiding the diary was also her way of not wanting to face that on some level she was scared of Jack? I change gears in the car. All that aside, the forest itself is still creepy, and this place really does feel haunted.

That's when I see it ahead, in the middle of the road. Lying flat. A black thing. Closer, I can see its feathers, rippling and fluttering a little in the wind. I stop a few metres from it and sit up straighter in my seat, stretching my neck to see over the steering wheel.

It is a dead bird. I know what type without getting out and examining it. I know if I get out and look down, I would see the glint of a beady crow eye, reflecting the high November sky. It is right in the path of my car as I am trying to leave the village. Of course, I know that it is no coincidence. Or maybe it is, but either way, I don't get out. Instead, I start the car again and swerve to the other side. I drive around it, and speed up, just in case. I don't look into my rear-view mirror until I am miles ahead, far away.

60

Two Months Later

Jack

The graveyard is quiet because the dead don't speak unless they are spoken to. The fog has lifted and the rain has stopped. Saoirse is holding his right hand and Wilberry is holding his left. Jack looks at the leaning stone wall, made up of rocks and boulders from hundreds of years ago. Everyone who died in Drumsuin is buried here, including the man in the village who used to take the betting money from Jack's father.

An old broken chapel points up to the sky, its steeple holding a bell which never rings. The graves are different shapes. Some are pointed and sharp, others rounded at the edges. Some have statues and others Celtic crosses. There are ancient and sunken ones with faded letters where the name is almost washed away by the rain.

Jack and Saoirse stand at the edge of the forest. The trees soar above them, snaking up the hill and covering the entire mountain. Once the trees reach the cliff edge, it drops off into the wild Atlantic Ocean, whose deep waters would wash away any secrets you had forever. If Jack turns, there are no trees behind him, only Aunt Bronagh's car and the graveyard. He takes Wilberry's floppy arm and waves it.

'Goodbye, forest,' he whispers.

Jack is excited to leave, and so is Saoirse. They are going to Dublin. *The big smoke.* They will visit their father, Cahill, for a weekend, and then go and live in a house Aunt Bronagh has rented near enough to Cahill, 'for now', she had said. 'Until we can sell the two houses here and to buy a proper place in Dublin.'

'Are there schools in Dublin?' Jack had asked on the drive to the graveyard to say goodbye to their mother.

'Yes, of course. Lots of schools. Plenty of shops too, and more people, not like Drumsuin. Not everyone will know our business. We will be anonymous.'

'*An-non-ee-muss?*'

'Yes, like no one knows who we are.'

Jack isn't so sure if you can ever leave a place like this behind, or if it stays inside you, like *tra-au-ma* or like ghosts. Maybe the haunting would come with them. Saoirse said that was not how it worked, that if they left Drumsuin it would all stay here. All the grief and sadness, and the haunting too. Jack feels he might miss Drumsuin, in any case. But he does feel happy, and excited. Especially to make friends and to show Pearl the dog a new place to go for walks – and to see the Irish Sea. Jack can't remember it from his trip to Dublin as a child, but he has seen plenty of pictures of it with its calm water with little ripples, the two red and white chimneys in the bay and the DART train that runs around from North to South. Saoirse said you could look out the window on the train and see everything all the way from Howth to Bray, including Dún Laoghaire where the boats went out and Killiney, with its beaches, hills, and coves. You could sit and listen to it *chuc-at-ta-chuc* and eat sweets and look out the window and no one would bother you. Then you could get out and wander down the busy streets of Grafton Street and O'Connell Street where there were hundreds of people and green double-decker buses, and people with funny clothes and tourists visiting from different countries, like America. You could cross the ha'penny bridge and wander around the little alleyways and shops. No one would know you, or who you were, because it was a city.

Saoirse takes both of Jack's hands and swings them as they stand at the edge of the forest.

'Thank you for waiting for me,' she says. 'Thanks for not giving up on me when people thought I might be dead.'

Jack looks up at his sister's face. Big sister Saoirse was almost all he had left in the world. He throws his arms around her and hugs her tight. He knew she would be home and that the game would end at some point.

'Are you coming back to the car?' Saoirse asks.

'In a minute,' Jack says.

'Okay, I'm going now. Come back when you're ready to go,' Saoirse says.

Jack nods and gazes into the trees. Searching, though he doesn't know for what. Until he sees it. In the distance. Human-shaped, larger than a person. An inky, shrouded figure – gargantuan, terrifying. It watches him back. Jack shuts his eyes and opens them again, but it is still there. Heart vibrating, he turns. *Is it? Surely it can't be?*

Jack sprints back to the car and bounds in breathless, slamming the door. Aunt Bronagh starts the car.

'We've got to get lunch, where will we go?' Aunt Bronagh says. 'Hope's Café, one last visit?'

'No,' says Kate. 'Let's drive to the nearest city and eat there.'

'Why?' asks Aunt Bronagh.

'Because Jack has waited long enough.'

'What for?'

'His first trip to McDonald's!'

They all laugh.

Saoirse turns around and smiles at Jack, fondly. The car begins to move and they drive away from the forest. Jack looks over his shoulder and watches as the trees get further and further away. Maybe it was the Creature. Then again, maybe it wasn't.

Acknowledgements

Where to start ... So many people have supported and helped this project get to where it is today – a published novel, hurray!

While writing, and visiting the fictional world of Drumsuin in my mind, I was almost always accompanied by one of my three cats, who lay on the table next to my laptop as I wrote during the pandemic and beyond. So Midnight, Gingey and Kitty deserve the first thank you for the many hours of feline companionship and support they put in from 2020 to 2025, (albeit in exchange for Dreamies and occasional chin scratches!)

Now for the thank-you messages to the humans. A huge thanks to my literary agent Stephanie Glencross of David Higham Associates, without whom this book would not be what it is today. Thank you for believing in this book and championing it right from the start. Your expert editorial input, insights and careful questioning expanded this novel in many ways and helped breathe life into what was a very rough draft!

To my creative writing tutor on the Faber Academy, 'Writing a Novel' course, Sabrina Broadbent, thank you for all your wise words and encouragement when *The Counting Game* was just a glimmer of an idea and the setting and characters were starting to form shapes in my mind. Similarly, to my first creative writing tutor, Jerry Hope, from the University of Derby, since deceased. Thank you for telling me I was 'good' at writing back when I was eighteen years old – I held those words close to me for twenty years and they kept me going throughout the many years of deleted drafts and doubt. Finally, to my primary school teacher Ms Morris of Rathmichael National School in Co. Dublin – thanks for encouraging us to read voraciously and even organising for us to edit real-life children's manuscripts back in the 1990s when I was a child. You may not have known it at the time, but the enthusiasm you showed for literature helped sow the seeds for me wanting to become a novelist one day!

Thank you so much to Genevieve Pegg of HarperNorth for your patience and help in the final editing stage, and to Daisy Watt of HarperNorth for your eagle-eye edits, commitment and tireless work on this novel. Also, to Megan Jones of HarperNorth for your assistance on this project. Thank you to Jess Haycox, Alice Murphy-Pyle and Emer Tyrrell of the HarperNorth and HarperCollins Ireland marketing team for your creativity and support in getting this book ready for the shelves and helping it get out and into the hands of readers. Thank you also to Molly Gregory of Simon and Schuster in the US for your brilliant insights and edits – not only for the US edition but for this UK and Ireland edition too.

Thank you to my alpha and beta readers and Faber writing gang for all of your writing feedback and support from 2019 – 2020 when this book was just a fledgling project: Jacqueline Sutherland, Scott Taylor, Blanka Hay, Shayna Wilson, Osman Haneef, Charles Adey, Katharine Ugeux-Lewis, Stephen Kenefick, Ruth Nares, Daragh O'Reilly, Paul Marriner and Yinka Ayeni. Thank you all for the laughs, the writing chats, the writing retreats (or is it wine retreats?), and the ongoing writing support. I thank my lucky stars I met such a kind and talented bunch of writers to support me along the way!

Thank you to the Garda Press Office, the Garda Síochána Retired Members Association, and John Kerin for your time, help and valuable insights into Gardaí procedures for missing children in the 1990s.

To my soulmates and friends: thank you to Holly O'Farrell, Kate O'Farrell and the extended O'Farrell clan (Brian, Caroline, Ben and the rest!) for your lifelong support and cheerleading, you've always believed I'd 'write a bestseller' – they say it takes a village to raise a child, and you were that village. Thank you to Becky McCann, Eugenio Costa and Joan McCann for all your ongoing love and support. Thank you to lifelong friends Zea de la Paz and Pauline McGough for your endless love and friendship. To my friends Jen 'Tony' Stannard, Kate Capocci, Joanna and Colin Priest, Jurate and John Wall, Thomas Curtis, Sheena Jeneesh Paul, Dawn Hewett, Sian Dodunski, Louise Guyett de Orozco and Kathryn Gibson. Lisa, Rich, Amy and Evie Lambert. Jen, Ron and Zoe Thornton. To counselling and psychotherapy colleagues who have supported me over the past few years – Daniel Dennehy, Sarah Comerford and Celine Coyne.

I'd also like to acknowledge the memory of deceased friends and family who were there for me over the years. Lara de la Paz, Rhoda and John Pearson, Fr Peter Nolan, Joe McCann and Breda Doyle. Special mention, also, to my half-sister, 'Annett Holliday' née Nolan, who was a writer and published three novels before passing away in 2005.

To my in-laws Geraldine, Patrick, Frank Holland and the extended Nolan, Pearson and Holland clan – thank you for your support and for being a much better family than the one in this book! Gary and Lindsey Nolan, Laura and Paddy Doherty, Patrick Nolan, Maureen Nolan and Eileen Nolan. Rob, Phil, James Mabbett, and Ian Pearson!

To my Mum, I feel lucky every day to have you, not just a mother but also a best friend. Thank you for always believing I could write a novel one day. Thank you for your endless patience, love, sense of humour, kindness, listening ear and wisdom about the world. To my Dad, thanks for your constant support and love, wisdom and integrity, and for always being there for me over the years.

Finally, thank you to Jason Holland, my husband. Thank you for listening to all of the book woes. Thanks for bouncing ideas back to me, and adding some ideas along the way when I was stuck on a plot point. Thank you for telling me to 'go and write' during the pandemic, and for being positive when I said I was going to attend the Faber novel writing course. You have been a rock throughout this whole process and life would be un-'bear'-able without you!

To my little 'cubby', thank you for sleeping peacefully in your pram and allowing me to finish the final copyedits for this book. You are the best baby anyone could wish for. You arrived and made me realise that women can indeed 'have it all'!

Harper
North

Book Credits

HarperNorth would like to thank the following staff
and contributors for their involvement in making
this book a reality:

Sarah Allen-Sutter
Fionnuala Barrett
Sarah Burke
Alan Cracknell
Jonathan de Peyer
Tom Dunstan
Kate Elton
Sarah Emsley
Simon Gerratt
Lydia Grainge
Monica Green
Natassa Hadjinicolaou
Emma Hatlen
Jess Haycox
Grace Howarth
Jo Ireson

Megan Jones
Jean-Marie Kelly
Taslima Khatun
Holly MacDonald
Alice Murphy-Pyle
Adam Murray
Genevieve Pegg
Amanda Percival
Dean Russell
Eleanor Slater
Hilary Stein
Emma Sullivan
Katrina Troy
Inigo Vivyan
Tom Whiting

For more unmissable reads,
sign up to the HarperNorth newsletter at
www.harpernorth.co.uk

or find us on X at
@HarperNorthUK

**Harper
North**